SLOE MOON

Sloe Moon Series

Volume 1: Tall Trees
Volume 2: Stoneharp
Volume 3: Crooked Hill
Volume 4: Eastbay
Volume 5: Halfway
Volume 6: Goldenlake

Novella

The Boy Who Played the Queen

Available soon:

Sun & Flame Duology

Volume 1: Everything the Sun Touches (Spring 2026)
Volume 2: Everything the Flame Heals

Content Warnings

strong language, violence, sex, gore, death, death in battle, brief mentions of suicide and assisted suicide, brief mention of rape

SLOE MOON

GOLDENLAKE

C. M. KUHTZ

WOLLSCHWEBER

PUBLISHING

Wollschweber Publishing
www.wollschweberpublishing.com

CREDITS

Copyediting: B. N. Laux
Production: C. M. Kuhtz
Cover illustration: @karlskunstkrempel
Cover design: C. M. Kuhtz
Logo design: Dorit Osang
Map design: C. M. Kuhtz

A catalogue record for this book is available from the British Library

ISBN 978-1-0683196-0-0 paperback
ISBN 978-1-0683196-1-7 ebook

for all of us who fail

THE LANDS OF THE FAMILIES

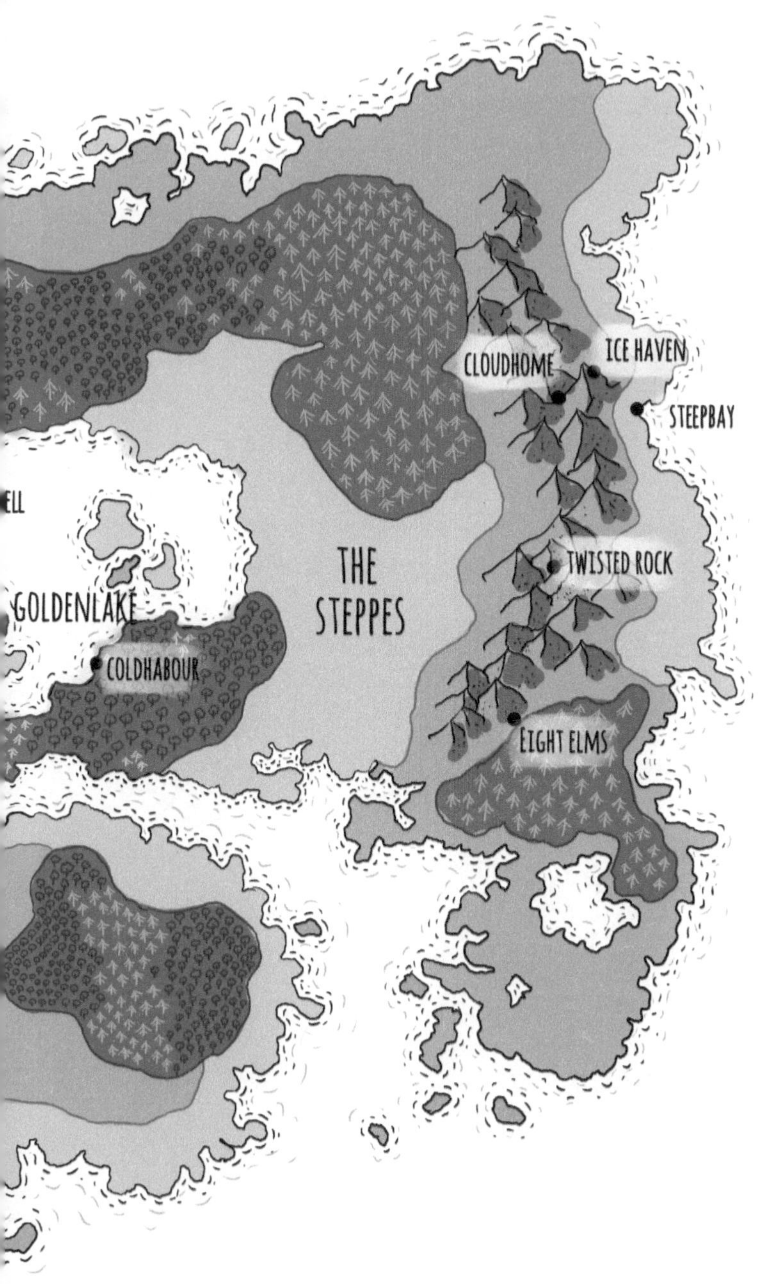
CLOUDHOME
ICE HAVEN
STEEPBAY
TWISTED ROCK
THE
STEPPES
GOLDENLAKE
COLDHABOUR
EIGHT ELMS
ELL

DRAMATIS PERSONAE

Pronunciation Guide

Vowels
A—as in 'marvel' (ā)
E—long, as in 'elusive' (ē) or short and flat (ə), as in 'energy'
I—like ee, as in 'feel' (ee), though sometimes more like a flat e (ə)
O—round, as in 'over' (ō)
U—like oo, as in 'moon' (oo)

Consonants
C and Q—like k, as in 'crown' (k)
J and Y—like y, as in 'yay' (y)
S—soft, as in 'zebra' (z)
W—like v, as in 'village' (v)

In Birkland
Bjor da Relian (Byōrr dā Rēlee-ānn)—a member of the Red House in Seagard.
Cathil (Kāthəl) Cloud—favourite son of the leader of the Clouds and famed warrior.
Cirvi (Keer-vee) Cloud—a wizard.
Cjanis (Kyā-nəs) Cloud—one of Cathil Cloud's sisters. Also a wizard.
Hano (Hānō) Bear—a wizard in Goldenlake.
Jaril (Yā-reel) Raven—Julas' sister in Darkwater.
Julas (Yoolās) Raven—a distant cousin of Sloe's.

Lilyis (Ləllyəs)/Nian da Nileon (Nee-ān dā Nee-ləōn)—Nivael's daughter.

Mayiel (Māyee-ēll) Magpie—an apprentice in Goldenlake. Qati (Kātee) Badger—one of Qes' cousins.

Qay (Kāy) Badger—Qes' aunt.

Qerla (Kēr-lā) Badger—the first wizard of Goldenlake.

Qes (Kəz) Badger—Sloe's cousin and best friend.

Qitli (Kətlee) Badger—runs the *End of the Road*.

Qor (Kōr) Badger—one of Qerla Badger's apprentices. Also Qes' cousin.

Rali (Rālee) Owl—a wizard.

Rawil (Rāvəl) Owl—the commander of a garrison of warriors in the west.

Raz (Rāz) Owl—Rawil's niece.

Rion (Ree-ōn) Owl—Raz's brother.

Rovan (Rōvānn) Owl—the commander of the Beakdig garrison. Rawil's ex-husband.

Saon (Zā-ōn) Moon—Sloe's ex-boyfriend.

Selan (Zē-lān)—a Moon warrior.

Silid (Zee-ləd) Moon—Sloe's oldest sister and heir to their mother.

Siran (Zee-rān) Moon—Siw's and Julas' baby.

Siw (Zəv) Moon—Sloe's sister, closest to them in age. A wizard's apprentice.

Sjunil (Zyoo-neel) Moon—Sloe's aunt and wizard of Tall Trees.

Sloe (Slō) Moon—the youngest child of the leader of the Moons and an aspiring wizard.

Sloe's mother—the leader of the Moons.

Sor (Zōr) Moon—Silid's child, living with Sloe in the Other House.

Tala (Tālā) Mouse—the ruler of the Mouse family.

Tarvi (Tārvee) Mouse—Torgall's twin sister, Cathil Cloud's sister-in-law.

Tjal na Tialin (Tyāl nā Tee-ā-leen)—a man of the Eastern Cities.

Torgall (Tõrgəl) Mouse—Cathil Cloud's husband.

Werid (Vĕrət) Wolf/Werid of the Far Side—a wizard from the Eastern steppes.

Yuna (Yoonā) Elk—a wizard running the administration office of the Stoneharp. Qarim Badger's ex-girlfriend.

In the Cities and at Court

Arif (Arəf)—one of the crown prince's retainers.

Bjalan da Relian (Byālān dā Rēlee-ānn)—the owner of Halfway Manor in the Hillakes. Bjor da Relian's uncle.

Fiolis da Nileon (Fee-õləs dā Nee-ləõn)—Nivael's daughter-in-law, Nian's wife.

Fjelmar da Faolin (Fyell-mār dā Fā-õ-leen)—Nuvalis da Nileon's betrothed.

Hilvis da Ozanil (Heelvəs dā Ōzā-neel)—Olas' widow.

Ila (Ee-lā)—a lady at Pietwood court.

Milavis (Meelāvəs)—one of Nuvalis da Nileon's companions.

Nalan na Nileon (Nālān nā Nee-ləõn)—a commoner, related to the da Nileons.

Naliris da Nileon (Nā-lee-rəs dā Nee-ləõn)—one of Nivael's younger daughters.

Nialis da Nileon (Nee-ā-ləs dā Nee-ləõn)—one of Nivael's younger daughters.

Nivael da Nileon (Nee-vā-ēl dā Nee-ləõn)—a man of the Eastern Cities and Prince of Crooked Hill.

Norvid da Nileon (Nõrvət dā Nee-ləõn)—Nivael's cousin.

Nurin da Nileon (Noorən dā Nee-ləõn)—the crown prince of Hillakes and Southclere, Nivael's eldest brother.

Nuvalis da Nileon (Noovāləs dā Nee-ləõn)—Nivael's eldest daughter.

Olas da Ozanil (Ōlāz dā Ōzā-neel)—a man of the Eastern Cities and negotiator.

Oyel da Ozanil (Ōyēl dā Ōzā-neel)—Olas' uncle, Norvid da Nileon's negotiator.

Qarim (Kāreem) Badger—Sloe's father, until recently presumed dead.

Revael da Relian (Rəvā-əll dā Rēlee-ānn)—a member of the Red House in Seagard.

Rikis (Reekəs)—one of Hilvis da Ozanil's companions.

Tjolvar na Tialin (Tyōllvār nā Tee-ā-leen)—a man of the Eastern Cities.

Tjovan na Tialin (Tyōvānn nā Tee-ā-leen)—a man of the Eastern Cities.

Valarel da Valarent (Vālā-rəll dā Vālārēnt)—one of Nivael's retainers.

Vilaris (Vee-lā-rəs)—one of Nurin's illegitimate daughters living in Blackfields.

BOOK ONE

THE PERFECT WAY TO FEEL BETTER

I stared down at the man who'd once refused to marry me.

"You need me to do what?"

I barely recognized him. In the year I'd been away from home, the closely cropped hairstyle of the Clouds had grown out and his dark hair fell down to his chin. His beard was unkempt and wet with tears. I'd kicked him hard, but what he seemed more afraid of was the tip of my girlfriend's blade at his throat.

"I need you to marry me," Cathil Cloud repeated, once the most formidable warrior in all the west, sprawling in the dirt of our guesthouse's floor at my feet. He'd stormed in and kissed me, without so much as a greeting, like the entitled dick I knew him to be.

"Well, I won't," I snarled. Not after everything that had passed between us. "It's fine, Lilyis."

She stepped back with a snort but didn't sheathe her longknife.

Cathil's face crumpled again and the sob that broke from him was pitiful to hear. I reached down to help him, but he turned away from me.

My friends, who'd come together at the late spring festival's evening to drink and feast, looked helpless. The only one who pushed through them was Qes, never able to resist a crying man for long, to kneel down next to him.

"We heard about your husband's death in battle," he said. "I'm truly sorry."

"He's drunk," Lilyis said.

"So am I," I said. "Or about to be shortly. Can we get him up?"

"Just leave him." Lilyis had a cold streak to her and perhaps how she'd reacted to Cathil's presence, ready to defend her territory, should've made me glad.

Qitli Badger, Qes' cousin and the landlord of the *End of the Road*, came out of the kitchen with the tray of delicacies we'd been waiting for. He sighed. "I wondered whether he'd put in an appearance. He's been haunting the camp ever since the separation."

"They separated before Torgall Mouse died?" Qes asked.

"The divorce was about to be finalized, but then it didn't need to be anymore. After Cathil's sister attacked the Mice, there was no way they could keep up the alliance. Torgall didn't hesitate to rid himself of his husband."

"He's right here!" Qes protested, still crouched over Cathil.

His cousin shrugged. "It's nothing he's not aware of. He's been scrounging beer off me for months, but my good will has started to run out."

"I'm sorry that I hurt you, Cathil." I rubbed my face, trying to figure out what to do. "To be honest, you're incredibly lucky that I merely kicked you in the pebbles and didn't blow your head off." I stepped over him and took Lilyis by the shoulder.

"Let's sit down," I whispered to her and looked at my circle of friends: there were the two Owls, Rawil and Raz, Eleas, the Cormorant wizard, Bjor, a man from the Eastern Cities, and Qati, who technically wasn't my friend, but Qes and Qitli's cousin, dour-faced and one-eyed, with the stitches keeping his lids closed clearly visible. I'd resigned myself to having him with us until we reached the forests, where we would offload him on the Badgers. Even if Qes had forgiven him for his past greed and cowardice, I wasn't half as charitably inclined.

The truth was that Qes loved few things more than a project, which was probably why he still tried to pull Cathil Cloud up instead of leaving him there to rot, after he'd rushed into the *End of the World* and kissed me without warning or consent. There'd been times when I might've welcomed the idea of being singled out in such a way and I would've been lying if I'd said I'd never fantasized about him pulling me into his arms like that. But things had changed and not just because he'd lost his status and had come to look more like a deranged werebear than the famous warrior feared by all the Owls.

In a way, he had a point. Everything had started when he'd refused my mother's proposal to wed me, to secure one of the longest alliances of the Moons. Cathil had preferred to marry Torgall Mouse, seduced by his beauty and wealth. I'd been glad to have missed out as soon as I met him in Goldenlake the year before. He'd been as arrogant as they come, full of a swagger that repulsed and fascinated me in turns, though for a moment I'd been lonely enough to consider giving in to him as the first cracks in his marriage started to appear.

But everything was different. I'd left Birkland with a company of men from the Eastern Cities, discovered my talents, and taken the position of Royal Sorcerer in the east. I'd met Lilyis and brought her with me on a business venture sponsored by the royal house of the Hillakes and Southclere, Lilyis' family, and had been banned by the wizard council of the west to ever set foot in the Stoneharp again, the one institution famous for educating the wizards of the families. It'd been my fault, but I'd hoped to have an evening of mindless drinking and feasting to forget about it all. Cathil's presence was a horrible reminder that the past was rapidly catching up with me. I'd tried to outrun it by leaving the lands of the families behind, aware of what waited for me upon my return—the whole steaming mess of it. I sat down next to Eleas Cormorant, the wizard the gods had pushed into my way.

She looked at me wide-eyed. "Cathil Cloud?" she hissed. "You actually *know* Cathil Cloud?"

"Not really. It's very complicated and not at all what I wanted to deal with today. Can we please celebrate?"

It was the day of the late spring festival. Outside the guesthouse a bonfire waited to be lit for the people who'd made their way to the camp below the Stoneharp, despite the war and the devastation visited upon the land not long ago.

I noticed Rawil Owl, the old commander, looking at me thoughtfully.

"What?"

"He's sort of right, you know," they said quietly. "It would be a good idea to marry him, to formally re-establish the alliance between the Moons and the Clouds."

"He had his chance."

"I suppose he did."

"And Lilyis would be all too happy to fuck him up properly, if I'd consider it."

"I can see that. Cousin Blade stands with her." A grim smile tucked at the mouth of the old Owl, who'd stepped into the space I'd held in my heart for a parent since I first met them. Rawil reached out and patted Lilyis' arm. "Give it some thought," they said. "It might be worth your while to start praying again."

Lilyis gave a little sniff, but relaxed and sat down next to me, taking hold of her beer bowl before draining it in one gulp. "This isn't over," she warned me. "At some point we need to talk about it in detail."

By the time we left the *End of the Road* to gawp at the bonfire, we were all unsteady on our feet. The light of the flames reflected in the waves crashing upon the beach; throngs of people stood around, squinting against the intense heat and the flying sparks, and I found myself clutching at the ornaments I wore around my neck, hidden under my tunic. Some of them I'd worn for a long time. One of them was the wolfstone, a rough piece of unassuming rock, always warm to the touch and wrapped in golden wire that had once half melted away and resolidified. For the short time I'd carried a sorcerer's staff in the Cities, I'd attached the wolfstone to its top, a gift that bound me to my master.

I mouthed the names of the gods it belonged to: *Sister Stone, Brother Flame. Please, please, please. Let my aunt be alive when I reach her. Take Cathil Cloud away to somewhere I never have to think about him again. Make Lilyis forget to grill me about him while you're at it* … As I lifted my gaze, I saw Eleas Cormorant looking at me. Her lips moved in her own prayer.

In the short while I'd known her, we'd discovered a lot of similarities. Lilyis had reacted with some jealousy to the wizard's closeness, though recently she'd seemed determined to shove us together to talk about our talents whenever possible. Eleas was tall and narrow-shouldered, her skin a deep brown, but with an unhealthy pallor. She wore an elbow-length cape fashioned from overlapping pieces of pearlescent shell, one of the luxury items her family was famous for creating. The council of the west had once sent her away to the furthest edge of her family's lands, but we'd still found ourselves standing side by side, sharing the attention of our gods. She had all manner of things to pray for, as had I.

Lilyis stood next to me, her arms crossed, a frown etched into her forehead. The light of the roaring fire turned her chestnut-red hair into a mane of flames. The heat spread a flush over her freckles. She was trying hard to ignore our friend Raz attempting to snog the head off Qati Badger.

Raz had tried to bring him around for a while and it was odd to see him finally relenting, his hands clawing at her back. Maybe he was finally drunk enough.

Rawil shot me a quick grin. They were more than familiar with the ease with which their niece went after what she wanted. I remembered too well the schooling Raz had given me last year.

"Don't tell me you're jealous," Lilyis said. "After the display I had to endure tonight."

"You want to do this now?"

"Why not?"

"This is supposed to be a night of reflection and prayer."

"Horseshit. It's a fertility festival, and Raz and Qati won't be the only ones trying to honour the spirit of it."

I felt myself blush and reached out to pull her close. She was smaller than me, her head barely reaching the top of my shoulder.

"Were you once in love with him?" she asked, pushing her palms into my chest.

"No, though being rejected by Cathil Cloud was painful. I hadn't met him then," I added quickly. "It was a political affront when the Clouds denied my mother's request to marry me off and join them. It's how things are done between the families. I was supposed to make a good match. As the youngest child of my mother I was destined to honour the Moons by marrying well. Rejecting Mother was as good as a declaration of war, but Cathil had made up his mind. He married Torgall Mouse instead. Back then, I thought it had something to do with me being undesirable or a personal snub, with my father's bad name among the families, but Torgall Mouse was the most beautiful man I'd ever seen. Cathil was greedy and stupid enough to believe he'd be able to force Torgall to fall in love."

"You're making me feel sorry for him."

"It was complicated, but essentially, Cathil's marriage caused a rift in his own family and everything in the west went to shit."

"You're saying, in a weird way, all of this is your fault?"

"Not my fault," I tried to assure us both. "Not really. I was just involved, without being asked. Being rejected in such a public way … I felt as if the whole of Tall Trees was laughing at me, as if it merely confirmed the bad opinion they'd always had of me."

"They didn't have an inkling of what you truly are."

"No one knew back then. Least of all myself."

"You don't want to jump him?" Lilyis asked quietly.

"Of course not."

"Even if it would be the perfect way to feel better about the whole thing?" She poked my chest.

"It would be the worst idea I'd ever had. It wouldn't solve anything at all, and apart from that, I don't want to. I love you, Lilyis."

"But he's … he's twice as big as me and if everything on him is to scale you might be sorry to miss out on the experience."

I reached down between us and found her length pressing into my thigh. "You're all I want, Lilyis."

"Can you two please find a room?" Eleas grumbled. "I am not drunk enough to enjoy the spectacle."

"Hear hear," Rawil Owl joined in. "Find somewhere far away to fuck, why don't you."

Lilyis pulled me along to the water's edge. The noise of the waves washing onto the pebbles was deafening. To the left of us lay the ship we'd crossed the Wild Sea with; the *Golden Drake*, in possession of the Honourable and Valiant Company of the Sun of Seagard, the company Lilyis and Bjor were officially working for. Smaller fires flickered close to its hull, built by the members of the crew on watch duty.

My head swam with the onslaught of the cold wind rushing in from the open sea, and my skin tingled as Lilyis turned me around and kissed me, greedily. She decided we still weren't far enough away from the others and detached herself from my mouth with a smacking noise, snatching at my wrist. We walked on towards the stretch of coast from where I'd left Birkland, until we reached one of the boulders sticking out of the surrounding pebbles like the back of a whale. She pushed me down and I fumbled with her belt and trousers, her cock springing free against my cheek.

"Show me that you mean it," Lilyis rasped, and I burrowed into her with a hunger kindled by shame about my own neediness.

$$\maltese$$

WORTH THE TROUBLE

"I'm getting cold."

Lilyis nuzzled into my neck. "Stop whingeing, Sloe. Pull up your pants."

"I must have more than five pebbles up my arse by now."

She grunted and rolled away from me. So far from the bonfire the spring night was still icy cold and I felt myself shiver as I fixed my clothes, while Lilyis lay stretched out under the stars, staring up into the luminous skies.

"That was more than I bargained for. It feels as if my bones have melted."

I buckled my belt and threw the blue cloak around my shoulders. "Do you need help getting up?"

"I'm merely commenting on how keen you were to show me I have nothing to be afraid of when it comes to Cathil Cloud." She chuckled. "Can you do it again? Not now, the gods have mercy on me, but … maybe tomorrow? After we've sobered up and had some breakfast?"

"You liked that, huh?" I sat down on the edge of the boulder, my boots pushed against the pebbles. "There's *much* more where that came from."

She laughed again, patted my right shin. "That's very good to know. Fuck—can you help me?"

I managed to hoist her up, so we were both sitting on the rock. She put her arms around me, snuggling close under the blue cloak. "I'll be so bruised tomorrow, but at least it's a good pain. Will I have some time to recover, or do you want to ride east straight away?"

"You still have business to attend to, haven't you? Oversee the unloading of the cargo and the transport into the storage yards?"

"I don't need to be here for that. I could leave Bjor in charge."

"I'm pretty sure Bjor would take it badly, being left behind to do the dirty work."

She breathed into my tunic. "I need to remind myself there are no princes in the Company of the Sun, but agents of equal rank. You're right, Sloe. It wouldn't be fair, and he probably wants to join us going eastwards."

"Probably."

"Will you be all right leaving Rawil and Raz?"

"I'll have to be." I swallowed. "They'll have everything under control around here and keep an eye on the *Golden Drake* before we return to the west coast."

Lilyis groaned. "Are you sure we should leave the ship here?"

"The crew will have plenty to keep themselves entertained— the camp will grow and grow over the next months."

"Despite the war?"

"Everything around the Harp lies under a holy truce."

"Really? What about …"

"The first fire was an accident. Supposedly. Though I don't know about the second, here is the safest place for them. Leave orders and put the most capable of them in touch with Yuna Elk and her people at the storage yard. With luck they'll sell all the cargo and buy enough goods to stuff the *Drake* up to the top deck before …" I didn't want to say it, and so I didn't.

The soles of her boots crunched on the pebbles as she stood up, massaging the small of her back. Under the light of the stars her face was as pale as milk. She didn't say it either.

Before you go back home.

"Back so soon?" Qitli Badger stood in his kitchen, wrapped in a grease-stained apron. "None of the others have come in yet. Do you need tea?"

"You don't want to go out and see the fire?" I asked him.

He barked out a joyless laugh. "I've had enough of Brother Flame's caprices to last me a lifetime. When the second fire happened, I'd almost finished getting the house back up and running, only to see it burn down again. I don't need a bonfire to be reminded of his particular sense of humour."

"But you're still here."

He dried his hands on a rag, fingers covered in burn scars, accumulated over decades of working in the kitchen. "Just because I was forced to acknowledge the strength of a god, doesn't mean I need to grovel before him. The camp is the place that feels most like home to me. It's where I'm closest to what I'm supposed to do. I can't imagine ever returning to Goldenlake. At least here the wizards are keeping well away. At the lake they're absolutely everywhere, like a grain beetle infestation." He grinned at me. "No offence."

"I understand what you mean. There'll probably be many more, now that the towers of the Harp are emptying."

"The power of the Harp has long resided outside of its walls. The public ceremonies at the camp aren't overseen by the wizards of the Harp, but by people who have come here, who have travelled across our lands to be housed and fed." He shrugged his broad shoulders again. "Whenever I've doubted that, the gods have been so good as to send me a clear sign. They let you survive the trip home and come back." His self-assured mask slipped, and he appeared utterly vulnerable. "They've let Qes come back, and they've spared my own life so many times I've lost count. Cousin Bowl has held their hand over my head to make sure I can be here to see all of you return, and the Owls have been very forthcoming and generous with their help."

"Ousting the Mice was an improvement?" I asked, eager to hear more about what I'd missed.

"The Mice have always been known for their greed. During the first years their rates were reasonable, because I was operating out of a tent, but as soon as I had the opportunity to take over one of the houses, they swooped down to pick my bones clean. For every basket of supplies, for every pile of blankets, they took their fees … They were extraordinarily inventive about how they could squeeze out more silver seeds. There have been complaints for many decades, but they became used to the profits and began to see themselves as the chosen family, the one entitled to take from the others. In time the Owls may go the same way, if there are no longer people like Rawil in charge, who have lived through a lifetime of border wars. Isn't it funny, how one little pebble can strike so many ripples?"

"I wouldn't dare call Rawil Owl a little pebble—not to their face."

"I'm not talking about Rawil, I'm talking about you, Sloe Moon of Tall Trees." Qitli took the pot off the fire to transfer the hot water into the teapot.

My heart skipped a beat. "What?"

"Didn't you save the prince's life? If he'd rotted away in a shallow grave in the forests, everything would've turned out very differently. Would you have married Cathil and been absorbed into the Cloud family, you would never have brought Rawil here to get involved with the council. Every little choice you've made in the last year has formed this place in some way. When Qes came here last winter, his scars still fresh and his eyes as wild as a foal's, he told me there was a person he needed to find, a person he loved, who had a part to play in the history of the families."

Lilyis drew nearer. She stood in the doorframe, her light-green eyes glued to Qitli's face. "He really said that?"

"Yes, he did. Ever since, I've seen you as someone who held the regard of the gods. If you can inspire such love, you are worth the trouble. Fire or no fire."

"Qes was desperate and wounded," I clarified.

"He was right, though," Lilyis said. "You have saved my father's life in more ways than one." She took my hand. "You need to learn how to take compliments."

"I can take the compliments, but I balk at the responsibility."

Qitli sighed. "Know that you are loved, by many people and in many different ways. The tea is ready."

"Do all innkeepers of the camp have such a philosophical bend?" Lilyis asked as we sat at the brazier in the common room, nursing our bowls of strong, bitter tea.

"Maybe you have to live through years of bullying by the Mice and many close encounters with death and destruction. All the people staying at the Harp have come here for a reason." I thought of Eleas Cormorant and her story. "Perhaps his wish is to serve the gods with good food and excellent tea." I took a sip, savouring the herby taste. "There could be worse calls to service, I suppose."

Lilyis averted her gaze. "You mean like yours?"

"In what way?"

"It can't be a coincidence that your Tall Gods cluster around someone who always thought of themself as pushed aside and judged for the shadow of other people's lives thrown upon them. They all flock to you—any god you're introduced to leaves something with you—something useful, no less. You might not be keen on the responsibilities, but I don't think you can deny something has started with you. The Bulls have come to Birkland to find someone like you." She stared into her bowl, on the reflection of flames in the liquid. "I can't begin to imagine the consequences if this had happened to someone like Cathil Cloud, can you?"

I swallowed. "How?"

"Everything you told me about him makes it sound as if he needed to fall on bad times. I've known many young men like him. I grew up amongst them, their rituals, and their powerful anxieties around what the Star preached at them about weakness and manliness. Have you ever thought about extending your talents on behalf of *yourself*, not on behalf of other people? Like my father, like my uncle, like me?"

"What are you saying, Lilyis?"

"That Qes and Qitli might well be right." Her fingers folded into mine. We both flinched as the door opened and we heard the laughter of Raz, trying to mask her nervousness.

"What are you two doing here?" she cried, pulling Qati Badger with her. Qes' cousin seemed stunned, as if he'd been slapped across the face, his mouth flushed from too much kissing.

"We came back a while ago," Lilyis said. "There's tea if you need to sober up."

"Oh, we've done a huge amount of sobering up already," she grinned. "Haven't we?"

Qati's eye widened like a hare's who comes across a fox. I felt a twinge of sympathy. Raz could have that effect on people. For someone who'd never expected to be made to feel like the most desirable person around, to fall in with Raz Owl ... When she'd taken me under her wing, she'd been kind and patient, and we'd giggled a lot.

"Sit," I said to him, patting the bench beside me. "Have you seen the others?"

"Eleas has gone to join the Cormorants at the *Golden Drake* and Rawil and Yuna tucked Bjor under their wing and made him try various festival specialties until he was green in the face. There are more people here than I thought and more are arriving as we speak."

"Were there any prayers?" Lilyis asked.

"Some." Raz sniffed. "Not that I paid much attention to them. Where's Qes?"

"You haven't seen him either?"

"Leave him alone." Qati's voice sounded rough, unused. "He knows his way around the camp."

"That's not what I'm worried about," I protested.

Qati smirked at me in a way that made my skin crawl. "I know what you're worried about. You can't stand the thought of him getting away from you."

"Fuck off, Qati."

"You're not satisfied with all you have. You always want more."

"Shut up," Raz told him, and lo and behold, he did. "You're still too drunk to know what you're saying." She stroked his cheek, and he flushed in anger. I underestimated him; maybe feeling wanted wouldn't be enough to make him a better person.

"We did it! We made him puke!" Yuna Elk blasted through the door, more dishevelled than I'd ever seen her.

Rawil hoisted Bjor into the common room. He actually did look green around the gills, as Raz had said.

"Don't torture my friends!" I exclaimed.

"Nah." Rawil made a dismissive gesture. "A little bit of adventurous eating has never killed anyone. No wait—it has, hasn't it?" They beamed at Yuna, suddenly seeming oddly young and mischievous. "Don't get your smallclothes in a twist, he's fine." They gave Bjor a little shove. "Just not strong enough to mix honey beer with fermented goat milk."

NONE OF THIS

We didn't go to sleep before the sun was well and truly up, and as I woke much, much later, the room was empty. Lilyis had left me to snore away in peace. The inside of my mouth felt furry and as I tried to roll around, there was something small and warm tucked against the back of my knees, unsheathing pearlescent claws in silent warning.

"Little Sister."

It'd been so long since Sister Stone had come to me in that form, a little grey cat with splotches of ginger fur, impossibly soft, its purr disconcertingly deep for something so small. I curled around her and her yellow-greenish eyes locked with mine before she closed them in a slow blink. In the Eight Kingdoms my Siblings had often been around me in their guises, but since I'd returned to Birkland, I'd missed seeing them, or feeling them so close to me. I started scratching under her chin and around her ears. She'd allowed other people to see her in her cat form, Qes among them.

"Tell me he's truly fine," I murmured, and she blinked again, a wordless gesture of reassurance, after which I must've drifted off again, because as I opened my eyes the next time, there he was, sitting on the edge of the sleeping platform, his blue-black curls a soft cloud around his face. He hadn't noticed I was waking up. His shoulders were slumped and his gaze on his open hands, as if he was studying the lines in his calloused palms, asking them the complicated questions he didn't actually want answers to, but needed, nonetheless.

"Qes."

"Oh, hey. There you are."

"What are you doing here?"

"I was waiting for you. To talk."

"What's wrong?"

"Nothing is wrong as such, but …"

"What did you do?"

"I might've slept with Cathil Cloud last night."

"Oh. I think I already knew that somehow."

"I hadn't planned on it! I … I felt so sorry for him, and we both had quite a lot to drink by the end."

"How are you feeling?"

"I'm not sure. I didn't want to hurt you."

"Qes, you are welcome to him."

"It was disappointing, if that makes it better."

"You don't need to assuage me."

"I felt as if I should." He reached out for me, and I took his hand in mine. "I think I kissed him first to make him shut up about how horrible his marriage was. I couldn't get a single word in about my own misfortunes with Nalan and he cried so much afterwards that I feel bad now." He folded up and I pulled him towards me. We settled against each other, my knees pushed into his and my arms around him. When we'd stayed in the old *End of the Road*, we'd shared a bed and had often slept snuggled together, before everything had become horribly complicated.

"I'm so sorry," I whispered. "I feel we've drifted more apart than we ever should have."

"You're happy—that's how it goes."

"It's going to be fine," I mumbled against his neck. "He'll understand you didn't mean to hurt him."

"But I did. Somehow, I wanted to punish him for what he did to you."

"He didn't do anything to me, Qes. It was all in my head."

That wasn't quite true, though. He'd once given his cousins the nod of approval when they'd been bored enough to use their prisoners for sport. If it hadn't been for Lilyis' father, I would've been raped back then. Not that I'd ever told Qes about that …

"It's going to be fine," I said again.

I saw Cathil Cloud that evening, as he slunk back to the *End of the Road* like a kicked cur, his hair as wild as his eyes.

"Can we talk?" he asked Qes, and my cousin left his place at the table.

Rawil, Raz, and Eleas hadn't come over; instead, they tried to recover at the *Pond*. Bjor was still pasty and had been steadily drinking bowl after bowl of strong tea while Lilyis spoke to him of the plans for the next days, about the logistics around transferring the cargo from the *Drake* to the Tower of the Sun, as Lilyis called it. Lilyis seemed the freshest, and I could see the pained expression in Bjor's blue eyes change to exasperation, begging me for deliverance.

I cleared my throat. "Lilyis, won't there be time to do that tomorrow? We have a whole platter of tasty leftovers to get through."

"We can't lose sight of why we came here, even if the ship of the Bulls has foundered during the crossing."

"I understand, but we're all hung over and exhausted today."

Qati groaned as if to support the statement.

"Fine," Lilyis snapped. "But you need to get me some of Qitli's cheese from the kitchen."

I pushed myself up. Again, I found our host close to his cooking fire, baking flatbreads on a stone. The smell was wonderful, of toasted grains and nuts.

"Have you talked to Qes?" Qitli asked, focused on the task at hand.

"Yes. I tried to make him feel better about it, but Cathil will ruin all my work, for sure."

"What will you do if this goes somewhere?" Qitli's dark eyes met mine with a challenge.

"Do I need to do something?"

"You know as well as I there are certain qualities my cousin is infallibly attracted to."

"As I said to him many times, I have no claim on him. If they can work something out, I'll be happy for them both."

"You're sure?"

"Absolutely."

Qitli breathed out. Knowing that Qes had someone who so vehemently took his side was a relief.

"I promised to wheedle some cheese out of you, Qitli."

"There's plenty up there on the shelf." He gestured to the side. "Cut some wedges. There's also cold meat left and some of the smoked fish."

"I need to apologize."

I glanced up from my breakfast tea to see Cathil Cloud standing next to me. His hair was combed, and his beard gone. I'd spent the last hour staring at the table, with everyone else running around the camp getting organized. I'd asked Lilyis if she needed me to do something, but she'd wanted me to stay put and wait for her return, so we could spend the afternoon walking on the beach together. Having Cathil surface was a strangely welcome surprise.

"Do you want to do it here?" I asked him.

His gaze flickered around the common room. "Better not."

I imagined Qitli softly cursing on the other side of the wall.

"We could go to the market and back again?" I suggested and Cathil shrugged.

"Sounds good."

As we walked away from the house, I asked, "Has Qes told you to talk to me?"

"In no uncertain terms. I assume he told you."

"Yes, he has. If you need me to say it, it's fine with me. We all do weird stuff when we're hurt, and sometimes it leads to the best things that ever happen to us."

"I don't think I need your blessing." A sliver of the old Cathil rose with the words and I forced myself to smile at him.

"Indeed not." My left hand folded around the blue stone bracelet, holding on to control. I couldn't get involved in that—though I still needed to know one thing. "Before we continue, I have to ask you something."

"Which is?"

"When you and your cousins brought us to Greycliffs last year, did you ever say to them that they were welcome to me?"

He scowled at me. "Welcome to you?"

"Two of your cousins came into the pigsty where I was kept, with the man from the Cities who was bound next to me. They said you'd allowed them to assault us."

He seemed genuinely shocked. "What?"

"Did they lie?"

"No one asked me—and I would never have consented to a prisoner of the Clouds being raped. That's what we're talking about here?"

"Yes. The prince and his negotiator intervened at the last moment."

He scratched at his temple. "I have always wondered what it was that made the prince change his mind about the scheme."

"Change his mind?"

"From one day to the next, he started to withdraw, to oppose my authority. I'm sorry. I didn't know about that. And I hadn't realized that me choosing to marry into the Mice would cause a lot of trouble for you at home."

It felt as if he'd kicked me. I'd expected him to speak more about barging into the *End of the Road* on the evening of the festival, not about the things that had happened in Tall Trees. "It did," I croaked, "and it made me feel really bad about myself. I thought there were other reasons behind it, good reasons. That's how everyone in the village saw it, at least. Qes mentioned it to you?"

"He did. I think he wanted to explain why you reacted so badly the other night, and why you have always kept me at arm's length, even before." He scraped the tip of his boot on a pebble that rolled away and landed against another one with a loud *clack*. "It's not always easy if you're the favourite child of a leader."

I found myself laughing at him. "Yeah. Sounds horrific."

"What I mean is that you're seldom told the truth about yourself and about the consequences of your actions." His voice had gone flat again. "It took a war for me to figure that out."

I stared up at him. The famed warrior prince of the Clouds, standing next to me in clothes that had seen much better days, and no longer dressed in the colours of either the Clouds or the Mice, without a longknife at his belt and boots that had started to fall apart. "I'm sorry for laughing. I never saw it that way."

"It can make you blind to everything but the things you want—being indulged since you first drew breath. I never knew the willingness of my mother to let me have my say in which husband I'd be given to would destabilize so many alliances. I'm afraid to admit that I never understood it for what it was—a political decision. I believed myself deeply in love, though I have come to think it was merely a story I told myself. Torgall never was interested in me, after all. I couldn't conceive of a world in which the gods would not grant me the favour of his love." He drew a deep breath. "Among the Clouds I knew myself to be the most important man, but when my mother was pushed aside ..." He stared out at sea and his nose wrinkled. "Cjanis didn't try to talk to me first. She roped in all my sisters to depose Mother and took things into her own hands. Since then, everything has so utterly gone to shit … while everything seems to have been improved for you. What's his name again?"

"Her name is Lilyis."

He arched a brow. "That's why she has come here with you?"

"One of the reasons. We had no idea how far things have progressed in the meantime, or that the Owls have taken over."

"Cjanis has only herself to blame. She thought to unite our family behind her, but she underestimated my eldest sisters. She always was the odd one out, really. Maybe she didn't realize that was what would break us in the end."

"Were you with Torgall when he died?"

"No. I wasn't allowed to fight with the Mice."

I blinked at him in surprise. "That's … exceptionally stupid."

"It was meant as a final humiliation—and it worked." He gnawed at the nail of his right thumb. "I can't tell you how well it worked. So you see, that leaves me stuck between the families."

"Is that why you've been haunting the camp?"

"Haunting?"

"That's the word Qitli used."

"I certainly tried to get as drunk as possible every single day. I ran out of silver seeds early on, though." He swallowed. "I sold my longknife at one point."

"I'm sorry to hear that."

"Sorry enough to consider changing your mind?"

"Not a fucking chance, Cathil."

He watched the waves crashing towards us, sucking in the smaller pebbles and broken shells as the tide started to run out. "It was worth asking," he said eventually. "Even if you'd be able to marry me now, it would be foolish of me to repeat the same mistake so soon—pandering to someone in the hope to be swept off my feet."

I chuckled. "Swept off your feet? I'm certainly not the weakest person around but …"

"Have you never dreamt of making a good marriage? Never planned out the day someone would choose you to further their influence and status and show you off before the world?"

"Yes, which was why being not considered hurt so much. It's the same all over the forests—my whole life I've been told it was my duty to support the Moons by marrying the person who Mother picked out for me, that the whole of Tall Trees would rejoice in the match and send me off with bags full of hides and richly dyed clothes to make a success of my life in another village." Just thinking about the hours I'd spent worrying about all that made me angry. "Only for someone to snub me so thoroughly that what little standing I had with my family was destroyed."

"I remember paying the fine the council of the east laid on me for your recompense." His eyes were narrow, his mouth set in a line. "It was an outrageous amount to ask for. Just because your aunt had the ear of the first wizard of Goldenlake."

"I didn't want to go and see the council! None of it was my idea."

"You still did it, though, and now you come back, filled with the experiences of your travels, with a whole entourage of weird people around you. I never expected the gods to turn against me in this way. If they hear me apologize, I might soothe their wrath and can make them listen to my prayers once again."

"Good luck with that. If I've learned one thing about the mess that was the whole last year, it's that whatever *you* do, the gods still do whatever the fuck they want."

CONTROL THE UNCONTROLLABLE

In the time the *Golden Drake* had been beached beneath the Stoneharp, an astonishing amount of the goods the Sun had brought to Birkland had been sold at the daily market. It'd been several months since the last ship from the Cities had brought the spices and dye plants I'd advised Lilyis to stock up on because they were widely used among the families. They'd already made her a small profit. The rest was loaded into carts and brought up the cliff. I would've liked to see the Tower of the Sun but my actions had made that impossible and the official ban been put in place, so I left Lilyis and Bjor to the Sun's business and met up with Eleas instead.

"Do you know what you're going to do yet?" I asked her, as we went southwards. It didn't take long for the Stoneharp to vanish behind the outcrops of rock and squiggly coastline. "Will you return to Westlight after all?"

"Technically, I am not supposed to leave the island, though they allowed me to enter the Harp and beg for forgiveness. My master is no longer here and none of the six wizards who are left within its walls scares me enough not to try and ignore them."

On our outing she collected shards of broken bowls from the beach, some of them decorated with intricate patterns cut into the clay, though some of them were glazed like bowls imported from the Cities. She'd wriggled out of her shell cape and stuffed it inside the bag she wore strapped across her chest. Without that reminder of status, she appeared like any other Cormorant, narrow-shouldered and dark-skinned, her green tunic splashed with seawater. Each piece of pottery she picked up seemed to hold an endless fascination for her, as if they embodied worlds of their own, revealing between her fingers the entirety of their history.

"I would like to come and see the eastern forests with you—if I may."

I felt a smile tuck at my mouth. "Are you sure?"

"We did not find much of a chance to trial our talents recently—obviously the camp is not the best place to experiment, but I think we should spend more energy trying to figure out what is actually happening. In the last weeks, I have heard a lot about this aunt of yours, enough to believe she might be able to help both of us."

"I'd love to take you with me and I'm sure Lilyis wouldn't have any objections. What are you doing now?"

She sat down on another rock, and I'd half expected her to lay out a spiral, as she liked to do, but she seemed to try and fit all the pieces she'd collected into the shape of one vessel. "Some of these might be as old as the Harp—and some as young as you, Sloe. If I could find a way of bringing them all together, into a … functional … unit …" She pushed a strand of silky black hair away from her face and smiled at me. "This feels like the life I'm trying to lead. Picking up broken shards from the waves, some bestowed upon me by generations and generations of Cormorants, others splinters of my own experiences, but it is like something that could work if the most important piece is found, something destined to remain missing, floating around somewhere in this most endless of seas." She laughed quietly. "Look at your face. I had expected to be miserable here, extremely miserable in fact, but it seems as if things have truly shifted. As if I can breathe for the first time in years and see things as they were always meant to be seen. The Stoneharp was built to be intimidating, to remind us of our own ignorance—seeing it so depleted … it is just a lot of stone. It means nothing but what I let it mean. My whole life

I have lived in fear of this place, even when I was residing here, trying to go through the Protocols. After they had marked me, I was still afraid all the time. But today … Perhaps it is because I have gazed upon the faces of two Siblings and realized how far they were removed from what I was led to believe."

"There's something in the air around here," I mumbled. "Everyone starts to spill, even Cathil Cloud. Aren't we far away enough from the camp yet?"

She mournfully studied her collection of broken pieces. "We should be."

I took her hand and she gasped, clearly fearful to hurt me with her gift, and I felt a slight shock jumping from her fingers into mine.

"Ow—Sloe!"

I held on. "It's fine. I'm still here."

"Yes, because you are used to dealing with gods!"

"Give me your other hand."

She frowned, but reached over. We both sat on the rock, clasping each other. She let out a soft whimper as my Siblings swam into view, as if through thick mist, circling us like a pack of wolves, all five of them: Sister Storm, wearing the face of Eleas' sister, Brother Brook, Sister Stone, the bulk of Brother Moon, and Brother Flame's likeness to the prince, causing me to breathe in deeply to handle the pain.

"Here they come," I said.

"I can see them. I still don't think they're people I know. Will they talk to us?" She sounded frightened.

"I don't think they need to—yet. They seem to want to watch you. Watch us. Brother Flame looks like Lilyis' father and Sister Stone like my aunt, when she was very young. Brother Moon like my father's master, the one who cut the mark from his skin."

Father's master had been a Badger and had the same eyes as me: one brown, one blue, the blue one in the same milky hue as the stone set into the bracelet the Queen of the Lakes had gifted me, unsettlingly round in a face that could be a lot like Qes'. As soon as Eleas released me, the mist swept our Siblings away.

"That was … weird," she said.

"Maybe they were already bored with us. They don't have the longest attention span."

"What would happen if we could find a wizard who is connected to Brother Rain in the same way? Would she be able to join in and bind Brother Rain to us?"

"If there are more who have escaped the council's notice, that might be a reasonable assumption."

"We could collect the strengths of all eight Tall Gods?"

I shrugged. "Maybe we don't need all eight of them. It depends on what you want to do."

"I do not want to burn people to a crisp." She squinted at me. "What do *you* want to do?"

"I want to protect my girlfriend from the Bulls."

"Do you need all eight for that?"

"Could it hurt?"

"It could hurt a great deal, if whoever we find to complete our circle has less benevolent plans. There are too many stories of wizards who have tried to use the good will of the gods for ill. We need to heed the warning and should be slow to advertise our curiosity." She wiped her palms on her trousers and pushed herself upright, the pebbles skittering away under her boots. "This could be another question to ask your aunt to help with."

"You're not tempted to try it?"

"I have hurt too many people I have loved, and only because you have forgotten how scary it can be to serve as a conduit for a strength that is not your own …"

It felt as if she'd slapped me. Suddenly I remembered kneeling on the floor of the House of the Sun all too clearly, trying to wash the blood off its walls. "You're right. I should be thanking the gods that they've allowed me to meet someone like you, someone cautious and strong enough to hold me back if the possibilities become too tempting." I stood up. "Do you think there might be wizards like us caged in the towers of the Harp?"

"They will have died of neglect long ago. There is no reason to keep them alive if they are not useful for the council."

I shuddered, still feeling my knees pressed upon the floor of the council chambers, my neck bent before them. But for my aunt it would've been the fate awaiting me: starving and half-mad, smashing my head against the walls of the Harp. Yuna Elk had once said that there'd always been cells in the Harp. Had the whole compound once been built to control the uncontrollable?

I'd hoped to be able to move into a separate room with Lilyis once most of the spring festival guests had left, but ever larger numbers of people kept streaming into the camp, as the weather was warming up. All of Qitli's guest quarters were packed. He didn't have much help, apart from a boy working in the small stable, and so Qes' cousin spent his days in the kitchen or sweeping the floors. Because everyone else was running around, I started to assist with the washing up and some of the food preparation.

My friends were accompanying the carts going up into the Harp and soon even Bjor and Lilyis knew their way around the storage yards. They might've been the first people of the Cities allowed within the walls who weren't kept as prisoners.

Distracting myself with work helped me not to think about the fact that I was no longer welcome there and led to a similar level of exhaustion when the others came back for their evening meal. Qes had started to collect provisions for our journey. I could tell he was getting impatient to leave. He spent a lot of time staring at the map Lilyis had brought with her, sometimes stabbing his fingers down, as if he needed to touch it in order to connect the lines and routes in red ink with the reality of the land as he knew it.

"I don't think we should bother with tents," he declared. "It's getting ever warmer and it would be best to travel with as few pack animals as possible, so we can reach the forests quickly."

"You're running away," I said, and he squirmed.

"I'm trying hard not to."

"Is this about Cathil?"

"What if I want to see some trees?" he asked tersely.

"Qes, what the fuck is going on?"

"He asked if he could come along."

The first thing I felt was outrage. "What?"

"I think he wants to run as well."

"Would you like him to come with us?"

"It's not about that though, is it?" Bitterness had crept into his voice.

"About what you'd like?"

"Yes."

"What gave you that idea?" It was difficult not to show how much his statement had hurt me.

He frowned at me. "This is supposed to be an expedition of the Sun."

"Neither of us has been officially employed by them, and the less it seems like anything official is going on, the better."

"Can you picture Cathil Cloud coming to Tall Trees?"

"It would certainly give my aunt the shock of her life."

"Right."

"But if you want him to come …"

"You're not serious!" Qes exclaimed.

"We've had a long talk. He must've told you. I appreciate he's had a rough last year, a year that has changed not only his life, but him. Don't forget that out there, there's still a war going on that can flare up any time. We could give him a longknife and he could make himself useful for once."

Qes squirmed. "Sloe … if this has anything to do with you still feeling guilty about what *didn't* happen, please don't … Don't tell me it's fine if you'd rather not see him ever again. I'll find someone else to care for, soon enough. Just because he's fucking gorgeous, though that shouldn't mean anything at all."

"It doesn't?"

"Well, maybe a tiny bit. I must've caught feelings for every man who burst into tears after I've kissed him." He groaned softly. "I suppose that was something you anticipated as well?"

"The thought had crossed my mind, yes. Cathil is welcome, as far as I'm concerned. Lilyis … I can't help you there, even if I wanted to. She'll continue to keep her knife sharp for him."

Eol stared at his wizard, stricken. "You want me to tell them that?"

Eleas lifted her shoulders. "You can make it sound better. Or you can throw me under the cart, whatever works best. This might be my only chance to travel to the forests and Lilyis is getting a fellowship together to go east. The preparations are almost done. You would be welcome to stay here with the Suns or return home to report to Ezil and Evi. I have done enough hiding, it is time to breathe."

"You can't breathe on Westlight? I can't tell them that I've lost our wizard!"

"I will be back at some point—and no one will blame you. No one can expect you to go against me when my mind is made up. You are on your own." She smiled at him softly.

"I can't believe I'll see you leave so soon," Rawil said, pouring out beer. "Can't you ditch Qati at least, so Raz can keep herself occupied for a while longer?"

We'd gathered on our last evening around the brazier; our things were packed and ready, Lilyis had left instructions at the *Golden Drake* and with Yuna herself. Our visit at the west coast had left me with a strange sense of regret, as if I'd failed to do what I'd planned to do, despite the Suns being set up at their tower.

"I'd be more than happy to leave Qati behind, but he seems determined to go back to the Badgers in Thorndell." I glanced over to Raz. "If Raz doesn't want to come …"

The old commander winced. "That's something I can't decide for her. I've kept her with me for a long time and I'd miss her, but in the end, she needs to know where her future lies."

SHIELD

Our eight horses stretched out across the grassland. We'd left the coast early that morning, after saying our goodbyes to Rawil Owl, who'd hugged us all and visibly teared up when bidding their niece farewell, while Raz seemed overjoyed to be allowed to go. With her, we had plenty of blades at our disposal. Comprising two people from the Cities, two Badgers, one Owl, one Cormorant, a Cloud, and a Moon, we certainly were one of the more mixed companies I'd kept.

I'd hoped to see Rawil hug Eleas, but our wizard had kept away from the commander, acknowledging them with a short nod before mounting her tall gelding. Unsurprisingly, the company fell into several pairings: Raz and Qati, Cathil and Qes, me and Lilyis, which meant Eleas and Bjor ended up riding close to each other. Lilyis' grey mare was forging ahead, and Cathil brought up the rear on my old horse.

Before we'd left, Eleas had gone on another one of her pebble hunting excursions, picking up eight flints smoothed into glossy blackness. I'd squatted close to the water line, seeing her weave a prayer over them, as she'd done at her village spring. I didn't need to hear the words to understand the ritual was meant for protection, something quite similar to the words I'd placed on the house in Seagard my family lived in. Her knees had cracked when she straightened up and retrieved the gleaming stones from the foam of the waves, before carefully placing them back. As the only marked wizard among us, Eleas rode in the middle of the group, bedecked with her shell cape and additional necklaces that made a faint clinking sound against it. Her spear was lashed to her saddle, but ready to be at hand in case anyone was stupid enough to try and stop her.

I'd expected at least one of my Siblings to show up during our last night in the camp, but none of them had drawn near and I felt itchy, as if one of them would surely take me to task the next time they materialized, though the breeze scrubbing over the grasslands let me breathe easier as we rode away from the threatening walls of the Harp, away from the council and away from Yuna Elk, who'd stuffed a pile of letters into my bag that I was tempted to read, though Sjunil would've throttled me if the seals arrived with her peeled off or broken. Leaving Rawil had been less painful than expected, a testament to the fact that I'd wanted nothing more than to leave for the forests.

During the last communication we'd had, Rawil had been distracted by other Owls, constantly coming in with messages and questions. The *New Pond* had transformed itself into a centre of command and was beleaguered by scores of people who needed urgent questions answered. Of all the rulers I'd known, Rawil Owl seemed to be the only one actually *doing* something and though they rolled their eyes, I could see that, deep down, they enjoyed themself. I'd left them thumbing through a pile of grass papers, a line of reed pens on the table in front of them, the young man who'd replaced Raz at their side and watching on admiringly.

Ahead, I saw Lilyis nudging her small mare into a canter. Lilyis kept pushing us forwards, in a way that reminded me too much of her father for comfort. With Nivael, I'd always sensed the feeling of dread that had spurred him on, and despite no red sails awaiting us at the Stoneharp, I could feel that the spectre of the Bulls had started to haunt her. Without knowing what exactly had happened to the Sun's rivals, she expected them to pop up behind every rock and cluster of birch trees.

She'd reacted weirdly calm as Qes brought up the question of Cathil Cloud and I'd almost been disappointed not to see her lose her shit. The days it had taken to empty the *Golden Drake,* but for the goods they expected to sell at market in the next few days, had separated us in a way; while I'd helped Qitli with his daily chores, she'd grown into her role of the expedition's leader, with more important things on her mind than petty jealousies.

On the first evening, we slept again under the wide skies of the western grasslands. She curled up at my side and went to sleep straight away, exhaustion coming off her like vapour. I extracted myself from the blankets and joined Qes and Raz on their watch. Lilyis had insisted on breaking up the pairings for the duty, well aware of how much I would've become distracted by her if we would've spent a few hours staring into the flames together. Qes and Raz welcomed me with freshly brewed tea and the leftovers from our evening meal.

"You need to talk," Raz stated, her mouth full of flatbread. "Why don't you sit yourself down."

"Are you nervous about going home?" Qes asked.

I pushed my palms towards the fire. Though the weather had become warmer in general, the nights still held a bite of frost. "Of course I'm nervous. I was never supposed to be away for such a long time, and Mother might not take well to the news that this isn't going to be more than a quick visit. She might've made more plans for me."

"You mean wedding plans?" Raz asked.

"She won't like hearing that I've made my own arrangements, and with someone royal who can't actually marry me."

"You think she'd be fine with it if you could officially join the da Nileons?"

"It'd be an alliance with a powerful family, even if they're based in the Cities. It'd make sense to her if I could spin it like that."

"You're afraid your mother won't take Lilyis seriously?" Raz snorted. "Everyone who spends more than a few moments with her must realize how seriously she needs to be taken."

"You can't expect to shield her from all the Moons," Qes interjected. "She'll live among your sisters in the House of Women and they'll have ample opportunity to interrogate her about anything they'd want to know."

"What if they won't receive us at all? Sjunil spoke to the council at Goldenlake about uniting the families against the men of the Eastern Cities only last year."

"Back then, it seemed a relatively simple task, despite the ancient feuds between us. Much has changed since then, and she knows it. She's seen you becoming attached to the prince, after all. She must know how deeply entangled we all are." Qes sighed. "Face it, Sloe— we could as well wear a yellow tunic and the sun sigil on our chests. We might not get paid as Bjor and the crew are, but …"

"… we still betrayed our families," I finished bitterly. "There'll be many people who see it like that. Siw … Siw might."

When I'd said farewell to my sister so many months before, she'd been reluctant to let me go at all. Before travelling to Goldenlake we'd never liked each other much, as there'd always been rivalry between us. I'd deeply resented her for becoming Aunt Sjunil's apprentice, a position I'd coveted as long as I could think, while she'd never felt called to serve the wizard of Tall Trees and didn't seem to appreciate my aunt. The only aspect of her apprenticeship that had suited her was the duty of the village healer. Siw was talented with herbs and poultices, teas and ointments, and many of the methods I'd employed when living in the Hidden Tower at Crooked Hill I'd gleaned from watching her care for Lilyis' father, when she'd done the actual work involved in saving his life. Siw would be disappointed in the path I'd chosen, the allegiances I'd entered into while I'd been away from the forest.

"Siw will calm the fuck down," Qes said. "Eventually. She still owes me for moving out of the way so she could get her hands on Julas."

We shared a smirk. Julas Raven was someone we both had experience with—in my case it had been a single kiss, for Qes weeks of a relationship fated to turn sour.

"What if Sjunil hates Lilyis—or the other way around? I don't know if I could bear it."

Raz grimaced into her tea bowl. "Your aunt strikes me as someone who knows you too well to be surprised that you fell in love with her. She's probably astonished that you didn't end up as her father's consort."

I blushed and Qes quickly smothered a laugh. "I can't deny there was a time when I would've been happy to consider that." I shot Qes a dirty look. "*Before* he pulled that shit in Goldenlake. Before I started to understand what and who he was." Back then, Nivael had sometimes spoken to me of his wayward son, had told me that I reminded him of Nian da Nileon, and not in a good way. Perhaps the gods had taken their cues from him after all.

"I wouldn't worry too much about Sjunil," Qes said. "Here's some more cheese for you." He handed over the bowl as well as a jar of pickled fruit. "You should go to bed. Lilyis spoke of reaching the river tomorrow."

"Which river?"

"The one that's closest on her strange little map. Knowing her, she won't rest until we can actually see it, even if I tell her a thousand times that the map is wildly inaccurate at best."

I tried not to wake her when I entered our bed but as I tucked the blankets in around me, Lilyis rolled around.

"You're afraid I won't make a good impression on your family?" she asked flatly.

"Oh—you heard that."

"Every single word."

"Ah, shit." My stomach clenched. "I'm sorry."

"I can understand that it must be difficult for you to be placed in this position—between the Moons and the Company of the Sun." I couldn't see her face in the darkness, but there was an edge to her voice. "We knew that would be the difficult bit."

"You're right. It makes no sense to chicken out now."

I felt her reaching for me, her left hand getting tangled in my hair as she leant over. She buried her face in the blankets covering my chest. "Do you want to hide our relationship from them? I mean, you'd still need to rely on Raz keeping her trap shut and that might be somewhat impossible, but …"

"No, of course not! My aunt would see through that straight away. I don't think I'm a good enough liar to deny how I feel about you, Company of the Sun or not."

I could feel her breathe out deeply. "I'm glad to hear it." She pushed in closer, and our noses bumped into each other. "We'll figure it out," she promised.

IF AT ALL POSSIBLE

"I admit, this bit was likely based on more solid information," Qes said as we halted on a ridge. Beneath us, a band of bright water meandered through softly undulating hills and patches of birches in their first leaves. Their colour matched Lilyis' eyes in their brightness.

The first maps of Birkland circulated in the Cities had been drawn up referencing information my father had once supplied to the men he'd encountered at the Stoneharp. He would've pointed out the stream to them. On Lilyis' map, it had the label *Bitterbourne*—she'd shown it to me that morning.

"Let's cross over and have the horses rest on the other side," Lilyis said smugly.

A shrug made the rounds in our company, and we followed her down the hill, the warm wind dancing in our hair. The Bitterbourne was shallower than it had appeared at first sight, its bed strewn with dark-grey pebbles as big as fists and difficult to navigate for the horses. We dismounted and made the crossing of foot.

Cirvi snorted and splashed, quickly darting her shaggy head down to drink and for a while I stopped and let her, watching the rest of the company reach the other side of the river. It was a warm day, reminding us summer was around the corner; the spray of the water felt deliciously cool on my face and a shiver ran through me, as if something in my bones delighted in the presence of it. I was too distracted to notice that my friends hadn't fastened the horses to the birches to allow them to rest as we'd planned, but pulled themselves back into their saddles. Cirvi lifted her head, and I could feel her draw a mighty breath before she let out a reverberating neigh, more a deep-chested bellow, shaking her muscular neck. I had to duck around her to see another group of horses, galloping towards us from behind the thickest clump of trees, their saddle cloths bright red. I started to pull Cirvi around, but she stayed put, as if rooted into the riverbed and trying to shield me from the arrows that started to fly.

Ten riders barrelled towards us; two of them were armed with bows. Cathil took the first one out within moments, rushing at him and flinging his knife into his throat. I heard the Elk come off his saddle with a sickening crunch. The second managed to fire two more arrows before Raz got too close to him, lopping his head off with a single stroke of her blade, then hacking into the next rider.

The party of Elks was made up of young warriors, clearly too inexperienced to realize they'd gone about their ambush in the worst way possible. Perhaps they'd seen Raz' hair bound up in the two knots of the Owls and it was enough to make them attack, or Lilyis and Eleas clothed in the colours of the Cormorants. It was likely that they'd seen a group of seemingly disjointed individuals crossing a river, their saddlebags bulging with provisions and one of them wrapped in the finery of a wizard.

It was an ugly fight, and once more I was left standing in a river, frozen to the spot and breathlessly watching as the rationale behind taking Cathil Cloud with us paid off. I saw him and Raz turn the fight around within a matter of heartbeats. They chased off the last of the Elks without me getting the smallest of fireballs in. Finally, Cirvi decided to move and started to pull me towards the shore.

Bjor was clutching at his left arm, an arrow fletched with crow feathers sticking out between his fingers. He was pale as I reached him, throwing Cirvi's reins at Qati. The arrow had pushed right through, blood trickling along his arm into the grass.

"I'll have this out in no time. Go and sit over there and I'll fetch my herb bag. Anyone else injured?"

"We should move on," Lilyis decided, sheathing her longknife. "Can you patch him up quickly?"

I cut the arrow shaft. Bjor hissed as I pulled it through and tried to stop the blood with a wad of moss and linen. "This will do for now. As soon as I can boil up some water, I'll have to check it more thoroughly. Do you need help getting back on your horse?"

He cursed as I pushed him up, but as soon as I was back on Cirvi myself, he swerved his gelding around and followed the others. We left the three Elks Raz and Cathil had killed back at the river, all too aware we hadn't been properly prepared to be attacked and that being able to drive the Elks off so quickly had been a fluke.

Lilyis only let us stop when the cover of birches got thick enough to hide us. "That was too close of a call," she said. "For all we know, there are dozens of raiding parties loose around us, eager to prove themselves." There was a glitter in her eyes that I'd seen at Smallclere. "The next time we might be too outnumbered to fend them off and it's a fucking wonder they didn't injure any of the horses."

We made a small fire and as the water boiled, I ground up herbs I'd seen Siw use in similar situations and unearthed a small pot of honey. As I peeled Bjor's sleeve back, ready to clean the wound out properly, I saw Raz rubbing the splashes of dried blood off her face and hands. Of all of us, she'd been most involved in the recent fights among the families. Staying at the Harp had made me forget how things truly were in the borderlands. There were so many new interests to factor in, and the Elks seemed to have a proclivity for operating in such a sneaky manner. I'd been more than useless, the last one to notice what was going on: Lilyis had been crossing the Bitterbourne into mortal danger.

Bjor cried out as I prodded him a bit too hard.

"Sorry," I mumbled. "I'll try to be gentler with you."

Eleas came over to watch me work, pointing out things from time to time. "If you tuck in the ends of the bandage like this …"

I found that I liked the way she made suggestions for improvement and followed her hints with relief. Werid of the Far Side, though nominally the master I'd associated myself with, had only taught me for a short time and I hadn't come to rely on their voice. While that made me vulnerable, it also meant I was grateful for anyone who felt the urge to bestow their wisdom on me. Though Eleas had shown herself to possess skills I'd never seen my aunt or indeed Werid demonstrate, widening my horizon to incorporate the techniques of the Cormorants would surely be a good thing.

Bjor pressed a finger to the bandage.

"Hands off," Eleas snapped at him. "Do not undo all the work Sloe has put into it. Thank your gods that they deemed you worthy enough to direct the arrow away from your heart, and for all of us to come out of the attack alive. We cannot expect to always be this lucky."

"Maybe the gods of the Star didn't have to trouble themselves too much on my account," Bjor said quietly.

I saw Eleas flush. "It would be nice to think that my wish to protect us all might have some influence upon your safety." She seemed genuinely pleased. "Evi would not forgive me if I would turn against you. She took quite a shine to you."

Bjor flushed. "I liked her too."

"I know." Eleas patted his shoulder, carefully. "Which is why I want to keep you with us."

That night, we hid ourselves away between the trees. Lilyis didn't allow a fire to be lit, so we munched on stale bread and dried strips of meat. We were still in Owl territory, as Raz said with some conviction, the next family lands we'd have to cross over on our way east belonging to the Clouds and then the Ravens, before we'd finally reach the westernmost parts of the Moon forests. Unless the borders had started to shift in the last year, in which case all bets were off.

I remembered my sister Silid scratching the outlines of the territories we were allied to into the soft soil of the herb gardens, to give me an idea of how wide Mother's powers spread. Back then I'd marvelled at the size of the world around Tall Trees, and had let myself be intimidated by the feeling of being the smallest bit of fluff caught in a vast net of alliances and treaties, some of them generations old, some new and liable to break. Just the thought of telling a younger version of me that I'd journey far beyond those borders made me tear up. Little Sloe wouldn't have believed themself capable of going so far east, and as for coming back amidst a tangle of people bound to me in love and friendship … impossible. Unconceivable.

Cathil and Bjor took first watch to afford Bjor the chance of getting as much uninterrupted rest as possible, and I'd given him another dose of the tea I'd prepared earlier, long since gone cold, with the instruction to only drink it once his watch had ended. Cathil himself sat furthest away from us, but I could make out his hulking form in the shadows among the trees. Moonlight glinted in the whites of his eyes.

Lilyis snuggled into my blue cloak, making the most of the warmth our bodies emitted. I stroked down her side, as if to assure us both we were still there after the attack.

"I felt so useless," I said to her as our company started to disperse and search out their bedrolls.

"You didn't need to do anything today," Lilyis said. "We had it very much under control."

Cathil cleared his throat with a rumble. "You took care of Bjor. What else can a wizard do when they're stuck in a river?"

I heard Lilyis chuckle into my cloak and poked her in the ribs with the tip of my forefinger. "Shut up, please."

Bjor drew breath, but seemed to think better of saying something.

"It didn't feel great," I said.

"You could pray," Cathil suggested. "That could help the next time. Pray that we'll be able to cross the Cloud lands without more raiding parties getting in our way. My sister has really fucked up, and they're all nipping at our heels."

"The Clouds can't be the only family who split after a disagreement on politics," I said. "There must be a way of pushing them together again."

"Yeah. Right. Can you imagine Cjanis backing down?"

"No. Not at all," I had to admit.

"Clouds are known to be almost as stubborn as Badgers," Cathil said. "She was never one to admit to her mistakes. After she got Cirvi killed …"

I swallowed. I'd been present at the gates of the Owl garrison when Cirvi Cloud had been stabbed. I'd inherited my piebald mare from him and called her by his name—how could I ever forget how calculating Cathil's sister had been, how ready to rejoice in getting rid of the older wizard?

Cathil continued, "After she got Cirvi killed, it all spiralled out of control, and while my sisters understood soon that Cjanis had merely acted out of self-interest, she still claimed that all she'd wanted was to serve the family, to ally us with an old enemy to raise us up without having to rely on the men of the Cities. When Lilyis' father sent his negotiator to me in Goldenlake, I truly believed that aligning our interests would give the Clouds an advantage, the chance to make us enough silver to compete with the Mice."

I felt Lilyis straighten up. "Hang on. Seriously?"

"My mother believed in my strategies and the prince's negotiator made some excellent points."

I sucked in a breath. "Because they didn't realize you weren't the one who held the power to decide on the family's course of action. It took Nivael long enough to understand that your sisters were the ones making the important calls. No wonder everything became so fucking complicated."

"It's not complicated at all," Cathil said coldly. "My sisters believed Cjanis long enough to depose my mother and have been fighting among themselves ever since. A divided family is a weak family."

"You're suggesting you didn't have any part in that? Any part at all?"

"That's not what I'm saying," Cathil grumbled.

"Sounds as if you are."

"Shut up, the both of you," Lilyis interrupted. "This is not the time to fall out over politics. Not when we're beset by Elks and Squirrels and who knows who else besides. Come on, Sloe—let's get some sleep."

Cathil huffed. "Do us all a favour and keep it down."

Eleas woke me as our watch began.

I'd slept badly, wondering for a long time if granting Qes' wish to take Cathil east with us hadn't been a terrible mistake, blade skill or no. The day's events had made us all jumpy and irritable.

Eleas handed me the waterskin as we settled among the trees. For a long time we didn't talk, the noises of the picketed horses the only sounds around us. The stars were out, and I shivered into my cloak, resentful that I'd had to struggle upright and leave my girlfriend behind. It took me a while to notice Eleas was praying.

She'd folded her hands together and pressed them against her mouth, but I could hear her breath brushing against her fingers. I couldn't recall the last time I'd prayed to my Siblings with such fervour. Being around them had both convinced me of their powers and disillusioned me further as to their true nature. If I'd learned something on my travels, it was that the Tall Gods weren't reliable. They'd let me gawp at my friends getting rushed by Elks.

"Tell me what is wrong," Eleas said, and I flinched.

"Sorry, I didn't want to interrupt you."

"You did not. But I can *feel* you worry."

"Sorry."

"Stop apologizing and talk to me."

"I felt myself getting jealous. It's been a long time since I've trusted the gods to have my best interests at heart."

"You are breathing. I would presume to count that as a win."

Ever since she made her decision at the Harp, I'd grappled with the realization that I missed her brooding, her hesitancy. Seeing Eleas Cormorant all self-assured and easy to smile irked me more than I wanted to admit. She seemed to have reached a level of peace that thoroughly eluded me.

"I'm scared. I should've been able to blast all of these Elks away, like I did before with the Bulls."

"And make them carry the news of your abilities back to their leaders? It might have been a stroke of luck that you were too caught up to react. We do not want anyone to know, or have you changed your opinion on that?"

"No. Of course not."

"Then what are you griping about?"

"It's the feeling of having no control. Lilyis is the leader of our expedition as she was always meant to be, and she didn't take my feelings into account when …"

"I think you need to keep the notion of Lilyis as the leader and Lilyis as your beloved apart from each other. She might well be forced to make decisions in the future for which she cannot afford to tiptoe around you. She holds the most difficult position and is trying her best. The least you could do is support her, Sloe. Tell her your honest misgivings but do not sulk if she has to forgo taking your advice. I have stood at Ezil's side for many years, and I have seen her struggle with many questions that had no easy answer." She narrowed her eyes at me. "As I recall, you told Qes you were fine with having Cathil come along. You cannot say one thing and expect us to hear something else."

BOLD

The next river we reached was deep and swift-flowing—a natural border to the territories of the Clouds.

"Do we have to expect the same kind of disorder on the other side?" Qes asked.

Cathil lifted his broad shoulders. "Fuck if I know. But given that I'm not the favourite person of any of my sisters right now, I should keep my head down. There'll be a ford somewhere here."

"Upriver or downriver?" Lilyis asked, prompting the same kind of shrug.

"The last time I crossed this far north into our territories, I was ten summers old."

"Let's try upriver," Lilyis decided. "I have no intention of taking us anywhere close to Greycliffs."

Turning north the wind blew across us, balmy and full of the beckoning scents of unfurling leaves and warming soils, of birches coming into the full strength of early summer. The feathery foliage of snow-weed edged the riverbanks, its first parasol-shaped blooms opening and creating wave-like patterns along the waters that hurried along with a silvery noise.

Brother Brook, I found myself thinking, *Brother Brook, please let us come to no harm in these lands. And please let me not freeze in panic again.*

We found the first ford one day's ride upriver, a wide stretch of storm-grey stones, the banks sloping on either side and their grasses cropped short by the goats, sheep, and cattle that used the place regularly, as well as the wild animals of the grasslands, its herds of deer and families of foxes, badgers, and wolves. If

I'd married into the Clouds, the lands before us would've been mine; I would've had the right to claim every one of the little purple stars of the winding weed knots that had woven themselves into the short grass. I rode next to the man who might've been my husband, but for one roll of the dice … Did Cathil feel the weirdness of our situation as much as I did? He slowly fell back to the end of our group, swaddled in Qes' cloak and a dark-blue shawl. Without the hairstyle of the Clouds, he was still too easily recognizable to risk riding about bare headed.

In the ford, the water barely came up to the horses' fetlocks; the pebbles were small enough to cross over comfortably and we held a quick rest to refill our waterskins and let the horses drink before setting out east again, over rolling hills covered in loose constellations of tall birches, the space between them kept open by grazing animals passing through the landscape. There, the name the men of the Cities had once chosen for the lands of the families made sense—that part of our continent was indeed a land of birches. They'd believed it to be the heart of us, the essence of what we were about, and other regions must've been deeply disappointing to them when the sweetness of our hills turned into empty grasslands, densest forests, dark and hostile, or the bleak waste of the steppes, to the east of the Golden Lake.

Even among such beauty, we moved though plenty of places perfect for another ambush and kept the longknives close. We rode in a tight huddle, clustered around our wizard and Bjor, who wore his injured arm bound across his chest. Raz and Lilyis led us over the hills, Qes and Cathil guarded our rear, but it was only a matter of time until we spotted a settlement that hadn't been marked on the map. We moved in wide loops to avoid any contact with the Clouds of the area. The houses we'd seen from afar had been fashioned from wood, thatched with dried grasses and surrounded by artificial ponds to keep freshwater fish and grow reeds to transport further inland. Herb gardens stretched out at the bottom of the shallow valleys and orchards were coming into flower, visible from far away and often the best indicator that we drew too close to a village.

From time to time, Cathil hazarded a guess as to where we actually were, and how long it would take us to reach the easternmost border. Despite the precautions we took, we were soon discovered. We'd tried to circumnavigate another village as we happened upon a hunting party, bringing back a couple of deer slung over the broad back of a horse: big animals, already gutted, their heads lolling over the side of the pack saddle.

Raz did the only sensible thing. She put on her most radiant smile, greeted the group of young Clouds, most of them women with the traditional topknot, and asked them for the best route, what their village was called, and whether there were more rivers we needed to be aware of.

"We're on our way to Goldenlake," she said, not quite a lie. "To attend the summer festival, now that things at the Stoneharp have gone tits-up."

The leader of the hunting party, a woman with narrow eyes and a soft mouth, smiled back readily enough. "Are things so bad out west?"

"You can't imagine the chaos. Most of the wizards have fled and the camp is in shambles. We'd hoped to take part in the public ceremonies, but no one can be arsed to hold them. The spring festival was an utter disappointment and …"

"So you're bringing your wizard to the Golden Lake?" The Cloud nodded. "You'll have a better chance to find the favour of the Tall Ones at the lake, though I'd keep more towards the south, to meet the Sweetwater ford."

"Thank you, that is most helpful. May Brother Rain keep you dry."

The Clouds reacted with gestures of thanks to her blessing and made no attempt to hinder our parting.

"That was well done," Eleas said as we were out of earshot. "An excellent tale to tell and the only sensible explanation for travelling in such varied company. Does this help you?" she asked Cathil.

"I know exactly where we are," he said. "We still have a fair way to go if we are to cross the Sweetwater. I'd hoped we'd gone around it somehow. Whatever excuse we offer up, the news of our party will speed through the lands. We better get our story straight."

"I've spent enough time at the Harp to have seen myriads of rag-tag pilgrim groups come and go," Raz said. "Most of them have at least one wizard among them who leads them in their prayers."

"Yes," Cathil agreed. "I remember Torgall mouthing off about them. They were notoriously difficult to control and some of them could get stroppy if asked to pay their way."

"'Stroppy' might be the best description for us that I've ever heard." Raz grinned at Qati, who scowled back at her. "Stroppy and scrappy. We should use the most direct way we can and stick to this excuse."

"There are many villages around these parts," Cathil said. "We might end up riding in circles if we try to avoid them all."

Lilyis scowled. "Then we should be bold," she decided after some deliberation. "Bold like pilgrims who see themselves as serving their gods' will. We can't waste weeks if there's the possibility of the Bulls beating us to Goldenlake."

"Right," Raz said, with a glitter in her eyes that made my breath hitch. "Then let's be bold as fuck."

Over the next few days, we drew a lot of attention. We were gawped at by Clouds herding goats, Clouds weeding their gardens, Clouds chopping firewood and fetching water. Eleas rode in front, her spear placed into a stirrup and pointing the way. She wore every single shell ornament we'd brought with us and a circlet of silver on her brow. Her face was closed off and as haughty as when we'd first met her.

Our company had gone from skulking around the hills to shouting out our presence.

We others wore our amulets openly, to signpost the fact that we believed ourselves on a mission to commune with our gods in the most ostentatious way possible. Qes carried a small silver pendant in the shape of a branch covered in stylized leaves that I'd never seen on him before and Qati seemed to have amassed his own collection of charms. Raz wore the likeness of Brother Moon and a large pin in the shape of a half-moon on her left shoulder. Every one of us had things squirreled away that made a glorious appearance. It was the first time since Eastbay that my own treasures were openly on display, and it was a strangely vulnerable experience. The families we belonged to might favour a certain Sibling, but who we actually prayed to was a private matter. I was astounded to see that Cathil wore the expected pendant connected to Cousin Blade, but also the loaf of Cousin Crumb, while Qati sported an amulet dedicated to Cousin Pearl, one of the Small Gods my ex-boyfriend Saon had favoured to support his creativity. I'd never noticed Qati engaged in anything artistic.

When we finally drew near to the ford where we planned to cross the Sweetwater, the sight of a group of tents at its banks made me break out in goosebumps. It was a good place to be, the only crossing in a long stretch of the river, and in the coming centuries there might well be a proper settlement there, taking advantage of passing travellers. A small cart waited for us, stacked with useful things: new saddle cloths and waterskins, piles of flatbreads, and rounds of salted cheese. A cooking fire burned among the tents, where fresh bread was baked and tea prepared, its scent drawing us in, and it only took a quick glance from Lilyis to let us dismount.

Raz bought some bread and cheese and chatted amicably with the Clouds running the cart and fire, telling yet another variety of our tale. I gave my reins to Qes and walked around the tents to find a place to pee. There were other carts and clothes hung out to dry, and a small group of goats as well as horses fastened to a picket line, most of them bays and chestnuts, though one of them drew my eye: a black and white piebald, similar to the mare I'd arrived on.

"Oh fuck."

As I spun around, a woman blocked my way.

"How did you think this could possibly work?" Cjanis Cloud was changed since I'd last seen her. She'd become gaunt, almost rangy, and the severe hairstyle of the Clouds exaggerated it. Her eyes bulged from her face. "You can dress my brother up as much as you want, but there'll always be people who know exactly who he is. It was a stupid idea to come back."

To my astonishment, my heart beat slow and even. There had been a time when just the thought about talking to Cathil's sister again would've sent me into a panic. "I'm beginning to realize that—alas, I don't have another option. I want to go home."

"I thought you wanted to go to Goldenlake."

"Yes ... after."

"If they're smart, they'll kill you."

"They can try."

Cjanis' longknife was at my throat before I could take another breath. I felt it bite into my skin. "I've dreamt of this moment, Sloe Moon of Tall Trees. On your knees. *Now.*"

"Speaking of bad ideas ..."

"If you want to see your friends live—kneel."

The blade bit deeper as I swallowed. I held up my hands and knelt in the grass, its dampness marking my trousers. "Cjanis …"

"Shut the fuck up. I don't need another word out of you." She stepped close and pushed my head down.

Suddenly a swarm of Clouds was around us, clad in silver-grey cloaks, though something on them looked different. They wore sashes tied across their bodies, embroidered with swirls and spirals. These were Cjanis' own Renegades, so many of them that I knew that we'd failed. It'd been a while since I'd been taken prisoner, but I had a certain amount of experience in being threatened. I could see the outrage in Lilyis' face as she was bundled among the tents. One of Cjanis' Clouds boxed Bjor in the bandaged arm and he collapsed with a bellow of pain. We were wrestled to our knees, ropes appeared. Our wrists were lashed together.

Eleas face was still, her long black hair falling across it like a sheet. The gaze of one dark eye bored into mine. We'd work together to free us. Cjanis might have a suspicion that I was capable of more than her bands of outcasts believed possible, but she had no idea about Eleas. I heard Lilyis groan as someone kicked her between the shoulder blades and my beloved fell forward, still furious, her anger shielding her from the coldness that settled in my stomach.

"I thought you'd finally learned your lesson, little brother." Cjanis gestured towards one of her followers to take care of me, while she focused on Cathil. She'd always loved to lay out her superiority, but as she strode across the grass to face him, I couldn't help but think she looked wild, like someone who'd kept themself alive by clinging to their convictions, despite the evidence that the water around them was rising. She was hungry, like one of the starving wolves in the stories. When Cathil lifted his chin to answer her, she kicked him in the face with all the strength she had.

ATTENTION DIVERTED

Cathil's nose broke with a *crack* so loud everyone flinched. Once I'd believed his sister to be a valuable ally, someone standing on my side. I'd even fancied her for a bit.

She kicked him again, and again—to the point where her Renegades started to appear uncomfortable, spittle flying from her mouth with the exertion of so much violence.

"Stop!" Qes screamed at her. "He's already passed out!"

She gave her brother one more kick and wiped her sleeve across her face, before turning to my cousin. I felt the attention of the Cloud who held the blade to my own neck slip as he watched his leader, waiting for her to explode once more. I needed to be careful. I needed to wait for the best opportunity to shake myself free.

"He's always found desperate men who are taken in by his shit," Cjanis yelled at Qes. "He's always survived on the lust and the awe of the likes of you." She bent down and squeezed Qes' face between her fingers, her nails digging into his scarred cheeks. "You are weak enough, I suppose. You might do for him until he finds the next fool to marry." She shot me a blood-flecked grin. I felt myself freeze. I needed her attention diverted; I needed her back turned …

"At least *you* managed to stay clear—or did you? He can't have let you go that easily." She spat on the lifeless form of her little brother. "All those months of being cast out must've made him less likely to do something stupid enough to anger you again. Don't be taken in, Sloe Moon of Tall Trees. He's made his bed and he must bear its filth." She moved her shoulders as if she gathered her strength for another assault. I braced myself—she wheeled around and punched Qes in the mouth.

"Get. Away. From. Him." The words came like blasts through my clenched teeth.

She shook out her hand and that bloody grin was back, the one I wanted to burn off her face. I felt my Siblings huddle around me, the protective scrum I'd longed for.

She laughed at me. "Is that a warning?" She gestured towards the Cloud who held me, and I felt another cut of the blade. Blood trickled into my collar, running across my skin in a line of drops. "Do you really presume to admonish me, on your knees and …" She sneered. "So utterly, utterly pathetic?"

"You haven't seen anything yet." I drew in a deep breath. "*Brother Rain, keep me dry.*"

He formed himself from the mass of his Siblings, a fan of hurling droplets, wrapping around the wizard and drenching her to the bone. I knew his face—a face that bared its teeth at me in a mischievous grin.

The blade slipped from my neck. I was on my feet before my thoughts could catch up.

Cjanis stared at me, her sleeves and cloak dripping, rivulets of rainwater running down the sides of her face. "No," she whispered, then started to screech. "No, no, *no*! Brother Rain is mine!" She fumbled for her longknife, trying to grasp the sodden leather wrapped around the hilt.

I instinctively brought up my arms, anticipating flame or wave—but another almighty crack sang out and Cjanis Cloud pitched forwards, falling flat on her face.

We all stared at the boy who'd snuck up behind her, wielding his knife like a club. Corlian Cloud, the boy Eleas had assisted in Greycliffs, gulped and started to shake.

"I'm so sorry," he whispered. "I should've been quicker."

"Why are you even here?" Eleas asked him.

"I was sent to meet Cjanis with some of my cousins." He sat slumped in the grass while the Renegades secured their former leader with the ropes that had been meant for us.

"What happened?" Eleas asked and I saw that she touched the boy's elbow, a reassuring gesture, and one she wouldn't have attempted when I'd met her first, for fear of hurting him.

"We were supposed to find out … but now I'm the only one of us left …" He rubbed his eyes. "Many in Cjanis' party have already gone and tried to join the side of her sisters again. Others have died, succumbing to their wounds over winter. When her back was turned, others spoke again of deserting her."

"They sent boys to spy on Cjanis?" Qati muttered, clearly shocked. As an outsider living in Greycliffs, he must've been witness to many of the recent troubles of the Clouds. He cursed under his breath, his narrow face filled with more compassion than I'd ever seen him display. "That's madness. Corlian, did you get hurt?"

"I was the lucky one. Again," the boy said with bitterness. "It only took her a few days to decimate her ranks. We fought her sisters a few miles' ride from here and were soundly beaten, before the news reached us that her brother had been sighted as part of a company of fanatics travelling to Goldenlake." He sniffled. "When I heard that the wizard with them wore a cape of shells, I knew it must be you," he said to Eleas. "I couldn't let her kill you." He blushed and I saw the wizard's eyes widen in dismay.

"We thank you for your help," she said, carefully folding her hands into each other. "It was a truly heroic deed and you saved us all." She glanced at me to continue and I cleared my throat.

"Thank you," I echoed. "Where will they take her?"

"Back to Greycliffs, I imagine. For her sisters to decide how she might be punished." Corlian's bottom lip started to twitch. The true implications of what he'd done started to hit home.

"Can we wrap this up?" Lilyis, her knees wet from being forced into the grass, laid a hand on my shoulder. "Could you see to Cathil and Qes so we can get the fuck out of here?"

I pushed myself up.

Cathil lay where his sister had left him. Qes sat bent over him, trying to wipe his face. My cousin had a bloody nose but seemed fine. As he glanced up at me, his dark eyes softened.

"His eyelids fluttered a few times but he's not conscious yet."

"Can we somehow get him up and on his horse? Lilyis is impatient to move on."

"I can't blame her. What a disaster." He glanced over to where Cjanis Cloud had been pushed onto an upturned basket, slumped, her topknot slowly disintegrating. "Though it could've been worse, I suppose. What will happen to the boy?"

"The Clouds will take him back with them, to report on what has happened here today. He'll be fine—he's only a bit shaken up. It's not every day you bash your wizard over the head with the hilt of a dagger. Whatever Cjanis' original intentions were, I'd say she's run her course."

"What did you do to her?"

"I turned her god against her."

"Oh. That was mean."

"You saw what she did to her own brother. She would've done much worse to you. Let me have a look at him, Qes."

Most of Cjanis' kicks had been directed at Cathil's face, which was swelling up rapidly, and there'd be lots of bruising around the neck. Knowing him, he'd probably end up more beautiful. "He's going to be fine—at least he's breathing." I pushed my fingers into his mouth. "None of his teeth seem to have come loose. Can you get me some water?"

While Qes left me alone with him, I tried to figure out how the attack made me feel. Could I have intervened much earlier, even with the blade at my neck? Did I want to see Cjanis wrath let loose on him?

Qes brought a leather bucket of icy water and the saddlebag that held my emergency herb kit. I soaked a rag and cooled Cathil's face, cleaning off the last of the blood. His lips were split, so I dabbed some of my salve on them. Cjanis hadn't been at the height of her strength; the skin was only broken in a few places, on his hairline and above his right ear. As I wiped into the wound on his temple, he flinched and his eyes flew open, as far as the bruised flesh would allow. A strangled sound broke from him.

Qes pushed me aside. "Cathil? Oh gods, Cathil!"

The west's most famous warrior scrabbled on all fours, tried to push himself up, mewling in pain.

"Can you ride?" I asked.

Cathil snarled, spitting blood. "Can't you give me one fucking moment?"

We left the Clouds behind shortly after. Eleas granted Corlian a hug and after everything that had happened, her gesture of kindness made me tear up. Cathil was able to mount his horse by himself, without any of us throwing out our backs in the attempt to lift him. We crossed the Sweetwater, deeply relieved to flee the scene of Cjanis Cloud's downfall.

I had a sour taste in my mouth. In the months I'd been away from Birkland, Cathil's sister had taken too many risks, and had caused the deaths of too many people. I'd sensed the poisonous ambition in her from the start, and had been attracted to it at first. It was no wonder that she'd succeeded in luring so many Clouds away from her sisters. However, I'd also felt the hesitation in the blade of the Cloud who'd held and threatened me. I lifted my hand to my neck and probed the shallow cuts that had already clogged up. I'd lost count of the times I'd been bled in such a way.

I shuddered in my saddle as I recalled the coldness of Brother Rain whirling out of the throng of the gods I walked with every day. He'd not given himself a face for my sake, but I'd recognized him anyway, in the set of his shoulders and the arrogance of it: Cirvi Cloud, the first wizard I'd seen getting killed.

In time, what had happened at the river would come to be known as the Sweetwater Rising, a few moments of mayhem that shifted the power dynamics in the lands of the Clouds for decades to come. One incident of violence against her own family, appalling enough for no one to intervene as Corlian had sneaked up on his own wizard. How fitting that Cjanis' demise was brought about by someone she'd underestimated.

The next two days, we barely stopped to catch our breath, trying to be neither especially furtive or to draw as much attention to ourselves. When we finally found ourselves in the lands of the Ravens, a heavy weight lifted from all our shoulders. No river guarded the border, but we saw a throng of shepherds from afar, dressed in dark-grey cloaks and wearing their hair long as Julas did. We'd passed over sometime during the day, leaving the chaos of Cloud family politics behind.

I saw Cathil breathe out in relief. Despite regular administrations of salve and cooling plasters he was pretty beaten up, the purple of the bruises starting to fade to green around the edges. He reminded me of the figs we'd been served in the Cities. I also noticed there were whole hours when Qati lost his scowl. It might've been due to the exhaustion that had settled on us like a leaden blanket, or because he'd had his first taste of what I was able to call forth if I wished to, the strength I could collect and use to keep us safe. As we made camp on our first day on Raven land, I saw Raz settling down next to him and wrapping her arms around him. For once Qati settled against her shoulder, his one eye closed, his right hand folding into hers.

"I think you need to allow us a day of rest," I said to Lilyis.

She herself had dark circles under her eyes, her braid was greasy and tangled. She ripped a flatbread in half. "Maybe tomorrow."

Bjor cleared his throat. "Sloe's right. The horses could use a break. There's grass and water here, some shelter. This is a spot as good as any."

"Are you saying I'm starting to run from my own shadow?" she asked him in the words of the Cities.

"I'm saying you don't want your own Cjanis Cloud situation on your hands," Bjor said flatly.

"Fine." She sighed. "On your head be it. I'm trying to keep us safe."

"We can't be safe if we fall asleep in our saddles," Bjor said. "The Bulls will be wherever they are—and we don't know if my cousins have made the crossing. Is this what you're actually worried about?" He smiled at her. "Or are you just nervous about meeting Sloe's family and want to get it over with?"

Lilyis gasped, narrowing her bright-green eyes at her compatriot. I remembered how much her father had hurried us along the roads of the Hillakes when he'd expected a bollocking from the king.

"Maybe," Lilyis said cautiously. "They might hate me on sight."

WAKE UP

We set up watches for the day so that the others could sleep or catch up on repairs. I checked Bjor's arm. The wound was closing up nicely.

"Thank you," I whispered. "I think she needed that."

"She seemed to be in a constant panic," he said quietly. "You have to keep an eye on that. Whatever the Bulls fuck up in the meantime, she can't be held responsible for what goes wrong before we're there to step in."

"I'll pay more attention to that," I said. "You're healing up well, by the way. How are you feeling generally?"

He moaned softly as I covered the wound with a fresh coating of salve. "I'm starting to appreciate why you felt so out of your depth in Seagard. This is different to everything known to me before. How could you ever make a success of it at court?" He smiled wryly. "Probably because families work in the same way, east or west. I can't wait to see Tall Trees."

I snorted in surprise. "Really?"

"I always thought the name of your home village to be very evocative."

"Evocative of what?"

"Forests?" He grinned and I had to resist poking the nail of my forefinger into the scab. "I always thought of gigantic oak trees, swaying, thousands of years old and watching over the Moons growing up beneath their branches."

"It's nothing like that." I wiped my sticky hands on a cloth. "It's full of chickens, goats, and bickering people. Smells like that too, especially in the winter. Perhaps my father had the right idea in turning his back on it after all."

"I'm beginning to suspect I could be much happier in Birkland than in the Cities," Bjor said. "It's quite beautiful."

"Still smelly."

"Everywhere is smelly. Have you forgotten about the stink in the streets after the snow melted in Seagard?"

I shuddered. "No."

"It's nice to see new people who don't have an instant opinion of me, because of my family name. People can reinvent themselves in Birkland—not just Lilyis."

"Are you thinking of staying here?"

"She'll need agents on this side of the sea, won't she?" He pulled the sleeve down over the fresh bandage. "Thank you, Sloe. You're getting rather good at this."

"I didn't hurt you that much?"

"Not today." He started to come to his feet. "I'll check the horses over."

"Qes already did that."

Bjor pointed his chin to the left of me. "They could use a second check."

I turned around.

Lilyis stood behind me, yawning, her face full of red welts where the folded cloak she'd used as a pillow had pressed into her skin.

"How are you?" I asked her, packing the paraphernalia into the herb basket.

"Even more tired than before."

"I'm sorry. I hadn't realized how much you struggled."

"You were distracted." She yawned again. "Is there tea?"

"I can make you some."

We went over to the small ring of stones and built up the fire. I emptied a skin of water into the teapot and gathered the other set of herbs from the kitchen pack Qitli Badger had stocked up for us.

"Why are you so worried?" I asked her.

She rubbed her palms through her face. "Because it dawned on me that essentially, we're doing the same thing as when we brought my sister to her future husband in Eastbay. It might be less formal, but it is a princess meeting the family of her prince for the first time. These people have known you your whole life, while I only have been a part of it for a short time. What will they say if you tell them marriage is not an option? Will they take us seriously at all? Will they go so far as to kick me out? I'm of the Eastern Cities, how can that not bother them?" She pressed her eyes shut. "None of them knows what we went through, how difficult it is to make it work every single day."

"You think it's that difficult?" I gave the teapot a poke with the firestick, not daring to glance at her.

"Does it feel easy to you? I mean, compared to living with Fiolis it's a walk in the rose garden, but … every day you do things that freak me out."

My stomach lurched. "Like what?"

"Like what you did to Cjanis Cloud. I know what you are, but I don't get a demonstration that often. That was something new, wasn't it?"

"Yes."

"Because you took something from her?"

"I think so. I'm not sure, but that seems to be how it generally works."

"At court you were the outsider, the one who stood apart, but here you fit in. Here it's me who needs to change her perspective, her opinions. Sometimes it's difficult to decide whether anything I held true is actually wrong or … You haven't grown up with the Star, you don't know how it feels to see all of its rules being so deliberately overturned. Even if I'm among those profiting from it, I can't help feeling guilty—and full of shame, when I'm not actively working against feeling like this. It's utterly exhausting."

"I felt it on the Continent sometimes, never understanding the rules in their totality. Always on the verge of committing the most awful blunders. There might be some who'll speak against you, but the only people in Tall Trees who are important to me are my aunt and my sisters. I can't see them taking against you."

"What about your mother?"

"I don't know what Mother is going to do. It might make sense to expect that she won't be thrilled to see her youngest child in love with someone from the Cities, but she might not be terribly surprised. Nothing she plans for me ever goes her way. It started with my name."

"Why, what happened with your name?"

"It wasn't supposed to be mine. My aunt blurted it out when she saw me for the first time, before the official ceremony had started. The word of a wizard is difficult to retract. Mother understood the gods had recognized me and that she couldn't change it if she wanted me to be found and heard by them again."

"Given your talents, she should probably have changed it. The Siblings find you a bit too easily." It was good to see her smile.

"I haven't had a very close relationship with my mother, in case you couldn't tell. She's always been busy with her responsibilities and so I was mainly raised by my sisters, until I chose the Other House to live in."

"You didn't have a happy childhood in the forests?"

"Not after my father was given up for dead. And before … I remembered some of the words he taught me and some of his stories, but mostly I remember him drunk. I think I clung to this spectre of him because I needed one parent who wasn't to blame for everything wrong with my life. I knew it wasn't fair."

"I understand. For me it was the other way around, my mother being actually dead." She watched me slip the herbs into the boiling water to steep. "It seems this is another thing we have in common."

"Like any member of the family, I worked with the animals and in the gardens as long as I can think back. There's no difference between the children of a leader and other family members in our work responsibilities. We played by the rivers and sometimes we were allowed to join hunting parties. Until I realized that I wouldn't become my aunt's apprentice one day, I looked forward to the ceremonies she held on prayer days. There were always many people around but somehow, I still think of that time as lonely. Isn't that weird?"

"I don't think it is. I've never felt more alone than on the day of my wedding, when the whole of Crooked Hill was crammed to the rafters with guests in my honour." She leant in to pour out our tea. As she handed me my bowl, her touch lingered on my hand. "I was kept apart from my sisters, and I hated most of my male cousins. Our lessons were endless, and they were all better at languages. They enjoyed seeing me get the whip for the mistakes I made. The only way I could take my revenge was to unleash all my fury on them in the training square, where my uncle found me talented and tried to single me out. It took a lot of split lips and scraped knuckles to assert my place. I know my sisters' lives weren't much easier than mine, just difficult in a different way, but I was jealous of them, especially of Nuvalis, who always has been my father's favourite. I hated that I was the first of us to be given away in marriage."

"I hated that I seemed to be destined to be the last. Apart from Siw, but future wizards are not supposed to be bartered with anyway."

"Really? Won't your mother accept that pertains to you? You, as the wizardliest wizard of them all?"

"No one in Tall Trees knows me like this, Lilyis. When I left home, I was Qarim Badger's odd brat who was stupid enough to end the only relationship they ever had, merely because their boyfriend made them feel bad. The one no one wanted to marry anyway, because of their father's bad reputation and their general weirdness." A sour taste crept into my mouth once again. "None of the Siblings had attached themselves to me at that point—that started much later. When I left, Mother gave me to Brother Brook, and though I'd prayed to him a few times before, I hadn't chosen anyone to give my favour to yet. I was still unsure which area in my life I needed the most help with. All of them, as it turns out. Perhaps that's why. Maybe they sense all the gaps in my soul that need to be stoppered and flock to me."

She sniffed. "Don't milk it."

"What?"

"Don't play dumb with me, Sloe. That's not the best explanation for why things have happened to you. Events in your life could have called them forth, and nothing much befell you before you left Tall Trees. You said that Crooked Hill sits upon a hill full of crystals that suppress the presence of your gods?"

I winced. "That's not quite right, but …"

"Tall Trees may once have been built on a similar reservoir. There must be good reasons why places are where they are. It took you a while to wake up to your potential."

"The wizards of Tall Trees have traditionally lived outside the village …"

"That sounds like a question to put to your aunt, Sloe."

I gulped. "Sorry, but you've blown my mind." I stared at the dark-green liquid that cooled in my clay bowl.

She smiled at me. "That's what I'm here for."

Eleas glanced up to me, her hands submerged in the water of the shallow brook we'd brought the horses to earlier. "This is the first sequence of movements I learned from my master." She'd squatted down and with her bony knees sticking out to both sides of her body she reminded me of a spindly frog. Her long-fingered hands caressed the water, her clean nails like pearls under its greenish surface. "Try it."

"Do I have to crouch like that? I don't think I can hold up my weight for that long."

"You can kneel if you want to."

I settled as close to the water's edge as I could. Goosebumps travelled up my arms as I stuck my own hands in. Next to Eleas' they were massive and rough, the little silvery scars more pronounced than usual. I tried to mimic the easiest of the water prayers. Despite my initial clumsiness the effect was beautiful, mesmerizing.

"Do it a few times to memorize the movements," Eleas said quietly. "Then we will combine it with the next one." She drew her hands back and watched me for a while, correcting me when I became too sloppy. "That looks good. For the second prayer, we start turning the palms upwards and down again—see, like this."

I watched her demonstration with bated breath. As I joined in, she gave a delighted laugh.

"Can you feel your heartbeat slowing?"

"No. I'm too anxious about doing something wrong."

"You will feel the calming effect of the practice as soon as you become more familiar with it. As soon as you do not have to think about the sequences and can combine them at random. It has often helped me to overcome … problems." She shook droplets from her hands and folded her arms across her knees. "Do it from the start. Both sequences after another."

I drew a deep breath and did as she'd asked me to do, and I could feel the coolness of the water calming me, drawing me out into its depth, the soft silt of the shallows, the swirling leaves that passed us on their way; spirals formed over my skin, making me sway, lengthening my breaths, and as my hands were finally met and pressed up to my chest, it took me a few heartbeats to realize that I should've expected him to answer in some way.

His hair was darker, plastered to his back and shoulders. There were drops in his lashes and his smile as suggestive as ever.

"You're almost home again," Brother Brook said, the smell of him hitting me after the words. "I am ready to be thanked for it. Properly."

EXPECT TO BE THANKED

Brother Brook's hands were still pressed against mine.

"What would you want from me?" I asked my Sibling.

"Not much." He grinned. "Oh, wait. There are gifts that are more … traditional." He released me and crossed his arms on the bank of the stream. I heard Eleas' breath rasping in shock as he beamed at us both.

"Traditional?" I prompted him.

"Many warriors have offered up their most valued weapons to me."

"I'm not a warrior."

"But you are. Haven't you understood that yet, Sloe Moon of Tall Trees?" He stretched out his dripping arm again and touched the tip of my nose, none too gently. "I've told them many times that you're the one we've been waiting for. Oh, and you." He winked at Eleas, who made a strangled noise.

"Whom did you tell?"

"My brothers and my sisters—some of the cousins. They thought I was mad to believe there was someone again, after all that time. Someone who can do what you do."

I felt my face distort into a confused frown. "What do I do?"

"You connect. You combine. You splice. You create. I knew it from the start, I *discovered* you." He sounded so self-congratulatory that for once he didn't remind me at all of Tjal na Tialin. "Don't get me wrong, there have been many people like your lanky friend here, or your aunt, for that matter—people who were pushed to the margins if they were lucky or imprisoned and written out of history if they managed to piss off the councils. With you standing among them, we have so many more options."

I blinked, trying to keep up with his words. "Wait—my *aunt?*"

"I once had great hopes for her, but she turned out to be too headstrong to manage."

Suddenly I remembered the day Sjunil saved me from the council, from Cjanis Cloud. She'd blown the door off its hinges.

"She never told me," I mumbled.

"See—I need to do everything around here." He sniffed. "Think about it. I will expect to be thanked." He pushed himself off the edge and sank, the shallow waters closing over his sleek head.

"Was he always so creepy?" Eleas asked as we walked back to join the others.

"He's definitely the creepiest of the Siblings I've met. As well as the most demanding."

"I suppose he is starting to feel left out if he was the first to walk beside you and now all the others have started to join in."

"Shouldn't a god be above it?" I thought it over. "You know what? Forget that. It's absolutely what gods are about, and he's only the most intrusive of them."

"You need to watch yourself with Sister Storm," Eleas advised, the teardrop-shaped mark on her forehead crinkled. "There is always a lot of subtext with her."

"It gets ever more complicated." I stopped walking for a few breaths. "I'm glad I have someone to compare notes with. Whatever caused us to meet, if it was the will of the gods or pure coincidence, I'm so glad we came to Westlight."

I heard her give a quiet snort of amusement. "You still believe in coincidence, after everything that happened? After everything he said to you?"

"I need to have some illusions left. If I came to understand there's no space for me to exercise my own free will, I don't know if I'd be able to breathe."

Her brows arched. "That is an unusual point of view to have for a wizard."

Biting my bottom lip, I admitted, "I'm still not sure whether I'm a wizard after all."

"You do?"

"I'm beginning to wonder whether there shouldn't be another name for people like us. People who can wield the powers of the gods, not just speak to them face to face. Especially now that the Stoneharp is starting to crumble away."

Eleas lifted her right hand to cover the mark on her forehead. "But this is me," she said.

I slept badly that night. My dreams were full of familiar faces that didn't quite match the people they'd been borrowed from, as if all the Cousins had decided to chime in with the song. At one point I woke Lilyis as I cried out in fear, feeling myself overrun with their presence, crowded out of my own mind. I only managed to fall back asleep shortly before Eleas woke me to start our watch.

We'd been given the last watch of the night. Usually, it was a good one: time to slowly start preparing breakfast and talk through some of my questions with her, but my dreams had left me raw and moody, so we spent most of our time together not saying anything at all. What would have been the point of scaring Eleas by recounting what fears had invaded my sleep? I was relieved as the darkness lifted and the first colours became distinguishable around us.

"Good morning." Lilyis bent over me and kissed the top of my head. "What's with the face?"

"It's my fucking face."

She huffed. "You did get your day of rest, didn't you? What makes you so grumpy all of a sudden?"

"Do not mind them," Eleas said and offered her a bowl of freshly brewed tea. "They have been in a strop for hours. There is bread and cheese if you are already hungry."

"I could eat." Lilyis knelt down next to the wizard. "So … having arrived on Raven land, is there anything specific I should know?"

"There are many ties between the Ravens and the Moons." Qes stumbled across the camp, with a yawn so wide his jaw crackled. "It might be a good idea to let Sloe ride in the lead with you." He took a toasted flatbread from the bowl next to my girlfriend. "We should try to stay in one of the Raven villages for a night or so to catch up on the most essential news."

Lilyis massaged the back of her neck. "A night sleeping off the ground sounds good right now," she groaned. "Didn't help that Sloe kept turning like a hog on a spit tonight."

Qes sat down next to me. "Bad dreams?" he asked.

"Horrible dreams. This was supposed to let us recuperate, instead I'm feeling as if a herd of cattle had stampeded across me."

"You are getting older," Eleas said, and I slapped her arm. "What? In our line of work we need to be grateful for every year the Siblings grant us. Every day away from the abyss is a good day. Tea?" she asked Qes, and my cousin nodded, his mouth already stuffed with bread. "I think you should hold a little ceremony, Sloe."

I glared at her. "Ceremony?"

"To give proper thanks to Brother Brook for guiding you home. We could do it at the next river we ford. That will hopefully keep him happy for a while, at least until you have actually reached Tall Trees."

"I've never led a ceremony before."

"This is what wizards do." She smiled at me. "Even wizards who are in two minds about their destiny."

The next body of water we reached wasn't a river, but a lake between wooded hilltops, with a small settlement at its southern end. Jetties had been built into the water and narrow boats jostled against each other, filled with baskets and painted with birch tar, some of them covered with hides against the rain.

"Brilliant. Two birds with one stone," Qes said.

"Can we get dry before I start with the prayers?" I muttered.

Lilyis shook the raindrops from her felted hood. "Yes, good plan. Is it always raining this much in spring?"

"Not every spring," Qes answered her. "We had a lot of luck with the weather before. Will you do the honours, Sloe?"

I fussed with my blue cloak. I didn't have anything on me bearing the sigil of the Moons, but there weren't many families who preferred to wear blue; it was much too expensive to dye, especially so far inland, with sporadic access to the necessary plants coming from the Eastern Cities.

We were spotted as soon as we came to the path leading eastwards around the lake. A group of children broke out in excited yips and a few men and women looked up. They were working on a row of boats resting on benches beneath the overhanging roofs of the village Roundhouse and began to walk towards us. Some of them carried their tools, sharp enough to do serious damage if our company should turn out to be a threat. I felt my heart hammer in my throat, my bladder twinge. Not that long ago I'd walked into state rooms in Crooked Hill, Pietwood, and Eastbay—riding into the village should've been nothing at all. On the Continent, no one had actually known me that well, but in Birkland I represented the whole of the Moons.

The first who reached me was a broad-shouldered woman with eyes as grey as lightest flint; in her right hand hung a short-shafted axe, its edge gleaming. "Where do you think you're going?" she growled.

"We would like to ask for shelter for the night. We're absolutely drenched."

"We don't get a lot of people travelling through here," she said. "Most are clever enough to leave us well alone." She eyed the others behind me. Rain ran over her face, dripped from her long dark braid. "You don't seem to belong together."

"These are my friends. We are on our way to Tall Trees, to see my mother and sisters."

At that she blinked. "You don't look like a Moon—more like a Badger."

"Half-Badger."

"My brother married into Tall Trees last year." I saw the Ravens behind her relax. "Maybe you know him?"

There were many Ravens on Moon territory, but only a few in Tall Trees. "You wouldn't be Julas' sister, by any chance?"

"Oh fuck," I heard Qes mumble behind me.

"So you do know him." A wide smile broke out on her face. One of her teeth was missing and a faint silver scar contorted the side of her cheek. "I'm Jaril Raven."

"Sloe Moon. Julas married my sister Siw."

"You are nothing like each other."

"Different fathers," I said with a hint of bitterness. Unlike me, Siw was lithe and beautiful.

"I don't think Ma would've allowed him to marry a Badger— half or not. Why are you with so many strange people?"

"As I said, all of them are friends. I've been travelling a lot recently, and these are people we picked up along the way. Qes and Qati Badger, Raz Owl, Eleas Cormorant, Bjor of the Eastern Cities, Cathil Cloud, and Lilyis Sun of Seagard."

She frowned. "Quite a collection you have there. I don't think we ever had an Owl or a Cormorant in Darkwater, and no Clouds since they started to kill off each other. What happened with his hair?"

"He left the Clouds a while ago."

"Ah. Come in from the rain then. Let us drink and talk, like family does."

The village of Darkwater had seemed deceptively small from the other side of the lake. Only a few houses stood close to its jetties; more had been built staggered behind them. The smell of smoked trout, the main commodity Julas' family traded with, dominated the village. The door of the Roundhouse stood open. It was empty, apart from a shallow brazier and a few folding stools stacked against the back wall. We left the horses under the overhang of its roof and entered one by one. The house had recently been used for a ceremony, which had left a hint of the sweet herbs burned during proceedings. Jaril lugged in a bench from outside and Qes jumped in to help. Another Raven brought beer skins and bowls, and someone coaxed the embers in the brazier back to life.

"Have you seen Julas since the wedding?" I asked his sister, once we were all in from the rain and sitting close to the brazier.

"No. You know how it is—I always planned to, but things happen. Snow falls, boats need to be patched up, nets repaired … the last thing I heard was that his wife almost gave birth on the feet of the wizard, she was that far along."

"The baby is alive and well?" I asked anxiously.

Jaril shrugged. "I suppose so. We'd have heard if something had gone wrong."

I loosened a deep breath of relief. "Thank the gods. I'd promised Siw to be back much earlier. She's going to be so angry with me …"

"She'll live," Qes murmured behind me. "She likes to complain."

"To be honest, we all thought Julas would've had more sense than to pick a wizard's apprentice," his sister said with a quirk of her left eyebrow. "He never was that good at sharing when we were children and now he'll have to share his wife with all of the Tall and all of the Small Gods. I suppose his time in Tall Trees will have changed him for the better."

Qes and I exchanged a glance.

"Maybe," I said cautiously. Julas and I had a complicated history, but it was nothing compared to what Qes felt towards him. "I think this a good time to give thanks," I said as bowls of beer were handed around and one of Julas' cousins brought a plate laden with flatbreads, smoked fish, and radishes that my companions fell upon like starving wolves.

"Darkwater is the best place for it," Jaril said, pushing her beer bowl against mine. "It's going to be a nice change to have a proper communal prayer. Since our own wizard died this winter, we haven't had someone qualified to lead us."

WHEN THE RAIN STOPS

"Did Julas tell you much about this place?" I asked Qes as we were brought to the guest quarters, a small house on the edge of the village that sheltered a collection of tools and nets lined up for mending. The Ravens had cleared some of the sleeping platforms for us, but there was no brazier. We huddled together, swaddled in our cloaks and shawls.

"No," Qes said thoughtfully. "He did speak about a lake, but I had no idea it was such a big one. It must be so beautiful when the rain stops."

We'd enjoyed the hospitality of the Ravens until late in the evening. I'd realized soon that I liked Julas' sister; she had a similar gruff charm. Since her mother had died a few years before, she had led the Ravens of Darkwater, but it was one of the smallest family villages and she longed to hear about our travels. At one point she'd sidled up to Lilyis and asked her some extremely direct questions about the Cities, shaking her head at the notion of the women of the Continent being kept from public office.

"How can they be that stupid?" she'd asked scornfully. "So many people wasted, who could well have the best ideas in the room. Just ask my husband who has the firmer grasp on reality in our marriage." She'd gestured to one of the men, and quietly burped. "Not that we had many of your sort in Darkwater. They always seem to miss us by a few miles and it's not as if much else is happening." She'd given Lilyis a good-natured shove with her elbow.

"Might he have been ashamed to hail from this place?" Lilyis asked Qes.

"The Moons have a lot of smaller settlements, just like the Badgers. I don't know what he could've been ashamed about. Perhaps he didn't want to talk that much about Ravens when he was living amongst the Moons. I wonder whether he has any other sisters. It's strange that Jaril should be the only one left in Darkwater."

"Or they have all married into bigger villages," Qati said. "Wouldn't you want to get out of here as soon as you could? The stench alone … it must be worse in the winter."

Raz gave him a slap on the shoulder. "Be nice. They've fed us as well as they could and aren't we lucky to have a roof above us?"

Cathil cleared his throat. He'd been rather quiet of late, and we all turned towards him. "We surely are," he rumbled. "The smell reminds me of home."

Qati huffed. "Look at you trying to ingratiate yourself."

Cathil glowered back at him.

"Stop," Eleas said. "Whatever this is turning into, we cannot have it. We need to stick together. I, for one, have never been among so many trees. Seeing the lake makes me feel calmer about that and gives me the space to breathe easier. We will all thank the gods for allowing us to come here. Is that understood?"

The whole company mumbled their assent before we paired off and chose our platforms. I heard Raz and Qati whisper some more, quickening breaths and fumbling, but it was over soon enough.

The Roundhouse's many small windows had been shuttered as we'd arrived, but they were thrown open the next morning to allow a view out onto the churned-up surface of the lake; the line of the woods around the water's edge rubbed into a smear of various greens. All inhabitants of Darkwater seemed to be present. The promised food and tea stood on a table at the side; people had brought their craft projects inside. Some whittled, others sewed shoes or patched up leather bags.

Jaril had brought a portable loom with her, warped with goat hair yarn in shades of yellow, black, and brown. It was threaded through tablets made from stiffened hide. The pattern she wove was astonishingly complex, like birds in flight on a ribbon as broad as my hand.

"Sloe, come and sit with me. Today is a day for staying indoors."

I poured myself a bowl of tea. "You think it's going to rain the whole day?"

She secured the thick row of tablets with a leather cord before she focussed on me. "It might let up towards the afternoon if we're lucky, but there's no chance any of us is getting into a boat before then. No one who doesn't absolutely have to. We keep ourselves busy in other ways."

I gestured towards the loom she'd placed between her feet. "That seems complicated."

"It's the warping up that's the worst bit." She grinned at me. "The rest is counting, really. I've always enjoyed doing it, ever since my Ma taught me how."

"I've done my share of plain weaving in Tall Trees, but nothing near as beautiful as this. Would you have some of the ribbons for sale?"

Her brows shot up. "For sale?"

"We've brought some things over from the west coast, perhaps we can exchange a few wares before we leave for the forests proper. Eleas has brought some shells with her, from Westlight."

"Westlight?" She beamed at me. "I always wanted to see the island."

"Lilyis carries some dye plants with her, if that's something you'd be interested in."

"I'll have a rummage through my stash and see what I can find. This pattern is a traditional Raven one and I've already promised it to someone, but I'm sure I have others squirreled away somewhere."

"I've rarely seen goat hair spun this fine. Are you producing that in Darkwater?"

"No, the yarn comes from my sister in Hollybrook where they have many master spinners."

"Hollybrook—I've heard that name before." Of course I had. Saon had talked about it a lot. The finest yarn he'd ever beheld, much better than anything he'd seen me make. "I know someone who praised it above all others." Though he'd been less complimentary about the colours it came in. "I never had much talent for anything that required so much precision. I liked to care for the goats. They always managed to cheer me up."

Julas' sister released the tablets again.

I watched her for a while, fascinated by the way her broad hands separated out groups of tablets, turning them this way and that, sometimes flipping them over. It was its own kind of magic. I noticed Lilyis was similarly caught up in the spectacle. I could feel her breath on my neck as she leant in closer and closer. My other companions had finished eating and were engrossed in their own projects or busy talking among themselves.

Qes had taken an interest in the Raven who worked on a pair of high-shafted boots, sewing with two bone needles simultaneously, while Eleas had pulled off her shell cape to lay it before a young woman for inspection. It was an unexpectedly peaceful scene, facilitated by the incessant noise of the rain and the knowledge that we were stuck in Darkwater.

I noticed Raz and Qati sat to the side, Qati with the troubled face I'd almost become used to, Raz with crossed arms. Based on the noises I'd heard them make the night before, I'd thought them to be in a good place but given the hard lines around Raz' mouth, Qati must've said something in the meantime to fuck it up again.

I knew Raz' patience to be on the thin side. She didn't need to try and change people around; she had plenty of offers wherever she was. She could always decide to attach herself to Bjor—or Eleas. Maybe Qati wasn't aware that she'd dump him before he could say 'I'm really sorry for what I said the other day'.

Why am I worried about Qati Badger's love life?

Just because I'd been pushed forward to represent the company in Darkwater, I wasn't responsible for the harmony between its couples! At least Cathil had the grace not to flaunt whatever had begun between him and Qes. The sound of yarn being twisted back and forth started to grate on my nerves and I excused myself with a smile, while Lilyis slid into my seat to watch the loom from up close.

I stepped outside of the Roundhouse, where a bench had been pushed against the wall to stay dry. As I settled down, I saw Raz had followed me. She made a weird movement, as if she was trying to shake off a fly.

"What's wrong?" I asked her.

"He's walking on extremely thin ice," she said. "Rian said I would regret choosing him, but I didn't want to listen. I never do, until it's much too late, and I'm weeks away from the coast— saddled with someone who'll never be happy to be with me."

It wasn't the first time Raz had come to regret choosing a boyfriend. Once she'd confessed to having singularly bad taste in people. "What did he do?"

"He's been whingeing since we left the Harp. Apparently, he feels uncomfortable with me being an Owl."

I stared at her. "It's not as if you hid that from him."

"He says I seduced him and he never wanted to start something. He said he should've kept away from me to wait until his family had found someone for him to marry."

"He should be so lucky."

"He doesn't mean it." She pulled a face. "He's trying to push me away because feeling good about himself makes him uneasy." She scrunched up her face. "He's quite like you in that respect, though you were much more playful." She sat down next to me and leant her shoulder against mine. "On the one hand he's jealous that Qes managed to pick up someone like Cathil, on the other he doesn't want to grant himself the same chances. I could strangle him sometimes."

"I never really liked him."

"Believe me, he knows that. He's jealous of you too."

I blinked, taken aback. "There's no reason to be."

She pushed against me again. "There is, even if you haven't grasped it yet."

We watched the patterns the rain made on the lake's surface: rings upon rings, thrumming into one another, painting chains across the water. A gust of cool wind scrubbed along the front of the Roundhouse.

"I've never been this far east," Raz said thoughtfully. "I know what Eleas meant, though. Sometimes all these trees look sinister, as if they want to push me from the saddle and stomp on me. I know that sounds weird for someone who has spent their life among them, but this *is* a relief. I never thought I'd miss the sea so much. I believed after spending so much time in the garrisons with Rawil, I'd be used to not seeing it every day. Still, it's a great chance, and I must thank you, Sloe. I didn't join the company for Qati, I also came along for you."

Lilyis gasped as Jaril laid out her treasures on the speckled deer pelt. "These are wonderful!" There were ribbons in many different colours, with many different patterns, and I saw Julas' sister blush with pleasure as Lilyis took them up one by one to inspect the coils. "I would take them all if I could."

Bjor cleared his throat. "Then the Company of the Sun would have to pay an appropriate price," he said.

Lilyis shot a glance over her shoulder. "Certainly. And commission some bespoke patterns too?"

I left them to their game and took another rolled-up bread from the table. The sky had lightened to the softest of greys and while I heard more saddlebags being opened and necklaces and bags of dried plants pulled forth, I chewed my way through layers of dough, fish, and herbs. There wasn't much in Darkwater that didn't have fish in it.

The enforced days of rest were shaping up to be Lilyis' first success. The Ravens would send their goods to the Tower of the Sun to be shipped across to the Continent.

"There'll be time for the ceremony before we leave." Eleas had donned her shell cape again, but I'd been too distracted to hear her approach.

"Yes," I said. "I wouldn't want to risk disappointing him after he had to be so direct with me."

Our wizard tilted her head. "It has almost stopped raining."

"Not quite though."

She took me by the shoulder and steered me out of the Roundhouse. The ground was a carpet of dark puddles in danger of merging into a single sheet, the water almost reaching the tips of our boots. Eleas lifted her right hand and made a gesture that I knew from the water prayer sequences. The thin veil of rain flowed apart, like a curtain, and we both stepped into its dry heart.

LOOKING INTO THE LAKE

From the inside of the Roundhouse, it must've appeared as we were merely walking onto the closest jetty.

"Thank him now. Before we ask the others to join in something more official. It is likely no coincidence that we have found our way here, where people are friendly and, as it turns out, family."

I clung to Eleas' arm as we passed through the whirl, Brother Rain bending around us both, the coolness of the water droplets making me shiver. The jetty creaked under our weight, but we continued to stride out onto the Darkwater lake, the ripples on its surface calming with our arrival.

"Brother Brook …" Eleas prompted me.

Brother Brook, thank you for bringing me so close to home, for letting me have the news that Siw and her baby are doing well.

Brother Brook, thank you for allowing me to have a wizard by my side with an open heart who understands me in ways few other people will. Who keeps the rain away from me while I pray.

Thank you for pushing Cathil into my way again so Qes can have another stab at being with someone who makes him happy.

Thank you for letting Bjor's wound heal well and for Raz and the opportunity to learn to live with someone like Qati, who might remind me a bit too much of myself.

Brother Brook, thank you most of all for being permitted to love someone like Lilyis, and to hear her say that she loves me back, to have her not laugh at me for how I want her to touch me, for being fearless enough to stand with me.

Eleas cleared her throat.

As I crouched down to touch the lake, I felt Brother Brook press back from the other side, though he didn't take on human form. He was just *there*, pushing ever so slightly against me. As I mouthed my last thanks to the deep beneath me and tried to straighten up, the jetty lurched. Eleas grabbed my arm, preventing me from pitching head-first into the lake.

"Careful," she whispered. "Do not let him claim you yet."

Lilyis' eyes widened as I rushed towards her, before picking her up and kissing her with a joy that almost strangled my heart. Back when Mother had first given me to Brother Brook, I'd felt so untethered, but in knowing Lilyis to be at my side, I finally had an anchor. She wrapped her arms around me.

"What was that about?" she asked as I set her down again.

"Just because."

"You're weird today, Sloe."

"Can't I be grateful for you?"

"You can, but a warning would be appreciated."

"When I stood out there, looking into the lake you were all I wanted to come back to."

"So much that you needed to interrupt our business?" She glanced at Julas' sister, who sat by with a grin.

"Oh, definitely."

She laughed and gave me a little shove.

"How long have you two been married?" Jaril asked. I saw Lilyis' face fall, and Jaril quickly added, "Not that it matters—at all."

"It's complicated," Lilyis said quietly and both of them went back to discussing their own potential partnership.

I had to admit that I hoped one day the news would reach us that Fiolis had succumbed to a sudden illness—nothing too painful, but something quick. Knowing her, her bitterness would preserve her well enough to outlive us all. Lilyis' sister's court was a far safer place for her than Birkland in the middle of the biggest change in generations. She would nourish herself with her prayers, entertain herself with berating and judging her sister-in-law, and quietly rejoice that she'd made it all the way back to her native Whiterivers, where the world worked in a way she was prepared to tolerate—most of the time.

Lilyis' sister Nuvalis had known full well what she'd taken upon her when she'd offered to make Lilyis' wife her permanent companion. Little love was lost between them but getting Fiolis out of the way had been her gift to her sibling, to give Lilyis a chance to experience happiness.

Fiolis had been brought up within the rigid customs of Whiterivers, clinging to the teachings of the Star with a strength of faith that had seemed almost admirable to me, if she hadn't inconvenienced me so much. It'd also made her treat Lilyis like dirt. I myself was about to arrive back home and be confronted with my ex-boyfriend, the one who'd gone about making me feel like shit in a much cleverer way. The coloured yarns on Jaril's loom reminded me too much of Saon. He would've approved of the pattern; he liked them ostentatious and attention-grabbing. Thinking about him made me feel queasy.

"Sloe," Qes said next to me. "Are you about to throw up?"

"I was wondering if Saon is still in Tall Trees."

"We must anticipate that," my cousin said with a deep sigh. He'd been onto Saon from the very start, and we'd spent far too much time discussing his every utterance, his every action. "I don't think you need to worry about him anymore. You're bringing *Lilyis* to meet your mother and sisters. Being in her presence every day, you probably forget how impressive she is. And how grimly determined to make this expedition work." He briefly touched my shoulder. "Even if he tries anything, we'll set Cathil on him.

Or Bjor. You've gained many friends who are willing to shield you from him."

"Thank you, Qes. I'll worry, though."

"Of course you do. Even when you're in love, you're still you."

We started the ceremony we'd promised the Ravens early next morning, as a thin layer of mist hovered over the lake. The air was crisp, but the promise of a warm, sunny day started to make itself felt. All Ravens living in Darkwater had come to the shore to see Eleas lead the ceremony and me pitching in with additional shorter prayers. I was grateful Eleas had made me get the personal stuff out of the way the day before, otherwise I might've been too afraid to dissolve into tears every time I spoke.

I could see our wizard was enjoying herself. Ever since leaving her village in Westlight, she hadn't had a chance to take up the reins. Her deep voice was firm and loud enough to reach every last one of us; she sounded trained and self-assured, and there was a glow in her face that swept us away. Qati was transfixed too. He'd grown up worshipping Brother Brook, and he'd spent enough time at the Golden Lake to witness the full majesty of him. Though the Darkwater lake was a fraction as long, it connected in spirit to the holy waters.

I found my thoughts drifting away to the Hillakes district, a landscape of steep bleak slopes and its own curving lakes, violent rivers, and hardy people. That was where Lilyis' family was from, where Brother Brook was revered in secret. As I watched her follow the ceremony, I understood for the first time our coming together might've been something that had been on the cards for a long time. Though Lilyis hadn't grown up in our faith, her ancestors had belonged to him, had to cling to him in order to survive, before eventually bowing to the strength of the Star.

I covered the blue stone bracelet with my left hand, the sliver of the Crown of the Lakes, Brother Brook's crown, that bound us.

"Are you sure?" Qes asked sceptically.

Jaril tightened the noseband on her mare's bridle. "I should've visited much earlier," she said. "Things will be easier for you with a Raven leading you across the lands." She was right. "And it will give Lilyis and me more time to hash out our terms." She patted the horse's flank and the dark-grey saddle cloth with the raven emblem stitched onto it in black felt. There weren't many horses in Darkwater, but all were black or dark bays.

"Thank you," Eleas said. "This is sure to be helpful."

We'd brought our horses to the lake to drink before we set out east again. The sky cleared more and more, and when the first sunlight streamed into the sodden village, its roofs dripping with moisture, we finally climbed into our saddles. Lilyis' mare pushed herself into position, ready to lead her herd again. Jaril leant down from the saddle to kiss one of the Raven men—not the one I'd thought was her husband—and made a noise against the back of her teeth to start us off.

I felt my stomach clench with anticipation as Julas' sister smiled at me. "Our next destination will be Hollybrook, and onwards towards the deepest of the forests."

We reached Hollybrook three days later. As one of the largest settlements of the Ravens it stretched across the valley, the houses clustered into many smaller groups within the whole. The dyers had their own quarter, as had the spinners and the weavers. Like Eleas' home in Westlight it was a community focused on their craft, allowing little else to disrupt them. It wasn't so much a family group but somewhere where artists came to live and work.

Given Lilyis' interest in her weaving, it made sense Jaril had brought us there, not only because it lay conveniently along the way. If the Company of the Sun was able to forge a direct connection to sell the coveted dye plants traded out of the Eastern Cities, the plan to build a mutually profitable relationship was well underway.

I noticed Lilyis' eye getting caught by the racks of drying skeins, the finished tapestries lined up on specifically cultivated hedges of holly and blackthorn, where they could be hooked onto the branches and held in place without causing damage to the fabrics, exposing them to the sunlight to mellow their colours and to give the effect of something more harmonious and older than it actually was.

I'd seen carpets and tapestries like that in the House of Women in Tall Trees, before I'd removed myself to the Other House, and there weren't only Raven patterns on show; some of them were covered in the stripy family emblems of the Badgers or the bulky forms of walking bears, though I couldn't spot a single Elk anywhere. There were limits to the Ravens' willingness to trade with the families in the forests. I felt myself tense up as I saw a narrow piece in dark blues and blacks, as long as Cirvi from nose to tail, covered in stars and the moon in all its stages. It reminded me of the pattern etched along the blade of my longknife. I would have to inquire after its price.

Jaril brought us to a central clearing where the community's Roundhouse sat like a huge squat mushroom. As the artists of Hollybrook worked in their quarters, the house was empty. One Raven was busy sweeping out dried leaves that had blown in and other bits of dirt and dead cinders, as if in preparation for a celebration. We'd been kept under close observation when we'd passed through town, and some inhabitants had followed us, while others came walking towards the company who'd arrived in their midst.

We'd barely dismounted as a woman who resembled Julas even more than Jaril pushed her way through to us.

"You're back so soon—has something happened?"

Jaril hugged her sister. "Nothing bad, don't worry. I'm on my way to see our brother's baby in Tall Trees." She rattled off our names, while the Ravens around us gasped. Owls and Cormorants were truly rare so far east and no one had expected a Cloud to show his face anytime soon.

"We would like to stay for the night," Jaril said. "We don't need much, and we come with a few interesting propositions." She gave Lilyis a meaningful nod. "But first, tell me—is there any more family news?"

Not particularly interested in catching up on the intricacies of Raven politics, I wandered back to where I'd seen the moon tapestry.

"Is this a commission?" I asked the grizzled Raven who'd come out to check on the drying process.

"Not that I know of. What does a Badger want with something like this?"

"Half-Badger, half-Moon."

Her grey brows rose sharply. "That so? Sor—this one says they belong to you."

Tears stung my eyes as I saw the Other I'd left behind in Tall Trees, so weirdly grown up within the year I hadn't seen them. We both hesitated, then my sister Silid's child rushed into my arms.

"You're back!" they cried.

"I said I'd come back."

"Yes, but I thought you lied to make me feel better about leaving me behind." Sor was wrapped in a dark-blue cloak, closed with a half-moon shaped silver brooch, their hair scraped into a bun held in place with a carved comb.

"Did you weave this?" I gestured to the tapestry on the blackthorn.

"No, but I designed it. I'm nowhere good enough to start work on something so ambitious."

"When did you leave Tall Trees?"

"Just before the winter. I couldn't stand to stay in the house any longer and when the option of joining the cousin exchange came around it seemed like a sign from the gods."

We'd shared the Other House in Tall Trees with a married couple, and I could well imagine that hearing them fuck each other's brains out every night had been as difficult for Sor as it had been for me. I hugged them again. "I brought Qes back with me, and a lot of new friends. I want you to meet Lilyis, my girlfriend."

Suddenly, Sor looked aggrieved. "Are you staying long?" they asked anxiously.

"No, we're passing through, but I need to talk to whoever wove your design. It would be the very thing to pacify Mother."

HONEYED LIGHT

Finding Sor in Hollybrook was the first taste of what it would be like to be back on such familiar ground. As I introduced them to Lilyis, Sor blushed deeply, before presenting her with something wrapped in a piece of barkcloth. It turned out to be a brooch made from gleaming cherry wood, laid in with silver wire to form spirals on the surface of another half-moon.

"That is beautiful, thank you so very much."

"I made it myself. Finished it yesterday."

"Thank you," Lilyis said again, her eyes sparkling with delight. "I will always treasure this gift, to remind myself of the first Moon I met who wasn't Sloe." She turned to me. "Instead of Eight Kingdoms there are a myriad here in Birkland," she said. "It amazes me to see that every single one is so distinct. Westlight and Hollybrook are not that far away from each other, and there's such a difference in cultural expression."

"This is why the cousin exchanges were started," Qes said. "To ensure the surrounding territories wouldn't feel strange to us, so we would create a web of friendships outside of our immediate families. Growing up in Thorndell I couldn't wait to be allowed out. These valleys in the forests can breed closed-minded people if we weren't required to stick our noses over the ridge from time to time. Though, to be honest, I'd always hoped to be sent to the Bears like Qati was."

"You had the better deal," Qati said.

Qes seemed to freeze. "I haven't forgotten," he said. "Even if I choose to forgive as much as I'm able to."

Qati swallowed. "Just checking."

"Why the Bears?" Bjor asked.

"My best friend growing up was half-Bear, and I loved her a lot."

I gawped at him. I'd assumed I knew everything about the man I'd called my best friend for quite some time. "Why haven't you told me about her?"

"Because she died before we were ten summers old," Qes said. "It was a long time ago, but we had enough years to tell each other the stories of our families. As a child I was mildly obsessed with werebears."

Sor gave a snort, noticed that Qes was serious, blushed again, and withdrew into the shadows of the Roundhouse.

"One day, you need to take me to Thorndell," I said.

Qes smiled. "It's nothing much compared to Goldenlake. It's barely larger than Darkwater, really. Our valley is too small to expand in the way this place has done, but it's a very old village. Our wizards always said it's one of the oldest in the east, of the same period as the first settlement on the Golden Lake reserved for the wizards. Before normal people were allowed to live there and visit the council. You people from the Cities reach Birkland and see a wide empty expanse, but every cluster of rocks has a story attached to it. Every stream is running over with memories of the families."

"I'm beginning to notice," Lilyis said quietly. She glanced at me and reached out to take Qes' hands. It looked as if my cousin would try to withdraw. I heard Cathil breathe in sharply, like a stag who's preparing himself to be outraged. "But I'm relying on you all to teach me, wherever you take me, whatever you show me—I need to learn, and I want to learn, anything you can give me, to make this venture into something we can all be proud of."

"Oh so noble," Qati huffed and Raz gave him a shove.

"I'll do what I can," Qes promised. "If the others help." He studied the faces of our company, growing more varied with every step we took on our way to reach Tall Trees.

Cathil harumphed but lowered his head in a way that signalled his consent. It was still strange to have him be so quiet around us, though I was grateful he didn't challenge me at every turn. He probably found it easier to accept Lilyis as the leader of our group. As a Prince of Crooked Hill there were some things you learned that didn't come easily to others: an entitlement Cathil himself was familiar with.

Lilyis turned to me and I helped her to arrange the folds of her greenish shawl to pin them in place with Sor's gift. They must've spent ages polishing it; the dark-red wood was soft to the touch. I leant in to kiss her after. I'd meant it to be more of a chaste peck, but she clutched me to her. I stumbled back in surprise, while the others laughed in relief. It might be the most we'd ever have in order to declare our love for each other, there among our friends.

It could've been a direct result of Lilyis' public display of affection that we were given a private house to stay in for the night, little more than a shed with a creaking platform built into its side, though it was heaped with pelts and blankets. It was meant as a refuge for newly-weds when the weather was too bad to make do with what the forests had to offer; there was no brazier, and the window was covered in dried hide which let in a fuzzy, honeyed light.

Lilyis threw her saddlebag into the corner closest to the door. "That'll do," she said. "Close it, Sloe. I don't want any witnesses."

I swallowed with difficulty. "What are you thinking of?"

"What do you think I'm thinking of? We haven't had the opportunity to be this alone with each other for a long time. Take off your cloak." She pulled away her shawl, new pin and all, then her cloak and tunic over her head. "Can you help me with the braid?" she asked, sitting down at the edge of the platform.

My hand shook as I tried to loosen the knot in the leather cord. I could not resist kissing her neck while I fumbled, breathing in her smell. As soon as the knot had come out, I wrapped my arms around her, nuzzling into the space behind her right ear, making her moan and lean back against me, while my hands were busy at her belt, opening it barely enough for me to reach in and check on the indisputable evidence that she wanted me. She shifted as I started to stroke her.

"Go slow," she asked me, barely loud enough to hear. "I've waited too long, and it might not take much."

I released her and rolled onto the bed we were to share that night, pulling the mud-spotted trousers from her as she toed off her boots. It was as if she longed to melt into me and needed to keep herself from dissolving too quickly. I tried to distract her with kisses, still fully clothed, caressing her sides and the softness of her muscles tightened by weeks of riding. As she started to rock against me, seeking my touch, I made her come with a single twist of the wrist, watching her eyes roll back. I cradled her against me. There was more than enough time to take care of me later.

"Sometimes I can't let myself believe," she whispered. "That I could finally feel so *there*. That sounds stupid, but it's hard to find words. As if I'd been finally allowed to *arrive* somewhere, not only searching and running and trying to find something unspecific but desperately needed, like in one of those nightmares when you're in a panic but there's no proper reason to be and it still makes sense somehow. It feels like I've been in this panic since I can think at all. With you I'm allowed a moment of respite, to finally stop searching."

"I think I know what you mean. I used to feel like that all the time at home." A film of sweat had risen to her skin, and I tasted its salt on her shoulder.

"Will it be enough for your family though?"

"It will be more than enough for my aunt, but I can't make any guarantees for my mother. I don't think I'll go back to living in Tall Trees." It was the first time the thought had come to me with such clarity. Speaking it aloud felt like someone taking a bite out of my chest. After all the miles I'd travelled since being sent away by Mother, I was far from the same person, and even less able to fit myself into the narrow slot allocated to me at home.

"What do you mean?"

"Tall Trees is but a stepping stone to the east. We'll go to Goldenlake as planned and then I'll decide. I can't see Tall Trees being big enough for me now. It already has a wizard and will have another one once Siw follows in Sjunil's footsteps. My sister is territorially inclined—she wouldn't like me to stick around."

"Maybe you could go with Qes, let him show you around Thorndell."

"Maybe. Watch him explain Cathil fucking Cloud to his own mother."

Lilyis cupped my face in her palm. "That sounds entertaining. Can you let me sleep for a bit?"

"You must be shattered with all these new things around you …" I felt her go slack in my arms and pulled one of the blankets over us, feeling my body moulding itself to hers. In the end I drifted off as well, though she made good on her promise when we woke up at sunrise.

Qes had managed to organize a pack horse for us as we prepared to leave Hollybrook the next day. Lilyis loaded it up with the skeins she'd bought off Jaril's sister, woven mats, and rolled-up pelts, among them the tapestry I'd acquired myself as a desperate try to assuage my mother before I dared to reveal my plans to her. Eleas had traded in a necklace for a new goat hair shawl, unbelievably soft and covered in a leaping fish pattern in greyish shades of blue. Bottles made from boiled bark and filled with birch syrup were stacked in the panniers as well as a generous supply of dried elk meat strips, exuding a strong smell of juniper and sour peppers. If that went on, we'd reach Goldenlake with a whole string of pack animals …

Jaril hugged her sister as they said their farewell and Sor flung themself into my arms again. I kissed their cheek, and they pressed another present into my hand. It was a hair needle, topped with a spiral that had been whittled to resemble the markings of a snail's shell.

"Your hair should be long enough."

I kissed them again. "Thank you. Do you feel as if you belong here in Hollybrook?"

They nodded, their dark eyes brimming.

I smiled at them. "I will tell your mother that you're happy."

Where the woods around Hollybrook had been open and welcoming, the thickets edging the road we followed east became ever denser. Julas' sister was careful to choose the right spot for us to stop for the night. While on family lands, we still had wild animals to consider: werebears, regular bears, lynx, and wolves could all decide to investigate us. Every valley was the perfect place for an ambush, and the gloom of the canopy in its darkening summer foliage came with a shiver of worry. I found myself at home in the smells though, of wet moss and the earliest mushrooms, sprouting from the dead wood half-buried in rotten leaves. It was cool and sunbeams stabbed through to light our path, announcing any clearings where we could let the horses graze.

When I turned around to glance at my companions, I saw Qati's resigned expression and Raz' awe. "It's as if the air itself is green," she said, with more reverence than I'd ever heard her express. "No wonder such powerful wizards come from the forests."

"No wonder they call us treefuckers," Qati said scornfully. "You can barely squeeze through without bumping into something, whether you want to or not."

Lilyis creased her freckled brow. "What does he mean?"

"There must be names you call the folks of Whiterivers or the ones from the heathlands? Mean names, hurtful names?"

"Uncle Nurin called Fiolis a 'Starbotherer'—does that count?"

"I suppose that's more aimed at her personally, but in Whiterivers they surely have expressions for you? What about the 'men from the twisted mountain'?"

"For the uncivilized men from the Hillakes?" Lilyis glared at Bjor, who suddenly seemed very uncomfortable. "Sure."

"It's something like that. There's generally not much love lost between the families of the west and east. Our company is unusual in that respect as well."

Raz rose in her stirrups to pluck a cluster of beech leaves that still bore the fuzz of new growth. She sniffed at them and closed her eyes in bliss. "It's beautiful and strange, if you're used to always finding the horizon around you. Whatever you might say to fuck it up for me," she said to Qati.

"I'm not trying to fuck it up for you, I'm just saying …"

"Would you shut up," Cathil interrupted him. "You've been complaining since I've met you."

"I want Raz to have the right impression," Qati sulked.

Eleas cleared her throat. "We should make time for a prayer. A *silent* prayer," she added, before winking at me. "Give the werebears a chance to rest their poor ears."

Qati scowled at her, but Cathil nodded in compliance, while I saw Lilyis and Bjor exchange a worried glance.

"Is she serious?" Lilyis asked me.

I shrugged. "Can't hurt to pray. If we come across a werebear, I hope to be able to get a fireball out of Brother Flame."

INTERNAL DISPUTES

The first sound we heard of Tall Trees was the screeching of children playing by the river, most of them quite naked, dangling from ropes that had been knotted into the overhanging branches of the oaks where the river formed natural basins, deep enough to swim and dive. In early summer, the river was peaceful enough, and had calmed itself after the yearly floods of the snowmelt. It hadn't been that long ago I'd been part of the noisy games and as we approached, I felt my heart hammer. I'd presumed my friends gathered from many other families would be welcomed, but what reason did Mother have to receive them with kindness?

As usual, a lookout had been posted to keep watch in one of the trees, and as they saw us draw near, they let loose a call of alarm.

Suddenly the children of Tall Trees were out of the water, grabbing the first weapons that came to hand: sturdy sticks, rocks from the riverbed, knives hidden in the piles of discarded clothing.

"It's Sloe!" one of them shrilled and the weapons vanished as quickly as they'd been taken up. The children were flooding towards our horses, shouting questions at me.

"Where were you?"

"Have you brought back sweets?"

"Where were you?"

"Who are these weird people?"

"Where were you?"

Cirvi, who usually wasn't easily spooked, snorted and started to side-step, trying to avoid the onrush of wet bodies; I saw some of them break off from the throng to run into the village and scream the news of our arrival at the first person they'd meet.

At that time of day, most Moons were busy with the chores the rota assigned to them, but many of them came into the village square to greet us and the doors of the Roundhouse flew open as we reached it, my eldest sister Silid standing on its threshold, resplendent as always in her dark-blue cloak and complicated coiffure studded with bone pins and amber beads. Smoke billowed out behind her, smelling intensely of citrus. We'd obviously disrupted another ceremonial cleaning of the house.

"Sloe?" Silid's high voice had an undignified squeal to it, and she let out an annoyed snort as she was elbowed aside by my youngest sister, carrying the smoke vessel.

Siw was furious. "Where the fuck have *you* been?"

I made a feeble gesture towards the east. "Over there, mainly."

Siw pushed the shallow pot filled with melting sap crystals into Silid's hands—the heir of Tall Trees stared at it as if someone had given her a shit-smeared infant to hold. It was a serious breach of etiquette, but Siw was too busy coming down at me to notice. "You have no idea what we went through because you didn't have the guts to stick it out at the Harp!"

"Errrr … you look great, by the way. Glowing."

Siw poked the sharp nail of her forefinger into the side of my knee. "No thanks to you, you ungrateful piece of …" Her voice broke and my youngest sister started to cry. "I thought you were dead!"

As I scrambled from the saddle to hug her, my cloak got caught in a strap and I almost strangled myself. Siw fell against me. Of all the things I'd expected to happen, that hadn't been anywhere *near* the list. She sobbed into my shoulder and I felt a sharp knot of anxiety melt inside me.

"I'm home," I mumbled, barely believing what I said. "Whatever this is about, it's going to be fine."

She sniffed angrily. "This is about you turning your back on us, you great big idiot! On all the Moons and all your sisters, just because there was a tiny chance to see someone again who didn't care if you thought him dead!"

"Father sends his best wishes, by the way."

She punched me in the chest, hard enough for me to gasp in pain and release her.

"What were we supposed to think?" She wiped a sleeve across her runny nose.

Silid had carefully placed the smoking vessel on the nearest bench under the eaves of the Roundhouse and stepped beside her, with crossed arms.

I felt myself back away, but my mare stood behind me. A whole village and a whole company of friends were watching me being yelled at. Not that I didn't deserve it. The bollocking had been a long time coming and was probably a test of what awaited me from my aunt, once I'd scraped together enough courage to go and see her in her hut in the forest.

"Why didn't you write?" Silid asked me.

"There wasn't time. We only were at the Harp for a few days, barely long enough to attend the late spring festival."

My eldest sister reached out to touch my arm. "Then you must stay in Tall Trees for Shortest Night. That's only two weeks away."

"Of course we'll stay." I sent a pleading smile to Lilyis that both my sisters noticed. "We can stay for that long, can't we?"

Lilyis pulled a face. "We can stay with your family if they want us here. The Bulls won't run away. Probably."

"There'll be time to discuss details later," Silid decided and pushed one of the hair needles deeper into her bun. "We have to prepare the house for the evening address. Mother wishes to speak to the family today."

"Did something happen?"

"You mean, before you and your comrades popped up like ghosts from the mist?" Siw suddenly had an expression on her face that I remembered all too well: her signature sneer. I hadn't missed it since we'd parted ways.

"Yes—before that."

"The news that has reached us from the west is extremely disconcerting," Silid interjected. "We need to prepare ourselves for unrest to reach the borders of our own territories before long. You might speak to what you have seen on your travels. You seem to have collected members of different families around you and it always is a good idea to hear from several sources. We are a long way away from the east and too many messages get misconstrued while they are passed on to us."

"We can all help with that."

"Use the Other House to stay in," Silid said, clearly keen to get us out of the way and back to business. It shouldn't have hurt but I still felt pushed aside. "It has been empty for months, since your last housemates left on their own adventure."

"That reminds me. We passed Hollybrook on our way and Sor sends their love."

Silid's face broke into a brilliant smile. "Thank you. We had many discussions before Mother allowed them to go and I am glad to hear they are well. You know where everything is. Come and find us when you are settled."

My heart beat so fast that I saw spots as I stood in front of the Other House of Tall Trees. The familiar smell of woodsmoke, wet blankets, and old boots greeted me from inside. I'd gotten off easy and would have to answer many more questions that evening. There were the introductions and more excuses to be made, and some meetings to get over with that I really didn't look forward to.

Qes pushed past me. The Other House swallowed him up; he tread a piece of split wood against the door to hold it open for the rest of our company. I knew the house had been used as guest quarters before, when big weddings had taken place and we'd had trouble finding space for everyone. While I wasn't permitted to set foot in the House of Women or the House of Men, the Other House had never excluded anyone.

My old sleeping platform still bore the blankets I'd folded up before I left Tall Trees, exactly as I'd placed them and very dusty. The corners of the partitions were covered in sagging cobwebs. The space belonged to another part of my life. Qes was the only one who came close to an idea of who I'd been then, how scared and unsure of myself. How strange to think it had been less than two years ago.

Qes didn't lose any time to sweep out the brazier and stack it with kindling for later. For once there was enough room for all of us, and the Other House went from a sad empty shell to being fully inhabited and filled with relieved laughter.

"Imagine—a thick roof over our head, at least until Shortest Night!" Raz cried. "Enough time to get to know your family properly and see everything you hold dear from when you grew up!"

I stood before the house, unable to step in. "Yeah. Imagine that." I felt ready to scream, or ready to sob, as I saw Lilyis carefully place her bags on the narrow table in the middle of the house.

"Which one is ours?" she asked.

I pointed to my platform. "This one. The one with the moon carved above it."

"Sloe, why don't you come in?"

"Qes will help you all to get settled, I need to … I need to try and find someone."

During the weeks at sea, I'd longed for Tall Trees in a way that made no sense to me. Perhaps I'd thought about the village of my childhood and not about the village where time had moved on since I'd left it, where everyone had an important job to do and no time for a triumphant homecoming. Maybe I'd wanted to be there because it'd been far away and at least familiar enough to allow me to picture it: the village square, the way in which the main houses and outbuildings had been positioned around it … But the life I remembered was the life of a child, without great responsibilities and without much agency. All that had changed. The people who crowded the Other House were there because I'd brought them with me. Because they'd followed me, or, better, the person they thought me to be, they *hoped* me to be.

The gently swaying trees around the empty square, the screams of the children back at play, everything was the same and still so different. There'd been no day when I hadn't known what to do, what tasks I'd been given in the gardens or with the animals—I was untethered in a way that felt deeply wrong.

I cleared my throat. "Is there anything I can do to help you?"

My sisters glanced up from the brazier. The clay vessel had almost finished spewing sweet smoke. The benches had been put up and mother's seat pushed in place, covered in many pelts to make her comfortable during lengthy proceedings.

"No." Siw drew bundles of dried herbs from her shoulder bag and lined them up on the bench closest to the fire. "We are almost finished." Her voice held a subtle accusation. Couldn't I have asked earlier?

"When will the family come together?"

"In an hour or so. Before the evening meal." Silid pulled a fold of her cloak back onto her shoulder. "We have time to get something to drink."

I felt myself breathe out in relief. "Could you take me to see Mother? I'd rather not do this in front of everybody."

My eldest sister scrunched up her face. "That might be sensible. Can I leave you to finish up on your own, Siw?"

"Sure. As soon as Sloe asks after the baby."

"Oh." A flush of shame made the top of my ears pulse. Once again, I'd been too caught up in my own fears to consider someone else. "I'm so sorry, I should've done that straight away."

"Yes, you bloody well should have."

"I hope everything went well?"

"Yes. They're with their father today."

"What did you call them?"

"Their name is Siran, and they have all the customary fingers and toes."

"That's … good to know."

"We're living here in the village until … until we know what's going to happen with Sjunil."

I felt the blood drain from my face. "What do you mean?"

"You knew she was ill, didn't you?"

"Yes." She'd told me very clearly that she wouldn't have survived accompanying me on my journey to the Cities and back.

"It's progressed a lot recently. I'll take you to see her. Sooner rather than later."

"Oh," I mumbled, helplessly. "Oh no."

"We thought it would be better to give her space and it makes more sense to keep Siran in the village, for them to grow up around the other children, not in a creepy hovel deep in the woods."

"Of course," I agreed.

I saw the lines around her mouth dig in. "Now you can go and meet Mother," she decided.

"Don't worry too much," Silid said as we approached the seats in front of the House of Women. "It will be some time yet until Siw will take her master's place. You know how incredibly stubborn Auntie Sjunil can be. She will cling on as long as she has to. Sit down, Sloe. I will tell Mother that you are here."

I was too afraid to sit. I closed my eyes, trying to calm myself. Whenever I had allowed myself to get my hopes up in the past, Mother had always managed to undercut them.

Silid was right, our aunt was one of the most head-strong people I knew, but that didn't mean she was supposed to suffer, to keep breathing until Siw had passed the Protocols.

"Sloe." Mother's deep voice drew me from my desperate thoughts. "Brother Brook has brought you back to us."

"He did." I touched the silver amulet she'd given me under my travel-stained tunic.

Silid held Mother's elbow to help her walk. Her hair had become fully white since our farewell, but she appeared stronger, more substantial than I remembered her.

I knelt down before her and she gave me her gnarled hand to kiss. It felt dry and firm in mine.

"They said you found your way home. The fine you petitioned the council of Goldenlake for has only just been paid. I should have seen that as a sign."

I'd all but forgotten why I'd left Tall Trees in the first place. "What took them so long?"

"We hear troubling news about the Clouds lately. It was likely to get lost among their internal disputes."

"You could ask Cathil what happened, I suppose."

Both Mother and Silid stared at me. "What?"

"I brought Cathil Cloud east with me."

"The one who rejected us?" Mother spat.

I smiled at her. "The one who made a mistake and knows it."

A BIG IF

"How could you do that?" Silid gasped.

Mother reached out to one of the seats and sat down with a sigh. "Why would you bring an enemy to Tall Trees? Repentant or not, the man has wronged you."

"Shouldn't we be prepared to forgive? He's paid the fine and now you're in possession of his silver. His life has changed almost as much as mine. His family has kicked him out and—"

"And you thought you needed to pick him up and make him a problem for the Moons again?"

"More a problem for Qes, really. They seem to have discovered a liking for each other."

"Qes? You brought the Badger back as well?"

"Two Badgers, actually. As well as an Owl, a Cormorant, a Raven—our company has grown much larger than expected. And I brought someone important to see you, Mother. Someone I need you to be nice to."

"You speak with such a different voice," Mother remarked. "That is very annoying."

I saw Silid swallow nervously. "Mother is right, Sloe. You are much changed."

Resentment bubbled up within me. "*You* gave me to Brother Brook," I said. "That started it all. He's kept me safe as you demanded of him, but he's also taken me on another kind of adventure. One that isn't merely about crossing land and water. It wasn't my idea at all, Mother," I said. "*You* sent me to Goldenlake, and it all snowballed from there. I travelled over the sea to the Cities, as Sjunil must've told you, where I found my father again and a half-brother I knew nothing about. Where I became part of another family and fell in love with one of them. It would take too long to get into details."

"I had feared as much," Mother said. "It is his voice I can hear."

"You're not relieved to know he's alive?"

Mother's dark eyes narrowed. "I'd hoped him to be dead."

Silid winced. "Mother, please."

"It is the truth. From the moment Qarim Badger came into my life, he has meant nothing but trouble for me. The Cities are welcome to him. These are too many distressing things to hear, Sloe. We will decide later what we are to do with the Cloud you have brought into our midst and how to hold you responsible for it." She made a vague gesture in my direction. "Bring me back inside, Silid. This has been a disappointing talk."

"What did you expect?" Qes asked as I made it back to the Other House, dazed and more shaken up than I wanted anyone to know. "You can't tell them something of that magnitude without providing any of the backstory! It must be a great shock for them to realize Qarim is still around. It was for you, too. You had plenty of time to make your peace with the fact that he started a new family in Seagard."

"Mother probably suspected it all along. She didn't seem surprised."

"Why did you need to tell them about Cathil?"

"I wanted to be honest with them."

He rolled his eyes. "Of course you wanted to be honest, and always at the worst time! Fuck, fuck, fuck, fuckity-fuck."

I stared at him. "That reminds me, I should probably not count on Sjunil's assistance to get out of this mess."

"Why? She seems to be the only one with enough clout around here to help."

"Silid thinks she's halfway to the land of the dead, and Siw has brought her family to the village to get her baby away from her." I noticed Lilyis hovered close enough to listen in, trying to seem busy folding her yellow tunic with the sun sigil stitched on its front. "You're right. I should've waited and thought properly about what information to share with them and when."

"I can't blame you," my cousin said. "You must be under a lot of pressure to dive back into Tall Trees after such a long time away. We'll find a way to deal with it, I promise." He patted my wrist. "Just maybe *don't* talk to them for the rest of the day."

"Should I join the assembly?"

"We will both go," he said. "Then I can do some damage control."

The Roundhouse was bursting at the seams. The news of our return must've reached all Moons in Tall Trees; people had brought food in expectation of something spectacular and the smells of root cakes, roasted bearnuts, and cheese were almost too strong. I couldn't wait for Siw to begin feeding her herb bundles into the brazier closest to her. In the first row I could make out someone who could've been Julas Raven. He was certainly broad-shouldered and the black braid hanging down his back long enough. The cloth knotted around him could have been a sling to hold Siw's baby in …

We'd tried to find seats further away from the representatives of the Moon government. My mother perched on her soft seat like a snowy owl, unblinking, while Silid prepared to open the assembly. How many of those monthly events had I experienced over the years? All of them seemed to fold into each other. I found myself getting breathless. Qes pinched my leg, hard enough to make me gasp.

"Concentrate," he hissed.

The Moons sitting around me couldn't help themselves but to gawp at us, though no one asked us any questions yet. I had the feeling they were all waiting to see us being officially told off—the ones who'd left the community of Tall Trees on family business but hadn't returned when they'd been supposed to, who'd taken the opportunity to flee that life and to become other people on the far side of the sea. They wanted us to be made an example of. No one was supposed to step so far out of line.

On Silid's signal, Siw pushed the first bunch of herbs onto the embers. The scent wafting up from the brazier brought me back to how wrong it felt to sit on those hard benches and not have a great future planned out yet. I found my left hand clutching at the bracelet I wore, the gift of the Queen of the Lakes. I had another family to go back to if it went wrong. I had Lilyis waiting for me in the Other House.

Qes pinched me again and I finally noticed that Silid was pointing at me. "Ow—what?"

"I have welcomed you back to Tall Trees," my mother's heir said disapprovingly.

"Huh … thank you?"

"We will prepare a feast in the next few days to officially celebrate your return, but it would be nice if you could pay attention to the goings-on in Tall Trees in the meantime, not dream about your adventures beyond the sea."

There was a fair amount of mocking laughter around me.

Qes sighed. "Don't look, Sloe."

"What now?"

"Saon is sitting right over there." Qes' chin pointed to the left, and there he absolutely was: wrapped in his shawl made from the brightest dyeing samples, overstitched with a multitude of spirals, his hair bound back from his narrow face. He was as beautiful as ever, more attractive than I cared to remember. "Oh fuck. I hadn't thought about him being here today."

"There's no reason why you should concern yourself with him," Qes said.

"At least he's not kissing anyone—yet."

Qes chuckled darkly. "That's the kind of optimism we need to survive this."

Silid had started with the official agenda for the assembly, the amount of wool and nuts sold in the last month, how many animals had been lost to predators, and that Siw would lead the communal prayers because Sjunil was too unwell. She didn't give any specifics, and no one seemed to regard it as news. Silid turned to our mother, who suddenly appeared to arrive back in her body, took a deep breath, and began to speak to the Moons.

"As all reports from the west have been of more divisions between its families and because there are yet no signs of a new peace, we have decided to move forward with this year's competitions. They will be held on the day of Shortest Night, in honour of the Tall Gods, to determine who will be given command of the warriors of the Moons."

Excitement bubbled up from the crowd, though I could see Saon rolling his eyes. He wasn't interested in any of it, so of course he deemed the question who'd be awarded with that particular responsibility to be stupid.

"Keep Raz away from the competitions," Qes said quietly. "We can't have an Owl complicating everything. Though this should distract everyone enough to give you a break."

"I think Raz is probably the least of our problems. We have four warriors among us who won't take it well to be banned from the fights."

"You should wish for them to be excluded," Qes said. "After all, we don't want a repeat of the Crooked Hill hunting party fiasco."

As the Moons left the Roundhouse, I noticed Jaril Raven waiting in the square. The man I'd suspected to be Julas rushed towards her. I could see that he indeed wore little Siran strapped to him, a bundle with a round face poking out, their eyes black and round, their hair standing up in tufts. Too small to walk yet, baby Siran still had a wide-awake stare that made me scared for them and the future they'd have to experience.

Julas hugged his sister and started to loosen the sling in order to hand his baby over. Jaril Raven took them from him with such tenderness that I teared up.

"I didn't expect anyone to visit before autumn," Julas said, the forked scar on his cheekbone flushed with pride. He'd kept the beard. In his sister's broad hands baby Siran seemed utterly vulnerable, but Jaril cradled them against her chest with much more expertise than I would've believed her capable of.

"I should've come to the naming ceremony," she said.

"We didn't have one as such," Julas admitted.

Jaril turned around to me. "Sloe—don't hover, come here and meet them."

Julas' eyes widened. "Sloe. How's the arm?"

I forced myself to smile at him. "I've almost forgotten about the scar, though in cold weather I can feel it twinge sometimes." I leant in to touch the downy cheek of his baby. "Congratulations. They already look a lot like their mother."

Julas blushed and I thought back in wonder that I'd kissed him once. Though I'd wanted to prove a point back then, there was Siran, trying to make a grab for the sliver of blue stone dangling from my wrist, then squealing as Siw stepped from the Roundhouse.

"When did you change them?" she asked Julas.

"Just before the assembly."

"There's a bit of a whiff coming off them, can you please check?"

"Will do." He scooped their child back up to find a surface to lay them on.

Siw seemed pleased. "He's been good about it all so far," she said. "It can't be easy being married to a wizard."

"Wizard?" I asked, feeling my stomach drop.

She made a dismissive gesture. "Not quite officially, but given my master's situation, I've taken on all of Sjunil's responsibilities. The Protocols will be a mere formality."

"This is Julas' sister, Jaril. We met her in Darkwater, and she decided to come along and visit."

Both women smiled. "It's nice to finally meet someone from his side of the family. He was worried no one was interested."

We all turned towards Siw's husband, who was making his way back to us.

"False alarm," he said. "They're still as dry as they can be."

"Thank you," Siw said. "Why don't you give them to me and make sure that your name is put down on the lists for the competition?"

He frowned at us. "Are you sure?"

"I'm sure. You should get another chance to prove yourself. If you want to."

A smile spread over his face and he all but ran away from us.

"Losing out the last time was hard on him," Jaril said.

"I know." Siw tucked the sling around her. I helped her to position the knot between her shoulder blades as she bounced up and down. Baby Siran let out a delighted cackle and clutched at my sister's necklaces.

"Did you know about Mother's plan?" I asked her.

"Nothing definite. She needed to come up with something to keep everyone's mind off the whole mess in the west."

"What if he wins? Will you allow him to lead the Moons in battle?"

Siw shrugged. "It's a big if, Sloe. We'll cross that bridge when we come to it."

❦

SANCTUARY

"I'm not saying it isn't beautiful." Lilyis took a deep breath. "But I can understand why you needed to leave."

It was early; we'd both been awake before sunrise and quietly dressed to leave the Other House. We'd walked through the village, witnessing the preparations for Shortest Night.

"What do you mean, exactly?"

She tucked a strand of red-brown hair behind her ear. "I mean that they all seem to have a very fixed idea of who you are. Did you tell them about your talents?"

"No. Siw would have a fit and I don't want to hurt her."

"She needs to know, Sloe. Who says that your aunt hasn't talked about it with her long ago?"

"Because she hasn't mentioned it to me yet. If something is bothering Siw, you will absolutely hear about it."

"And if it doesn't bother her that much?"

"How could it not? It'll be another reason why she shouldn't have been apprenticed to our aunt, and as much as she used to complain about it, she seems to take real pride in following in Sjunil's footsteps. I can't take that away from her. It wouldn't be fair."

Lilyis took my arm. We walked down to the river to a small group of birches, where I'd spent much time talking to Qes about my ex-boyfriend. Their silver-white bark flashed up from the valley at us and the noise the wind made going through their serrated leaves reminded me of the standing stones in the grounds of Gard Manor, of birches that had self-seeded themselves to shelter an ancient place of worship. The moss-covered boulders along the river had never been dedicated to Sister Stone, but I shuddered as we drew closer to the ones Qes and I used to sit on. I saw traces of the ring of stones we'd made our fires in to cook, when we'd spent whole summer nights down here, glad to be away from the other Moons. It was like a separate world to me, one I needed Lilyis to know.

She drew a deep breath and sat down on the soft moss. "This feels like a sanctuary."

"It was. And one of the first places I showed Qes when he arrived. Thankfully I never took Saon here."

"Is he the one staring at you as if he's willing your head to explode? The one with the aggressively colourful shawl?"

"Yes. We used to see each other for almost two years, but looking back on it I always drew the shortest straw with him. I expected him to be long married."

"What would he do if he knew of your accomplishments in the Eight Kingdoms?"

"I don't know—laugh at them, probably. Tell me I made it all up to get some attention."

"I don't need to be jealous?"

"No, you really don't. He didn't treat me well and I have no intention whatsoever to repeat the experience."

"Good. It sounds as if he and Fiolis would hit it off."

I had to laugh at that. "He's not interested in women—or he wasn't back then." I felt myself scowl. "I probably don't know him well enough to make such presumptions. He was always most devoted to his art."

"What art?"

"He aspires to be the master dyer of Tall Trees. He made this cloak." I fussed with the sky-blue fabric that was starting to become decidedly scruffy.

"He made it for you?"

"No, not specifically, but he gave it to me at Silid's behest, before I left. He hoped to have others ask about it in Goldenlake, to make more of a name for himself."

Lilyis nodded slowly. "That sounds horribly familiar."

We fell silent for a while. I lowered myself to the ground next to her. "I think whenever I've felt homesick last year, this is the place I truly wanted to be—not in the square, not with my family—but here, between the water and the trees, alone and able to clear my head."

"Thank you for bringing me." She drew me to her, and I buried my face in her shoulder. Her hand was cool on my cheek. "Will you take me to meet your mother today?"

"If she agrees to it. We didn't start our visit off in the most harmonious manner. It's possible she will first want to see me sweat for a bit. She'll expect me to crawl back, broken and repentant. It hurts to know that."

Lilyis kissed my forehead. "I felt the same coming back to Crooked Hill. I was supposed to make a big deal about apologizing as I'd done before when things had gone wrong. In a weird way, I think Father was relieved when I didn't."

"That sounds like him. He's the most unpredictable man I've ever met. I miss him—is that weird?"

"You saved him and put your life in danger for him more than once. It creates a bond. He'll be preparing for his wedding. I hope to all the gods that I'll miss it. Hmmmm ... this moss isn't as dry as it looked." She pushed a hand under her arse to check how damp her trousers were. "Should we start to go back?"

I climbed back to my feet. "We'd better. I don't want to miss breakfast."

She scrunched up her face. "Look at me, Sloe."

It was strangely difficult to meet her eyes. "Yes?"

"We don't need to stay here. We can leave, if it gets too much for you. You don't owe them anything, do you hear me? You have a whole company at your back, you don't need any of them."

Breakfast was brought into the Other House by none other than my sister. She was in full wizard get-up. "I'm going to bring you to Aunt Sjunil's today," she said. "You better eat quickly."

"Does Mother know about this plan?"

"I assume so. Silid suggested it, and I need to stock up on supplies from the cottage anyway, so it all works out."

"Can I bring Lilyis and Eleas?"

"If you want to. There's not a lot of room, though. Some of us will have to sleep in the stables."

We left Qes in charge of the company and fetched the horses as soon as we'd chewed down some bread and cheese. Sjunil's house was a few hours' ride away, so it made sense to stay the night. I packed additional blankets and smallclothes, bracing myself to find my beloved aunt much changed. When we'd parted at the Harp, she'd as good as shoved me away from her. She hadn't seemed especially sick to me then, but I'd seen her suffer before. It wasn't a new complaint, but an illness that had gnawed at her for a long time. Even if our visit meant I'd postpone the next confrontation with Mother for a few days, I felt my stomach clenching in terror.

Siw rode fast, eager to get it over with and return home to her own family. She still used the black mare she'd travelled to Goldenlake with, a swift animal that often left our own horses behind. For once, Lilyis kept her own mare at the back. I wanted her to meet my aunt, but I needed her support more, knowing her to be at hand in case I'd break down. We crossed two rivers on our way, both starting to run shallow as the height of summer approached. Siw must've made the way too many times to count, but it impressed me that she didn't hesitate once. She knew the woods much better than me. From time to time, small groups of deer jumped out of our way, fleeing a few paces, before turning their necks and enormous leaf-shaped ears around to watch us pass.

We reached the hut before noon.

I'd always imagined it as a tiny rickety dwelling, but it was as big as the Other House, with a stable at the back, standing on a knoll above a bubbling stream. The trees around it had been cleared and gardens stretched out in the sun, bursting with purple-flowering herbs. Butterflies swooped across them, and someone was there, in between the beds, wearing a silvery scarf knotted around their mass of brown hair.

As they saw us approach, my master flung away the hoe made from elk-antler, pulled up their long tunic, and sprinted down the path to meet us.

"Sloe!"

Werid's beautiful face was distorted with relief as they almost ran into Cirvi.

I fell down into their arms and all notions of self-restraint were forgotten. We both started crying. The last time I'd seen my master had been on the beach beneath the Stoneharp, when they'd waved Qes and me off to flee towards the Eastern Cities, and neither of us could've been certain to see the other again.

"We'll stay back here for a bit," my sister said as Werid pulled me up the path to the door.

The hut was clean and smelled of tree sap and drying mint. There was a table, already set with clay plates and wooden bowls, decorated with a jug stuffed with the purple flowers rampant in the gardens. Shelves ran along the wall behind the table, crammed with a multitude of baskets, stoppered pots, and bundled grass-paper scrolls. It was unexpectedly light and airy, the sleeping platforms built into the back of the house and divided by a chequered curtain woven from goat hair, with the same design as my aunt's signature cloak.

"Sjunil?" Werid pushed me through the curtain.

My aunt lay curled up on her side, her hair covering the pillows. I knelt in front of her, and she pulled my hands to her chest.

I wasn't sure she knew who I was, but a slow smile spread over her lined face. "You brought them all with you," she said, almost too quiet to be heard. "I can see them around you, looking at me. Judgmental little fuckers."

With my help, my aunt made it to the table while Werid started on the tea. The flesh had fallen away from Sjunil's bones, but her eyes were as bright as ever. As Siw brought the others inside, she gave her master a wary frown.

"Should you be out of bed?"

"Fuck off, Siw. It's fine. Tell me who you brought to see me."

"They're Sloe's guests, not mine."

Both Eleas and Lilyis were muddy and sweaty from our ride, as well as absolutely terrified.

"Sjunil, this is Eleas Cormorant, a wizard of Westlight. We met her when we almost broke our ship apart in a storm that pushed us off course."

Sjunil shot a quick glance towards Werid, but smiled as graciously as I'd ever seen. "She's welcome here."

"And this is—"

"Ah. Don't tell me. Someone you fell in love with back in the Cities?"

"This is Nivael da Nileon's daughter, Lilyis—and yes, we're very much in love, thank you."

A tentative grin made its way over my aunt's gaunt features. "Oh, Sloe. Never knowingly under-complicated. You are certainly the most extraordinary visitor this humble abode has ever had the honour to receive, Lilyis."

She bowed, probably more of an instinct than a conscious choice. "Thank you."

"For what? You won't find this at all easy, I'm afraid. With all the freedoms the Cities lack, the families play by a different set of rules. I can't imagine that a Princess of Crooked Hill has been allowed to remain unattached. Sloe would never have brought you here if they weren't serious about the relationship, but my sister won't stand for it."

"I know," Lilyis said quietly. "It was still worth a try."

"Does your father know about this?"

"Yes."

"Hmhm. He continues to out-fox me, all the way from across the seas. In any case, you can always stay here, if things in Tall Trees get too uncomfortable."

"Everybody sit," Werid interjected. "Tea is almost ready."

As we found our places around the table, I saw my aunt keeping an eye on Lilyis, while I helped my master to fetch more drinking bowls and set out some bearnut cake soaked in honey. As they were ready to pour the tea, Werid's dark fingers closed around my wrist.

"You need to tell us," they said.

So I did.

"This was what I was afraid of," my aunt said, clutching her bowl though the tea had long since gone cold. I still had problems accepting the way in which her collarbones stuck out from her tunic. "Thank fuck we got you out of the Harp in time."

"What do you mean, 'that's what you were afraid of'?" I asked, noting Siw scowling at me over her tea.

"I couldn't have anticipated the extent to which they caught up with you, this is quite unusual. But as you know by now, you're not the only one with a similar experience." She stared at Eleas. "Though most of us stick with one Sibling. We don't suck them up and keep them as you seem to do."

"It's true then. This …" I rattled through a list of appropriate words in my head, "… *curse* comes from our side, not from the Badgers?"

"It's probably the result of a combination of circumstances, but yes—there are precedents for this sort of talent among the Moons. It's not a curse, Sloe."

"It feels inconvenient to me, most of the time."

"It might be inconvenient, but it has also brought you back home to your family, after all the trials you have survived of late. You should be a tiny bit more grateful."

CONSTANT CONTACT

"Yuna gave me these letters." I pulled the sealed, squashed tubes of grass paper out of my shoulder bag. "And sends her love, obviously."

A light flared up in my aunt's eyes. "I didn't think she'd take the trouble to write. Not after we said our goodbyes at the Harp. Yuna was angry with me, but with every day I spent there, the sense of dread became stronger. I knew I couldn't possibly stay and die there. Just imagine, my ashes being stored in the Stoneharp for all eternity? Ridiculous."

"Things have changed at the Harp," Eleas said. "Most members of the council have left to re-join their families when the war came too close for comfort. You might have become stuck there if things had worked out differently."

"Though the Owls now rule the roost," Werid said with a smile. "You don't expect the wizards to return?"

Eleas shook her head. "It feels like a place that is sinking, and it will be left behind in a few decades."

"Serves them right," Sjunil said. "It should've happened years ago. They've long become too fixed in their attitudes. If they'd reacted to the emergence of people like Sloe with more flexibility …"

"They were scared," Werid said. "To acknowledge the return of these talents would've meant conceding that an untrained treefucker can surpass them, only because of how they were born. No work, no dedication."

"Hey," I protested, and my master held up their hands.

"I'm just saying. Siw, how do you feel about it?"

My sister had been silent throughout my confession. My initial hesitation to confide in her might've been based on a healthy instinct.

"It feels intimidating," she said eventually. "Terrifying, if I have to be honest, and infuriating, that Mother could've made such a crucial mistake."

"I'm sorry, Siw. It wasn't Mother's fault. She acted on a promise given to someone she believed to be dead. Or not—whatever suited her, I suppose."

"I'm not angry with you." Siw held out her hand, calloused and stained from the herbs she worked with. "I've been unhappy with Mother's choices for a long time, but I've come to love some aspects of it." She smiled as I took her hand and she squeezed my fingers.

"You'll always be an exceptional healer, Siw. I have much to learn from you."

Sjunil cleared her throat. "Can you do all that later? We need to decide how to continue your education."

"We need to?" I released Siw's hand.

"This is why you came back, isn't it? Your father probably wasn't much help—as expected. I don't have much time left and you'll want to travel on to Goldenlake before my dear sister gets more ideas concerning your immediate future. There are still plenty of eligible bachelors around, and though you kick and scream, she'll find someone new."

"What do you suggest?" Werid asked sourly.

"Sloe should stay here for the time being. Until Shortest Night. That'll give us a chance to cram an apprenticeship into two weeks."

"No …"

"You can't have been under the impression that any of this would be easy. Sister Stone might not always be willing to assist you. You need some proper herblore and at least an introduction to the basics of the Tall Mysteries."

"Help," I whispered.

A grin had appeared on my master's face that I didn't like the look of. "You wanted to be a wizard. You have a lot to catch up on," Werid said.

"I don't deny any of that but trying to do it in two weeks is utter madness!"

"Thank fuck we can divide up the lessons," my aunt said. "Siw will take herblore, Werid can do the mysteries, and I'll tackle the rest." She turned to Eleas. "You can take over if one of us needs a break. If you'd like to stay here for now."

Eleas swallowed. "It would be my honour."

Lilyis' eyes wandered from face to face. As the only one present not in touch with our gods, she had to feel excluded. "What about me?"

Sjunil sighed. "If you promise not to distract Sloe too much, you may stay as well. Herblore is useful for everyone to know, and we need to turn the compost heap. You must be good with a shovel."

Lilyis opened her mouth to protest and gulped. "That sounds fair."

As Siw was expected back in Tall Trees, she didn't dawdle. After tea, Sjunil went back to bed and Werid and Eleas saw to the dishes, while my sister took us with her into the herb garden.

"Don't you dare complain," she said and gave me a little shove. "You have absolutely nothing to moan about."

"I'd hoped for a tearful reunion and a few useful tips, not to be indentured."

"Don't let her fool you. This is one of her good days—on others, she's barely able to open her eyes."

"Is that why she's in such a hurry?"

"I think she waited for you to come back, and now that you're here, we might lose her very quickly."

We three stood amidst the flowering herbs buzzing with insects, the sun burning down upon us. It was difficult to disregard the teeming life in the garden and contemplate saying farewell to one of the most important people in my life.

"You should make every breath count. Don't waste any of them on whingeing. Let her give you what she needs to give you."

"I've never heard you speak so well of her," I whispered.

She half-turned to the house. "Don't tell her this, but I might love her almost as much as you do, though she wasn't the best master I could've wished for. I've always found Werid much more sympathetic, so you might've had more luck there. I don't believe I can envy you for the burden the gods have bestowed upon you, but I can be jealous of Werid's presence in your life."

"I don't think they'll stay much longer after Sjunil has … gone."

"You underestimate how worried they've been for you. Whenever I came back to stock up, I was treated to a few hours of anxious speculation." She rolled up her sleeves. "At least they know you'll have someone to watch out for you." She smiled at Lilyis, with more warmth than I'd expected. "Right. No time like the present. You'll have noticed that the way I've grouped these plants is based on their use. Internal or external, teas or poultices …"

I pushed out a deep breath. There was nothing left to do but to succumb to the lessons.

"I like your friend Eleas," Werid said as they took over. "She strikes me as an extremely useful sort of person."

"She's had my back since I met her in Westlight, and she's already taught me a few things. Things I hadn't heard of before, like water prayers."

"Westlight is a different world with different traditions, but I think you'll need all the help you can possibly get. You should try to keep her at hand. She told me about Sister Storm, and about her history with the council." Werid had brought me to a little room attached to the stable, a second kitchen where Siw handled the smellier ingredients for her salves and potions, which was filled with piles of baskets and empty clay jars. That part of the lesson plan I'd have to survive on my own. Whatever wisdom my master was about to lay on me, Lilyis wasn't allowed to listen in. "She told me you were able to combine your talents."

"That seems to be correct. Whoever god I meet sticks with me."

"You're a connector."

"Is that the technical term for it?"

"No. There's no official term for what you are. No records have survived that describe this sort of gift."

"You're sure it isn't a curse after all?"

"That depends on what you make of it, Sloe. I can imagine it is immensely scary for you, because you don't feel in control."

"That's true."

"I'm sorry but I have to ask. Have you killed someone yet?"

Tears rose to my eyes and I furiously tried to blink them away. I hadn't allowed myself to think much about Tjal's horrible brother and what he'd tried to do to me. "I've killed someone, but I don't think the gods were involved." My voice had gone scratchy. "I've injured a fair few, during the raid on the House of the Sun."

"When you defended your friends and family. Who did you kill, Sloe?"

"Do you remember Tjal?"

"Yes."

"He had a brother. He'd cut down a good friend of mine and I found myself acting. Maybe Sister Stone kept my heart steady, I don't know. I try not to think about it."

"You need to talk about it, though. You must've been shocked. You never struck me as someone tempted by violence."

I swallowed hard. "Not to inflict it, no."

"What do you mean?" Werid moved closer to me, their elbows pushed on their knees, their hands folded in front of them.

"That might be a question Lilyis could cover," I croaked, blushing.

"Oh. I understand."

"I don't think you do."

"You ask your girlfriend to hurt you?"

"No, no that. It's more about knowing that she'd be *able* to hurt me, if she wanted to. It's difficult to explain."

"I don't need the particulars," they said calmly. "There are things that are allowed to remain undiscussed between masters and apprentices."

"Thank fuck."

"Quite. My point is that you're not a person running around trying to kill people. Even if you admit that taking out Tjal's brother wasn't an accident, it's not something you find yourself tempted to do more of, right?"

"Right."

"When you hurt those people at the raid, you felt as if control slipped away from you?"

"I was utterly gone," I whispered. "It was pure luck that no one died of their injuries. The blood … the blood splashed right up to the ceiling."

Werid's fingers flexed. "I can see this must've frightened you. It would be strange if it hadn't. Control is something Sjunil will have to focus on in her teachings, so that's good to know. That's the practical side, what about the theory?"

I heard myself give a relieved chuckle. "What theory? I know the tales told around the fires in Tall Trees and there's the one scroll Sjunil liberated from the administration centre when we were at the Harp, but that's literally all I know. With our wizard living outside the village, and only present from time to time, I never spent more time on all that than any other inhabitant of Tall Trees."

"They're not called the mysteries by chance," Werid said softly. "The knowledge is closely guarded. You must've realized there are several ways to engage with the gods. Most wizards remain on the first level. They pass the Protocols and serve their villages as healers and leaders of the ceremonies, as advisors to their government. This is mainly a political position. They interpret the signs around them to determine the will of the gods, but that's where their powers end. All of your life, this is how you have understood wizards to operate. Some of us ascend when we come face to face with the Siblings and the Cousins. As far as we know, there's no rationale behind who gets picked to talk to them. Some of us are contacted often, others only experience it once or twice in a lifetime. I appreciate that nothing about this is new to you yet. You have *experienced* it before you *knew* of these things, and that isn't the way it's supposed to go. Though we don't know for sure. There have been centuries of speculation and the most widely accepted theory is that gods will come to people of certain bloodlines. None of the Siblings have officially confirmed it, but it seems reasonable to assume so." They sniffed. "The Badgers came to rule the territory around the Golden Lake because they've always had many wizards among them who ascended, and once the Owls laid claim to the lands around the Harp because it was similar for them. The reason why they're back in power might be purely because of their prowess with longknife and bow, but they once held the right to their privileges because their family brought forth extremely talented wizards."

I felt dazed. As a regular apprentice, I'd have been granted years to wrap my head around the intricacies and trying to take it all in at once felt near impossible. "I didn't know that."

"Because our power has receded behind those of our leaders. Today it's about worldly influence, not so much about spiritual strength. This was once a different land, when high-level wizards were numerous enough to be in charge. Our numbers have declined for a long time, and we're often seen as the exceptions. That it was once the other way around is something the councils don't care to remind us of. Once there weren't as many wizards in existence as we required, and so this shift might've come about to satisfy demand. If ascended wizards are treated as such, it's no wonder that the next level up is seen as a bigger threat."

"That's how it feels to me."

"To be in such constant contact is something threatening. You can *speak* for the gods but can also *act* on their behalf. Given what we know about the nature of their characters, we should all be scared shitless."

DESTINED TO HATE

Lilyis and I slept in the stable, while Eleas was allowed to share Siw's room. The distinction between non-wizards and wizards was being upheld, as was proper, and I was too exhausted to be offended anyway. I'd talked to Werid until darkness had fallen over the knoll. Sjunil had long since gone to bed and we ate our evening meal quietly before retiring for the night.

Lilyis touched my temple. "You didn't expect to fall into this face first, didn't you?"

"No. I thought it'd be more of a quick visit and that we'd return to Tall Trees after a few nights away. I shouldn't have been so stupid."

"Don't beat yourself up about it. This place is beautiful, and it gives us a respite from your mother's demands. Siw will have to explain to her that you won't be back until Shortest Night."

"Oh, I didn't think about that. That somehow makes it better."

She laughed quietly. "Don't be mean. You'll face her soon enough."

"I know. But my head hurts from all the information. I didn't know half of the herbs Siw showed us today."

"I made some notes, and you're welcome to borrow them. You should get some sleep. Tomorrow will be more full-on."

"I might sleep better if we'd do something to take the edge off first …" I rolled over my shoulder to kiss her.

"Then tell me what you need me to do."

Afterwards, Lilyis slept like a log, while I was still juggling all the blasted plant names in my head. I felt sticky and a bit ashamed remembering what I'd said to Werid during our lesson.

In the gloom of my aunt's stables Lilyis tucked herself close to me, as if expecting me to protect her, when in fact she was the one to bite everyone away who dared to touch me, commanding my pleasure—which might have been why we'd been sent to the stables in the first place. As foulmouthed as my aunt was, her cottage was hallowed ground, a place of learning and spiritual devotion, not for desperate pleas stammered into tangled straw. I pushed the blanket back under my hip. Lilyis and I had been together for long enough for her to know me, but she could make me shiver with the strength that broke from her, never unexpected, never without me prompting her, but still … It took an eternity for me to drift off.

Siw woke me as she came in at sunrise to feed the horses, nudging me with the tip of her boot. 'Get up,' she mouthed. "Let's squeeze in a lesson before I leave." She made a forbidding gesture. "Don't wake Lilyis. We need to talk."

A faint mist rose from the stream below the cottage, snaking around the grassy ground and the garden.

"Werid has been a great help around here, but they have a predilection for decorative flowers. Usually I'd never let the hawkspurs bloom." Siw flicked her nail against a tangle of pink star-shaped blossoms. "The buds are much more potent than the petals. I suppose I will have ample time to get the garden back on track once Julas and I move here."

I felt annoyance creep over me. I was exhausted, the few hours of uneasy sleep having done little to help. "You wanted to talk?"

"Yes. Are you planning to stay around?" Her blunt question felt like a punch to the throat. Ever since we'd been children, Siw and I had chafed against each other, and she seemed determined to take up the dynamic I'd hoped to have left behind.

"What?"

"I know that you're off to Goldenlake on Lilyis' mission, but afterwards. Will we have a problem?"

"No. Siw, I never wanted to step on your toes."

"You're going back to the Cities with Lilyis?"

"I don't know. I haven't decided yet."

"You know that she loves you?"

"Yes."

"You're willing to let her sail away again?"

"It's not like that."

"It never is in the end," she said. "If you stay, it won't be in Tall Trees?"

"No—about that I'm certain."

Siw grimaced in disappointment. "Our home has become too small for you."

"I can't cope with Mother breathing down my neck. She's tried to control everything in my life for so long, and even if she'd relaxed her grasp now, I wouldn't be able to live as I need to live. I don't want to marry anymore. At least no one else but Lilyis and she isn't free to do so. If I serve the Moons, I'll do it on my own terms, not on Mother's. Silid would have a conniption if I told her."

"Silid has borne the brunt of Mother's actions and opinions much longer than either of us. She'll surprise you. When I came back from the west, pregnant and scared, I found an unexpected source of support in her."

"That's nice. I never had that sort of relationship with her, though she raised me as much as Mother did. Siw?"

"Yes?"

"Are you happy?"

She smiled at me, the rising mist settling drops of dew in her dark hair. "Probably as happy as I can be. I have a plan, and that always helps."

"What's your plan?"

"Live in this cottage, extend it, have some more children, try to keep them safe. Serve Silid once she's taken over full duties. All this depends on what will happen with your friends from the Cities."

"You mean Lilyis and Bjor?"

"No, I mean the others who will follow them if they manage to keep their foot in the door. You realize that your intentions might be laudable, but that the consequences will result in the families being put into danger?"

"I'm trying to steer them into a less destructive direction. You can't put the responsibility for their character at my feet. Men from the Cities have come to these lands for many years, though the Company of the Sun goes about it in a different way."

She huffed. "Be aware that your name will be implicated if all goes tits-up."

"Believe me, I'm *well* aware. This is why we need to get to Goldenlake."

"Fine. Perhaps Tall Trees has always been too small for you, but you didn't know it. Maybe that's why you were always awkward, with everything around you."

I was ready to cry again. "Is that what you thought of me?"

"I thought we were destined to hate each other, and you made it easy for me. You always seemed uncomfortable, even when you finally decided on the Other House."

"I hoped no one else could see that."

"Seriously?"

We stared at each other in silence. I had the choice of digging in deeper, but felt too vulnerable to take more of her spite. "What about the lesson?" I asked eventually.

"I'll be back in a few days. Now that the competitions have been called, there'll be many things to do to prepare the village.

Until then, you should familiarize yourself with the plants in this garden, and …" She pulled a thick scroll of grass paper from her cloak. "These are my own notes from back when I started my apprenticeship. They are based on the layout of the beds and nothing much has changed. A few of the most useful recipes are included and I strongly recommend that you copy them or learn them by heart. I'll need my notes back."

"Thank you so much, Siw."

"You'll have to practice your sewing and learn more about the position of bones and flesh. You should ask to help slaughter the pigs. I found that quite enlightening." She grinned. "People and pigs are not that different, and you can hone your knife skills on them as well, in case you need to intervene in more drastic ways."

I gulped. "Right. Do all wizards have to attain this level of knowledge?"

"I have a special interest and healing is where my talents lie, though there's little I can do to aid my master at this point, besides drugging her to help with the pain." She looked afraid. "I'll assist our mother when her time comes and you might be in a position to see many people die yourself, to ease them over into the land of the dead. A wizard is first and foremost a guide. This is how Sjunil has always explained it to me. A guide to a realm beyond what we can see, a connection to the gods in whatever way we are suited to fulfil the role. In the end, all that we do is about the land of the dead. To ensure that we have lived a life without regrets, so that we can pass on to the next adventure. I should probably have left this for Sjunil to say," she added, with a nervous glance back towards the cottage.

Our aunt had always struck me as well-prepared to take on any adventure she chose to consider, but in that moment the burden of our position fell heavily upon me.

Siw noticed me slump. She smiled. "Let's pick some herbs for tea and help Werid with breakfast."

While we ate, I thought about my sister's words. Without being aware of my aunt's beliefs I'd acted out that side of them for a long time. I'd made it my task to speak for other people, to get involved on their behalf.

Werid hadn't woken my aunt to join us for the meal, so we tried to be as quiet as humanly possible while we had more toasted bread, herb pastes, and thick slices of crumbling cheese from last year's batch. Siw left after we'd cleared everything away, not waiting to say farewell to her master. While Eleas took Lilyis to the garden, I followed Werid back to the storage shed, bracing myself for more disturbing revelations.

"I don't know when Sjunil will be strong enough to give you a practical lesson, so I might try to do what I can. Do you have any questions about what we talked about yesterday?"

I tried to find a comfortable position on the low seat I perched on. "Based on what you said, Eleas and I fall into the third-level category?"

"Eleas seems to. I have my suspicions that we need to find a new category for you."

"So … the wizards of old, the sorcerers in the tales of the Eight Kingdoms, they were like Eleas, allowed to use the power of the Sibling they were associated with?"

"Right."

"And people in this category have been suppressed by the councils why? Because they are afraid to lose their own influence?"

"That's how I can explain it to myself, Sloe."

"While here in the lands of the families we were pushed aside and hidden, on the Continent we were celebrated, until the priests of the Star arrived from further east to convert the people of the kingdoms. We were given positions at their courts and taken into service to consolidate the grasp of their royal families with the strength of the gods. Has there never been a time when we were granted similar treatment here?"

"The stories that come to mind have only survived in obscure sources. Some of them have been fashioned into origin myths in which the boundaries between gods and wizards get very blurred. It's difficult to say, Sloe. I don't have a definitive answer for you, but the councils have been in power for a long time, and it's undoubtedly in their interest to destroy any material that speaks of a time in which it was different."

"Isn't it weird that the attitudes towards us can be so diverse?"

"To me it speaks of the fact that we were once spread across the whole known world, and that, in this way, the people of the Eastern Cities were part of the families too, despite their changed beliefs. It makes sense to strive for an arrangement between us that considers both sides—none of us can claim the higher ground."

"Unfortunately there aren't many people in the Cities who'd feel happy with this conclusion. The Star teaches them that having embraced a new set of gods makes them morally superior."

"Have you met any of their new gods?"

I stared at my master. "No."

"Have you spoken to any of the priests, asked them if they can talk to them in the way we can to our Siblings?"

"No."

"This might be the thing you need to find out. Otherwise we have to assume that the gods of the Star might not exist."

I gasped. *Not exist.* Werid's words echoed through my head. I couldn't even imagine how it would feel to be confronted by such a statement when it came to the Siblings, to be told that everything I'd learned about them since becoming aware of being a member of the families, was built on a pile of lies. "The Continent is full of people who believe in them with every shred of their soul," I countered. "Lilyis' wife is a good example. If I dared to suggest this to her, she'd try to eat my heart."

"The councils and the Star seem to have quite a few things in common," Werid said. "They both want us to believe without questioning them in any way that undermines their hold, though they are choking the life out of us."

STRAIGHT INTO THE FLAME

As I'd anticipated, Sjunil asked me to come to her bedside the next morning.

"It's strange to think that you're actually here," she said, reaching out to touch my hand. "I used to pray every evening that the gods would keep you safe and hurry your return. How are you keeping up?"

"I feel overwhelmed."

"Something you share with every apprentice. It's part of the process, believe me."

"Break you down to build you up?"

She grimaced. "As I said to you once before, that's an approach I don't condone. Our situation is somewhat unfortunate and if there was more time to train you, I'd give you all the space in the world. I'm under no illusion concerning my state of health and knowing that I had at least a chance to help you on your path will make these last months mean a lot more. Stop sniffling, for fuck's sake."

"You did that on purpose!"

A ghost of the old fox-like grin appeared on her face. "Maybe I did. Right. Buckle up, buttercup. There are things about me that you need to know." She took a deep, rattling breath. "My Siblings came to me early, but my master had warned me it might happen. Most of the Moon wizards have ascended very young. Thankfully, I had guidance to get through that time and wasn't as scared as I could have been, as scared as you were. When I was an apprentice in this house, I was one of three and didn't understand until later that not all of us were expected to survive."

"Did the other two die?"

"They did. One of them caught a fever, so that was a bit of a let-down, but the other one … the other one was my best friend. They killed themself after the gods came out to them."

"Wait—what?" It felt as if someone had knocked the wind out of me. Werid had spoken before of would-be wizards who'd been broken when they ascended, but hearing my aunt talk about it so bluntly came as a shock.

"They longed to be spoken to and when it finally happened it was too much to bear. It was different for me. I'd had ample time to get used to the visitations before I noticed that something was a bit off. Years … and as soon as it happened to me, I understood why I'd lost them. You didn't have much of a breather either, but you were around wizards who knew what they were seeing and would've been there to get you out. It's highly likely that my friend's talents were more advanced, and that they burned up, like a moth flying straight into the flame."

"How did they die?"

"They poisoned themself."

"Oh, Sjunil. I'm so sorry."

"They came from the smaller villages and were more Bear than Moon. They were strong and seemed capable, but there always was a vulnerability to them that I didn't really understand. They must've been so afraid, and I feel guilty that I couldn't make them feel loved enough to try and live with … it."

"What was their name?"

"Sloe. They were called Sloe Bear."

I blinked, desperately trying to keep up. "What?"

"You must've heard the story of how I named you."

"Of course, but …"

"They had blue eyes—very unusual for a Moon, more so for a Bear. When I saw you brought out into the sunshine, I said *their* name. The name they'd given themself, not the name their own wizard had bestowed upon them. As soon as I'd spoken it out loud, it made sense to stick with it."

"Did Mother know that you named me after someone? After a Bear, no less?"

"Yes, but …"

"This is why she didn't speak to you for months afterwards."

"I think she thought I'd cursed you—and maybe I did, given how things progressed."

"Why did no one tell me?"

"Because it wasn't a story that would've helped you along. Not with your father doing his best to inconvenience everyone around him."

"You need to tell me more about Sloe Bear."

"They were kind and shy and liked to look after the chickens. They'd been taught to read and write but had been trained as a warrior first, because their village was a dangerous place to live, quite close to the steppes and the Hedgehog clan. They were most at home on a horse. They'd switched houses a couple of times before settling on the Other House in the end, though they weren't completely sure. I think there must've been some violence in their past, but they never talked about it. When the third apprentice died, they took it hard, as if they saw it as a betrayal by the gods. This place wasn't large enough for us three and I was weirdly relieved but Sloe … sometimes I wonder if they'd managed to hold on for a bit longer … or if this hadn't happened before, if they hadn't felt themself fated to die as well, to leave just one of us. There are so many questions I'd like to ask them today. There might've been a chance for them to be alive, though I probably wouldn't have gone to finish my education at the Stoneharp if they'd still been with me, never met your father and never mentioned him as a good choice to your mother, so there's that. I've had the idea in the past that you remind me of them in more than name and eye-colour, you know, and that has made me afraid for you from time to time. In general, you've handled your ascent far more gracefully than I expected. Instead of pushing the gods away you seem to have reached a balance with them. I can't describe how different you are to me now. I know your travels can't have been pure joy from start to finish—there must've been times when you feared for your life or for the lives of your friends, but you seem so much more *there* to me. Am I making a mistake?"

"No. No, I think you're right. The Princes of Crooked Hill gave me an idea of how I could fit into their world. They made space for me, offered me the opportunity to learn more, to *seek* knowledge, not just to be subjected to it. It seems wild to me that I might never have come this far if I'd tried to fit myself into the hierarchies of the Harp. All of this might come back to haunt us, when other Companies have set out to bring back a wizard from Birkland ..."

"It's not your fault you made such a good impression." Her lungs gave a strange rattling sound again. "I understand how you could feel responsible for this development. We might see the dawn of a new age of wizardry in the west—and it might all have started with one lonely Moon travelling on a ship to the Cities. Wouldn't that be something?"

"Do you think they'll find what they're searching for?"

"You found Eleas, didn't you? Even if we assume that the Siblings have had their dirty paws in the pie, if they search for them at the Harp or in Goldenlake, they're probably going to be disappointed. Deep in the mountains of Cloudhome they might find wizards eager to deny your existence, but if they scour the furthest regions, they might find them after all. I don't think we can rule out that some of them, or at least one of them, could be in possession of a gift that has evolved to bundle others."

"From what the Siblings said around me, it seems as if this was an unusual situation for them as well."

I heard my aunt swallow thickly. "Really?" Then she said what I'd longed for her to say since I'd arrived. "Fuck, fuck, fuckity-fuck."

As much as I loved to hear her spit out those words, I could see that I'd scared her deeply, and after all she'd disclosed to me, I couldn't help but dread the future awaiting us.

"How is she?" Werid asked.

"Asleep."

"Ah, that's good. It's not always easy for her to actually sleep. Many nights she spends in a daze. You talked for a while."

"There's much to tell."

"So I gather."

"I'll have to re-evaluate some things that I've heard about her over the years."

Werid smiled sadly, pushing the dried roots aside on the wooden board to make more space for the next batch. "I've been with her for some time and every day she says something that changes all that came before. She's the sort of person who always keeps you on your toes. You'd think living in the depth of the forest, tending to the garden and a dying wizard would be boring, but it never was. Not one moment feels wasted."

"Thank you for being here for her, Werid."

"I couldn't leave Siw alone with her."

"Has either one spoken about why the wizards of the Moons live so far away from Tall Trees?"

"Sjunil mumbled something about the changing course of the rivers, that Tall Trees was much closer to this house at some point, before it was destroyed by floods and rebuilt several times."

"Oh. Really?"

"But maybe I've got the details wrong."

"No, that would make sense. When you were a wizard in the steppes, did you live among the Wolves or apart from them?"

"I lived with my family, but in my own tent, always on the edge of the camps. They kept the animals away from me, to comply with the old rules we follow in the steppes. Some restrictions might not make much sense nowadays, but once they were based on practicality. Most people feel restless around us and safer if they know us to be separated off."

"Did you often feel alone in the steppes? I mean, you had your wife with you, but …"

"I still felt alone most of the time. Why do you think I've delayed my return so many times? There would've been opportunities to get away, but I know that she hasn't waited for me. I have no reason to believe that she would have. I might arrive with the Wolves to find myself divorced by proxy. She warned me once—and I believe her."

"Werid …"

"This is a chance for me to be involved in something bigger," they said, glancing down at the knife they used to chop the vegetables. "*Proper* wizard stuff. Can you give me the leeks?"

The leeks had been harvested in winter and stored; their outer leaves had shrivelled to brown paper. Werid stripped them ruthlessly, their movements pointedly brutal, daring me to say more. They'd never talked much about their wife with me, but the fact that they were still around told me enough about their marriage. Werid presented a captivating front, all gleaming hair and stunning frocks, but most of the time the glamour served as a mask.

"I will dearly miss your aunt when she has left us behind. These months under her tutelage have been some of the best of my life."

"Tutelage? Really?"

"We have spoken a lot about our notions concerning the land of the dead. She hasn't tried to spare me and I'm grateful for the opportunity to fulfil my vocation as a guide for someone this distinguished, this … revered."

I frowned at them. "Revered?"

"Your aunt has a reputation that reaches far beyond Tall Trees. She'll pass into legend. Only because she chose to give all her attention to a place like Tall Trees doesn't make her less influential. You've seen her on the council in Goldenlake. She held the respect of all those wizards, and the love of some. Do you know that Yuna wanted to come with us, but Sjunil forbade her to give up the Harp for her? They have said their goodbyes and she was a pain to live with afterwards."

"That doesn't surprise me. Yuna still loves her, but she also seemed angry."

"There's a lot of history between them." Werid shot me a meaningful glance. "Can you put the sausage in, please?"

I scraped the slices into the pot hanging above the kitchen brazier. "I'm glad to have you here, Werid."

"You should be."

"It might not be how I expected to be taught but I wouldn't forgo it for all the world."

"Make sure to show your gratitude," Werid advised. "Sjunil is holding on for you and she needs to know that you appreciate the effort."

As steps sounded behind us, we fell silent.

Eleas ducked under the lintel of the front door, carrying a brace of plump birds.

"Oh, well done!" Werid's face lit up. "We'll have a feast tomorrow! Can you pluck and gut them for me, please? Where's Lilyis?"

"She wanted to stay outside for a while. Your girlfriend is a talented archer, Sloe."

"Yes, she's been in training all her life."

Eleas made a gesture that caused me to exchange a look with my master and leave the kitchen after Werid had given me permission with a nod.

I found Lilyis close to the house, perched on one of the mossy rocks at the water, the sun blazing down on her hair, her collar dragged open. She hadn't cooled down after the successful hunt; her face was flushed beneath the freckles.

I stopped a few steps away. "Did you want to talk to me?"

"Did Eleas say something to you?"

"Not really."

"I asked her to keep her trap shut."

"Lilyis, what's wrong?"

She leant forward and scooped the ice-clear water up in her palms. She stared down into the leaking vessel, as if she expected her own face to stare back up at her. "It's starting to feel like a dream," she said. "A beautiful dream, but with every day I spend in these woods I realize this isn't my world—it's yours. All these lessons … I know that you need them and that I'm standing in the way. When Siw comes back to check up on us, I will return with her to Tall Trees."

THE BRAVEST

Before we left the hut, there was much to do. For the next two days the weather held, so Werid taught their lessons among the flowering herbs, while we weeded or picked buds and leaves to process them later. As Werid was busy with me, Eleas took it upon herself to sweep out the cottage and search for small things to fix for them. Apart from the option of providing food for us, Lilyis had little else to do but dry the dishes. I couldn't blame her for wanting to get out. In Tall Trees she had Bjor to talk to and all the others; she could watch the training for the looming competitions and teach a few blade tricks. On the knoll, the quietness could feel oppressive at times.

Siw came back sooner than expected and I saw my love breathe a deep sigh of relief.

"You can't imagine the number of scrapes I've had to deal with," my sister said. "Everyone and their dog want to compete for the chance to command the Moons. I'm all out of throttleweed salve. I need to make a massive batch to take with me."

"Can you bring Lilyis along?" I asked my sister.

"Is she already going up the walls?"

"Yes, and I can't stand to see her so fidgety and unhappy."

"There's plenty for her to keep busy with in Tall Trees. All those little boys could use some pointers."

"Thank you, Siw. You'll keep an eye on her?"

"Certainly."

"Don't let her know I asked you to, for fuck's sake."

During our last night spent in my aunt's stables, we mostly talked.

"Promise me you'll not miss the festivities," Lilyis said. "I need you there at Shortest Night."

"I'll try to come back a day early if I can," I promised. "By then I'll probably be so desperate for a break I might burst into tears as soon as I hear the drums."

"What drums?"

"There'll be music."

"Oh, right."

"And honey beer and roasted pork and …"

Lilyis winced. "Sloe?"

"Yeah?"

"Please try not to piss off your aunt too much. She's sacrificing a lot of her time for you, and I can see how it costs her."

"I'll be the best student there ever was."

She scoffed. "That doesn't reassure me as much as you believe it does."

I frowned. "You think I can't be a good apprentice?"

"I think that's not the way you learn. You need to get your hands dirty for stuff to stick, and this set-up isn't designed to do that." She snuggled against my chest.

"Can you promise me something in return?"

"What?" she asked sleepily.

"That you won't enter the competition."

"I'm sure I'm not allowed to."

"Then don't try to find a loophole."

"You don't want me to have fun?" she asked, mockingly.

"I don't want you to shame the best of our young warriors."

"It's sweet of you to think I'd be able to." I felt her mouth twitch against my neck.

"I've seen you on the training square often enough, and I've stood and watched the Tall Trees competitions almost every year. I know that you'd have a chance to best them all. This type of thing is seen as a big affront—Julas lost in his last round a couple of years ago and he's not over it yet."

"I understand. It's the same at home, in case you've forgotten."

"No, I only …"

"You don't trust me to behave?"

"I know Cousin Blade takes a special interest in you. He's a very seductive god."

She pulled away. "You're serious, aren't you?"

"Yes. Yes, I am."

"If we start like this, I'll never be able to leave you alone. You're surrounded by all of them, apparently!"

"I'm saying that I get it, but we can't afford to disgruntle the youth of the Moons. I'm getting cold, please come back to me."

"All right. I *promise* that I won't try to take part in the competitions. Not even a friendly fight?"

"I defer to your common sense."

She gave me a small shove before settling down against me once again. "I like knowing that you worry about me."

"Just because you're not here with me doesn't mean I won't hold you in my thoughts."

"I know, but you'd be forgiven for getting distracted by all the things you need to learn." She kissed my shivering skin and silenced us both for a while.

"It actually improves my opinion of her," my aunt said, after Lilyis and Siw had left us. "She knows that if this is supposed to work you need to trust each other, even if you're apart. Sometimes it will be a forest, sometimes it will be an ocean." She patted the edge of the bed. "Sit down, Sloe."

"Are there many more revelations to come?" I asked sourly. "So I can brace myself for anything life-changing."

"Don't be a cunt, Sloe."

"I'm really trying." I sat down as I was bid. "How are you feeling?"

"Tired. It wasn't the best of nights, but I think it's time that we get them all together."

"You mean ..."

"I mean that I can give them both to you. Sister Soil and Sister Sun."

I found myself reaching for her. "Why didn't you say something before?"

"Because I specifically didn't want the council to know. You'll have all eight Tall Gods around you when you go back to Tall Trees. I can't speak for the Cousins though. They are too unreliable."

"Do you have a favourite between them?"

"I thought I taught you to forget about the F-word."

"Right, sorry."

"Let it be said that I've had my fair share of handling high-maintenance women." The ghost of a grin flashed over her face. "I'm sure you'll be able to claim them both in time. Don't be disappointed if they require a bit more attention for now."

"I meant to ask you, when you blew up the door in the Harp's council chambers ..."

"There are many things they can provide you with. Sister Soil *loves* a good explosion."

"Oh. You're saying that could be helpful in a fight?"

"Among other things. She usually comes with a few suggestions." She took my hand in hers. "Maybe we're in luck and they'll bear me enough love to accept you straight away."

They stood around my aunt's bed, still swathed in the black mist they'd appeared from, all eyes glued to her face. The two women closest to her were so beautiful that my breath hitched: one of them with very dark skin and tight curls, the other short and muscled in a way that reminded me of Julas' sister, but pale like something living in a cave for most of its life, with eyes as milky and flat as the stone in my bracelet. A smell came off her that had nothing on the fecund riverbed tang Brother Brook brought with him. Whomever those two forms had once belonged to, I could immediately see why Sjunil would've fallen for both of them, and I felt myself swallow, not sure how to speak to anyone so breathtaking.

Eight Siblings crowded silently around us, waiting for something to happen. For someone to start talking.

Brother Brook, always first to lose his patience, sniffed loudly. "This is awkward."

"It doesn't have to be," my aunt said.

He shot a glance across at Sister Sun. "Yes, it does. There are questions we have avoided for a long time."

"You started it!" Sister Sun hissed at him across my aunt's blankets. "And you *know* it!"

"Perhaps we can hold off on the family squabbles," Sjunil said, with a mocking tone that made all of them freeze. "Sloe, these are the goddesses I spent most of my life with. They both bear the faces of my deepest regrets, when I was young and stupid enough to assume the world owed me something in return for my pains. Let me see …" She pointed at them one by one. "Tjal, and the prince I recognize—who's that?" She inclined her head towards Sister Stone, who looked a bit sheepish. "Is that supposed to be me? I was never that cute. Who's this?"

"One of Eleas' sisters."

"And Cirvi Cloud as Brother Rain? That's quite fucked up. And him? Who's Brother Moon?"

"My father's master."

"Ah." The excitement gave her more colour than usual. "Thank you all for coming. This is a special occasion, indeed. You'll have all noticed this isn't a normal case of master and apprentice contacting the gods. This is an introduction and, in a way, a change of regime."

"Regime?" I whispered.

"Shut up, Sloe. This is my speech to make." She was obviously enjoying herself. "Today I'm delivering Sloe Moon of Tall Trees into your hands, and I charge all eight of you to watch out for them to the best of your abilities. If any one of you fails in your task, I will find a way to return from the land of the dead to make things difficult for you."

I blushed. I'd been at many of my aunt's public ceremonies, and she'd always had a specific way to make her expectations clear, but that was extraordinarily reckless. Perhaps it was knowing she was close enough to the land of the dead to smell it that let her find those provoking words, but one by one, I saw the Tall Gods lower their heads in assent. Brother Brook was the last one. He'd surely felt pressured into it, but in the end he bowed to my aunt, who beamed up at him as smug as a cat sprawled in the only available strip of sunlight.

"Thank you. We can talk about the details later."

They began to step back into blackness.

The last one to linger was Sister Soil. She bent down over my aunt to kiss her cheek and said, "You are the bravest I have ever known."

Werid almost dropped a tea bowl when I told them about what Sjunil had done for me.

"That was … I don't have words for it. They actually came to her side? All eight of them?"

"They did."

"You know that might've been the first time in the history of the families that a wizard saw them all together?"

"Are you angry that you weren't there to witness it?"

"Gods, no. I doubt my heart would've taken it." They didn't sound as if they were trying to make me feel better, and I allowed myself to believe them. "As I said, your aunt is an extraordinary person, Sloe. There probably won't be enough days in a year to tell the secrets she's chosen to keep from us all and the true extent of her power. She could've been one of those ambitious sorcerers who once ruled at the side of the kings of the Continent."

"I think you're right."

"She could also have made a career for herself on both councils, or taught the most talented apprentices at the Harp, but that isn't what she chose to do with her life. She served her sister and her family. I need you to understand that is a valid choice."

"I understand perfectly. I know I'm not strong enough to make the same decision. Whatever happens with Lilyis, Tall Trees isn't the place for it."

"You'll try and settle in Goldenlake?"

I grinned at them. "Can't I be some sort of travelling wizard?"

Werid put down the dishrag. "You might joke about it, but that might be simultaneously the safest and the most dangerous option available to you. Safest, because it limits the possibility of a leader instrumentalizing your talents to overthrow the other families—dangerous, because … I don't think you're cut out for the life of a wanderer. Ever since we met in Goldenlake you have been on a desperate search for someone to attach yourself to. Tell me if I'm wrong."

"You're not wrong. That was definitely me back then. *Desperate* seems an accurate description."

"Back then?"

"A lot has happened to me since."

"As we all can tell. People usually don't change that much in a year. Technically, I'm still your master, Sloe."

"I'm still beyond grateful for it."

"I should come with you, then. As soon as the situation here resolves itself."

"I don't know if we can wait that long."

"I'm not expecting her to last beyond Shortest Night."

"But that's … that's only a few days away," I whispered.

"I think she will ask me to prepare a draught to help her."

It felt like a kick to the heart. "A draught to do what with? Kill herself?"

"It's another important lesson, Sloe—to accept when the game has been played."

"But after what happened with her friend …"

"She's allowed to choose. It's a wizard's privilege."

BEFORE I LET YOU GO

When I asked my aunt about her plans, she smiled with a shrug. "I don't owe anyone more pain than I'm prepared to give."

It'd taken me a few days to gather my courage and question her outright, after torturing both Eleas and Werid with my pointless musings. "And you're sure?"

"For now, I'm sure. There are few times more auspicious than Shortest Night and thanks to you, I've seen all their faces. There won't be a big surprise waiting for me in the land of the dead."

"That still sounds risky to me."

"It's what comes to us all, Sloe. I've tried to push it away for years, but I'm at the end of my tether. I'll do my best to prepare you, but you need to go to Tall Trees and join the others when the time comes. I might decide to wait."

"As you said, it's your choice."

"Now where were we?"

"We don't need to do this today."

"Haven't you listened to me?" She pinched my arm hard enough to make me yelp.

"All right, sorry!"

"I will ask Werid to accompany you to Goldenlake."

"They already said it might be a good idea."

"Wonderful. Qerla Badger owes me a shitload of favours so maybe she'll do this one for me. It should pay off to have almost married the most powerful wizard at the lake, shouldn't it? Today I want you to try and call to only one of the Siblings. We should start with one you're already familiar with, but I think we shouldn't needle Brother Brook too much. What about Brother Flame?"

"Sounds … doable."

"Good. I know it goes against all the principles being taught at the Harp, but you've earned the right to be a little demanding."

I closed my eyes and called to him.

Nothing much happened, then the cover at the side of the open window started to flutter. Sjunil's dark eyes widened as the cloth blew inwards and the kite swooped into the cottage, closer than I'd ever seen it, much bigger than it had seemed circling above me on the Continent. It landed at the end of her bed; a sharp-edged feather dislodged itself from the wing and sailed slowly to the floor, sawing back and forth.

"Holy fuck. What kind of bird is this?"

"It's a red kite."

"I've never seen one of those before."

"It's at home in the Hillakes—I think."

We both stared at the animal in front of us, who returned our gaze with unblinking yellow eyes.

"To be honest, I don't know if this works for what I had in mind," my aunt whispered. "Though he came when you called."

"Could I ask him to change?"

"Try."

I held out my hand to the massive bird perched in front of us. My fingers shook as the kite stretched out its neck and the feathers brushed against my skin, oddly cold and sleek.

Please. Show us your face.

The bird folded out its wings, to the full width of my aunt's sleeping platform. As I blinked, the human form of Brother Flame became apparent, sitting on the blankets with crossed legs, dressed in clothes belonging to another continent, his copper-coloured hair falling over his shoulders and forearms. As always, seeing him gave me a tug of pain around the heart. In so many ways my story had started when I'd met Lilyis' father in the woods, though

Brother Flame didn't copy him in all details: his left hand didn't show any signs of its fingers having once been broken.

"Why do you need to see my face?" he asked, putting his elbows to his knees. As he so often did, he tried to imitate a human man but didn't quite pull it off, as if there was another body inside, working against the form inflicted upon it. Of all the Siblings he appeared to be the only one who had that specific problem.

"Because I like to see it," I said.

My aunt tried to push herself upright. "If I hadn't expected one thing to happen these days, it's having a man in my bed. I always assumed I'd learned enough from past mistakes not to open that pot of maggots again. Thank you for coming, though. There are a few things I'd like to ask you and maybe a few things we could try to do."

"Start with the questions," he said.

"When exactly did you attach yourself to my student here?"

"I was given to them."

"When?"

"When the wolfstone was gifted to Sloe, me and my sister came with it." He glanced at me. "We have felt responsible for them ever since."

"Why?"

"Because that is what we do." He seemed genuinely astonished. "What we have always done."

"Surely you don't attach yourself to just anyone who's wearing a wolfstone."

"No. That would be impractical."

"What prompted you to step to Sloe's side?"

He frowned. "I don't know. It happened."

"All your Siblings were gifted to you," Sjunil said. "Your mother entrusted you to Brother Brook and things have been gathering momentum from there."

"Yes, that's what I figured."

"The question remains: why do they *stick* to you? Why are they able to share you without getting into conflict? No offense, but the Siblings have a well-earned reputation for being somewhat possessive."

The yellow eyes latched onto her face. "None taken," he said, with a hint of iciness in his voice.

"Why do you all stay and why are you able to hand over your powers?"

"We don't hand them over as such. It's interesting to see what Sloe makes of them. How they combine our strengths into what they need them to do."

"Have you had dealings with many people who were able to do this?"

"No. Sloe is the first."

"Would your Siblings say the same?"

"I expect so. As you said, we are all territorial creatures, and we do not take too well to sharing attention. There is a creative element to whatever this is, that is quite fascinating. In addition to the fact that Sloe took us back to the Continent. It was a re-awakening to another world, something half-forgotten and I, for all that it's worth, am grateful for the experience. Things are changing, and chances are there will be continental wizards again." He nodded at me, as if we were both aware of the implications of his words. "I do not have any answer as to why the task has fallen on Sloe specifically. There might not be one." He made a strange movement, as if he had a crick in his neck. "Is that enough for you? Can I leave?" He sounded impatient, as if he couldn't wait to fly again.

"Of course," Sjunil said. "Thank you."

He flickered like a flame, glowing into this bird shape and catapulting himself off the bed, folding his wings to his body to fit through the window.

"Why did you let him go?" I asked my aunt. "I thought you wanted to do some practical exercises."

"You saw how antsy he became all of a sudden, so we should find someone else for the next part. To divide up the attention more evenly. Do you have any preference, Sloe?"

"We should go with someone *you* know well. What about Sister Soil?"

"Right. You can't help but be curious about the latest powers you'll have to play with."

Her smell hit me first. On her own, it seemed less green to me. She wore the same face as when the Siblings had gathered around my aunt's bed the last time, and as she smiled, I saw dimples in her cheeks.

"You have exhausted yourself already," Sister Soil said in her deep, raspy voice. "You need to be more careful."

"There isn't much time left, and too many things I need to know before I let you go."

"Such as?" She sat herself down on the edge of the bed.

"Show me what Sloe will be able to do with your help," Sjunil asked. "Will it be like … like what we did together?"

The pale blue eyes swivelled towards me. "That may depend on the elements we can combine it with," she said gently. "There might be options to explore that haven't occurred to me either. It should be easier to make things explode if Brother Flame is around. I can provide some of the ingredients, but we might have to find others first. They'll certainly have a better time growing their herbs from now on and to find their feet in unfamiliar places."

"That sounds helpful."

"Which is all we can strive to be," she said, arching a thick brow. "It will be strange to lose you."

Sjunil's face went slack, as if she had to deal with a sudden onslaught of intense pain.

Sister Soil continued, "But I understand why you want to pass us on while you have the chance to do so with full deliberation. I have always hated how little time we are allowed to have with the people we come to love and, in a way, rely on." She took my aunt's hand. "How do you want to do it?"

Sjunil narrowed her eyes at me. "Are you prepared to find out?"

Both of us stared at the smoking remains of the window frame.

"All right—this was a mistake."

I heard Werid and Eleas running in from outside.

"What the fuck was that?" my master called across the cottage.

Sjunil grinned. "Turns out we should've taken the lesson into the gardens."

"Are you mad?" Werid protested. "You can play around all you want, far away from the gardens and the buildings, but don't you dare do something stupid in the house again! What the fuck did you do?"

"Sloe seems to be talented in more ways than expected. They didn't need half as much oomph as I usually do."

Werid turned on me. "This will be your job to repair, curtains and all."

"I'm sorry—and I'll sort it out."

"You can start sewing during our next lesson."

It'd felt strange, quite unlike anything else I'd experienced before, like a flammable purplish mist creeping up around my ankles that could be squashed together and formed into an ignitable entity. Once again, I'd asked Brother Flame for assistance, and he'd certainly delivered. It was a wonder I still had my eyebrows.

The experience left me tingling, like goosebumps that didn't want to go away, covering my arms and shoulders; tiny beads of sweat continued to break out on my forehead and temples. I would've liked Sister Stone to make an appearance; the presence of a soft, purring cat would've done much to slow down my heartbeat, but I was left alone in the stables, missing Lilyis more with every breath.

I watered the horses, fed them their hay for the night, and raked together a few pitchforks of shit to lessen my workload in the morning. The last time I'd tried my hand at sewing I'd worked on my wizard costumes for the functions in Eastbay. Replacing the curtains I'd destroyed so efficiently would be a relatively easy task. The window frame was another matter. I possessed no carpentry skills. I didn't look forward to trying my hand at it; the memory of the almighty crack still made me shake and my ears had barely stopped ringing. It was a dangerous talent to possess, something that would take Qes and Lilyis by surprise, something the Bulls couldn't have dreamt about, and unless they found themselves a wizard who possessed both the love of Sister Soil and Brother Flame, it could turn out to be an undeniable advantage …

"I can hear you thinking from all the way over here." Eleas stood in the door of the small stable, while I stared down at the tines of the pitchfork buried in a heap of soiled bracken. "Though you do not seem to be afraid anymore."

"It was rather exhilarating. I don't want to imagine how I'd feel if there was a human being on the receiving end of it, not just a piece of wall."

"You probably cannot be too careful," she said thoughtfully, "and should try and put in some target practice. I could find you some half-rotten baskets and chipped clay jars to blow up."

"That sounds amazing."

"Are you sure you want to keep sleeping here? I could make some space for you in the house."

"No, thank you. This feels right. I have lots of work to do before I'm anywhere near worthy enough to take my place among real wizards."

Reducing said baskets and jars to splinters and the tiniest fragments of clay felt satisfying. It took me a few times to aim the blast in the right direction and it didn't help that both Eleas and Werid stood at the side with crossed arms, watching me like proverbial hawks. After the last basket had disintegrated, I set the heap aflame with a burst of blue fire and nothing was left but pale ash that I doused down to ensure nothing could kindle itself on the remnants of my trials.

"Do you feel more in control?" Werid asked. "Are you starting to get a grip on it?"

"Yes, but this isn't close to being in the midst of battle. When the shit hits the ceiling, I might not be able to keep a hold on the reins."

"You should use every moment you find to practise," Werid said gravely. "Until you don't have to think about it."

Eleas shot them a glance. "I am sure Sloe knows that already. Go on, you two—I will clean up meanwhile."

Werid brought me into the herb kitchen where we processed the plants we'd picked during my first days at the cottage. Werid showed me the proper technique to pestle them into submission in my aunt's big mortar of roughened clay, to create a paste of much smoother consistency than I'd managed to achieve before.

"I understand that battle magic is more exciting than what I have to teach you," my master said, with a strong flavour of disapproval in their voice. "But you need to learn to heal the wounds you inflict."

I gave the fastleaf another pounding. "I'm aware, Werid. You don't need to worry about me forgetting what damage I'm learning to do here."

"You wouldn't be the first one seduced by a new skill," they grumbled. "Still not fine enough. You can't risk the skin getting irritated by all the lumps you leave in."

They were especially hard on me for the next few days, something Eleas watched with a worried expression. Between Werid's attempts to keep me humble, my aunt's blunt questioning of our Siblings that made me very tense indeed, and the target practice, there was barely time to breathe. In the evenings I worked on the new curtains and the window frame that I had to start over after managing to make it too small *twice*.

"You need a day off," Eleas said one morning. "I will take you fishing."

"But ..."

"You will burn yourself out. I doubt one day will make the difference between life and death at this point. I will talk to your master."

She stayed true to her word. We left the cottage after the morning's chores had been done, following the course of the stream on foot. During our time there Eleas had scouted out a few places along the banks where the best conditions for catching trout were met and we walked a surprisingly long way until she stepped underneath a wall of overhanging rock that offered a sheltered spot for us to stack the gear and settle.

"Do not fret about catching anything today," Eleas said. "It was merely a good excuse to get you away from the dragons."

I heard myself giggle. "Don't ever let Werid know you called them a dragon."

"I do not intend to. Enough is enough. You are starting to look rather strung out. You should curl up in the moss and sleep for a few hours. I will watch over you," she promised.

I found dry leaves under the rock, pushed together in a way that made me suspect Eleas had used the place for a secret nap from time to time. The smells of Sister Soil and Brother Brook hovered around me and as soon as my head hit the leather bag I'd brought, I felt my eyes close. I could hear Eleas hum to herself, songs I'd never heard before and that seemed vaguely familiar nonetheless, mimicking the silvery gurgle of the swift-flowing water. I was asleep before I knew it, for once untroubled by disturbing dreams.

As I came to, I found myself alone and almost bashed my head on the rock above as I sat up in alarm. I spotted the parcel of clothes folded up next to the stone Eleas had sat on. The water basin was deep enough for her to submerge herself up to her chest. Her black hair lay wet against her shoulder blades. I must've made a noise, because she turned to me.

"Apologies—I did not mean to wake you."

"You didn't. Why are you in the water?"

"Because it feels good, and I did not get a single bite anyway. Do you want to come in?"

"I don't want to know what happens if I actually dunk my whole body in there."

She shrugged her naked shoulders. "It might be good to find out."

I thought back to the fight against the temple guards in Smallclere. I'd been in full panic then, not thinking straight.

Eleas smiled at me. "It is your call—I am not your master."

She might not be my master, but she was my friend and correct to assume it was a situation I needed to prepare for. I wiggled out of my tunic. Though the day was warm, the water was decidedly not, and I had to grit my teeth to keep from squealing as I stepped off the bank. The ground was soft and silty, the smell of the water almost overpowering. I forced myself to duck down and felt my hair lift above my head, my whole body being suspended for a few precious breaths, the coldness of the water reaching into me with many-fingered hands, exploring, poking. I felt something from him that I'd never felt before: *love*. Brother Brook might've always been the snarkiest of the Siblings and the one quickest to complain, but he held me with great tenderness. I felt the tears starting before I'd come up for air.

"Is something wrong?" Eleas asked, a question all my friends had posed to me at one time or another.

"I had some sort of revelation."

"Can you talk about it?"

"Not quite yet." I pushed my wet hair out of my eyes. "You're right—it feels good."

She lifted an arm out of the water and swam a few strokes away from me. She was used to swimming in the sea; I'd never seen someone move with less effort through the green-tinged ripples. It was a full-body water prayer. I felt a shiver running down my back and glanced down at the soft folds of my belly disappearing into the depths, the goosebumps covering my chest. I'd never look as elegant as her, but that wasn't the point of the exercise. I could *feel* the same as she did, and in that way, we could be one in an immediate form of worship. I stilled myself, closed my eyes and gave myself over to my Sibling's embrace: *I love you too.*

"You look like a stewed prune," Werid said. "Did you go swimming?"

"Yes. Eleas thought it might be a good idea to try and get used to feeling water all around me. This time, I didn't start to glow."

"Congratulations," they said. "Have you fed and watered the horses?"

"Yes."

"Swept the stable?"

"Yes."

"Sjunil wants to see you. You can take some tea and bread in with you."

"Thank you."

Their brown eyes narrowed suspiciously. "For what?"

"For not giving up on me. You must've wanted to so many times."

"Well, Wolves are nothing but persistent," they said, but there was a smile lurking somewhere, waiting.

As I brought the tray into my aunt's bedroom, I gasped. Overnight all colour had been drawn from her face and hair, as if she was fading away in the light of the as of yet unreplaced window. The joy I'd felt that day was sucked out of my bones; the tray clattered to the storage chest, with some of the tea spilling when I rushed to her side.

Her eyes could barely open, but with sheer force of will she managed to turn to me. "Our lessons have tired me," she rasped. "Much more than I wanted to admit to myself. I don't know how much more I can give you."

"Please—*please* don't worry about that. Every day I was allowed to spend with you has been much more than I expected. If you need to go, you go."

"I might not have to make a choice after all." The corner of her mouth dug in a fraction. "You need to know I was sure you'd come back to me before I died. It has been a great privilege to watch you explore the path, Sloe, but I think I need to rest."

"Why are you back already?"

"She sent me away."

Werid drew in a sharp breath. "You've seen it too, right? It's as if she's halfway across."

"It comes so suddenly ..."

"Oh, Sloe—it really doesn't. You haven't been here. You haven't seen her in all these months. She perked up a lot when you and Lilyis came to see us, but it was bound to be over soon. I think we should prepare ourselves to say farewell today."

"What about Shortest Night?"

"Sometimes the gods have their own idea of what is befitting, and we have to roll with the punches. It's our job as wizards, and as members of the families."

"I'll tell Eleas."

"Do."

I found my friend storing the equipment away, her hair still damp. She took a deep breath. "Is it time?" she asked.

I started to cry, and without hesitating, she hugged me, without fear of how touching me would affect either of us. I folded up against her. It'd been a long time since I'd cried like that, not able to hold anything back, full-on snot and wheezing. How could one day hold both the best and the worst moments of a life?

We gathered around her bedside and waited in silence, Eleas' hand clasped in mine. Sjunil died as the sun came up the next day. Eight Tall Gods stood at her side, looking down at her face when the land of the dead claimed her.

"We need to bring her to Tall Trees," Werid said as we sat in the kitchen hours later, none of us able to sleep.

"We can build something," I said, thinking of the contraption of saplings and tent fabric Julas had created to bring the injured and unconscious prince along with us.

Werid inclined their head. "I think you should also take some of her ashes with you to Goldenlake, to give her back to the holy waters."

I sniffled but felt too drained to start crying again. "She would've liked that."

We clutched our tea bowls. Sjunil had been silent at the end, no pithy last words, no curses, no wishes. Her strength had simply run out. I wondered how Mother would take the news, as the older sister. And Siw.

"Let's try and leave tomorrow morning," Werid said. "We'll sort out the cottage for your sister to take on and …" A tear spilled down their dark cheek. "That will be that."

The air in the house had changed. Our world had become much smaller without her in it.

It should've been my life. It should've been my legacy; but for a few different turns of fate, I would've stepped up. Parts of me were deeply relieved I'd been spared that duty. I was allowed to escape and take away the memories of those few days, of the dizzying whirl of emotions that had formed the experience on the knoll, that felt more than ever like an island to me. The tides of time crashing up against it, trying to pull it down to its destruction. I was granted the privilege to extricate myself from all that, to follow a different path, while the place would continue to hold my sister with all its associations of an apprenticeship full of regrets and doubts.

I saw my own master take a shuddering breath, wiping the back of their right hand against their face. "There's so much to do, but I … I feel overwhelmed by it."

Eleas cleared her throat. "Then let me help. We will make a list and divide the tasks up between us." She reached across the table to take Werid's hand. "It will get done."

Werid gulped. "Sloe, we need to check what supplies from our stores might come in useful for our journey to the east. We should pack an emergency kit. I'll talk to your sister as well, to see what she might need help with before we leave her behind, and … fuck. I hadn't realized I loved her so much."

We looked towards the part of the cottage where my aunt lay wrapped in her blankets, her body washed and ready to travel one last time.

✤

BACK INTO THE DIRT

We arrived in Tall Trees three days before Shortest Night. We'd buckled the body of our wizard in tightly, draped in her signature chequered blanket, and suspended between her grey mare and Werid's horse. Eleas and I were flanking her to ensure we brought her safely to my mother.

The bonfire that would become a pyre had already been built, the square around the Roundhouse divided up into sections for the competitions. Some of them were already churned up, with remnants of broken practice weapons pushed to the sides or splatters on the partitions that reminded me too much of blood for comfort.

Again we were spotted a long way off and the news had been brought to Tall Trees well before we dismounted in front of the Roundhouse. The Moons streamed to my aunt, some of them started to wail, and drew my sisters out of the House of Women.

"Impeccable timing as always," Silid muttered as she stepped close to me. "Trust Auntie Sjunil to go out as soon as the wood had been gathered anyway."

Siw panted close behind her. When she spotted the body, her face shuttered. "I thought she'd hold on for a while longer."

"The gods kept calling to her," Werid said, before we turned to see the leader of the Moons come out into the square, at the elbow of one of my other sisters, her face as hard and unmoved as Siw's. We waited for her to say something as she drew closer, but she only reached out briefly to pat the cloth above Sjunil's shoulder, before she nodded at Silid. Given how long she must've known about her sister's illness, it was reasonable to assume that a plan had been in place for some time.

My eldest sister frowned. "We will bring her inside," she said to us.

Eleas was the only one permitted to follow them into the House of Women. I saw Werid touch her arm lightly, in an unspoken gesture of thanks.

As I glanced up, I noticed my friends standing at the side of the Roundhouse, armed to the teeth, and Julas carrying baby Siran in their sling against him. Our arrival must've interrupted a training session. They seemed a bit worse for wear; Lilyis sported a black eye. It'd been stupid to assume she wouldn't get involved somehow. Qes, Cathil, Bjor, Qati, Raz—all stared at me.

"Oh, Sloe. I'm so sorry." Lilyis came to hug and kiss me. "How are you feeling?"

"Horrible. In the end, she still managed to take us by surprise." I wrapped my arms around her and held her as close as I could, until she made a strangled sound and I released her.

"Come," Qes said, his dark eyes shiny with unshed tears. "Let's go and get *really* drunk."

"Losing a wizard is always terrible," Cathil said as we'd settled against the wall of the House of Men, where benches had been placed for the fighters to take their breaks between sessions. Skins of honey beer had appeared on the table between us as well as a pile of chipped drinking bowls. "And usually precedes many changes for a village."

"Siw has been taught well. She'll know what to do." Qes filled my bowl again. "While you were away, we started to get stuff together for our journey. I thought you probably wouldn't want to wait long until we leave."

"To see Julas finally win—or not."

"Have you spoken to your mother yet?"

"No. I still need to gift her Sor's tapestry, but today… today that's the last thing on my mind."

Raz sat next to me. Two of the nails on her right hand had turned black and there was a long scrape down her wrist. They must've taken turns to prepare my sister's husband for the fight ahead. The only one who didn't sport any injuries was Qati. No wonder Siw had needed to come back for supplies.

In the section in front of us the next training session started, young warriors assembling to practise for their chance at glory. A fever seemed to have swept the Moons; everyone turned out to challenge their luck, even Moons much too young and inexperienced to have a realistic shot at commanding anyone.

I absent-mindedly turned the blue stone bracelet around my wrist. Watching them beat the shit out of each other was a good distraction from the grief that choked me.

Watery sunshine illuminated the training ground while we sat and watched the prospective contestants. I noticed that Qati and Raz kept mostly out of each other's way, while Qes and Cathil touched each other much more than was strictly necessary. I detected an air of cautious happiness around my cousin that reminded me of the time his relationship with Nalan na Nileon had been at its most hopeful. Circumstances in Birkland were much more likely to make their relationship last, and if Cathil's relaxed body language was anything to go by, he'd either managed to keep his true identity under wraps or the storm had already washed over him and moved on.

Qati sat on the edge of the table, working on his third bowl of beer. His skin was grey, the lines around his mouth deeply dug in. I promised myself to talk to him properly soon. Every single member of our company had their fair share of horrible experiences, though Qes' cousin was the one who bore his open for everyone to see, stitched into his skin.

The fighters changed partners again, but I couldn't see Julas joining them. He probably had his hands full, since his wife had her master's funeral to plan on top of everything else. Qes jumped up and vanished for a while, to return with more beer skins slung over his shoulder and a basket stuffed with bread, cheese, and cakes made from dried berries and crushed beech nuts, held together with thickened honey: the first of the festival delicacies for us to taste. I had no idea which of the specialties my aunt had liked the most but the thought that she wasn't able to eat them ever again made me lose my appetite. In a few days we'd see her burn, for everyone to witness her passing on, her body to be released to follow her soul into the land of the dead. Cathil was right, losing a wizard was a traumatic experience for the whole of Tall Trees, though I couldn't help but wonder how many of the Moons around us had secretly despised her for her foul language and tendency to be a bit scruffy around the edges. Precautions needed to be taken to ensure the gods would still be able to hear our prayers. All duties would fall on Siw's shoulders. I felt a spasm run through me.

Lilyis' hand tightened on my leg. "What?"

"I think I need to try and find Siw."

I caught up with my sister in the storage area attached to the Roundhouse, where she was busy stacking firewood and bundles of dried herbs.

"Siw?"

She flinched, and though she tried to hide her face in the shadows, I saw tracks of tears on her dusty face. "I don't want to talk to you right now."

"Listen …"

"No. Go away."

"I won't."

"Fuck off, Sloe."

"I can't imagine how you must feel—but I'm here for you, whenever you're ready. I'm more than able to help. Don't let Mother and Silid bully you into taking on more than you can." I gave her a curt nod and turned away.

"Sloe, wait." She caught my wrist. "I might hold you to that offer."

"Fine. Go ahead."

"Can you help me get the firewood stacked in the Roundhouse? Towards the back on the left, so it's on hand for the ceremony?"

"Of course." I held out my arms. "Load me up."

While I'd been at the cottage, my things had remained stashed in the Other House. It felt strange rifling through what I'd brought over the sea and all the way over land. Even the rolled-up tapestry wasn't worth much in the end. I looked down at my palms. I'd managed to get a few splinters while storing the wood.

"Here you are." Lilyis closed the door of the Other House behind her. "I was getting worried when you didn't come back. What happened to getting drunk with the others?"

"I don't want to get drunk."

She came closer and sat next to me on the edge of the platform. "I can see that you're hurting. Do you need a cuddle, or would you rather be alone?"

I curled up, laying my head into her lap. "I wasn't prepared to lose her yet."

"Everyone could see that she loved you very much, and you must've loved her, too. We can hide out here if you want." Her fingers were in my hair, stroking me, soothing me. "I remember when I lost my mother … it was a horrible time. I can't promise you that you'll get over it anytime soon."

"I know. I'm grateful I have you here with me." I felt her warmth seeping into me.

"We should have some time until the training finishes for the day. If you want to …"

I didn't feel like drinking the feelings away. Fucking them away sounded much more tempting. "Yes. Yes, please."

Her hands cupped my face, before she bent over to kiss me. She didn't hurry me but pulled my clothes off slowly, and we slipped under the blankets, pushing my treasures down to the clay floor.

She rolled between my knees and settled herself into me, her hair like a curtain around us. She made love to me gently and deliberately. I felt something inside me break loose from its tether, while I laid on my back, the rafters of the house trembling above me, and the sensation I'd had floating in the river came back down to enfold me in its embrace.

If I'd thought Werid had been driving me hard, it was nothing compared to what Siw put me through over the next few days. She had me running around Tall Trees like a headless chicken, and there was absolutely no way she'd have been able to do all of it on her own. Shortest Night had always seemed like a lot of faff to me, but that year it was absolutely ridiculous. A whole scroll of prayers had to be recited in a highly specific order, to ensure that all Siblings received their fair share of attention, and the Cousins wouldn't feel short-changed on such an important occasion. The edges of the village square were full of lines of freshly washed clothes, drying before the big day. With me trying to be everywhere at once, it was simply unavoidable that I was cornered one day.

Saon appeared in front of me as if he'd casually stepped out of the wind, in his signature shawl, his glossy hair swept back from his face. "They said you wouldn't be back until Shortest Night."

"Well, I'm obviously here—sorry, but I have so many errands to run for Siw …" I tried to push past him, but he wouldn't let me.

"I think we need to talk."

I snorted in disgust. "Seriously?"

"I bought some of the yarn you lot brought back from Hollybrook."

"Good for you. I'm sure Qes made you a fair price."

"He said he would speak with you."

"About what?"

"About us."

"*Us*? Do everyone a favour and piss off, Saon. I don't have any more time to waste on you."

He blinked and suddenly, in the midst of so much grief and panic, my heart opened. I felt laughter bubbling up inside me. Mother was right—I had a different voice; I was a different person. I had other friends, if you could call Cathil Cloud and Qati Badger friends, and I only had to think back on how safe and loved Lilyis had made me feel the other day to realize that there was nothing, absolutely nothing that Saon could offer me. I saw anger seep into his features.

"So now you think you're special?" he hissed. "Coming back like you're so much more important than all of us, trying to play at being a wizard without ever having been chosen to be one? You're as pathetic as you always were, and just because you had a sniff around the world, you're not suddenly a better person—or one worth the bother." He puffed himself up like a blue tit in winter, his eyes alight with hatred.

I smiled at him. "Right back at you. You must've pulled a lot of strength from holding me down. I can't imagine how bad it must feel to lose that power if there's nothing else to keep you afloat. I'm sorry I have to take it away from you, Saon, but I'm sure you can use the disappointment to further your art. I always thought there was something lacking in your designs. Maybe it will be the making of you."

He gasped for breath, and I expected him to start yelling, but instead he charged at me, as if he thought he could run me off my feet and throw me back into the dirt he'd once picked me up from. I felt myself reacting without thinking, as I'd hoped to do one day. My hand closed around his throat as I held him away from me.

"I'll laugh at you again," I warned him.

He clawed at my fingers, his beautiful eyes bulging out of his face.

"I don't need to hurt you, Saon. I will let you go, if you calm down." There was no tremor in my voice, no trace of the fears he'd so often brought forth in me. "One, two, three …" I released him and he stumbled back, his face beet-red.

"You're a monster!"

I grinned. "Even monsters have certain standards."

INTO BATTLE

The body of Sjunil Moon presided over the celebrations, wreathed in garlands of summer flowers that had taken the help of all the children of Tall Trees to make, who were now wearing their own flower-crowns. Some of them might go on to remember that particular Shortest Night as something out of the ordinary, the year when everything had a strange sombre undertone, or perhaps none of it meant that much, because there were so many other exciting things to consider: the cakes that were only prepared for the festival, the spit-roasted chickens that had been fattened up especially, and the games that would be played, when everybody was relieved of their chores for the celebrations and there was plenty of fermented milk and beer to go around. My own memories of Shortest Night weren't that happy and seeing the children whizzing around would've filled me with anxiety anyway. It was the night most of us had their first experiences, but for me it had never happened as easily as that, and I still carried a lot of shame around it. There was music, drums and flutes and people singing, because they were already half-drunk.

The competitions started in the afternoon as the shadows of the houses fell across the village square and tempered the heat of the day. There was no division per age group and more fighters competed than ever before. Each one had tried to make themself appear as intimidating as possible: painting their faces, braiding their hair, most of them wearing Cousin Blade's amulets openly, while Julas had opted for a wash and a firm knot at the end of his long braid to avoid it coming loose during the fights. His boot laces were new, and he wore leather wrist guards. On the

Continent contestants had donned protective gear, including helmets—none of the Moons would've wanted to be caught dead in those. Any blood that was shed would be spilled in honour of the gods. Seeing the young warriors swagger around the square made me cringe.

Qes had managed to keep a good spot for us to watch from and again we settled with plenty of food and beer. Julas wasn't the oldest one; it seemed as if most men of Tall Trees had felt bound to sign up. Siw stood at the fence with him, carrying their sleeping baby bound to her back. I mumbled a quick prayer that Julas wouldn't take any stupid risks.

Raz, next to me, let out a groan. "Can they please start? With so many of them it'll take ages anyway."

Bjor pointed to the far end of the square. "I think they're about to."

I saw Mother step from the House of Women, my sisters around her, dressed up as spectacularly as I'd ever seen them, covered in amber beads and silver, and Silid wearing one of the shell necklaces we'd brought from Westlight. Cheers greeted them. Lilyis grabbed my hand excitedly. It was what they'd been training for, though none of them but Julas were allowed to compete. While I prepared myself to be incredibly bored, the others were on the edge of their seats. The only one who rolled his eye was Qati Badger, and I felt an unexpected surge of solidarity. I stood up and changed seats with Bjor, to give him a better view.

"Have they been this obsessed while I was away?" I asked.

Qati shrugged. "It's probably a useful thing to become obsessed about if you need Julas Raven to win." He glanced towards Siw. Julas' sister stood with her, and it seemed as if Jaril tried to comfort her, to assure her that Julas wouldn't stick his neck out too far.

"I wouldn't say that we *need* him to win—though it might make things easier."

"Won't there be trouble if a Raven tries to command the Moons?"

"Not if it's a Raven married to the wizard of Tall Trees. Everyone will know he has the favour of the Tall and the Small Gods. What happened with Raz?"

"Ask her yourself."

"What if I want to hear the story from you?"

"There's nothing to tell. People break up."

"But why?"

I caught a glint in his eye. "Because Raz likes her people scarred and broken, but only to a certain extent."

"Meaning that you are too damaged, even for her?"

"When you look at me, what do you see?" He sounded bitter. "Someone who has made a lot of stupid mistakes—but I don't regret all of them, though starting something with an Owl definitely doesn't belong to those."

The first round commenced. Four fights were held at once, but Julas wasn't one of the combatants. He stood there watching the others with narrowed eyes, trying to gauge which ones he was likely to encounter in later rounds.

"Did Raz tell you that we used to have a thing?" I asked.

Qati shuddered. "I know about that, yes. I can probably guess how it ended."

"She seemed so sure about you," I said, and he made a strange noise. "I suppose Raz is always sure in the beginning. She wants to be a good person and never plans to hurt anyone."

"I know. This is not so much about her as it is about me."

"Because you have problems trusting people?"

"Because I'm not sure why we're doing all that if we can't get married in the end. I'd rather stop it now, if it doesn't lead to anything."

I felt my heart clench. "You've pushed her away," I realized.

He scowled furiously, which made me suspect that I'd understood his motives too well. "It saves us both a lot of bother."

"I'd say you both are immensely bothered right now. I wish you'd appreciate how lucky you've been to have her, if only for a little while, and that she followed you this far. She wouldn't have left Rawil Owl behind for just anyone."

"She would've come because of you."

"I don't think so. I wish you'd rethink your decisions. It'll take us a while to reach Goldenlake, and you should talk things through. It won't be much fun travelling with you two otherwise."

"There are enough people in the company to avoid each other successfully—and, as you said, it won't be the first time Raz has been broken off with before."

I glanced at her, at the deep line dug into her forehead. "I think before she always initiated the breakup. This might be something new for her."

"Please don't get involved, Sloe. There's no reason why you should. We are all grown-ups."

"Whatever you think you're trying to do, it doesn't strike me as particularly grown up. It's self-defence, but not in a good way."

"Look who's fucking talking."

A ribbon of blood flew towards us, spattering across the sandy ground. I saw Qati recoil. One of the contestants stumbled back, clutching her forearm. First blood had been drawn and she was out of the contest.

"You don't seem keen on all this," I noticed.

"Not everyone can be a warrior," he said. He'd paled, though the cut wasn't much to write home about, compared to what we'd be expected to stomach in the final rounds. "You'll need people who are better with numbers than blades."

"What have you done in the days I've been away from Tall Trees?"

"Not much. Thinking, mostly."

"What about? Goldenlake?"

"That too. It wouldn't make much sense for me to return to the Bears. I've never felt as if they cared much about the cousins they allowed to come to them, apart from what work they could squeeze out of us. You never went on exchange, did you?"

"No. Mother didn't believe it a good idea and none of my siblings went, either. I think she feared we'd get ideas about marrying for love, if she'd allowed us to run too far. Considering how things turned out, she was right to be worried."

"It must've been complicated to grow up as the child of a leader." At first, I thought he'd said it sarcastically, but there was no sneer to accompany his words. "Sometimes I forget everyone's life is disappointing and that even Cathil Cloud has gone through tough times. Though he always seems to fall back on his feet, the lucky bastard."

We both turned to where Qes and Cathil sat engrossed in the fights, barely breathing. Julas drew their attention. Bets had been placed on the outcome and he was one of the favourites. I remembered watching my sister's husband when he'd been no more than a Raven cousin, nice to look at but not known to me. Things depended on him surviving the day. I saw Siw standing next to Jaril Raven, fiddling with the knot of the sling she held baby Siran in, worrying her lip with her teeth.

"They've put him through his paces," Qati said. "There's no doubt that he's well prepared."

There was something understated about the way Julas held himself; he seemed much more relaxed than his opponent, the tip of his blade pointing downwards, his eyes never leaving the face of the warrior before him, a man almost as tall as Julas and painted around the eyes to make him appear like a wildcat, his hair braided through with glittering silver rings. Compared to the other pairings, their encounter was slow. They were still trying to figure each other out—until Julas made an almost lazy step to the side, brought his blade around behind him, and cut his opponent across the calf. The Moon who'd kept an eye on the score sounded the rattle that proclaimed the end of a fight. The painted Moon first looked stunned, then the pain filtered through, and he let out a bellow of frustration. Neither had broken a sweat, neither of them had uttered so much as a grunt.

Lilyis elbowed Bjor with a smug smile. She'd taught Julas some of their tricks. He rose quickly through the rounds, staying calm throughout, unimpressed. The preliminaries were barely worth getting excited about.

At some point I stood up to rub some life back into my arse.

"I'm going to get more cake."

No one paid any attention, so I slunk off on my own to where the food was given out. As I joined the queue, Eleas came over.

"Are you already bored?"

"Nothing explodes—of course I'm bored. My own training has spoiled me thoroughly."

She crossed her arms. "Werid has chosen to catch up on sleep before the bonfire is lit. They could not bear to sit through this either."

"They might've made the best decision today. How are they holding up?"

"Could be better. Your sister has made them feel as welcome as can be expected. It will be a difficult night for us all. Do not worry too much if you are not able to enjoy the competitions."

"I hadn't thought Qati Badger would be the one I'm most in agreement with."

Eleas smiled. "What do you want to do?"

"Jump ahead to when all of this is over and done with and I don't need to see any more blood for a while."

"It is an important day for your family," Eleas said. "Get out of the way, Sloe."

"Would you come with me, or do you want to see the fights?"

"Where do you want to go?"

"Let me get some cake and after that we can walk down to the nearest river."

"Fine." Suddenly she seemed worried. "You should tell Lilyis though."

"But they're starting to get interesting!" Qes protested.

I kissed Lilyis' scraped knuckles. "I'm not saying that I don't understand why you're enjoying it, but …"

"You need some time away?" Lilyis said. "We'll be here when you and Eleas get back."

"Do you want to place a bet?" Raz asked. "There's still time."

"No, thank you. I don't care who wins."

"Spoilsport!" Raz laughed. "Don't you want your brother-in-law to succeed?"

"There are some fighters that might get dangerous for him," Bjor said and Cathil nodded in agreement. "This isn't over yet."

"I've seen him fight and lose the last time—I know."

I turned to Siw again, who'd pulled baby Siran around her body to feed them. She saw me watching and made a face at me. The last rounds wouldn't be fought until first blood; there was a chance of everything going seriously wrong.

I hugged Lilyis to me. "I'll go and talk to Siw first."

"Tell her we're praying for him."

I walked around the fence to where my sister waited for Julas to step into the fight again.

"You're not having fun?" Siw asked.

There was only the soft noise Siran made as they suckled. "Do you actually want to be here?" I asked. "What happens if he loses again?"

"Then he'll have yet another year to train. Why would I want him to lead *anyone* into battle?" she asked, her voice sounding oddly small.

HUNGRY DREAMS

It felt like an appropriate time to pray for my sister. We were back among the birches but hadn't bothered with a fire, merely shared the fresh cakes and sat there, staring into the swirling waters.

"I don't want to remove myself from them," I confessed eventually. "I don't want to be impatient and … pessimistic."

"I know, but this is inherently what a wizard is," Eleas said. "Someone who stands outside of most of it, someone who provides another perspective. That can be painful, especially for the people who love you. I would wager your sister appreciated that you did not allow yourself to be swept away in the excitement of the competitions. That there is someone in her family who knows what she fears for him. She is aware that she is one of the lucky ones. If something happens, she will have a whole village to help her raise her child."

"That makes me feel a bit better."

"This is why I am here."

"No. You're still on your pilgrimage."

"Who says I cannot do a few things at once? Let me know when you have had enough. We should not miss the end of it—or the lighting of the fire."

"One more prayer before we go back."

"Good."

I tried to suck up the calm surrounding us, the noises of the small leaves fluttering against each other in the wind, of a couple of small brown birds bathing in the shallows at the edge of the stream, flinging water droplets about with their wings.

Brother Brook, don't let him die. Don't do this to my sister. Please. Brother, please.

As we returned to the village square, it was eerily quiet. Most of the fences that had divided the space up had been removed to leave but one, which had been modified to a rough circle, to allow everyone in the first rows to witness the spectacle.

Four contestants were left to fight in the last two rounds, but they were all the worse for wear. One of them could barely see out of her right eye as it was almost swollen shut, and another was bleeding from a shallow cut on top of their head. Julas wore a make-shift bandage around his upper left arm. The unconcerned attitude had left him. His mouth was a white line in his carefully trimmed beard and wisps of hair had come free from his braid, sticking to his forehead. Though he'd been one of the favourites from the start, the Moons closest to us supported the fourth one: a smaller, wiry man, older and with more nicks and scars than Julas. I couldn't recall seeing him before; perhaps he'd joined my family in Tall Trees while I'd been away. He was darker skinned than most of us, with his hair braided back without ornament. As with wizards, where plain clothes usually signalled someone secure enough in their abilities, all four of the finalists hadn't put in much effort. They wore sleeveless tunics and scuffed boots with new laces, the legs of their trousers bound with strips of woollen fabric. Maybe the next year all the younger contenders would wear the same, to signal they were serious about winning.

Julas was lucky to be paired with the woman with the swollen face, though it still took him some time to beat her. The second favourite came through as well. He fought in a way that reminded me more of the competitions I'd seen in the Eight Kingdoms; he was as fast as the warriors of Crooked Hill had been and though he looked nothing like Tjovan na Tialin, a bad taste began to creep up into my mouth, more prayers to my tongue.

Julas watched the man dance around his opponent, scrunching the rag he'd wiped the sweat from his face with his hand. I saw the muscles work in his cheeks, the forked scar beneath his eye a fiery red. It was difficult to imagine he was the man I'd once kissed and then refused, whose face had been in my hungry dreams for a good while after.

Cheers went up as the other finalist had reduced his second-to-last opponent to a limping wreck and the rattle sounded the end of the fight. As I glanced at my sister's husband, I saw him staring at me. He made a beckoning gesture. It took me some time to get through the throng of the Moons around the circle, but after shoving some of Saon's friends aside, I finally reached him.

"I need your help," Julas said. "Come with me, Sloe."

"Whatever do you need my help for? I barely know which way is up on a longknife."

"Exactly." He took me by the shoulder and pushed me towards the man he'd have to fight. His opponent was barely out of breath, though sweat had dug furrows into the dirt on his face. He glanced up and smiled as Julas approached, pulling me along with force.

"Sloe, this is Selan. He came to Tall Trees after last winter."

"I've heard of you." Selan's voice was higher than expected, and once we stood before him, I saw that he wore linen bandages beneath the tunic to flatten his breasts. "The wizard who isn't a wizard." He dabbed a bit of blood from the shallow cut above his right knee. "This might not be the best time to get properly acquainted, but I'm sure we'll have some time later." He stared at Julas. "Are you ready?"

"That's exactly it. You don't leave enough of the others to make a fight for third place worth watching." Julas unbuckled the sheath of his longknife. "I'd rather fight for the Moons when the families of the west threaten us than being beaten to a pulp today."

I felt my jaw drop.

Selan narrowed his eyes. "Really? All of Tall Trees has waited a whole day to see us fight each other. They'll hate you."

"I'm married to their wizard. They can't afford to hate me."

"You're either the bravest or the stupidest man I've ever met." Selan sucked blood from his teeth and spat it to the ground.

"I don't mind what version they'll choose to believe," Julas said quietly. "What use would I be if I let you clobber me to an extent that's enough for *them* to accept my defeat? I've trained with Sloe's friends from the Cities, but I don't think that will help me much against you. Would you be happy to command the Moons?"

Selan blew up his cheeks. "Fuck. Yes, I'd be happy—but are you sure? This isn't a decision you're likely to recover from."

"The last time I lost because I fainted. I've had them laugh at me since."

"What about showing them that you can win?"

Julas turned to me. "Tell him, Sloe."

I stared at him, confused. "Tell him what?

"You know what."

"That the opinion of others isn't worth dying for in a stupid way? That a competition doesn't in any way represent real battle? That it would be a good story to tell your baby when they're big enough to understand?"

Julas flushed a violent shade of red. "All of that."

"This isn't how things are normally done," the future commander of the Moons said.

Julas stared towards the bonfire, the body of my aunt, covered in flowers. "It's not a normal Shortest Night anyway."

"What the fuck did you say to him?" Lilyis asked.

"Having him pull out of the competition wasn't my idea."

"Do you understand how many hours we've spent to get him ready?"

I pulled up my hands, my palms apologetically turned towards her. "It wasn't my decision, and you know that. You bet on him, is that the problem?"

"Yes—yes, I did but … not a lot. It's the principle!"

"The principle of what?"

"Honour?!"

"It was an honourable decision to quit."

Bjor seemed as confused as the others, but not as angry as Lilyis, Raz, and Cathil. "I think we should go and congratulate him on his second place in the competition."

"The fuck we will," Lilyis said.

The whole square of Tall Trees was filled with grumbling people.

"That's actually a good idea, Bjor." Qes led the others away, but Lilyis wasn't prepared to give in yet.

"Why did he change his mind if you didn't have anything to do with it?"

"You saw who he would've fought, and you've seen enough of these play-fights to know he'd have lost in the end."

"Play-fights?" She sounded scandalized. "Just because you never wanted to be a warrior doesn't mean this isn't to be taken seriously!"

"I understand that. Julas is right—there'll be plenty of opportunity to fight against the families of the west. We need every longknife we can get to defend Tall Trees and the Moons. How long will it take the other finalists to recover? Will they be ready if the village comes under attack in a week's time? There are no walls like in Crooked Hill, Eastbay, or Seagard. We might be able to rustle up a serviceable palisade, but we need enough people to hold it. I'd say Selan will make a competent commander and he was favoured by many Moons anyway. I think Sjunil would've approved."

"Of course she would've. Because she was a wizard, not a fighter." Her eyes flashed with anger. "I'm sorry, Sloe, but we won't ever see eye to eye about this."

"Do we need to?" I asked, suddenly scared.

She crossed her arms. "I would like you to agree with me. To know that we are of one mind."

"I wonder whether that's useful," I mused.

"I hadn't expected to find myself on Cathil Cloud's side anytime soon, but sometimes it's fucking impossible to love a wizard and not want to strangle them."

"I'm sure Julas would agree with you there."

Her forefinger flicked up, pointing at my face, and she seemed desperate to counter with something mean. She took her hand down. "We'll talk about that later. They're coming to light the fire."

I turned around to see a procession of my mother and sisters, each one carrying a torch dipped in birch tar, Siw leading the group across the square from the House of Women. The Moons stepped back to let them pass. In her other hand Siw brought a smaller vessel, the citrusy smoke of burning tree sap perfuming the air, billowing out like breath. To my astonishment I saw Eleas and Werid at the end of the procession, both carrying bowls with treasures that would be burned with my aunt to guarantee her body's transition and to become useful to her in the land of the dead. Werid had chosen an light-brown robe, falling in heavy folds and lined with red fox fur, pinned close with a brooch in the form of a running wolf, their hair built up into a construction that must've cost them hours to secure with golden pins. Eleas wore her shell cape and a short cloak of the finest, most lustrous goat hair, silvery like a wave in moonlight. No one had asked me to be a part of it. I wasn't a member of Mother's government, nor officially apprenticed. None of the Moons would've understood why I should be walking with them.

I turned around to see Lilyis' eyes wide, her mouth open. She'd never seen my master as Werid of the Far Side before, the shine of gold surrounding them. Their unearthly beauty took many of the spectators by surprise and I could see the adoration in their faces. Werid was like Sister Sun made flesh. In their presence the idea of Tall Gods coming out to speak with wizards wasn't quite as strange and forbidding. Their face was blank, while Siw had trouble keeping back the tears, the smoke wavering this way and that as she finally reached the pyre.

Mother gave her torch to Silid, who slipped a folded square of cloth to the ground, and the leader of the Moons knelt for the first time in a long while before her younger sister. The light of the torches flickered on her white hair studded with amber pearls. Werid and Eleas brought forth their gifts, bowing in front of her and Mother pulled out a chain of gold and handfuls of silver seeds, to place them beneath the pyre with a silent prayer, before she held a hand out to Silid to be helped up again. Drums started a driving rhythm as Siw pushed the smoking vessel in with the precious metals and straightened her back, the grief on her face constricting my throat.

Lilyis took my hand as my eldest sister started to speak.

"We have someone to give to the gods, someone who served her whole life to make the existence of the Moons better and purposeful, to bring us into alignment with the wishes of the Tall and the Small Gods, who worked tirelessly to speak for us all. With Sjunil Moon we have lost our most important representative on this side, but we ask her to continue giving us her love in the lands she now travels, to bestow her devotion upon our parents and grandparents, on all the Moons of Tall Trees who have gone before us and all who will follow. May we meet her again when the time comes. May the Tall Gods bring us news of her safe arrival before long."

As the torches were pushed into the pyre, I heard the call of the kite echoing through the valley and the smell of earth rose up to my nose. I sensed the promise of rain, wind, and the soft touch of the moon on my brow as the flames started to lick up, to grasp what was left of Sjunil Moon and to escort her into new life.

BOOK TWO

LAKESIDE

"It looks incredibly different." I pushed myself up in my stirrups to study the placid surface of the sacred waters of the Golden Lake stretching out in front of us, with swathes of birches in their deep summer green fringing its banks. "Like a normal lake."

"It is a normal lake," Qes said. "All in all."

"You know what I mean. Is it weird that I'm disappointed?"

He gave a snort. "I know what you mean. Excuse me, I think I should see how Cathil is taking all this. The last time we were here he was in such a different position …"

"Go ahead. I can't imagine how your boyfriend must feel."

Cathil Cloud and I had first met in the Roundhouse of Goldenlake, and I'd really hated him then. Like Qes, I was slowly coming around to seeing him with less of a bias. We had both been different people two years before.

I shuddered as I turned around to the others. The weather had been fine for our travels, so warm in fact that we'd had to rest for a few hours in the middle of most days to wait for the heat to subside. Our last days in Tall Trees had been tense, to say the least. Julas' decision to pull out of the final fight had caused the predicted problems, though Siw was as relieved as I'd hoped she would be, and both had left the Shortest Night celebrations rather abruptly. I'd managed to catch my sister in the morning as she'd checked the ashes to collect anything that was left of her master.

"Thank you," Siw had said, clutching the wooden container to her chest. "Nobody knows yet and it might come to nothing, but there might be another baby on the way. Despite me still feeding."

"Oh. That's … awfully quick."

"I know, and I'm half hoping it will keep him grounded. It wasn't an easy decision for him, Sloe."

"Believe me, I know. I've spent the rest of the night defending it to everyone. He was brave to choose you over everything else. Many people would have caved under that sort of pressure."

"He didn't know when he signed up for the competitions. I wish I could come with you and see the lake again—to bring Sjunil to the waters."

"I'll do it for you."

"She would've loved that it's you."

We'd smiled at each other. "Please be careful out there," Siw had said then. "Things are getting so scary, so unstable. If all what we hear is true …" She'd glanced towards the side of the square, where Julas stood, talking to the baby strapped to him, his face alight with love. Siw would have a hard time protecting her husband in the next months. In the end she'd given me the wooden box, secured it with a checked ribbon and multiple knots that held the remains of her master. "Don't let Mother push you into coming back if you don't want to," she'd said softly.

I'd presented our mother with the Hollybrook tapestry, my sisters gasping as it was unrolled and laid out before her in all its glory. It could find its way into the Roundhouse, or she'd keep it in the House of Women. We all understood it was my concession to the authority of a leader. Tall Trees might've become too small for me, but I still had to navigate the complications that came with being born into its ruling family. I remained part of it, even if I tried to lengthen its leash.

For the moment, it stretched all the way to the Golden Lake and the elevation next to the road that granted access to the town built along the lakeside, the clumps of thatched buildings that were disappointingly dingy and bleached in the harsh light of the summer day, with torn nets hanging across drying racks and boats pulled up on the pebbles, some of them starting to rot away.

"This is it?" Lilyis asked, and the way she tried to keep her voice from dipping made me realize that she felt as I did. Nothing pointed towards the place being special.

We'd been to Eastbay together, we'd seen the enormous dome of its city temple, and then the Stoneharp was … the Stoneharp. There was nothing before us to denote status, though the waters were beautiful enough.

"You'll see," I promised, looking back at my other companions.

At least Raz was impressed. "This is nice," she said. "I imagine it'll be even more stunning when the leaves of the birch trees turn in autumn and are mirrored like swathes of golden cloth in the lake."

"I don't expect we'll be here by then," Cathil said.

Eleas' gelding was the last of the nine horses to come to the ridge. We were dusty and sweaty, the hardships of travel starting to wear on us, but she smiled radiantly as she joined us. "How amazing. It is almost like the sea. Calmer, but wonderful." She rubbed her sleeve across the mark on her forehead, as if she wanted to make sure it showed up on her skin. A breeze came up from the water and made me shiver, though sweat ran down my temples. Why wouldn't Eleas feel instantly connected to the lake?

"You can't see it from here, but there's a boat station at the end of the headland and Coldharbour all the way over on the east coast of the lake." Qati's voice sounded unused. He'd kept to himself for most of the journey, taking his watches with Bjor. I couldn't imagine those two had much to talk about, apart from their current relationship status. But Qati had lived in Goldenlake longer than all of us.

"Have you ever been to Coldharbour?" Lilyis asked him.

"A few times, on supply runs for the Bears. It's nothing much, mostly storage huts and more boats." He squinted against the glare of the sun on the water. "I don't particularly recommend it."

"At least we'll have a roof over us tonight," Cathil said flatly. "There were so many midges last night, I counted seventy-two bites on my left leg alone."

"I can't see any sign of the Bulls," Lilyis said.

"You wouldn't," Qes said. "This is merely the waterfront, the town reaches quite far inland and unless they're stupid enough to proclaim their presence with a big red banner they'll live somewhere in one of the quarters, like everyone else."

Bjor sucked in his breath. "Knowing my family, a big red banner it is."

Lilyis huffed. "Your words, not mine. Remember that."

Werid pushed their mount past us. "Right then—can we please get a move on, Sloe? My arse could use a break."

Coming towards Goldenlake the road became ever wider, and it didn't take long for us to find ourselves on the outskirts of the most important town in the east. The ground around the houses was baked dry, the thatch on the roofs brittle, but from there the size of the place was much more apparent. Lilyis had stopped grumbling when she became aware that Goldenlake was many villages, all squashed together, with every family presiding over a quarter, their different sigils painted on every wall. The Roundhouse stuck out of the town, with the wide square in front of it bearing the traces of three enormous bonfires that had burned at Shortest Night, torn paper decorations lying against the walls of the surrounding buildings. We'd arrived too late for the tail-end of the celebrations. All the food had been eaten, the specially brewed beer consumed. The smell of cold ash was in the air, of rancid grease and smoked fish. Of all the times to be in the holy town of Goldenlake, it was probably the worst.

We stopped in front of the Roundhouse that stood empty, its doors thrown open.

As I looked around, Qati sighed. "Let me handle it," he said and dismounted, giving Qes the reins of his horse to hold. He disappeared between the houses. As we waited for him to return, Eleas studied the square.

"Everyone seems to be recovering from the festival," she mused.

"Some people had fun at Shortest Night," Cathil rumbled.

Qes slapped his shoulder. "Shut up," he said. "We had fun."

"Yeah, right up to the moment when the last fight was cancelled," he said sourly.

"I can't talk about this again," I groaned. "Where has he gone?"

Raz was busy loosening the straps of her saddle to make her horse more comfortable. She certainly was trying hard not to care about Qati. "He's probably fucked off and left us to it. Wouldn't surprise me in the slightest."

"Get over it," Qes said. "He wouldn't do that to us."

"You're sure? He's already stabbed you in the back once."

"His horse and his bags are still here," Bjor said. I was relieved to hear him take Qati's side.

"There he is," Eleas said.

Qati made his way back to us, with two people walking behind him. One was Qes' cousin Qor, apprentice to the highest-ranking wizard of Goldenlake, with the same hair as Qes and a facial expression that turned decidedly hostile when she spotted my master standing next to me. Werid's flamboyance singled them out wherever they were, and some people simply had to disapprove of someone so beautiful.

"What are *you* doing here?" Qor asked them.

"I have returned," Werid said coldly. "You can inform your master that I expect to be attended to as is befitting."

I was grateful for Werid pushing themself forward and distracting Qor. The other person Qati had brought back with him was another apprentice I hadn't seen yet, who might not remember any of us.

"Qor!" Qes disentangled himself from the horses and came forward to greet his cousin.

"Qes. I didn't expect you back anytime soon after the disaster last time. Did you manage to find them?"

"Yes. They're right here, Qor." He pointed his thumb at me.

"Huh—so they are. I didn't expect to see them alive after the bastards from the Cities dragged them off into the woods."

I heard Lilyis draw breath and took her wrist to hold her back.

Qes groaned with disappointment at his cousin's reaction. "It's all turned out rather unexpected," he said quietly.

PIECES OF YOUR STORY

It was the same house they'd given us last time; the same wall Lilyis' father had been fettered to, barely healed but still so dangerous. The stable at the back had been prepared with hay and grain for our horses and fresh layers of dried leaves on the floor. A small stack of firewood and a basket of provisions had been brought to the house. The last time I'd slept there, Tjal na Tialin had been alive. The thought sent a chill through me. There were more of us, though Qati was likely to seek a bed elsewhere. We were on Badger land and there was nothing holding him back from splitting from the company.

"Let's go to the water," Werid said, pushing the hood that protected their hair back from their brow.

Eleas signaled her agreement.

"As dirty as we are?" Lilyis asked.

"That's what water is for," my master said in their best stern voice. "To cleanse us after we have travelled through the wilderness."

"I thought these waters were holy."

"The place is holy—and that includes the soil and the people who dwell around its shores."

"We obviously have a different understanding of the concept," Lilyis muttered. "How can we be holy, with all our basest needs and urges?"

"Because we are of the elements," Eleas said calmly, "and the elements are of the gods."

"Do I need to prepare myself for more discussions of this sort?" Lilyis asked me.

"Goldenlake is a place for wizards and most of them love to debate the finer points."

"Most of them?" She poked me with her elbow. "You mean 'most of us'."

"Those are claims I'll have to be careful with while we're here. You've seen the face on Qes' cousin Qor—she wouldn't forgive any indiscretion. When we were at the Stoneharp, you didn't get to see it at full capacity. Many of the wizards who have fled the Harp might well have settled here or will arrive in time."

Werid rolled their eyes. "You can talk later," they admonished us. "Clip-clop."

At least the guesthouse was close to the shore, so we soon stood to the left of a thicket of reeds and the remnants of an old jetty long fallen into disrepair.

Werid's long coat brushed along the pebbles as they walked down to the water. They carefully pressed it against their stomach as they crouched down to lift some of the lake water to their face to clean off the dirt of the road. Their long braid fell over their bent back, trailing behind them. As they so often did, my master appeared like the embodiment of a person in the legends, a graceful god, and I heard the intake of breath from my companions as Werid lifted their wet hand above their head and let the drops fall. As Werid of the Far Side turned back around to face us, the lines that had been around their mouth since I'd found them in my aunt's cottage had smoothed themselves out. Werid passed us and returned to the town without a word. I saw Eleas swallow, but she grinned at me and started to run into the lake, fully clothed.

Lilyis laughed. "What the fuck?"

I pulled off my cloak, Bjor was hopping on one foot as he toed off his boots—and then we all walked in.

The water was unexpectedly warm close to the shallow shore. I saw Qes hanging off Cathil's neck, trying to get him under water, and though Lilyis didn't seem comfortable with the use we put the lake to, she washed her face and watched us splash about, until Raz started to pull her further in. Back then, I'd left Goldenlake in winter, when the lake was frozen hard enough for people to skate and build snow lanterns on it. The smell coming off the waters made my nostrils flare as I scrubbed at my arms and neck, trying to get off the old sweat and horsehair. Qes screeched as Cathil finally managed to pluck him off and wrestled him down, kissing him hard.

"This is so weird," I said, as I made my way back to shore. "Everything is the same, but it couldn't be more different."

"You should be happy you made it back," Lilyis said, reaching out to stop me.

We embraced, standing knee-high in the lake. "I am, believe me. But it's still … It feels like a dream to me."

"A good one?"

"In most aspects, yes." I turned back to the guesthouse where my pack with the ashes lay waiting. "Werid and I might have some sort of arrangement, but no one here will think of them as my true master. I'm nowhere close to where I was last time, and back then I had a very specific reason to be here, a task put upon me by my mother."

She pushed against my chest. "Serving the Company of the Sun is a task," she reminded me. "Just because we're in Goldenlake, that doesn't mean we have achieved anything yet."

"You've already met a lot of new people."

"Those relationships will have to be maintained. Don't look at me like that—there'll be plenty of time for wizard activities. I'm getting cold."

A cloud had moved in front of the sun and we both shivered in our soaked clothes. We left our friends frolicking about and turned back to the house, collecting our cloaks and boots along the way.

Werid had started the fire in the brazier and pointed to a construction resembling a small net-drying rack. "You can hang up your clothes here or take them outside. Are you feeling better?"

I shrugged off my wet tunic. "No. I still feel as if none of it is real."

My master glanced at the tangle of ornaments on my naked chest. "Are you so astounded to find yourself in doubt? This has always been a place where the veils between what is, what could be, and what was are very, very thin." They came towards me and touched the wolfstone in its half-molten cage of golden wire, the silver pendant of Brother Brook, Qes' pebble and, at last, the key to the Hidden Tower. "Isn't it amazing that you've brought all these with you?" They stretched their hand out, the empty palm towards the ceiling, and I laid my wrist down so they could touch the sliver of blue stone in the bracelet. "All these treasures, all these pieces of your story. You must've fought for them." They smiled at Lilyis, who stood behind me, watching us. Werid was close enough to me to make me feel strange about it, and Lilyis might not be happy to be witness to a talk between master and associate.

"I'm the last person who should be allowed to speak on the problem of attaching too much value to objects," Werid said with a deep sigh. "I have mourned the fading of every single dress I've ever owned, but you need to be careful. Your aunt never put her trust in ornaments, as you well know."

"You gave me the wolfstone."

"I know. But you've started collecting." They finally released the bracelet and stepped away from me. "I need to speak for both your aunt and me, when it comes to you. You're a long way off from finishing your education."

"Will you talk to Qerla Badger about me?"

"I'll have to."

"Is there any chance she'll summon me?"

"Qerla loved Sjunil—or did so once. I think she'll understand what we're trying to do, but I don't want you to blurt out anything yet. Go and get dressed, Sloe. You have goosebumps on your goosebumps."

We ate a simple meal of flatbreads, cheese, and raspberries sprinkled on soured cream. The house was full of drying clothes. The only one missing was Qati, and I felt strangely resentful that he'd chosen not to be with us that evening. Qes and Cathil checked and fed the horses, and the quiet lapping noises of the Golden Lake accompanied the soft crackles from the dying fire. Raz and Bjor started to yawn, setting each other off again and again, until Lilyis snapped, "For fuck's sake, go to bed!"

"You'd better," Werid said. "We've come a long way and tomorrow things might get complicated."

"What do you expect?" Qes asked.

"Council business, and there might be trouble coming our way from the Clouds residing in town." Werid looked at Cathil. "Don't tell me you haven't taken that into account?"

"I've been somewhat distracted," Cathil admitted, glancing at my cousin.

"It's time to pull your finger out and prepare for what might happen if the news spreads that the man who managed to strike such a rift into his family is right here and not exactly well-protected. You might all be confronted with members of your own families. I've seen Owls in Goldenlake, though no Cormorants, as far as I'm aware. Take care, everyone. We shouldn't let Lilyis and Bjor wander around on their own, until we know if many men from the Cities are in town." There was a new tone in Werid's voice as they addressed us over the empty bowls and baskets. As if they tried to think about what my aunt would've said to make sure we were kept on our toes.

Everyone nodded at them; only Eleas frowned. In a town of wizards she was the only one of us who had the authority to poke that particular bear. Like in Tall Trees, we divided the sleeping platforms between us. The last time I'd spent my nights there alone and knowing Lilyis would be next to me helped me to breathe easier. I'd try to keep a grip on my own fears, the memories that welled up between the walls. It was where my gods dwelled, in the soft sounds of the waters washing against the land, in the way the embers offered up their deep shades of red and rust and the wind whistled through the rafters of the roofs. I remembered speaking to Tjal for the first time in the same house, seeing him cry for his brother. I gulped down the last dregs of my cold tea. Goldenlake hadn't been an easy time in my life then, and it likely wouldn't be now.

$$\raisebox{0pt}{\scriptsize ❦}$$

ON MY WATCH

As I awoke the next day, my master had already left the house, but I could hear familiar voices outside the door. Qerla Badger, who must've been informed of our arrival.

I rolled out of bed and pulled on my clothes as best as possible, before pushing into the sunlight.

The elderly first wizard of Goldenlake was in full regalia, her staff studded with freshwater pearls and glistening ribbons. She had the same eyes as me, one blue, one brown, though her hair had long since gone grey.

Werid stood before her, as if they'd felt compelled to protect us, Eleas next to her with her arms crossed and wearing a deep frown.

"Sloe!" Qerla lowered her staff to push my master out of the way. "Is it true?" There was a hitch in Qerla Badger's voice, usually so authoritative and unflappable.

"Yes. We've brought her with us."

She breathed in slowly. "Were you with her at the end?"

"We were all with her, but Werid has spent the most time at her side. They can tell you about everything that happened."

"But they are no Moon," Qerla said disapprovingly. "We need to have a ceremony—a celebration," she decided.

"We already did that in Tall Trees."

"There are many people here who will want to pay their respects. Your aunt made a name for herself in the east, Sloe, and we have always honoured the greatest of us in Goldenlake."

Werid looked mildly annoyed to be pushed aside, just because they were a Wolf, and I could see their brown eyes narrow, calculating how to approach the situation. "A ceremony would be good, Sloe. To ensure that the gods hear Sjunil Moon's name echoed throughout our world once more. It might be the perfect opportunity to introduce you to the wizard community."

Qerla stiffened and again lowered her staff. She used it like an extension of her arm and when its gnarled top pointed at Werid's chest, we all took an instinctive step backwards.

"Why?" Qerla asked, dangerously quiet. "What happened?"

"We shouldn't talk about it out in the open," Werid said.

"Fine. Let me come in, before everyone's ears are glued to the walls."

Werid hesitated before moving aside to let the older wizard pass. Most of us were still sleeping. Qerla commandeered the seat closest to the brazier, while Eleas started to revive the fire, to drive out the dampness of a night close to the shore.

Werid glanced at the staff resting against Qerla's seat. "Sloe, do you want to tell your story?"

"Are you sure this is a good idea? Didn't Sjunil say that we should be careful with the information?"

"Your aunt is no longer here. If you can get support in Goldenlake, this is the way to get it. Qerla needs to know things have changed and will continue to change, if people like you and Eleas are starting to make an appearance."

"People like you?" Qerla asked.

"Should we show her?" My mouth was awfully dry.

Werid smiled. "Don't blow up the house, please."

I moved closer to the brazier, letting the blue stone bracelet fall down my arm, so I could touch its links with my fingertips. I reached out with the other hand and as the blue fire enveloped my skin, Qerla Badger made the most astonishing sound: as if someone had stamped on a cat's tail, half-hiss and half-scream. It woke the rest of the company.

"No. That *can't* be."

I doused the flame with a spurt of water from my right hand. "I'm afraid it is."

"Sjunil swore to me that she was the only one."

"Wait." Werid leant forward. "You *knew*?"

"Don't be absurd, Werid—I knew. We were together for quite some time and people share secrets when they're happy. She said she didn't know why she was inflicted in this way and why the visitations always took such a toll on her strength. So it is something that came through your mother's side?"

"That's what we assume."

"Is that all you can do?"

"We've been starting to train, to make it a bit more … reliable."

"No wonder you didn't want it to be talked about in the street. The apprentices should be shielded."

"That's what we figured," Werid said softly. "And why Sjunil wanted us to be discreet about it all."

"The apprentices are not my only concern." Qerla had started to massage her hands, as if her fingers had gone numb. "We have heard other news from the west, and we are all wondering what will happen. Many members of the western families have left their quarters and only few representatives behind. People are starting to get nervous."

"Are there men from the Cities in Goldenlake?" my master asked.

"There always are—as you well know."

"Some who arrived only recently?" I jumped in.

"There is no telling," Qerla said. "We have never counted in the travellers. Goldenlake is open to all, Goldenlake doesn't have gates." She stared at me. "What are you afraid of?"

"If they haven't arrived yet, there might be a group of them coming soon that isn't so much concerned with the material riches of the lands of the families but the talents of its people. Specifically, they're interested in wizards."

Qerla blinked. "Why? Every single man from the Cities I have ever spoken to has laughed in the face of the Tall Gods."

"Because they haven't made the connection before," I admitted. "Wizards play a large part in the stories that are told on the Continent, though they have different names for them. For us."

"Let me guess," Qerla Badger groaned. "Someone saw your little tricks and decided that all wizards are able to show off in the same way?"

"That's pretty much what happened."

"Fuck." She started to massage her hands again. "That could be a disaster for Goldenlake."

"We are aware," Werid said flatly.

"Until now they were only interested in silver, gold, and pelts— you're telling me they could start buying *people*?"

"We don't know what they have planned, and they might not find many wizards like … like me. But they might not stop to find out, or unearth untrained family members with grudges against their relatives, who might be persuaded to serve them."

Werid sniffed. "We always thought people like Sjunil, Sloe, and Eleas to belong to an age that has long gone by or only be the figment of a fractured imagination. It seems that the council at the Stoneharp has been suppressing news of them, has silenced everyone who didn't match their idea of what a wizard is. If there are already three of them among people we know, there might be many more."

"What are you asking me to do?"

"To keep an ear open for any information about traders from the west who are asking to employ wizards, and to take rumours about a new kind of wizard seriously," Werid said.

"A new 'kind' of wizard?" Qerla scoffed. "I would call them 'cursed'."

I felt the impact of the word hitting me like a kick to the gut.

"They aren't 'cursed'," Werid disagreed, making an appeasing gesture towards the Cormorant.

"No?" Qerla reached for her staff and pushed herself up. "One day there may dawn a time when these abilities are as accepted as the extraordinary feats of learning and wisdom we expect our apprentices to perform before they take on the wizardship, but it won't be while I'm still alive and breathing. I saw your aunt suffer, Sloe. You can't tell me this will not affect you two. You will burn out soon, like she did. If you ask me, the less you fiddle about with it, the better. And for introducing you to the community—this cannot happen. This will *not* happen, not on my watch."

"You shouldn't have told her," Lilyis said as she finished plaiting her braid.

"As the first wizard of Goldenlake, she has a right to know. I understand why Werid wanted her to."

"She'll keep an eye on you, and she might get suspicious once she realizes that you're here with two people of the Cities. I can't let you talk yourself into danger, can I?" She glanced up at me. "I know I don't understand everything that's going on around the families, but you don't need to give me that look."

"What look?"

She narrowed her bright-green eyes. "Careful—you don't want to get onto thin ice with me."

"Because you're of the Sun, or because …"

"It has nothing at all to do with the Company, Sloe. This is purely about you being a dick again."

A spike of anger leapt at my throat. "*Again?*"

"We should talk about it later. Didn't Werid ask you to join them as soon as possible?"

"They'll understand that I need a while to catch my breath after this disaster."

"What did you expect? The first wizard of Goldenlake must have an awful lot to lose."

I pressed my eyes closed. "Why … why are we fighting, Lilyis?"

"You tell me."

"Right." I turned around. Even on board the *Golden Drake*, when tensions had run high, we'd snarked at each other at times, but not like that. It was a new development. She'd changed towards me since Julas' withdrawal from the competitions.

I barged through the door onto the street. Werid would wait for me at the Roundhouse, as they'd promised. My feet brought me to where water met shore, and I walked around the broken boats and splintered wood washed up by the lake's timid summer waves, the ropes of dried grass and fish bones picked clean by birds and other scavengers, thinking about her. How it had felt to step into the lake the day before, and then be refused by the wizards once again.

I wasn't the only one with the idea to use the lake for reflection: where the centre of town was closest to the water stood other groups of people, and one man in a felted hood, who looked out towards Coldharbour with a scowl. He wore woollen trousers and a nondescript tunic and perhaps I wouldn't have noticed anything odd about him, but my gaze slipped down to his feet. He wore sandals of a kind I'd only seen on one type of person.

YOU TELL ME

"Sloe—slow down." Qes took my arms and squeezed them so hard I gasped. "What was that about shoes?"

"Not just shoes—sandals."

"So what?"

I suppressed the urge to roll my eyes. "I need to tell Bjor and Lilyis. Where did they go?"

Qes and Cathil smiled at each other and shrugged. "Off to explore, I suppose. Why?"

"The priests of the Star wear those sort of sandals, Qes." Cathil opened his mouth, but I talked across him immediately. "It's not a coincidence. It can't be."

Qes groaned. "You're saying that the Bulls brought priests to Goldenlake?"

"It might not have been the Bulls but another group of travellers from the Cities, but the thought of one of them at the lake …" I felt my stomach drop to my feet.

"He might feel close to his own gods here," Cathil said, and I was ready to slap him.

"There are enough temples on the Continent. We don't need any priests here. You know what they'll try to do. They want to ruin everything. If Nivael had brought priests with them back then, there'd have never been a chance of us beginning a friendship."

"But he didn't," Qes said carefully. "Breathe, Sloe. Did you talk to Werid?"

"No, but you're right, I should. Could you tell Lilyis that I need to speak to her when she and Bjor come back to the house?"

"Will do," Cathil said in a tone that made it clear that he was deeply relieved to see me go.

My master reacted to my news with a suitably deep frown. "Why would they need to bring their priests to Goldenlake?"

"I've met these priests and commonly assume they want to avoid having anything to do with the Siblings. That they are afraid to be influenced in ways they fear to be unseemly. Or sinful."

"Sinful?" Werid grimaced. "What could be sinful about the Siblings?"

"Both of us, for example. According to the Star our lot would've been set on a fixed path when we came into this world, with no chance of choice between the Houses."

"Well, then they can fuck right off." Werid took me by the arm. "You seem truly worried. This is one man in sandals."

"Because Qerla is right. Goldenlake has no gates. There could be thrice as many men of the Cities hidden away here as sailed on the ship of the Bulls. The council needs to be made aware that the Star might … try to do something. They once came to the Continent to drive out our gods. They could try and do the same here."

"I don't think they understand how vast the lands of the families are, Sloe. You call the council of Goldenlake the council of the east, though technically the Golden Lake sits more towards the middle. To the Wolves you are of the eastern families."

"Every fire starts with a single spark, and even if this one is a pair of sandals, I want to take it seriously."

"Of course."

"The damage the Star could do to the families, to all of our wizards …"

"Who have given you a definite 'no' for an answer, Sloe."

"I can still want to protect them, can't I?"

My master pulled a face. "Why does it all have to be so complicated? That's not a question for you, just …"

"… a moan towards the gods?"

"Something like that. Right, what do you want to do?"

"I want to find out how many men we're dealing with."

"How? You're not the best choice to infiltrate an enemy camp, and it stands to reason that Lilyis' face is known to them. What about your other friend from the Cities?"

"If there are Bulls among them, they'll recognize him straight away."

"But he'd still be the best candidate to check up on them."

"Probably. As far as we were aware, the Bulls didn't take any priests on board, so either this one joined them under false pretences, or …"

"… he does belong to a separate group." Werid touched my arm again. "Go and find him, Sloe. Everything else can wait. I'll have some tea with Eleas and see what she comes up with."

I breathed a huge sigh of relief when I found Lilyis and Bjor back at the house.

"Of course I'll do it," Bjor said. "Werid is right, I'd be able to assess who we're dealing with the quickest, and we can't risk Lilyis getting mixed up with them if we don't want their heads to explode."

"Thank you."

"This is why I came with you, Sloe, to be at hand for these situations. Don't worry about it." He beamed at me, flushed with enthusiasm. "Let me go and see what I can find out."

As he left us, Lilyis turned to me. "You think it's a good idea?" she asked pointedly. "You know he'll do anything to feel useful to you."

"Do you want to have that talk now?" I sat down at the table, pulling a half-eaten flatbread to me, trying hard not to sound bitter. "The one we postponed earlier?"

Lilyis made a face. "Lately we don't seem to agree on many things, and I must say this is what I feared would happen. As a member of the Sun I've come to these lands with an agenda, and you are starting to resent me for that."

"I don't resent you, Lilyis—I love you."

"These feelings are not mutually exclusive."

My hands ripped the bread into manageable bites. "It goes deeper than that," I admitted.

"Deeper how?"

"I think we have different ideas about a lot of things, and how could we not, having been raised on different continents, though we might be considered to hold a similar status on paper."

She crossed her arms, her brows drawing together. "What are you saying?"

"That some things are standing in our way, and we either learn to live with them or consider them as too great an obstacle to go on as we are."

"You want to break up with me?" She sounded angry.

"No!" I cried out, aghast. "No, I really don't, though recently you have started to make me feel bad about ... about how I see the world sometimes."

Her pale face set into a snarl. "Is that so?"

"We need to be able to talk these things through, without everything escalating into wrath and ..."

She closed her eyes. "I'm obviously not good at this."

"You aren't, but I'm not either. All the relationships I've been in so far have been quite one-sided, or not serious enough to try and put a lot of work into it."

"You're right," she conceded. "We both don't know what we're doing here. Living with Fiolis wasn't much at all. I'm not used to constantly being around someone who means that much to me, though I should be allowed to tell you when you're making a mistake."

"In fact, I need you to call me out on things," I said. "As long as you give me permission to do the same for you."

"I'm sorry, Sloe. I didn't want to make you feel bad. I wish I could blame it on getting adjusted to Birkland, but I think I'm having trouble handling that you're so in demand here," she said quietly. "I feel myself getting jealous a thousand times a day and there are always too many people around for us to truly be with each other or find time to get as close as I want to be with you. It has to do with the inconveniences of travelling, but also with the way the families live their lives most of the time. I don't always want to roll around in the dirt. I wish we could have a proper bed from time to time."

"I feel the same way, you must know that."

"I can't read your mind, though."

I looked around us. "We're alone."

"We are." She smiled at me, almost shyly.

As I stood up, she blushed, reached out to me and I pulled her into my arms. Her kiss hurt a bit, and I found my bones go to jelly, ready to collapse to the floor. I was able to steady myself against the table.

"You make my knees go all wobbly," I rasped.

"Good." Her hands buried under my tunic, into the soft ridges to both sides of my spine.

The door flew open.

"Oh, sorry," Bjor said.

"It's fine." Lilyis sounded deeply disappointed as she released me. "I suppose whatever you've come to say is more important in the big picture."

Bjor blew up his cheeks. "The men of the Cities staying here in Goldenlake are not Bulls."

"Are you sure?"

"Yes. They are Whiterivers men, and they haven't brought one priest, but five."

"Whiterivers men?" I pulled my tunic down.

"I'd recognize those stupid hats anywhere."

"Fuck." Lilyis kicked the leg of the table in front of her. "That makes it more difficult."

"Why?" I asked, trying to flatten my hair.

"Because there's a good chance of the Bulls trying to reach Goldenlake, if they made the crossing, and the last thing the families should be exposed to is a war between Whiterivers and the Hillakes fought out on their territory."

"Your sister *and* your father have married into Whiterivers to prevent exactly that from happening!"

"How long have you known people from the Cities, Sloe?" she asked mockingly. "Usually the men who are drawn to seek out such adventures as they expect to find here are able to come up with a quick excuse to start hostilities far away from home. They probably left Whiterivers before we travelled to my sister's wedding. With so many priests in their company how high are the chances they understand what the Sun is trying to do here? You tell me."

LIFE CHOICES

"I can keep an eye on them." Qati flashed an unexpected grin at his own joke. "Raz and Cathil can help to stake them out, also Qes, if he wants to."

"I want to." My cousin nodded eagerly. "If we all work together, we should get a good idea of how many Whiterivers men we're dealing with and have Bjor's back in case they start to ask uncomfortable questions. What story did you tell them?"

Bjor licked honey off his fingers. "Member of a trade delegation, got separated in the forests and made my way to Goldenlake to catch up with them. I thought I'd better keep it simple and as close to the truth as I can."

"How did they react?"

"As if I needed saving from the savages. Told them that I'd been taken in by a group of family members on their way to the lake and they didn't like that one bit."

"Even as a man from Southclere?"

"I think they care more about my belonging to the Star than about my family name. For now, at least."

Lilyis scoffed. "For now," she echoed. "They are bound to show their true beliefs sooner or later. You think you can join them?"

"I told them I'd get my things and be back before nightfall."

"Good," Lilyis said. "This is a brave thing you're doing here."

"I've been waiting for something brave to do."

Werid had listened to us discussing Bjor's plan in silence, seemingly busy combing out the fringe on a shawl. "I assume you are aware of the risk of taking on the priests? If they find out you retain such close connections to the families, what would they do to you? Separate you from their gods? Exclude you from the Star?"

"I'm not too bothered about that. Not after seeing what the Siblings can let Sloe do. They might be the safer bet anyway."

Lilyis gave a quiet snort at that. "Sounds as if you have already separated yourself."

"The Red House education has always favoured weapon training over religious education. No one in my family should be surprised. Whatever the priests try to do to me, it doesn't scare me. If they had the temple guard with them that would be different, but this isn't the Continent. They don't have any right to hurt me in Goldenlake."

"I doubt they'd see it the same way," Werid said. "I'm glad you're ready to help. The families have long memories." They tilted their head at Lilyis. "It would be better if you kept away from them though."

"I know, and I'm not exactly chomping at the bit to get into a discussion about my life choices with five priests. Especially, as they might have connections with my wife's family." She gave me an apologetic glance.

"Then everyone is clear on what to do, and as soon as we know more about them, we'll petition the council. At least Eleas and I will. I'm sorry, Sloe, but it will probably give you more time for training and—"

"I can do my bit. I look like half the Badgers in town. If there is one place in Birkland where I'm not standing out like a sore thumb, it's here."

Werid exchanged a worried glance with Eleas. "Please be sensible. Don't get sucked into a situation in which you could get hurt again."

"My circumstances have changed significantly," I reminded my master. "And I'm right next to one of the holiest places of all."

"No need to get cocky," Werid said. "The less attention you draw to yourself, the better. Think of your task as supporting Bjor."

We posed as a group of friends getting amicably drunk to pass the time on a street corner. Cathil was in possession of a skin of honey beer that we passed around, and we took pains to appear like family members of lower rank. I'd hidden my amulets under my tunic again and pushed the bracelet so far up my arm that it vanished under my sleeve. I'd bound my hair up in a knot, not a style I usually wore, as had Cathil. We chatted between sips of beer, each of us observing a different section of the busiest street in town.

There were quite a few other groups like us, just people talking. Raz and Qati had positioned themselves in another quarter and I supposed they would have no problem posing as a couple spiralling into a fight about their relationship. Raz had suggested Qati and though he'd seemed as surprised as the rest of us, had agreed to the scheme. Something we'd spoken about must've made him reconsider the situation he was in and why he'd tried to weasel out of being close.

It was amazing how much was going on in the streets at any given time, how many different families were present in Goldenlake who all lived their lives in their own quarters, visiting the small markets in other parts of town or bringing home fish from the boat station. Most of them seemed to be preoccupied with food. The last time I'd been there, I hadn't had much chance to be involved in the day-to-day of Goldenlake. As a hostage of the men of the Cities I'd been confined to the house they'd stayed in for most of the time.

There were people who ran errands on behalf of other, more important people. Not many of them lived there permanently, but as with the Stoneharp camp, high summer was the busiest time at the lake. Most of them must've come for the Shortest Night celebrations and many would leave within a few weeks. At that time of year, the markets were starting to overflow with fresh greens and summer fruit, eggs and soft cheeses.

Goldenlake was where many families brought their own specialties, where other nuts were available and flatbreads made from different kinds of flour, where dried mountain goat from the eastern ridges was sold at horrendous prices to delegates who longed too much for a taste of home to resist.

I didn't see as many children running about as in winter. No one seemed to recognize Cathil, even if at one point we were passed by a group of Clouds in their signature grey cloaks and severe hairstyle. I noticed Cathil tensing up and turning his back to them. Qes picked up the clue, leant forward and kissed him, to further obscure his face.

Cathil hissed, "Now they're definitely looking at me."

"Why?" I took another sip of beer.

"Being kissed by a man as beautiful as Qes is bound to draw some glances."

Qes blushed with pleasure, while I felt an unwelcome spark of jealousy. After all that had happened to Qes since we'd left Tall Trees, it was mean of me to begrudge him a boyfriend who was able to make such compliments in public.

I forced myself to smile. "Calm down," I said to the man who'd once been chosen to marry me. "They've already gone, without giving any of us a second glance. You can kiss all you want."

"Please don't encourage him," Cathil said, but his grin belied his words.

"Do you want me to leave?" I asked.

"No." Qes gave Cathil a little shove. "We're here for a reason, even if we haven't seen a whisker of the Whiterivers men yet."

"There's the priest again. Don't look." The man had appeared behind a house with the emblem of the Magpies painted on it, and he wasn't alone. Two men were with him, both in the unflattering headgear they'd made me wear during my stay in Whiterivers, a woollen cap above a linen covering that left no hair on show. One of the men wore a tunic with a sigil above the heart I was very familiar with: the dogs of Eastbay.

"We know where they've sailed from," I murmured.

My time in Eastbay, and everything that had happened while we'd been in the city, was something I didn't particularly care to remember.

"Where are they going?" Cathil asked.

"They're heading towards the northern quarters," Qes said. "Qati can ask the Bears if they are hosting them again?"

"You could be forgiven for expecting the Bears have learned their lesson after last time," I mumbled.

"That might not have been a disaster for everyone involved," Qes said, turning to his boyfriend. "Were the Bears compensated for what they did to Sloe?"

Cathil flushed with annoyance. "I assume so. You'd have to ask Lilyis' father. He promised anyone involved an awful lot back then."

"Maybe the Bears count on another financial opportunity," Qes said. "Let's hope Qati can guilt them into divulging a few helpful details."

"Did you find out anything?" Raz sounded excited as we met up at the guesthouse.

"Yes, nothing incredibly important but it could lead to more information," I said. "Where did Qati take you?"

"We went to the boat station first, and it was positively swarming with them."

"Swarming?"

"They've received a shipment from Coldharbour, mostly casks of syrup. They had three carts full of them. You were right, the hats are really stupid. Why don't they realize they make them stand out so much?"

"Because they're wearing them to protect their modesty."

Raz snorted. "They could do so less conspicuously."

"It's a cultural thing with them. Have you found out whether it was the first shipment or if they're doing this regularly?"

"Qati is on it. He seems to like to skulk around. I've rarely seen him so animated. I need to get a firm grip on my heart, I don't want to fall for him all over again."

"Hmhm. They don't seem to expect to be under observation and as long as they continue to be careless …"

"They're not doing anything forbidden," Raz reminded me. "According to Qati there have always been traders in Goldenlake who profited from the crowds gathering for the festivals. What could you accuse them of?"

"Everything hinges on what they brought the priests for," Eleas interjected. I hadn't seen her approach. "And if the council can be persuaded to see them as a genuine threat."

AS IT WAS NOW

During the high season Goldenlake hosted many public prayer ceremonies, most of them in a designated place on the shore that was regularly cleared of debris and marked with a heap of stones. During summer it was festooned with garlands of flowers and over time the waves of the lake would disperse the offerings and the stones they'd been placed on.

I found myself getting bored by the public prayers; they tended to go on for ages, and it seemed that the Whiterivers men stayed well away from them too.

"They're having their own ceremonies," Bjor confirmed a few days later. "Three times a day, in the house they're renting from the Elks."

"The Elks …" Qati said. "I suppose that makes sense. It sounds as if the Elks lost out last time."

I turned to Lilyis. "Your father said the guide he had with him and who was killed with his companions was an Elk."

"But what about Yuna?"

"Rules are different at the Harp. Yuna is an administrator of the Stoneharp, she isn't supposed to be involved in family politics."

"The Elks have made it further up the list of families to watch out for," Werid said with a deep groan.

"As long as they're only renting out the space …"

"But there's a connection that's likely to extend beyond a single handshake. It stands to reason to assume they're using the Elks' contacts to procure the syrup, or buying it directly off them. The Elks might store their reserves in Coldharbour, like many other families prefer. As Raz said, everything they're doing is perfectly legal," Werid cautioned. "Traders from the Cities have come to the lands of the families for hundreds of years, and we can't be sure when all these threads first came together. When your aunt asked for the families to unite against the Cities, I doubt that she knew how complicated all of it already was. You seem to think the men from Whiterivers constitute a special threat, but to the families all men from the Cities would've been the same."

"Given the prejudices Whiterivers folk hold against the Hillakes, a kingdom that has been bound to them by many a royal marriage, it seems plausible to me that their arrival in Birkland is more recent. Could you try to find out?" Lilyis asked Bjor.

Bjor spent most of his time with the Whiterivers men and had only snuck out to meet us after a few days had gone by. Our breakfast meeting had a conspiratorial flavour. While we'd kept an eye on Bjor's new friends, Eleas and Werid had tried to change Qerla Badger's mind about holding a big ceremony for my aunt.

I'd kept as far away from the wizards as possible and after giving up on the public prayers I'd gone down to the lake by myself, studying the reflections in its waters, the subtle changes of colour brought about by different times of day. Whenever I stepped close to the lake, I could feel the longing gather around my bones, the desire to run into the water at full tilt, seeking the embrace of the gods again. Playing about with my talents was much too dangerous, especially in sight of the makeshift altar at the centre of town.

Having Bjor live somewhere else served as a constant reminder of what my aunt must've felt when agreeing to give me up as a hostage to the prince's men. After travelling such a long way together it felt as if a piece of our company was continually missing. Werid had said that Sjunil had taken the prince's betrayal hard, and I'd seen her on her sickbed with my own eyes, as we'd finally been reunited after weeks of uncertainty. I hadn't fretted that much about her, more about Qes, who I'd presumed to be dead … Being back at the lake felt like watching two images: the lake as it had been then and the lake as it was in the present, sometimes overlapping, but more often than not showing two different realities, with my memories serving as the setting for one of them, one inner and one outer world touching.

"Sorry, I didn't want to intrude." Lilyis had stepped up behind me. Though her boots must have shifted on the pebbles, I hadn't heard her.

"I wasn't praying."

"Oh good. I never know with you."

I stuck out my arm and she took my hand as she joined me in my contemplation of the holy lake. "It must be strange for you being the only one of the Cities in the house."

She squeezed my fingers. "It is at times, especially when everyone else seems to be so busy, and I can't join in with your little spying missions." She wore a felted hood drawn up over her hair, her long braid snaking around her neck to keep it out of sight. "It must be nice to feel useful." She sounded bitter.

"Did I tell you they wouldn't let me leave the house when I was living as a hostage with your father's company? Because I was to be treated as his counterpart, I wasn't supposed to work, or do anything else but sit inside and be demonstratively idle. I wonder whether the thing with Tjal would've started if I hadn't been bored out of my mind."

"You must be reminded of him here," she said quietly.

"Sometimes. He was the first to ever claim falling in love with me, so that's bound to stick." I saw a muscle twitch in her cheek. "He's dead. As dead as both of his brothers."

"He can still be important to you, and even if knowing about him stings a little, I can't be the one to complain, being married and all." She moved closer to let the waves wash over the tips of her boots, pulling me with her, as if she believed to be further away from the people around us the closer we were to the waters. "I don't want to be jealous of a dead man," she said. "Though I can't always help it."

"I understand."

"It gives me something to latch on to while I'm in a land I don't understand. Despite all the weeks spent on my research to help Father. I never gave you enough credit for being out of your element on the Continent."

"Don't worry about it."

"I do, and you need to let me." She pulled me down for a brief kiss. "I can't push all of that down. Imagine having been raised with a golden spoon in your mouth and struggling when it's suddenly taken away. At first it feels like a new and utterly wonderful freedom but … in the last weeks I've been less comfortable than at any other point in my life. I can see it will probably make me into someone better in the long run, but often it feels like having less." She leant into my side. "This is your world and your home, and I want to find myself happy here. How could I not be, with such beauty before me?" She smiled at the Golden Lake stretching out towards the horizon. "But then you get lost in wizard talk and are so far away from me, or you walk off with Qes and Cathil, leaving me behind because of who I am, though I've tried to get rid of Nian da Nileon as much as I can. I get scared when he catches up with me."

I wrapped my arms around her shoulder. "Of course."

"I hate him—for being the stupid, entitled, spoiled brat that he is. I teased you about being the one with the blue eye and the one with the brown eye, but I was talking more about myself."

"Hmhm." I made an encouraging sound.

"I can see that you're struggling as well. Why can't they recognize you for what you are? A sorcerer who could flatten this whole town if they wanted to? Can they really be so blind?"

"They're blind because they're afraid. On the Continent sorcerers were revered and this awe has made its way into the myths. Here, claiming to share the Siblings' powers is seen as hubris, as trying to be someone one shouldn't be, and aiming too high for others to be comfortable. Can you remember Eleas how she was when we first met her? As if someone was constantly trying to put her down?"

"You mean bitter and disappointed?" Lilyis asked quietly. "And at odds with the family she was supposed to care for?"

"That's exactly it," I said. "This is how they make us feel. As if there was something deeply wrong with us. I've felt it all my life, as if it's a moral failing on my part. I'm used to it, but I'm digging my way out every single day. Eleas seems to have found a method to cope with these emotions, and I hope that our talks and training have helped her as much as me. A few hundred years ago your ancestors would've killed me for what I can do, and I'm under no illusion that I was only given the position in your uncle's court and the key to my tower because such a long time has passed. Though the Star thinks their grip on the Hillakes and Southclere is getting stronger, they've never had as much influence there as in Whiterivers, and they'll probably never have when Nurin gets his arse on the throne. You must have expected the wizards in Birkland to react with the same wonder and excitement, not as if Eleas and I were annoying impostors, clamouring for unwanted attention. Maybe there will come a time when people like my aunt don't have to hide their talents away for their whole life, to find a place among the wizards, when they aren't sent into exile like Eleas or locked away as I almost was. I might actually be safer in the Cities, as weird as that sounds, but there I don't get to have the other side of it, the learning I came to appreciate first."

"You don't need to explain," Lilyis said. "I get it. Are you ready to let your aunt go? They're waiting for you."

VARIABLES

I'd relinquished the wooden box earlier that morning. One of Qerla Badger's older apprentices had collected it from the house and I'd felt bad handing it over without making a fuss. Though my head was firmly convinced that I'd already done everything to see Sjunil off into the land of the dead, to be reunited with her body so she could travel its hills and valleys, the box still held something valuable. It continued to feel connected to what my aunt, who I'd only fully started to love once I'd been given to her to guide into the east, had meant to me. Which part she'd taken in getting me to where I was, how I was able to feel about myself.

I let Lilyis lead me along the shore to the pebble altar, where the congregation was already gathered, and Qerla had arranged the other high-ranking wizards to pay tribute to the woman she'd once wanted to marry. The apprentices stood behind their masters, dressed to impress, with their staffs, complicated hair, and painted eyes. As was their habit, Werid had subverted expectations and was clothed in a long grey robe, their hair braided into a simple, unadorned crown, with not a single golden pin in sight, and merely the necklace of clunky wolfstones on their shoulders. Qerla had stationed them at the edge of the group, with Eleas standing behind them. The Cormorant seemed happy to serve as Werid of the Far Side's apprentice on the occasion, though her forehead was marked, like almost all other wizards here, her hair pulled back from her brow to display the tattoo with pride.

Our company had found a spot among the congregation and Lilyis brought me to them. Surely Qerla hadn't waited for me to arrive, but the score of apprentices carrying small drums started the ceremony off as soon as I took my place next to Qes.

The news that a famous wizard was being celebrated had attracted many people who'd probably never seen my aunt, never spoken a single word to her or hadn't heard her name before that day. They attended for the spectacle, while I heard Qes start to sniffle beside me. He hadn't known Sjunil Moon particularly long either, but she'd kept us both safe during our travels. After I'd been taken and he gravely injured, she'd firmly tucked him under her wing. Though for us it was the last ceremony in a row, I could feel him struggle to hold on. When I reached out to him, our fingers twined around each other.

"She would've hated this," I said and saw him desperately press his lips together. "The costumes, the drums, and the wizards who were irritated by her at the best of times, now making out that they are oh so bereaved."

He squeezed my hand and I saw the scars on his beautiful face blaze, as if they were barely healed over.

It was difficult to hear the words of the first prayers over the drums; we were standing too far removed from the altar. Essentially, it was an occasion for the wizards, not for the rest of us, or maybe the drums were deliberately employed to exclude us.

Qerla Badger was grey-faced with grief. My aunt's ashes had been transferred from the box to a much grander vessel, laid in with various woods and mother-of-pearl, which had been given centre stage on the pebble altar, with a garland of pale-yellow flowers placed around it. None of it had anything to do with the person Sjunil had been. Qerla did it for herself; it was her personal farewell, and as soon as the notion struck me, I found that I was able to tolerate it much easier, the prayers and the singing, the fucking drums ... I finally noticed my master watching me.

Werid had probably come to the same conclusion as me, and I saw their elegant brow arch pointedly. Of all people present, Werid should've been in the middle of it, but they allowed themself to be pushed aside. If there was ever a chance for me to get officially recognized, we needed to keep Qerla Badger happy, or as happy as possible under the circumstances. Tears streaked the first wizard's lined face as she bowed to the ashes, preparing to open the lid.

The song the apprentices started to fall in sounded familiar; as if the wizards of the west had sung it from the walls during the battle at the Stoneharp. The wind freshened, blowing the embroidered cloaks of the attendants around, wreaking havoc with their hair. The sound of beads clicking and rattling reminded me of chattering teeth. The warmth of high summer had been snatched away. We shivered. Patterns appeared on the surface of the lake, and I could see Qerla freeze, as if she considered the secret she'd kept all those years to protect the woman she loved. The most powerful wizard in the east was clearly apprehensive, and as she flicked the box open, the ashes of my aunt rose from it in a silvery spiral. A communal gasp thrummed through us; many fell on their knees to pray, some of the apprentices throwing themselves into the water with their instruments still slung about them.

Qerla spun around to glare at me, but all I could do was to shrug back at her.

The spiral danced away, borne along by the wind, out into the distance, uncoiling more and more, until it resembled the winding spine of a snake, or one of the dragons in our oldest myths. Many people were weeping openly. The ceremony would be talked about a lot during the next weeks, months, and years— it would be another opportunity for Sjunil to become legendary.

"Holy fuck," I heard Cathil Cloud mutter, loud enough for Eleas to turn to us and wink.

"You need to tell me—did you do that?" I asked.

"I do not *need* to tell you anything." Eleas' smile had a blandness that made me more suspicious than a self-congratulatory smirk. "Let's say that dead wizards do not get punished."

"What's that supposed to mean?"

Werid pushed past us. "You're both playing with fire," they hissed. "You'll be lucky if there are no repercussions."

"You don't think this was the appropriate opportunity to remind everyone that there's still *some* magic about?" I asked.

Werid sniffed. "It was nicely done, but whatever reaction it was supposed to bring forth, there'll be some that won't appreciate the thought that they are by no means as intimately connected to the Siblings as they believe themselves to be."

"Everyone will remember it," Qes said, wiping his eyes. "And not for the boring prayers and the endless chanting."

Werid sighed. "Can you please run everything else any one of you might plan to piss off the council by me first? I'd like to be kept in the loop, if you don't mind. And you ..." They turned to Eleas. "Nice touch. She would've like to see them on their knees like that."

"It wasn't me," Eleas said.

"But let's say, in case it was—Sjunil would surely have appreciated anything that disruptive. Sloe, come with me." My master held their arms behind their body, their fingers folded into each other as we walked away from the water. "I had the opportunity to pose a few questions today," they started our conversation. "The group Lilyis is so concerned with has been here since early spring. Since, others have left Goldenlake to travel back west to meet their ships. There have been consignments coming over from Coldharbour for months, and it's said that the Elks are supporting them—and the Hedgehogs."

"The Hedgehogs?"

"That suggests they have made their way across to Goldenlake from the east coast. There's no way Lilyis will be able to control them if their contacts extend so far into the steppes. This is clearly a large operation."

"Who told you that?"

"The apprentices. Most of them are grateful for any attention to come their way."

"Werid …"

"You know I can handle myself," they said.

I'd seen my master weave their own enchantments many times. "What I'm saying is that the Bulls might have received a warmer reception on the east coast, and never planned to land at the Stoneharp but instead to make their way to Steepbay. They could've already crossed the mountains or have dug in at Cloudhome. There's no knowing where Bjor's family is trying to trade out of. Are you sure there are no treaties in place between the men here and the Bulls?"

"We can't rule it out, but it seems highly unlikely."

But then, the Bulls were much in favour of Southclere's independence, and any resentments that were harboured in Eastbay towards the royals from the Hillakes would serve as tinder to let old tensions flare up.

Werid cleared their throat. "I don't envy the situation Lilyis will find herself in before long. Even when her father left there was little chance of kicking them out once and for all—now it seems an impossible task. Many will side either against all people from the Cities or with the traders they've had dealings with in the past. The Suns are something new and not everyone will understand what they are trying to do. The Moons might find themselves sidelined if their association comes to be general knowledge."

"What's your advice for me?"

"I don't have any to give. Apart from trying to gather more information before deciding on one way forward. The success of the Suns depends on too many variables and I'm getting more and more scared for you." They took my wrists. I could feel the hands of my master shake. "This has stopped being a game a long time ago."

TOO MUCH TO GAIN

"Werid seemed worried." Lilyis cleaned the brush against the corner of a dividing wall and continued to work over her small grey mare. "Have you talked things through with them?"

My throat constricted as I recalled the helplessness I'd felt when Werid had spoken to me. "Yes. They suspect the Bulls never meant to go west in the first place, perhaps because they knew this is where the crews from Seagard have often gone before. They might be further east, which makes me wonder if it would be warranted for us to travel to the mountains. I've never been farther east than Goldenlake, Lilyis. I have no idea what we'd find, apart from that all stories mention the wild dark forests, stuffed with dangerous creatures, and that the mountains themselves are so high that they touch the sky."

Lilyis snorted but noticed the pained expression on my face. "Oh. Sorry, I didn't mean to laugh at your concerns."

"Even before we reach the forests or the mountains, there are the steppes to negotiate."

"I thought Werid came from the steppes."

"Everything they've told me about their family hasn't filled me with confidence that the Wolves wouldn't turn on them. Lilyis, please take it seriously," I begged her. "You should let the Bulls be."

"You know we can't," she said, shaking her head. "Not if there's the smallest chance of them connecting with the Whiterivers men. This is quickly becoming about the future of my family, about the possibility of revolt."

I sighed. "Walk me through it."

"You know what I'm going to say."

"I want to hear you speak it out loud. You owe me that much," I added tersely.

She put the brushes aside and took a deep breath. "There's going to be a war between at least two of the Eight Kingdoms. You've felt it as we were travelling to Eastbay—something is slowly coming up to a boil. My sister is trapped on enemy territory, isolated from Crooked Hill. If Father hasn't managed to stall developments on his own marriage, he'll be in a similar situation. The Red House has too much to gain from my family's fall not to take an interest in supporting any venture that could sponsor the war. Every copperling they earn from the syrup they buy in Birkland will go towards their efforts to reinstate the da Relians as the rulers of the south, and these are just the most obvious complications. I agree it isn't fair the families are getting into the middle of a conflict between kingdoms that are not even *officially* here."

"Then make it official," I suggested. "It's time for you to let your name be known. It was always meant to be a diplomatic mission of sorts, wasn't it?"

"But who speaks for Birkland?" Lilyis asked softly. "There are too many families here, I can't visit them all."

"You can start with the Badgers. Goldenlake is the centre of their family's influence, and you know someone close to their ruler."

She frowned. "Who?"

"Qes. You always knew he was a prince, didn't you?"

I saw her mouth fall open. "I always thought that was Father exaggerating for Grandfather's benefit."

"He didn't. Status-wise Qes and Cathil are quite evenly matched."

When confronted with the prospect of dropping in on his own family, Qes appeared less than enthusiastic. "You don't want to do that." My cousin swallowed nervously. "I can't recall anyone in Thorndell ever having a kind word to spare for the Eastern Cities, though my mother likes to eat sour peppers with absolutely everything."

"Having the support of the Badgers would mean an awful lot," Lilyis said, pouring out more honey beer for him. "Are your concerns about me visiting your mother or about presenting Cathil to your family?"

"A bit of both. Thorndell is different than Tall Trees, Sloe."

"How could it not be? Isn't it strange that I've never been, if my own father grew up there?"

Qes groaned. "You're making this very difficult for me, Sloe."

"You know Lilyis is right."

"It isn't her plan, though. It reeks of your strange schemes and not everyone can be as easily wrangled as would suit you."

"Oh, I'm aware."

"Are you? Let me ask Cathil first. Please don't spring that on him. Getting him anywhere close to Thorndell would be a big step for him."

"Fine," I said. "But don't wait too long. We'll have to start preparing for our departure."

"You really can't wait to flee," he said, clearly disappointed.

I gulped. "What do you mean?"

"Just because the wizards have denied you at the first try, you'll have plenty of chances to pester them into reconsidering. Goldenlake is where you belong, Sloe."

"I'm not so sure anymore. Not if no one is prepared to listen. You've seen them react, and you've seen how I was treated on the Continent. Am I wrong to expect more from the families?"

In the days after my aunt's ceremonial release, the weather turned muggy and grey, with an oily film spreading on the waters of the lake. Every little movement coated us in sweat and life in town quietened immediately; everyone seemed to want to escape inside and sit still as much as possible. We didn't get to see Bjor for a while and there were no sightings of his new companions, which set my teeth on edge. The suspicions we harboured were unsubstantiated; he was the only one who could've spoken to whether we were starting to get spooked by our own shadow.

The whole of Goldenlake felt as if the pressure was building. I noticed that I'd begun to scratch myself under the queen's bracelet whenever I needed to get rid of a burst of nervous energy. It wouldn't take long for me to eventually break the skin.

Qes was right—I wanted to flee, to spring loose from the town I'd longed to get back to so much. It was bound to happen with any place we'd travel to: me itching to reach it and desperate to leave it behind only days later, never again able to settle and rest, a wandering wizard who wasn't accepted anywhere.

At least having time with Lilyis meant more opportunities to sleep with each other, though I caught myself getting distracted several times and prayed Lilyis hadn't noticed that my thoughts drifted away from her and the pleasure she tried to provide. I couldn't help feeling guilty. When Raz asked about me being in a weird mood, I knew it was pointless to deny that something was wrong.

"Maybe it's the weather, or that I'm getting worried about Bjor, but in the last few days I've been struggling to feel sufficiently grateful that I made it back home to Birkland."

Raz handed me a summer plum. "Explain."

"I don't want to," I admitted. Especially, I didn't want to talk with someone I'd slept with once. "I feel horrible enough as it is. What about you and Qati? How is he coping with being back in Goldenlake?"

"I'm not sure. He doesn't talk about it either, though he seems to be running a lot of errands lately, as if he'd slotted back into place with ease. I'd hoped we'd be given a second chance, but I'm not so sure anymore. Wherever we're going from here I doubt he'll come with us. He said as much when we first started seeing each other. That he only wanted to get back, nothing more. I can't complain."

"What about you? It seems that Lilyis has made up her mind to travel on to Thorndell and probably further east towards the steppes. Would you lend us your longknife and your blade skill?"

"Are you sure you want me?"

"What's that supposed to mean?"

"That I don't always feel like I belong."

I knew so well what she alluded to that I rushed on, "In the steppes no one will be—apart from Werid. Though I'd never presume that you'd shake off the opportunity to return to your own family and Rawil Owl's side, you will be always welcome at mine."

"Even if Lilyis starts to blame me for your behaviour?" Raz asked, sceptically.

"What? Now I'm confused."

"She's the jealous type, and sometimes I'm not sure that she's convinced the thing between you and me lies in the past."

"I'll talk to her," I offered.

"I don't think that's going to do as much good as you imagine. Without Qati as a buffer she might well resent having me around."

"We need you, Raz."

"You'll have Cathil."

I shook my head. "Cathil Cloud might decide to piss off back home at any moment."

"You're still having trouble trusting him?" she asked.

"There's too much history between us. I'm giving him the benefit of the doubt, for Qes' sake. I'd love to have you join us again."

"I never noticed before that you can be an extremely persuasive person if you want to." The old familiar grin lit up her face. "Who knows if there isn't another Badger in Thorndell worth having a second look at? So, there's going to be Lilyis, Cathil, Qes, and Werid?"

"Eleas, if she agrees. We also have to disentangle Bjor. Lilyis will need someone with her who can pass as an official retainer of the Princess of Crooked Hill."

"You're not worried that will get her into trouble?"

I felt a nervous laugh creep up my throat. "We're already in up to our necks."

"*Deeper* into trouble, then."

"She's on a mission. Really, I'm mostly there to hold her back by the scruff of the neck in case things go bad."

"Things go bad how?"

"My father didn't have the best of reputations, and his affiliation with the Eastern Cities might well have caused a lot of anger among his relatives. The Badgers might be the closest of the most important families in the forests, but they're also stubborn and deeply suspicious. I could either be taken into the heart of the family or rejected again."

"That sounds as if your presence at her side would cause problems, not help to resolve them."

"Maybe both," I said, wincing. "But Qes still hasn't agreed to any of that and who knows what arguments he'll bring forth to avoid seeing his own mother?"

A CLEAR MESSAGE

Cathil blocked the light coming through the door. "I think we need to talk again, even if it's uncomfortable for both of us."

I looked up from the map I'd been studying after Lilyis had pushed it at me with an impatient groan. "Do you want to do this here or somewhere outside?"

"There's no one here, is there?"

I glanced around the guesthouse. "No, there's something going on at the Roundhouse, so they've left me to it."

Cathil closed the door behind him and sat down. "As I understand, visiting Qes' family was your idea?"

"Sort of, yes."

"Sort of?" Cathil made a sceptical noise. "I'm aware that Qes is worried about me meeting them, what with everything that has been going on with the Clouds lately."

"And because the Badgers have stayed true to the Moons throughout the whole mess."

He moved uncomfortably on the hard bench. "That too. Be that as it may, if I go to Thorndell, it will send a clear message to his mother and aunts. To all the leaders of the Badgers, in fact."

"I thought you wanted to marry again."

He frowned at me. "Marrying into the Badgers is a different proposition than marrying into the Moons."

"Says who? The family who cut you loose?"

"They still have some hold over me, and now that Cjanis has been brought back on course, things might change once again. What I need you to tell me is, if I propose to Qes, would you oppose it?"

"Me?" The breath caught in my chest, and I dreaded whatever he'd say next. "Why are you asking *me*?"

"Because Qes has told me everything."

"*Everything* everything?" A shudder raced down my spine.

"Yes. I need to know if you would see yourself in the position to change your mind about him anytime soon." His sigh was a low rumble. "Given the restraints you experience with Lilyis Sun, do you think you'd want to reconsider? You know I wouldn't have a chance to make things work with Qes if you did."

"I don't know what to say. You shouldn't ask me that."

"But I must."

"If you want to marry Qes, you should ask him, despite what I might feel about it."

He bit his bottom lip. "I'd hoped you would say that but couldn't quite bring myself to rely on it."

"Since when have you been considering other people's feelings? And since when have you been thinking of proposing?"

"A while. He's been working through his feelings for his ex-boyfriend. And for you."

I closed my eyes. Trust Qes to be unnecessarily honest about what we'd fought through. "Has he told you everything about Nalan na Nileon as well?"

"I think so."

"It didn't end well between them."

"Yes, I know. So you're saying …"

"I'm saying, ask him what you want to ask him, and don't be surprised if he starts to cry."

"Thank you."

"But don't hold it against him if he finds a thousand excuses why you shouldn't get engaged. He *will* try to sell himself short."

"Thank you," Cathil said again. "For not ripping my head off—now, and then." He stared at my hands. "I'm trying to stay on your good side, Sloe Moon of Tall Trees."

"Why? You, the most famous warriors of the west?" I grinned at him, but he didn't smile back.

He was weirdly twitchy. "Goldenlake might not realize what they are letting go for years. I'm not the sharpest blade on the rack, but I know when things are changing, and I recognize someone dangerous when I see them." He stood up and backed out of the house, as if he didn't want to be alone with me any longer.

Lilyis had listened to me ramble on about Qes and Cathil, her eyes getting ever wider.

"You can't tell anyone else about it!" I begged, my voice sounding shrill. "Just because I couldn't bear not to talk about it ..."

"I won't." Lilyis turned away from me towards the horizon, so unendingly flat and hazy.

The wind rippling the water was disappointingly warm, as if it had scrubbed over the sun-scorched steppes to reach us, bringing their heat into Goldenlake. All the stories I'd ever heard of the eastern steppes had been tales of warning: the steppes were Birkland's wild place, uncompromisingly hostile in summer as in winter, their people shrouded in mystery. There was new conflict to expect beyond the lake.

As Lilyis faced me again, her mouth was set in a line. "It bothers you, doesn't it? Even if we're far away from Tall Trees?"

"What bothers me?" I asked, hoping not to be called out.

"Don't play coy with me," she snapped. "That this can't be our story. The engagement, the good wishes, and ..."

"I've always known about that, so how can I complain?"

"You can still feel bad about it. You know I would divorce Fiolis if I could."

I swallowed. I'd hoped that was how she felt about our situation. "Even here divorce is not an easy process to go through. It's shameful, because it means that there is discord not only between two people but between two families, that alliances are being put in danger, or sometimes break apart completely. There's no easy solution and who knows if you're not secretly relieved about these obstacles standing in our way before your first year in Birkland is over."

"Meaning?"

"If I have trouble putting up with me, how can you be expected to?"

"Is that why you've been acting so strange lately?" She pushed her hair from her face and crossed her arms. "Because you're going into one of your self-hate spirals?"

I felt my shoulders draw up, as if my body wanted to shrink before her. "Maybe."

"It's this place, isn't it? It certainly is beautiful but—excuse my language, are all wizards such cunts?"

"Most of them."

"Was this the same reaction you had from them at the Stoneharp?"

"Pretty much. Though we certainly took more of a risk with Qerla Badger, hoping that she'd understand."

"Believe me, Sloe, this has nothing to do with you, but everything with their own fears of finding themselves demoted to insignificance."

"My head knows that but my heart …"

"Your heart needs to pull its finger out." She smiled. "There are enough people on two continents prepared to punch anyone who talks bad about you, and I'd be in the front line." She stood upon the tips of her toes to lean in and kiss me, her braid whipping around with another gust of hot wind. "The sooner we leave, the better. There's enough going on without you losing your mind over the expectations of some crusty old wizards. Eleas is someone you should listen to. She knows more about how it feels to be you than anyone else around. She should be the only one allowed to judge. Hang on—can you hear that?" She released me and spun around. "Was that a scream?"

Another piercing sound rose above the roofs of Goldenlake.

People started rushing from the shore into town. Calls echoed between the houses.

"Something is going on. Should we go and look?"

"Yes," I agreed. "We'd better."

She took my hand and pulled me with her. More and more people left their houses to check on what was happening. The central square was beginning to fill up and I pushed in front of Lilyis, to shoulder my way through the gathering crowd.

Blood had been spilled at the Roundhouse, trickling towards the staring people of Goldenlake. Something had been strung up under the circular roof of the meeting place, no, not something—*someone*.

Images flashed into my mind of mauled bodies suspended from branches, and there was a gaping throat again, cut with something blunt, its edges raw and ripped. The man wore a bag over his head, stiff and glistening with his blood, but I knew the boots the rope had been lashed around. I'd seen them many times.

Cathil ran past me, drawing his longknife as soon as he was clear of the first row of onlookers. He cut the dead man down with a single slash of the blade. He sliced the bag open, and a face appeared, made almost unrecognizable by the gag.

"No." Lilyis pushed herself off my chest.

Bjor's blond hair was clumped with blood, his features distorted. They'd covered him with clothes that weren't his own, but the boots ... he'd been beside us in those boots for a long time.

I could feel myself getting numb from top to toe as Lilyis cradled Bjor's head in her lap. I knew there was no urgency. Our friend had been dead since before we'd run back into town. The colour of his skin reminded me of the three men we'd once found hanged in the woods.

I spotted Qes, standing not far off. I made my way over to him. "We need to check if the Whiterivers men are still here," I said, my voice calm in the way I knew. The way that made me afraid of myself.

Qes was pale, his scars livid. "Yes."

The streets around the square were deserted. My breath rattled in my chest as we ran. The quarter of the Elks was empty, but the doors of its House of Men had been thrown open. The signs of hasty departure were unmistakable: a broken bowl and a shirt trampled into the floor, the embers in the brazier still hot, spatters of blood at the door, and a red handprint on the table.

He started to shake. "This is our fault. We let him do this. They knew he was put among them to wheedle out information—"

"Qes." My voice was icy. "They can't have been gone long. Let's check the boat station and ask if they are crossing over to Coldharbour or if they've left on horseback."

His dark eyes went wide, and I saw that he was close to falling into panic. "Wait. I'll check the stable first."

The men from Whiterivers had taken their horses with them.

"Fuck," Qes said. "Could they have shipped the horses over to Coldharbour?"

We heard someone else arrive: Qati Badger, red in the face and panting with exertion. "They were seen leaving town on the northern road. They didn't go all at once. Some of them went a few days ago." He pushed his palms into his knees, to prevent himself from doubling over. "Do you want us to hunt them down?"

I drew a deep breath. It felt as if I'd been encased in a thin sheet of ice, and if I moved too much it would splinter and lay me open to the pain. "Let's think about that. The council might have an opinion on this matter. You don't spill blood at the Golden Lake."

COOL OFF

Werid was visibly shaken by the events. It felt wrong to be the only one dry-eyed and steady-handed, chains of frost drawing ever closer around my heart as my friend was brought into one of the nearest houses to examine.

A whole gaggle of wizards had made their way over to get involved, all outraged, scandalized, as if Bjor had been killed in such a public way to besmirch their personal honour. Perhaps it was the only way they could understand what had happened, the damage that had been done.

"Why would they do this to one of their own?" Werid asked. "Didn't you say you suspected them to sympathize with Bjor's family?"

"We shouldn't have let him go by himself," Lilyis said, staring down at the body wrapped in a shroud of watermarked linen.

"If you had gone with him, you would both be dead," Eleas said matter-of-factly. "It is pointless to berate ourselves when we do not know why it was done to him."

"We need to wash him, prepare him," Lilyis whispered. "We need to do *something* to avenge him." She was pale and shivery. "He was an official member of the Sun, and suffered an inexcusable act of aggression."

"I doubt any one of them has heard of the Sun," Qes interrupted. "I suppose they pretended to befriend him, and he must've said something that … that betrayed him." He leant over the corpse of our friend, tugging the linen aside to study the clothes they'd put him in. We saw him frown, poking the swollen skin beneath the cloth.

"Qes!" Werid protested.

"Come here," my cousin said quietly. "Look at that."

We crowded around him. Qes had pushed Bjor's shirt and jerkin up to expose his side. There was something red sticking out. No, not sticking out, but sticking *to* him. Werid pulled the shirt off and we all gasped, taking a horrified step backwards.

Bjor's upper body, tide-marked by the sun and wind of our travels, was covered in burns. Some of them were older, some of them fresher, but all of them in the unmistakable form of a five-pointed star. As if someone had used their amulet to mark him.

"They tortured him," Lilyis hissed. "They hurt him before they killed him, in the most humiliating way possible, strung up like a pig to bleed out in front of everyone …" I heard her knuckles crack as she clenched her fists. "Who knows what they made him confess to."

"There are older rope marks around his wrists," Werid confirmed, before they checked his open neck. "And bruises as if he'd been choked."

"He was only a few streets away from us," Cathil said, sounding utterly stunned. "They must've kept him gagged the whole time.

This could've happened to me.

"Sloe?" Lilyis drew close, her face pale underneath her freckles. "Are you all right?"

I gritted my teeth. When her father's men had taken me hostage back then it could've happened at any time, and if there'd had been another man to lead them, not someone halfway decent like Olas da Ozanil, I might've lasted only a few days.

I made a horrible mistake. I underestimated them.

"These were men from Whiterivers," Lilyis interrupted my thoughts. "Not our own."

Uncomfortable glances were exchanged between us of the families.

"Many won't see a difference," Werid said. "Your compatriots don't tend to distinguish between us either. What worries me is that we don't have much to go on regarding motivation. Did they kill him because he associated himself with the families? Because he was with Lilyis? Or did it have no meaning at all, merely misplaced bloodlust?"

"They branded him with stars. I'm pretty clear on their motivation," Qes gritted out. "I've lived among them and experienced their zeal, though Sloe might speak more to the general character of Whiterivers people."

"The people we met there certainly upheld more rigid ideas about their faith," I confirmed.

"If they wanted to burn the Siblings out of him," Raz said, her voice thick, "and they treat one of their own like this, what would they do to someone like me? Or Eleas? How can we allow them to live?"

Werid breathed in deeply. "We don't know for sure that this was what they were trying to do. Though the argument is convincing."

"They left someone covered in star-marks in front of a Roundhouse filled with wizards," Qes scoffed. "They must've known that Bjor was employed by the families to spy on them and their priests."

Eleas tilted her head. "Which makes the fact that they have taken advantage of the freedom to reside in Goldenlake all the more horrible. We will not find a solution to satisfy all of us. Werid is right, we should wait for the council to comment. It does not make much sense to try and catch up with them."

"Could they have tried to poison the well?" Lilyis asked.

Eleas frowned. "What do you mean?"

"Try to burn all bridges behind them so there won't be any others from the Eastern Cities allowed to stay with the same trading privileges."

"You might overestimate the amount of planning that went into this gesture," Cathil mused.

"I'd rather over- than underestimate them, even if it throws out some of my other theories." She clenched her fists again. "I hate that no one of us was close enough to help him. This should never have come to pass. It can never happen again."

Werid crossed their arms. "It *will* happen again—in some way or another. We're all in shock." They reached out and touched Bjor's pale shoulder. "Cover him up, Qes. We need to make sure he reaches the land of the dead with all honours we can bestow on him."

Qerla Badger was furious, which took at least two decades off her.

"The gods have been insulted," she fumed.

Oil lights were grouped around the body that had been cleaned and checked for other traces of mistreatment. I'd personally combed Bjor's hair and plaited it with golden wire, trying hard not to break as I prepared him for the land of the dead. He'd been clothed in tunics and woollen trousers like the families. We all claimed him after his death.

Werid and Eleas stood with the first wizard of Goldenlake; on the square a group of apprentices held torches dipped in birch tar, their faces carefully blank. Everything depended on Qerla's decisions.

"All men of the Cities residing in Goldenlake will be rounded up and questioned," she said, pointing her staff out into the darkness. "We will start to patrol the road in case more of them seek to hide themselves away."

Werid scratched at their temple. "Is that truly what you want? To start restricting access based on where someone was born?"

"Do you have a better idea?" Qerla snapped at my master. "At least they are easy to spot." She glared at Lilyis.

"He was my friend!" Lilyis drew herself up, preparing to attack.

The wizard's staff lowered to her throat. "You are fortunate that you have enough people vouching for you, and though the victim wasn't a man of the families, the intent cannot be misunderstood—to burn their faith into us all!"

"Wait, wait, wait." Werid slowly shook their head. "Your solution is to build a fence around the town?"

"As we should have done a long time ago. A few months back, Sloe Moon was taken from Goldenlake to meet a fate that could easily have been as bloody. The Eastern Cities refuse to take us seriously, and it is time to retaliate."

"Qerla, what would Sjunil have advised?" Werid asked.

"You heard her speak at the council when she was here last. She asked us to unite against the Cities—even then."

The temperature in the house seemed to drop. "I don't think she meant for us to lose our heads," my master said. "This man won't be the last to horrifically die if we can't begin to think straight."

Qerla snarled, "What do you suggest?"

"It might be a good idea to find out who is here now, but to do so in a measured, rational way. In the light of day. By all means, post guards in case more people try to flee, but don't pull the whole of Goldenlake from their beds."

Disappointment showed in Qerla's lined face, as if she'd often longed for an excuse to call the wrath of the Siblings down onto her town.

"You want us to act with restraint when they have dared to humiliate us?"

"They believe us to be savage people. I merely wish for us to subvert their expectations."

"To play by their rules?"

"No, to ensure that we play by ours. These are our lands, and we have the strength to slap them from their high horse whenever we wish to do so. Let's behave like the ones who don't need to stoop to their level, Qerla. I want nothing more than to gut the men responsible with my teeth, but I would advise letting things cool off first." Their gaze shifted from the first wizard of Goldenlake to me and for the first time since we'd discovered Bjor, I felt my heart lift. "We are much stronger than they imagine."

Qerla's eyes went wide, the blue and the brown, a mirror of my own, connecting me to her, to all the Badger wizards that had come before us. "What do you want to do, Werid?"

"I want to put the fear of the Tall Gods into them." My master signalled to me. "We have the means to stake our claim."

"That sounds like another dangerous idea."

Werid of the Far Side smiled their most beatific smile. "Ask the apprentices to prepare to search the town in the morning, calmly and without frightening the families who have come for the festivals. We need a pyre, higher than the ones for Shortest Night. I want him to reach the land of the dead as a hero, worthy of the legends."

KEEPING SCORE

"You haven't cried yet," Lilyis noted.

"I know it's weird."

Lilyis glanced up to the tip of the firewood heap, where the bier had been leashed fast to a sturdy frame of oak that would take eternities to burn down and cast a light across the waters for hours.

"To be honest, I expected you to break down."

"Oh, I will—at some point." Even as I said it, my voice sounded utterly strange to my ears. "Usually when I hit my elbow against the door or after something similarly ludicrous. That happens to me sometimes. I always thought it was Sister Stone's influence and maybe it is. She wants to protect me from myself. We have somewhere to go. I can't collapse."

"I wonder whether the others know how to take it, or if they wonder if you actually liked him."

"Bjor and I went through a lot before we became friends. Qes knows that very well."

Lilyis pulled a grimace but opted to not question me further.

The atmosphere was appropriately sombre. No doubt there'd been music and celebratory songs when the Shortest Night bonfires were lit merely a month before. Over the last two days, all houses in Goldenlake had been inspected and a few Elks interrogated. It transpired that Lilyis was indeed the only person of the Cities left in town. The people gathered in the square to attend the funeral squinted at her with suspicion, despite being in her Cormorant colours and surrounded by her friends of the families. Things in Goldenlake had changed overnight.

Questionable activities were suspected around every corner; there were fewer children around as before, as if they'd been told to stay indoors or at least in their own quarters. No Elks were to be seen. Even with their notable confusion about how the guests had behaved before their untimely departure, no one believed the Elks not to have noticed that someone had been tortured beneath the roof of their own House of Men. Though few had so much as seen Bjor da Relian before he'd been killed, every inhabitant of Goldenlake had an opinion on what had happened to him and didn't hesitate to proclaim it loudly. Our company found itself at the mercy of the whole town.

I saw Qes huddling into Cathil's side. Werid and Eleas were somewhere with the wizards, while all others waited for the ceremony to start. I noticed that Raz and Qati stood next to each other, not touching, but close enough to seem friendlier.

"This needs to be the last funeral for a while," Lilyis said. "With Qati staying behind, we'll be a sorry lot if we continue to lose companions at this rate."

"Seven is a good number," Cathil said, before he kissed the top of Qes' curls.

My friends were close to utter exhaustion. With the temperatures of high summer upon us, all preparations for the ceremony had to be made as quickly as possible and so we'd spent a lot of time running around. Whenever I drifted off to sleep at night, I saw the dead men lined up on the branches, under the rafters, their distorted faces, mauled throats … I'd merely slept a few hours since we'd found him, my head desperately trying to make sense of why it had happened. If it had been a signal of some kind, or a cruel joke.

Bjor's body had been bound with colourful ribbons. Bunches of wildflowers had been laid at the bottom of the pyre, left by members of the families who hadn't known him but wanted to pay their respect.

A hush fell over the square as the apprentices left the Roundhouse in formation.

"This is so fucked up," Qati said, and we all turned to him. His eye was hard as flint. "Last week they had no idea who he was, and they're acting as if he served them."

"They think he died for the gods," Raz said disapprovingly. "Let them have it. Shut up and watch."

The prayers rang out across the square. Seeing how the whole of Goldenlake came together to mourn Bjor da Relian made my stomach burn. The feeling that my world had gone madly out of kilter joined the sense of being trapped. When Lilyis started to cry as silently as she possibly could, I berated myself for feeling numb. Of all my friends, Bjor had been closest to me. I'd been with him in Blackfields and Eastbay, with Arif … my nails bit deep into my palms as I balled my fists. Arif, whom I also lost.

Brother Brook's smell reached me before he did.

"It shouldn't have happened."

"It still did." For once, Brother Brook's green eyes held a spark of pity. He sat on one of the boulders close to the heap of broken boats that had been placed there to be repaired during winter. His hands folded into each other, his elbows pushed into his knees in a rather human pose. "It will make him more important."

"More important?"

My voice sounded cold, but something started to crumble within me.

"He was given up by his family. He could have been a useful member of your girlfriend's company but hardly anything more."

"You don't think that would have been enough?" I asked angrily.

"If I've learned anything about you all, it's that you always want more, even if it's downright *impractical.*" He made a face as his head turned. "There he is. Brother mine!"

Someone else walked over the pebbles, meandering between the land and the water—not drunk, but looking lost in thought. The luminous eyes of Brother Moon alighted upon his Sibling and me. "I've always loved this place." His smile transformed the broad face. "Is there any way I can help?"

I turned to Brother Brook and he shrugged his shoulders.

"Where are they now, the men from Whiterivers?" I asked. "Are they heading eastwards or are they trying to reach the coast?"

Brother Moon winced. "You don't think that's cheating?"

"In what way? I'm using all methods at my disposal. They'll do the same. It's not my fault if they can't talk to their own gods, is it?"

"They're sending a shipment of syrup and tar towards the coast but the men who killed your friend are trying to go around the lake. It will take them a good while. They have split up into several groups."

"Why did they kill him?"

"I'm sorry, Sloe, but I don't know. These men don't belong to me. They don't speak to me." Brother Moon leant forwards and I thought he'd touch my shoulder. Seeing his Sibling's glare, he pulled back. "He's not the only one who will die when you fight them."

"I understand that," I said. *Do I? I will cause more pain to more people.* "I do think that Werid is right, and that we need to be cleverer than what they give us credit for. I don't want to drag Lilyis further to the east and find out that they turned towards the Stoneharp after all. Can you see the ship with red sails?"

Sadness swept over Brother Moon's large face. "I can, but I can't be sure it's the ship you're searching for. I must ask you to keep this information to yourself."

"Why?"

"Because there are limits to how much I wish to intervene."

Brother Brook snorted. "Since when? You've never let a good opportunity go by to play a trick on your kin. You've always swooped in to pick up the leftovers. Sloe's father being a case in point."

Both Brothers crossed their arms.

"You weren't good for him," Brother Moon said sternly, "and you knew that. He was about to break and to be lost to us. This is an old quarrel and not the place to warm it up."

"It's the perfect place, though it might not be the most opportune time."

"What about the ship?" I interjected.

Both Siblings narrowed their eyes at me. "There's a fine line between being assertive and being cocky," Brother Brook said.

"Point taken."

Brother Moon moved his broad shoulders as if in a shudder. "There's a ship with red sails lying beached in Slatelight."

"Slatelight?" I fumbled in my tunic and pulled out Lilyis' map. "Whereabout is this?"

Another one of the warning glances shot between my Siblings, but Brother Moon's forefinger pointed to a squiggle in the roughly sketched line of Birkland's east coast, far below the dot Lilyis had painted in to signify Steepbay. "On the other side of the mountains."

"Fuck. This was what we were afraid of. I should've asked for your help much, much earlier."

"It wouldn't have made the path you're on easier. Remember that you left your own ship a long way over in the west, and if I know anything about people, it's that they don't like to stay put."

"Why can't I tell the others?"

Brother Brook rolled his green eyes. "Because none of you can afford to try and use us as glorified messenger boys. These are large debts to incur."

"You're keeping score?" I asked, surprised.

"Of course," he said with a derisive snort. "Who do you think we are?"

We left Goldenlake two days later, riding out of town towards the northern forest and in the same direction the Whiterivers men had gone to circumnavigate the waters. Raz had kissed Qati as we left him behind, saddled with the task of keeping his eye on the wizards around him. We'd actually clasped arms before I climbed into Cirvi's saddle, nodding at him, before Qes moved in for a bear hug.

"I'll see you soon," he'd promised his cousin, kissing his cheek.

I'd seen the doubt in Qati's eye and unease in the way he'd held himself. He was probably the one who'd best learned to read the atmosphere in town, and if he was worried, we might as well be.

When we reached the curve in the road where the last dwellings had been built, we saw the guards with their spears standing in the shade under the roofs, watching us.

To our right lay the expanse of waters, where Bjor's ashes mingled with my aunt's and many others the wizards had deemed worthy of entering the land of the dead from the holy shores.

THE WORST POSSIBLE MOMENT

I didn't expect Thorndell to be as close to the lake as it was. We only spent one night out in the open; all the while, I could see Cathil getting more and more jittery. Without Qati and Bjor, our company fell into new groupings: Qes and Cathil leading us onwards, Lilyis and Raz chatting behind them and the two wizards bringing up the rear. I had the impression that they'd surrounded me, that I was the one the company closed their ranks around. It was an unexpectedly lonely feeling to have, and I didn't dare to call on my Siblings after the talk of debts and scores I'd been subjected to.

Temperatures were less oppressive under the canopy of ancient trees lining our path and shadowing the campsite. Exchanging the openness of the lakeside with the closedness of the woods felt like a relief in some ways, but my gaze kept returning to Cathil's broad back. I waited for the best opportunity to finally speak up. I managed to catch him on the morning before our arrival.

He was finishing the last watch of the day and I urgently needed to pee. After relieving myself as quietly as possible, I returned to the fire and the teapot coming up to the boil.

Cathil's face fell into a wary expression. "Don't you dare pressure me."

"You want to wait for the situation to explode around you?"

"He lost another friend, mere days ago."

"He'll need some good news."

"I don't want him to say 'yes' because he needs to make himself feel happy. I thought you of all people would understand." He pulled five generous pinches of tea leaves from the bag and stirred them swiftly into our well-used pot. The smell rising from it was wonderful, rich and earthy, and my tongue attached itself to the roof of my mouth, impatient to taste the first bowl of the day.

"It won't be easy for him," I prophesied.

"You act as if I don't know. Can I advise you to keep your big nose out of my business and focus on your own? Lately, your girlfriend seems to find more to talk about with Raz than with you. I thought I'd have to strangle both of them at one point. They wouldn't shut up."

"Lilyis needs to be distracted, and Raz is exceptionally good at that."

"Don't be stupid, Sloe. Now that Qati has left her, she needs another person to give her attention to."

"Fuck off, Cathil," I barked, "and pour out the tea already!"

Qes' home village was an old place, moulded into its surroundings. The houses had been built into wooded hillsides, with only doors and two windows on their fronts. Trees grew out of their roofs or the walls had been built around older oaks, making use of their gnarled roots to give shape to the dwellings, thatched with compacted bracken and interlocking branches. The Roundhouse took up an entire hill, had various entrances and bore a thicket of brambles on its roof, clustered with green fruit and the last pale-pink flowers.

"Amazing," I heard Raz say and Qes blushed. "Like a whole town underground. Are all settlements of the Badgers like this?"

"Just the oldest ones," my cousin said. "There have been Badgers in this area for thousands and thousands of summers. Some of us believe that we are the oldest family in the forests and all others branched off from us. If you ask me, that's probably too convenient, but it gives my mother a certain authority around here."

"Your mother rules this part of the woods?" Lilyis asked.

"No, technically her sister does. But my mother has always been her closest advisor, with strong opinions and so involved that most of us consider it a joint reign. Are you ready to meet the rest of your family, Sloe?"

"No, so let's get it over with."

Riding into Thorndell, a thousand reasons why bringing Nivael's daughter into a town entrenched in the old ways of the families was probably one of the worst ideas I'd ever had popped into my mind, and that the talk we never had with my own mother in Tall Trees was to be staged under less favourable circumstances. I knew no one apart from Qes. Our so-called family would judge me for the one man they could connect me to, and knowing my father, he'd probably managed to enrage most of his relatives in some way or other.

"It must've been wonderful to grow up here," Raz said. "All these places to hide ..."

"Yeah. It was truly magical," Qes said drily. "Apart from constantly being under the thumb of a whole herd of sisters destined to get involved in the leadership. Real fucking treat."

Qes had never spoken much about his childhood, though I'd always had the impression he shared my situation—not fitting in but being too high of rank to simply fade into the background.

"It's going to be fine," Cathil said. "If it doesn't work, we haven't lost much."

"Easy for you to say." Lilyis reined in her grey mare and waited for our two wizards to join us before we dismounted in front of the Roundhouse. "Where is everyone?"

"They must know we're here. They'd never let us get so far without keeping a close eye on our progress ..." Qes turned around, a deep frown etched into his brow. "Maybe they are busy with a celebration, or ..."

"The Roundhouse appears to be empty," Eleas remarked after peeking into one of its windows. "Though embers are glowing in the braziers, as if they'd come together a little while ago."

"Let's go down to the ponds," Qes said to me. "Raz and Cathil, would you mind staying with the horses?" He turned to Lilyis. "You too? I think Mother wouldn't appreciate me bursting into one of the ceremonies with a whole entourage of strangers."

"We'll all stay here," Werid confirmed. "But take Sloe."

"What's going on?" I asked him quietly as we walked away from the rest of the company.

My cousin was pale and sweaty. "There are few occasions when every single inhabitant of Thorndell is required to attend, but if this is what I think it is, things will get more complicated than expected."

"Now you're scaring me." I grabbed his elbow. "Qes, talk to me."

During the time I'd known my best friend, he'd never been so clammy and close to panic. "The presence of the whole family is essential for two things. Swearing a member of the family into government—and for a ritual drowning."

"Wait, what?" I shuddered. "You think they've all gone to the ponds to watch an execution?"

"I told you my family likes to do things the old way. Thorndell may look quaint but … Sloe, it might be time for you to understand that your father had good reasons to leave his family behind and build himself another life. You've grown up among progressive people, but Brother Brook has always had a much more fearsome face this deep in the woods."

"You can't be serious."

"Come, let's hope that I'm all kinds of wrong here."

We heard the sound of the drums wafting towards us.

"Fuck." Qes pulled me with him, and we started to run up the next ridge, then down, pushing through the trees, thin branches ripping our clothes and whipping our faces, until we were right above the ponds of Thorndell, where the closest river had been dammed and formed into a series of oblong pools. The crowd gathered below spilled around the edges of the ponds, wearing striped cloaks and shawls in all available colours; everyone was dressed in their finery, and amidst the throng of Badgers we saw a cage balancing above the dark water, a huddled shape inside.

Wizards lined the banks, with staffs and badger pelts wrapped around their shoulders, their faces painted to continue the stripes of the family emblem. The drums were played by five women in sleeveless vests. We'd arrived in the middle of a highly regulated procedure.

"Is he already dead or about to die?" I asked.

The man in the cage lifted his head and began to scrabble about, as if he'd woken from a drug-induced sleep. We were too far away to see his face, but again, his priestly footwear was unmistakable.

"How the fuck …"

Qes started to sprint down the hill, spraying dead leaves and clumps of dark earth behind him. "No no no no no no no no …"

I slipped on the root of a beech as I tried to follow him, threw my arms backwards to regain my balance and fell on my arse, skating down the steep slope in the most undignified way, my tunic riding up and leaves getting pushed in, scratching against my naked back.

The Badgers at the bottom stepped back as I landed among them with a squeal, while Qes shoved through his extended family to reach the wizards at the pond. I groaned, hauled myself up with bleeding palms, and shook the debris out of my clothes. My arms were covered in dirt, my arse was wet and somehow, I'd managed to bump one of my knees. I felt all eyes on me as I limped along. As first impressions went, it couldn't have gone more wrong.

I heard Qes scream at someone, his voice breaking under the strain. The woman he yelled at resembled him and my half-brother in Seagard so much that it felt like stepping into a dream. All of the wizards wore the tear-drop tattoo, scrunched up in outrage as they clustered around him. The wizards who'd come together to kill a priest of the Star had my eyes and the mark. Becoming aware of my presence, all six of them suddenly looked up at me.

The two-coloured eyes had been less pronounced in my father, but the wizards were truly like me. For the first time I understood why so many people reacted to me the way they did. Broad-shouldered and square-faced, every one of those wizards could surely punch my nose in without breaking a sweat. Five of them had blue-black hair like Qes, but one of them a shaggy brown mop, like my own. I'd arrived with the people I'd always wanted to find—at the worst possible moment.

BLOOD AND TEARS

The wizard who pushed herself forward was powerfully fat, her black and grey hair braided into thick plaits. I knew who she was: Qes' auntie Qay, whose eyes were the other way around, with the left one blue and the right one brown. The blue was as bright as a kingfisher's plumage, her gaze as unsettling as any I'd ever experienced.

"They attacked Tanglebriar a week ago." She poked the butt of her staff between the branches that had been steamed and woven into place in the manner of a gigantic eel trap. The man in the brown cloak and sandals flinched away, as if he'd come to expect pain to follow her touch. "Are we to keep still and play dead like a frightened cub?"

Angry murmurs arose.

"There's a great difference between playing dead and drowning someone in the ponds!" Qes panted, facing the formidable wizard bedecked in silver amulets in front of him. "There must be an appropriate reaction, but you proceed straight to killing him?"

"Qes." An older woman standing behind the wizard cleared her throat. "When did you come back?"

He pulled up his shoulders. "Just now, Mother."

She frowned. "You didn't think to write? The last thing we heard was that you followed a mad Moon to the west and then nothing, not a breath to inform us of what was going on. You made your point, but you can't expect to barge into a holy ritual and disrupt the sacred—"

"Seriously?" His voice cracked again.

"Get the cage moving," his mother said, turning away from us.

"Sister, wait." Qay Badger scowled. "The ceremony has already been stopped. Let's hear him out."

"Have you tried to talk to him?" her nephew asked.

"He doesn't have our words," one of the other wizards spat.

"And you're sure he was part of the raiding party that attacked Tanglebriar? You saw him there?"

"Yes, we saw him there. Stop wasting everyone's time, Qes."

"Can I talk to him, Mother?"

A shocked silence spread over the Badgers.

"What? Why?"

"To find out why our villages are targeted by the men of the Eastern Cities after decades of peaceful trading."

Qay smiled and jabbed at the prisoner again. "We always knew that it wouldn't last long. Plenty of people warned of them turning against the families for eternities and now everyone is pretending to be surprised. How do you come to know the words, Qes?"

My cousin shot me a desperate glance and I came to the rescue. "Because I'm the mad Moon he followed west. And east, crossing the seas." All wizards but Qay made a hasty protective gesture. "We both learned to converse with the people of the Eastern Cities, so we might be able to get a few valuable answers out of him."

"You are Sloe Moon," Qay boomed with derision. "Qarim's cursed child."

"Hang on."

"No wonder they called you mad. You look like him, only more so."

"Does that even make sense?" I muttered.

Qes' aunt was getting into full flow. "Who gave you permission to raise a voice among the Badgers, someone we have never seen before? I warned Qes against associating himself with you before he left us and should've known that he wasn't strong enough to avoid being tempted."

Qes blushed violently. His first words to me had once been: *They told me to watch out for you.* I'd always interpreted it as someone telling him to find me, not to warn him away …

"Is that true?" I asked him, not able to hide my anger.

"I wanted to make up my own mind."

His mother squared her shoulders under the wealth of amber necklaces she'd donned to attend the execution of the priest. "Qay did what I'd asked her to do. My uncle has always had the reputation of being a few leaves short of a branch, so no one here was surprised in the slightest when he died in as much shame as he did." Qes shot me another pleading glance, beseeching me to keep my mouth shut. "I suppose every family needs the one crazy uncle. For a while, we still hoped for him to make a passable wizard."

Qay snorted, but her sister continued, "Don't expect to be treated like more than the spawn of a disgraced man around here."

I felt myself smile, though I hadn't planned on doing so. The blue stone bracelet adjusted itself on my wrist. I gave it a little shake and Qes' eyes went wide.

"No! This will end in tears, Sloe—*blood* and tears. Can we continue the unpleasantries later, Mother?" He sank into a crouch in front of the cage, pushing his aunt's staff aside. As he spoke the first words of greeting, the priest flinched again, but he lifted his head. His face was encrusted with old blood, his mouth swollen. He had quite a few teeth missing.

Qes repeated the words, reaching out for him. The man hissed and scrambled back as far as the wooden cage allowed. I heard what he'd said to Qes, but I also saw what he wore under the brown cloak: a tunic of red, the bull's head emblem embroidered over the heart.

"You have no right to do that!" Wails of protest went up around us.

"I have a voice in this town." I'd never seen Qes so angry. Every single curl vibrated, his scars stood out in dark-red lines. "It's of the utmost importance that we find a way to retrieve the information from him—just think for *once*, for fuck's sake!"

Some of the surrounding Badgers started to jostle against the wizards, but Qay lifted her staff above the throng and the pressure started to subside.

"We will have silence at the water," she said, and I felt the hairs on my neck lifting. Qay Badger was unquestionably the first wizard of Thorndell. Her sister hesitated before she took her son by the elbow.

"This will have consequences, Qes. You are not a little boy anymore. You can't charm your way out of every mistake you make."

"I'm well aware, Mother." He stood a full head taller than her and half a head than Qay, but I could sense his fear. He was able to square up to the Badgers he'd grown up with because our travels had changed him. "I'm claiming the prisoner for interrogation."

Qay made a disapproving noise. "You truly wish to risk that much for one of them?"

Qes studied the man in the cage. Under the hood of his cloak and the blood his hair was blond like Bjor's had been, and though he must've been clean-shaven when the Badgers caught him, he had the patchy beginnings of a reddish beard.

"He won't thank you," Qay prophesied. "He will stab you in the neck as soon as he has the chance."

"At which point you're welcome to stick him back into the cage," her nephew replied softly. "This is bigger than Tanglebriar."

"Yes, that's what we're trying to tell you," his mother said. "An example must be set."

"Can't you do that *after* he's betrayed his people?"

The two most powerful women of Thorndale exchanged a glance, before Qes' aunt gave an annoyed snort. "You have two nights to make him talk. That would be a more auspicious day for an execution anyway."

Unsurprisingly, we found our company surrounded and kneeling among the horses, the blades of Badger warriors at their throats.

"What's going on, Qes?" Cathil's hands were folded around the back of his head while Lilyis did her best to shrink into her felted hood.

"That depends. It may be a stroke of luck, or the start of a total disaster." Qes turned to his aunt. "Tell them to release my friends."

I walked behind the man who'd been freed from the cage, holding on to his bound wrists. No one trusted me enough to take their eyes off Qarim's cursed spawn. Drawn longknives bristled behind my back.

Qay gave a signal and our company was permitted to push themselves back to their feet.

Raz dusted off her knees with a smirk. "Not quite the welcome you expected, Qes?"

"On the contrary, it was all I feared it to be. Don't worry, we'll take care of it." He turned around to me and the Badgers stepped away from the priest. I saw Lilyis' mouth set into an expression of triumph deep in the shadow of her hood; a sight that made me shiver with an onrush of anticipation.

"Bring him in here." Qes pointed to the low door of the Roundhouse, and I bundled the priest in. "It's better if we do this bit where no one is watching."

Qay couldn't be brushed off that easily. She studied the various members of our company. Werid didn't wear the mark as Eleas did, but the resentful entitlement oozing off them was unmistakable.

"You must excuse our eager warriors, but in times like these you can't be too careful with strangers coming into town without any warning whatsoever." She made a beckoning gesture, and our two wizards adjusted their cloaks painfully slow, before following the invitation into the Roundhouse.

The embers were still glowing, the smell the same, but we were ushered beneath the trees at the edge of the central mound, some of the exposed roots blackened with the fragrant smoke from the braziers, the ceiling much higher above our heads as we walked deeper into the assembly space of the Badgers. Half the crowd who'd been waiting to see the execution earlier was stationed in front of the door—all armed, all disappointed.

Qay Badger pulled the door closed after then and flung her staff to the ground. "Cut the crap, Qes—who are your friends and what the fuck do you think you're doing?"

"If I may." Werid steepled their fingers and the smile on their face had something of the predator about it. "It's a complicated situation but one that I am happy to explain." I saw something flash in my master's eyes, something I hadn't expected to see again: Werid of the Far Side had spent the last months cooped up with Sjunil Moon; it made sense that some of my aunt's mannerisms would've rubbed off on them. It gave me a jolt, simultaneously of joy and ice-cold dread.

TALK TO YOU

"You actually thought bringing a princess of the Eastern Cities to Thorndell would be a good idea?" Qay Badger scoffed at her nephew. "I can't remember your mother dropping you on your head when you were small."

Qes squirmed. "Which is why we need to know more about the men who attacked Tanglebriar. In this matter, the Company of the Sun stands with the families."

"Badgers are not usually known for being gullible," the first wizard of Thorndell sneered. "You seem determined to work against your family attributes to spite your mother."

"Hey," Werid said gently. "It's not his fault. In fact, it's none of our fault. Sometimes the gods follow their own plans. We should thank them that they have brought Qes home in time to prevent a horrible mistake from being made." They turned to the prisoner who'd slumped back into a dirty heap on the floor, apparently not aware that one of his captors was of the Cities.

"The only chance to shed light on the whole mess is to obtain more knowledge from him. We need to get a better idea of what we're up against if the Bulls have already reached the central woodlands."

"Listen to you. Suns and Bulls and so much outlandish gibberish. How can you care—a wizard of some renown?"

Werid crossed their arms. Every trace of my aunt's grin was wiped off their face. "Because Qes was right. This is bigger, and much more dangerous than any of us know yet. It isn't just a matter of the Badgers taking revenge into their own hands. This is something we need to consider carefully, to be of service to all the families that might fall victim to the greed of the Cities. And you were right as well. None of us should be surprised that they have started to take with force what we won't offer for free. We have long known them to follow a different set of rules, a different faith that allows them to dismiss us as worthless to the gods of the Star. I'm not saying they shouldn't be stopped."

"It sounds like you're expressing exactly that," the Badger wizard said flatly.

"I'm saying that as much as we don't want them to make no distinction between our families, we need to afford them the same courtesy. Within reason."

"Your princess can be arsed to respect the way of the families?" the wizard asked, sarcasm tainting her rich voice.

"As much as anyone of the Cities can be. Her family has tried to stay on our good side. Most of the time."

"That means nothing to the Badgers, and a Wolf signing their name to this … venture won't surprise anyone much. Forgive me, but your family never had the best of reputations, and no one was shocked that you yourself prefer to be known as Werid of the Far Side, instead of Werid Wolf."

My master flushed, rather unbecomingly.

Eleas cleared her throat. "You cannot dismiss the fact that there is also a Cormorant here, and an Owl and …" Her gaze found Cathil, and he gave a small nod. "And a Cloud."

Qay's face froze, before she hissed, "You brought a Cloud to Thorndell?" She narrowed her striking eyes at Cathil. "Can it be true? He doesn't look like a Cloud."

"Hair can grow, and alliances can shift. We all wear different colours sometimes." Eleas drew herself up. She was much taller than Qay but must've weighed half as much, if that.

"My sister will not like it," Qay said. "Though I agree. If so many different families can be persuaded to vouch for this princess of yours, I can at least assume that my nephew was not easily duped into believing the false promises of a stranger. Though the question remains, why did you bring her here?"

Qes breathed in deeply. "For Mother to meet her and grant her if not support, then the promise of abstaining from aggression towards her."

The wizard turned slowly towards the collapsed priest. "Giving her access to this man would count as support?"

Lilyis cleared her throat and pushed back her hood. "Yes. It doesn't require much to help me on my way, and as soon as I'm finished you'll be welcome to him, if your gods require him to die." Her accent had never sounded more charming to me, but her words made my heart shiver.

"Oh good." Qay laid her palms together. "How nice that we can speak directly to each other, without my nephew translating and twisting our words."

I'd noticed that the priest had moved slightly, trying to sneak a peek at Lilyis without being observed. Perhaps he'd recognized her voice, or noted the different intonation in it. I shuffled closer to him, in case he'd dared to try anything stupid and planted my foot firmly on the hem of his soiled cloak.

"Have at him," Qay said to Lilyis.

Our friends stood in a half-circle around us, the three wizards clustered at the side.

Lilyis pushed up her sleeves. "Fine. Let's begin." She crouched down in front of him, though keeping a sensible distance.

"You landed on the east coast," she said in the words of the Cities. "To be fair, I didn't expect that. Were you blown off course as we were?" She sounded friendly.

A tremor ran through the man's body, but he was determined to remain face-down in front of her.

Lilyis grimaced. "Please pull him up for me, Cathil."

Qes' boyfriend grabbed the priest by the shoulders. The man gave a *whoop* of surprise as he was put onto his feet.

"Thank you." Lilyis switched words once more. "You will do me the courtesy of looking at me," she said softly. "We are the only two people of the Cities here and I do so enjoy conversing in my own language for once."

The priest stared at her, scraping together his remaining defiance, his swollen mouth pulled into a sneer. "I should imagine someone as degenerate as you would feel quite at home among the savages, Nian da Nileon."

Qes groaned and I felt my heart skip a beat.

"Someone as … degenerate as me?" Lilyis repeated.

"You might not be aware of it but the whole of Southclere is familiar with your reputation, with the shame you have brought upon your family with your escapades."

When I saw Lilyis' mouth set into a line she seemed so much like her father that I was starting to feel nervous about what she could be provoked to do. "Escapades?"

"The gambling and the whoring," the priest blathered. "The wasteful manners of a spoiled prince."

Werid leant towards me. "What is he saying? He seems very passionate all of a sudden."

"I'll fill you in later," I promised, my foot still on the priest's cloak.

"Not all sins on this list I can put my name to," Lilyis replied. "But I suppose that's always the case with rumours. People enjoy blowing things out of proportion, that is half the fun. Why did the Bulls need priests to join their expedition?"

The prisoner blinked. "You didn't take any members of the Star with you to the west?"

Lilyis ignored the question. "Were you the only one? You look enough like a da Relian and I've heard that some of the more distant cousins were pawned off to the temple in Applebeck."

"I was not pawned off!"

Lilyis smiled at him. "Right. So the Red House didn't pay their debts for five years of wines and spirits in flesh? Is that another one of those pesky rumours?"

The priest gasped.

"I thought so. Seeing as we find ourselves in a similar situation, I hope we can help each other out."

The priest bit deep into his bottom lip.

"You won't mind me saying that you have the look of someone who is in a smidge of a pickle. If my friends hadn't intervened on your behalf, you'd be feeding the creatures of the woods by now. Or be displayed somewhere in the village for all to gawp at. I suppose there are ghastlier deaths than to be drowned in a cage, but not many come to mind."

"I am more than willing to lay down my life for the Star."

"Which does you credit, I'm sure. Though there was no one there to see it and to spread your story among our people. It would've been a somewhat pointless death."

"The gods will know ..." Doubt had started to creep into his voice.

"I might not always have been the most observant member of the Star, but I never had the impression that our gods bothered much with details. What good does it do for them to lose a believer, after all? You'd think they're all about numbers." She turned to Cathil. "He's starting to slouch. Can you make sure he stands up straight, please?"

Cathil pulled the priest's shoulders back, reminding him in no uncertain terms of who he was at the mercy of, and that the conversation could easily be abandoned in favour of a more *physical* interaction. I'd never seen Lilyis play that game before. She'd been watching her Father and her uncle Nurin all her life, men ruthless in their own ways, men who enjoyed the dance.

"I'm offering you something here," she said. "A way to prevent bloodshed on all sides. Let us start again. You landed on the east coast?"

The priest's shoulders slumped; Cathil pulled him back up.

"The Cities have traded with Birkland families for centuries. Why are you torching villages all of a sudden? You must know how much damage that will cause for existing relations. Unless the Bulls do not concern themselves with future profits, only with what you can grab on this voyage? I would have imagined that the da Relians have so much as glanced at a map before setting sail. This continent is vast, and by now you must have realized that its families are highly organized and very skilled in blades craft and tactics of trade. I can only assume that things went wrong for the Bulls early on and that they resigned themselves to brutality from then onwards, though as a member of the Applebeck temple I must also expect you to be familiar with the Book of the Star and its teachings. There are many passages within its pages that ask us to be if not kind, at least polite to each other."

"Shut up!" the priest wailed, crumbling under the onslaught of Lilyis' words. He tried to cover his ears, but Cathil wrenched down his elbows. "Please. Just … shut up."

"Hmhm," the Princess of Crooked Hill murmured. "Be assured—I really could talk to you all day."

TOO MUCH LIKE HIM

"What did she say to make him break down like that?" Werid asked.

"Nothing specific. She talked at him. You were there."

Eleas crossed her arms and leant closer to me. "What has she found out?"

"There were three priests with the Bulls. One fell overboard during the crossing, one was killed at Tanglebriar, which leaves him. Apparently, one of the eastern families took issue with the Bulls holding a ceremony of the Star and a few Bulls died in the ensuing fight. Since then they've moved westwards, preying on farmsteads and travellers, trying to steal enough riches to warrant the costs for the expedition. I don't think the Suns need to fear being outdone concerning the cargo they bring back east, but the slash-and-burn approach will obviously spoil things for everyone who comes here next year and ever after."

"If the Suns want to establish a permanent trading post at the Stoneharp, it could do irreparable damage," Eleas concluded. "Was she able to find a link to the Whiterivers men?"

"Give her a bit more time," Qes said sourly. "I've never seen anyone do so much without drawing the smallest blade."

Qay Badger pulled an approving face. "This is the way of the wizards. What promises has she made him?"

"None that I've heard. She spoke of 'help', but she didn't specify."

"Clever." Qay studied my face. "You are too much like him," she said then, a crease forming over the bridge of her nose. "I don't like it."

"You don't have to like it."

"It makes it hard for me to trust you."

"What did my father do that was so horrible?"

"You must remember that they cut the wizard's mark off him." A shudder ran through her broad body and she glanced away from me to keep an eye on Lilyis. She was squatting next to the priests she interrogated, while we had started to talk among ourselves. Cathil stood by, ready to assist in dealing out punishment.

Qay continued, "There haven't been many people who were subjected to that kind of humiliation. You could count them on the fingers of one hand. I'd always had my doubts about Qarim and should have spoken up against him being apprenticed when I had the chance."

"Essentially, you blame him for your lack of initiative?" I asked, incredulously.

"I blame him for dishonouring Brother Brook in a way that couldn't be excused." She touched the teardrop shape on her forehead, as if she had to make sure there was still skin there, no silvery scar speaking of shame. "I have no idea how he managed to blab his way into a position where he was able to wed your mother. While my heart says that is hardly your fault, my head reminds me that some unfortunate traits run in the blood."

"My blood is my business."

"It isn't. Not if you wish to be accepted in Thorndell as part of the Badgers." There was a shine in her blue eye that reminded me of ice blinking in sunlight.

Lilyis came to her feet. "I think he needs a breather," she said. "And my tongue feels funny."

Qes handed her a bowl of beer. She smiled at him as she took it, tucked a strand of reddish hair behind her right ear. "That was much more rewarding than I thought it would be."

We stared at the sobbing bundle on the Roundhouse floor.

"How did you get him to fold so quickly?" Raz asked admiringly.

Lilyis lifted her left shoulder. "He's always doubted himself and his motivations. He resents his family for sending him away to the temple. It would've taken much longer if he'd been a different man. Younger sons in Southclere all have a similar fate to wrestle with and some of his concerns are also mine. Many men pride themselves on withstanding pain that's inflicted upon their bodies but present much easier angles of entry than they are aware of. It probably helped that he's starving, frightened, and well aware that he was about to be killed." She emptied the beer bowl. "Let him eat and drink something when he stops crying. We have a lot of time left before the wizard's ultimatum." She reached up and patted my cheek. "Well done for not getting involved."

I turned my head to kiss her palm, and saw Qay Badger's face light up, as if the gesture had provided her with a clue she'd been missing so far, which made me nervous for what was to come. She stepped back, opened the door of the Roundhouse, and beckoned two of the Badger warriors over to give them instructions.

As the priest quietened, Qes helped Cathil to sit him down on one of the benches, where he continued to bemoan his betrayal with whimpers and sniffles, his hands and feet dirty, some straps of the sandals snapped. How easily could Lilyis have been in the same situation? If some of her sisters had been born as brothers and she'd found herself as surplus to requirement, she could've been passed on to a temple to clothe and house and be kept out of the way. And how easily could this have been Bjor? It wasn't a good thought to have; it quenched the empathy I'd felt for him. As lucky as we were that Lilyis had quickly found a way through to him, one of the most important questions was still open: did the Bulls know about the Whiterivers men?

We were brought some basic provisions but not invited to leave the Roundhouse yet. The space in front of it was filled with armed

Badgers, who seemed inclined to wait it out. The first wizard of Thorndell was not prepared to leave us out of her sight. We might be forced to spend the night right there, in our dusty travel clothes and treated like intruders. Knowing that Qes' aunt held such an unfavourable opinion of my father that it couldn't keep from influencing her view of me, hurt. They were the wizards I so dearly wanted to belong to, after all, and I'd always hoped that things would fall into place for me among the Badgers. Had Qarim possibly made the right decision to burn the bridges behind him and stay in Seagard?

"What's wrong now?" Raz asked me, once again.

"This isn't like I expected it to be. I mean, at all."

"You never wondered why Qes didn't talk much about his childhood?"

"I was too busy with my own problems to notice how little he spoke about it," I confessed, my face heating with discomfort.

"I've realized you tend to do that," she murmured, and a muscle twitched in her cheek. "Don't get me wrong, but that hasn't changed since you've gotten together with Lilyis. She keeps you on your feet, but ..."

I scowled. "But what?"

"You can be very self-involved. That's probably a requirement for anyone striving to be a wizard. I don't blame you at all." She gave me a little shove.

I knew it was meant as one of her jokes, but it felt like a hard pinch to the soul.

Raz snickered. "You're still alive, so it must work for you. Have you noticed that there's something happening with these two?" She pointed her thumb over her shoulder at Werid and Eleas.

"What do you mean? They must stick together, they're our wizards. Werid is married, anyway."

"Werid has said openly that they don't expect their wife to wait for them. They make an exceptionally cute couple, wouldn't you say? Both striking in their own way …"

I felt my jaw sink. "Really?"

"Which makes me the only unattached member of the company, and that is a very odd arrangement."

"You don't know …"

"I have fucking eyes, Sloe, and unlike you I'm not too distracted by my ambitions to pay attention. Since Qes is too focussed on Cathil to call you out on stuff, this thankless task seems to have fallen to me. Again. Whoop-de-fucking-doo." Her next shove wasn't quite as friendly, and I felt myself cringe.

"I'm sorry, Raz."

"Don't be. Take off your blinkers once in a while." She grinned, then glared past my shoulder at Lilyis who stood quite close to the priest again, leaving me contemplating how many other recent developments I could have missed.

Everyone in the room shifted to watch her sit down next to the Bull, waiting for him to start talking. Not able to bear her silence for long, he asked, "Are they still going to sacrifice me?"

"Sacrifice?"

"I was warned, you know."

"About human sacrifices?"

"Before I boarded my uncle's ship in Seagard, our first priest invited me and the others to dine with him. It was an honour that was hard to come by in Applebeck." Speaking the name of the place aloud seemed to pain him. "It soon transpired that all he wanted was to scare us straight."

"What did he say to you?"

"That going to Birkland was like jumping into a pit of demons. Demons that would prey upon our innocence and tempt us with promises beyond what could be dreamt of in the Triangle. That we needed to be aware that sin was lurking behind every beautiful face and that we must be strong and resist. That we would encounter barbaric practices and unspeakable brutality, that human sacrifices were common among people who still worship the old gods." The priest appeared young as he confessed, unbearably young. "We promised him vigilance, but as we joined the others at the harbour the next morning, my brothers were so excited to be allowed on this adventure … and now … now I am the only one left." He swallowed, rubbing across his swollen mouth. "When we were in the Red House, we used to dream of the lands we would like to see in the east. I haven't found Birkland much to my liking." He scowled. "Why are they living like this if they could come to the Cities? There is a lot of dirt here."

I saw Qes biting his lip, determined not to scream with impatience.

"It takes some time to get used to the circumstances," Lilyis said kindly. "Everyone would struggle with that."

"How can you bear it?"

Lilyis shot me a quick glance. "The reputation that precedes us is not often based on our true self. Sometimes we need to run a long way to escape. You wouldn't believe how tiresome it is to be married to a Whiterivers woman."

All colour drained from the priest's face.

DAMAGE CONTROL

I noticed the shift in Lilyis' demeanour. There was a predatorial edge to her that had been well-hidden before. She gave us a taste of her excitement.

"Speaking of Whiterivers … am I right to assume that the Bulls have laboured within a certain understanding since they arrived here in Birkland?"

"Understanding?" He repeated the word so slowly it was obvious he was trying to hold off the inevitable.

"As one of the only two priests left to the company, I must suspect that you were privy to some of the discussions among the expedition's leaders. Was there any talk of meeting up with another group of travellers? Coming from the west, perhaps?"

The man licked his lips, nervously. "I can't recall …"

"It's far too late in the game to start fucking with me," she reminded him in the disconcertingly soft voice she'd already used on him to good effect. "Far, far too late indeed." She gave Cathil a signal and Qes' hulking boyfriend moved closer to the bench they sat on. The priest leant back and paled even more. Whatever the Badgers had done to him after his capture worked in our favour.

"There was some debate around ensuring the hierarchy would be enforced as soon as the groups met up," he croaked out, "and concern that the Whiterivers men couldn't grasp the reasons why … why support was granted. I heard them talk of lines that needed to be drawn and …" It was as if the young man had only just understood what he'd been involved in. That there, in a primitive structure at the edge of civilization, a member of the royal family of the Hillakes and Southclere sat before him, while he divulged the existence of a conspiracy against the rule of Crooked Hill.

"Yes," Lilyis said. "Indeed. So must we assume that communication between the Red House and Whiterivers has been happening for quite some time, that there was some coin exchanged for the promise of …" She encouraged him with a smile.

The priest kept his mouth shut for once.

"… inside support should Whiterivers invade," Qes suggested and everyone stared at him. "What?" He held up his palms. "I lived at Crooked Hill court long enough to have picked up on most of their basic concerns. They wouldn't have married so many members off to the east if it wasn't the kingdom they were most worried about."

The priest had likely only understood the words 'Crooked Hill' in any of it, but he was closing up like a clam, when it was decidedly too late to do any damage control.

Lilyis stood up and turned her back on him. "We know that instead of Bjor infiltrating the group from Whiterivers in Goldenlake, they knew exactly who he was to begin with. His name and description must've been circulated."

"That's a hasty conclusion to come to," Qes interjected.

"Though one we must keep in mind. Given the confirmation of our fears some of the things we noticed while travelling through Whiterivers to my sister's wedding make more sense. None of it has only just happened. It's been long in the making."

Perhaps it was hearing Lilyis speak in the words of the families again that set off the priest or it was a desperate attempt to wrest back control, but suddenly he was on his feet, his hands stretched out towards Lilyis. He grabbed her braid and pulled her backwards, not considering how close Cathil was to him. I'd never seen someone so big move this fast: Cathil's arms shot out, the left under Lilyis' shoulders to keep her from toppling over while the right swung in a wide arc, thudding into the priest's chest.

We stared at the hilt of Cathil's eating knife poking from the man's body. The priest looked down, up; Cathil gave the pommel a *thump* with his palm, and the man fell against the wall, blood starting to rise between his teeth.

"Was that necessary?" Qay Badger groaned. "We could have still drowned him if he was half-dead."

Lilyis massaged the roots of her hair at the back of her neck. "He was helpful. We can call this easy death a reward for his services."

"He's not yet dead," Raz said.

"Give it a moment," Cathil growled, bent forward and pulled out his knife. A great gush of blood followed, soaking the red tunic with a darker stain. The priest made a choking sound, scrabbling for a hidden Star amulet among his clothing. He didn't manage to reach it before he sunk back, his neck at a weird angle against the earthen wall of the Thorndell Roundhouse.

"Can't we spin this somehow?" Werid asked. "Would it have to be death by drowning?"

Qay shrugged. "I can try, but there will be much disappointment."

I watched Cathil clean his knife on the priest's cloak before sheathing it. He seemed unruffled, and Qes to take the particular death more lightly than usual.

"I'm sorry," Lilyis said. "That was stupid of me."

Qay ordered two of the Badger warriors to remove the dead priest from the Roundhouse and brought our company out into the open. The square was full of gawping people, waiting to hear what had transpired in the secrecy of the bramble mound. Whatever story Qay would come up with to placate them, as the body was brought out, the brown cloak covering the distorted face, an angry hum arose from the crowd. Apparently, everyone had looked forward to seeing someone drown to honour Brother Brook.

Our own company was herded towards the living quarters of Thorndell. Qes' mother waited in the place where audiences usually took place, the group of benches clustered under a protecting roof of bracken and pine branches next to the House of Women. She was ringed by some of Qes' sisters and frowned impatiently at her son.

"I'm waiting to hear a good excuse from you," she said.

Qay gently pushed her nephew aside. "You can lay off him," she said. "I sanctioned the intervention, and you can assume the gods are assuaged."

"Never mind the gods," her sister huffed. "Barging into a ritual like that is a grave offense. Have you learned these kinds of manners from the Moons?"

"No, Mother." Qes kneeled in front of her. "I beg for forgiveness."

One of her advisors hauled him to his feet again. "Don't be ridiculous," she hissed at her brother. "This is not the time for your drama."

Qes squirmed and I realized the Qes I loved was quite different from the Qes known by his family. He brushed the dirt off his knees. "I should have sent notice."

His mother's face darkened. "Yes, you should have. After all the discussions we had I should have never allowed you off the leash at all. You should have been married last year, but all the men I'd earmarked for you have been given away."

"About that …"

"We will find someone to take you quick," she said. "Now that you are back, we can organize something in a few weeks. I have always liked an autumn wedding."

"Mother!"

I saw Qay biting down a grin. "Let him speak, sister."

Qes' mother scowled. "He had his chance to sniff around the world, it's time to honour his fate."

"Fate?" Qes sounded half-strangled.

"This has gone on long enough. The cousin exchanges were always supposed to be a temporary arrangement, surely you are aware of that."

"This is not the time, Mother. The lands of the families are about to burst into flames. Tanglebriar won't be the only village reduced to ashes if we don't stop ..."

"We do not concern ourselves with other lands," the leader of the Badgers said. "Politics is not a game for Badger men who weren't chosen to be wizards. You will serve to strengthen our alliances—not with the Moons, but there are some promising candidates among the Bears—"

"Mother," Qes said again, his voice sounding firm. "I can't marry a Bear. I'm already engaged."

A deathly silence fell over the benches in front of the House of Women. His mother leant forward. "Come again?"

I saw Cathil fighting hard to control the surprise on his face.

"I'm already engaged, Mother." Qes sent a pleading glance over his shoulder and Cathil stepped up and bowed before her.

"Who is he?" The leader sounded thoroughly put out. "What family does he belong to?"

"My name is Cathil Cloud, formerly of Greycliffs."

Qay rolled her eyes. "Oh, we have heard of *you*. Even so deep in the forests the news about the Clouds' predicament have reached us. Seriously, Qes? After all I've done to pull your neck from the noose?"

Qes was red as a beet. 'I'm sorry, Cathil,' he mouthed.

"Don't be." Cathil took his hand. "This is perfect."

"Aw," Raz said next to me and I felt myself grinning from ear to ear.

"You can't marry a Cloud!" Qes' sister bellowed at him. "A *disgraced* Cloud!"

"He won't," his mother said. "Not if he wishes to retain the protection of the Badgers."

I saw Qes' knuckles go white, so hard did he clasp Cathil's hand in his. "Don't worry, Mother. I won't make any claims to your favour in the future."

"Have you come back to ruin my life?" his mother asked icily.

"Actually this was supposed to be a diplomatic mission," Werid interjected.

Qay barked out a laugh, but Qes' mother wasn't amused. "Is that a joke?"

"No." My master pushed themself to the front of our group. "But things have moved on rather quickly."

"Consider your mission failed," the leader ground out. "I should never have let myself be persuaded to trust the Moons to keep my son safe." She looked at me directly. "Your mother will receive a sharply worded letter, Sloe Moon of Tall Trees."

"She probably expects one anyway," I said, speaking up for the first time in a long while. "We didn't exactly leave Tall Trees with her best wishes."

The leader of the Badgers took a deep breath. "And you need to leave Thorndell, before I decide to stick you into the empty cage."

✿

WHAT REMAINS

"That probably went as well as it could," Qay Badger said drily.

Dusk started to fall over the town, not the ideal time to be kicked out. Our horses stood at the ready and we had many spectators who wanted to make sure that we left. Qes was flushed and sweaty, as if he barely managed to keep everything together. He tightened the girth strap once more and pulled himself into the saddle.

"I didn't want to cause pain," he said.

His aunt patted his knee. "She'll calm down. Give it a few years before you come back, I'll see what I can do." She turned around to face the wizards of our company. "I assume you'll move on towards the steppes?"

Werid pulled back their thick braid. "That seems to be the plan."

"I'm sorry we didn't have the chance to pray together. My sister can be abrupt, especially if her entertainment is spoiled. May the Siblings be with you." She glared at me and Lilyis. "The best of luck for your endeavour," she said. "I hope you are more successful in the steppes than in Thorndell. It would be a good idea to visit what remains of Tanglebriar before leaving the area. Though I wouldn't advise spending the night there."

"Thank you," Lilyis said. "I appreciate all you have done for us today."

Both women smiled at each other, then Lilyis urged her small grey mare forwards, next to Qes' gelding.

Raz and I were the last riders in the throng. The deep shadows of evening seemed filled with hostile presences. The path we followed led us into the valley of the ponds, where the empty cage stood on the narrow strip of soil and the surface of the water looked oily, like a barely contained threat. How many people had been drowned over the centuries that Thorndell had been settled? How many lives had been claimed by the hungry god lurking in the darkness?

"How big are the fish in there?" Raz asked.

"It's not a trap—not for fish, anyway."

"Oh. Would Lilyis have let him go back to that?"

"Probably."

"Thank the Siblings for Cathil's reflexes, then." She shuddered. "I'm glad we won't have to stay the night with the Badgers."

"Don't rejoice too quickly."

We camped in a clearing not far away from Thorndell, building a small fire and silently waiting for the water to boil. Qes and Cathil had volunteered to sort out the horses and had not yet returned. They obviously had a lot to talk about. Lilyis sat next to Eleas and Werid on the other side of the flames, while Raz and I were on tea and bread toasting duty to provide some sort of meal after a most eventful day.

"Do you think I could've done something?" I asked my friends, suddenly afraid that concern was exactly what Raz had talked about earlier. "*Should* I have done something?"

Werid shook their head. "No. It was wise of you to keep out of it. Throwing your weight around would've made everything more complicated."

"I feel bad."

"We all feel bad. I had no idea the Badgers are so difficult to deal with."

I nodded. "It certainly clarifies my father's decision not to go home and face his family."

Lilyis lifted her gaze to me. "Would your mother have reacted to me in a similar way?"

"That's quite likely."

"Qes must feel awful."

"He got himself engaged," Eleas snorted.

"And lost the love of his family," Werid reminded her. "Whatever happened between him and his mother before this day, this can't be easy for him, and it might cause complications for all of us later on." My master smiled at me. "You probably attract people like us, Sloe."

"What do you mean?"

"The only person among us who isn't at odds with their family is Raz."

Raz laughed. "I've had enough spats with my own mother, thank you very much."

Eleas made a gesture that reminded me of a water prayer. "That may explain why we try to choose to build a new family with such desperation. The question is, what will happen to Qes and Cathil?"

"We'll find somewhere," I said, with more conviction in my voice than I actually felt. "There'll be a place for all of us."

As I awoke next to the cold ashes, mist was creeping into the clearing. The horses stood huddled together on the spot where enough grass grew to keep them entertained. Eleas had the last watch and gave me a little wave as I hoisted myself up. I went for a pee and joined her at the edge of the camp.

"An unexpectedly quiet night," she said. "Have you had any disconcerting dreams, Sloe?"

"Not that I could recall. I was probably too exhausted." I glanced back at my companions. Qes and Cathil slept under Cathil's cloak, entangled in each other.

"We will have a wedding to plan," Eleas said drily. "I will have to fight Werid for the opportunity to officiate."

"Can't you do it together?"

"Maybe …" There was a smile around the wizard's mouth that made me remember what Raz had said, but before I could ask, I heard a yawn behind me. My master stumbled across the clearing to take care of their morning needs.

"Have you presided over many executions?" I asked Eleas.

"I was the wizard of a small community, and not for many years. I was spared that duty."

"When Qes and I arrived to pull the priest out of the cage, the wizards present were so disappointed. I can't recall witnessing anything like that in Tall Trees."

"I don't think Tall Trees is as old as Thorndell. The Badgers cling to traditions that have never been part of life among the Moons."

"They have a reputation for great stubbornness."

"There you go."

"If we could have kept the priest alive, Qes' mother would've likely been in a better mood."

"It is hardly your fault, Sloe."

"I still feel responsible."

"It might be difficult to hear, but you are not *that* special." She scrunched up her nose. "You must allow us to be held accountable for our own mistakes."

"Hear hear," Werid muttered, who used the hem of their cloak to wipe their hands. "The old ways were cruel in many aspects. In Goldenlake they have already turned away from many of the old rituals."

"They used to drown people in the Golden Lake?" I asked, horrified.

"Of course they did."

"That isn't a lie spread by the Star? To excuse their violence towards the wizards?"

"The important thing is that times have changed, Sloe, and these prejudices need to be discussed before the men of the Cities set fire to every village they happen upon. We must prepare ourselves to see some horrible things in Tanglebriar."

An eerie silence pervaded the forests as we approached the site of the Badger village, though the most noticeable change was the smell of smoke and charred flesh, of dead things starting to bloat in the heat of high summer. The Bulls must've come across the settlement by accident. It had been scarcely more than a farmstead, reduced to little more than a heap of smouldering ashes, with a separate pyre to burn the dead after the raid. There were signs of the lives that had been lost: unusable tools strewn about, half-burned tapestries nailed to collapsed structures, a single boot, curled up from the heat. Although the Badgers had removed the family members, and there were no bodies to be seen, vomit rose into my throat as we witnessed the destruction visited upon the idyllic spot at the side of a mossy brook.

The Bulls hadn't needed many men to raze Tanglebriar; the settlement hadn't been fortified. Its inhabitants must've counted on the closeness of Thorndell for protection.

I managed to hold it in for a few more moments, but as I struggled for breath, I knew it was pointless. I just about made it out of Cirvi's saddle before I started to throw up. My companions remained on their horses, watching me turn out my insides. Merely imagining what had happened in Tanglebriar was too much. There'd been children there and old people. It hadn't been a garrison ...

Lilyis kicked her resisting mare forwards to move closer to the remnants of the houses. "The Bulls must've taken their dead and wounded away. If they were any." She bent forward and pulled the shaft of an arrow from a piece of collapsed roof, studying the fletching. "These are not family-made. They came from the Eight Kingdoms. Sloe, are you quite finished?"

I wiped my mouth, eyes and nose running, before another heave pulled me to my knees.

"There can't be much left," she remarked but I was too exhausted to quip back.

"Leave them be," Qes said. "It's going to stop eventually. They usually puke."

He was right. I'd reacted in much the same way when we'd found the prince and his dead companions. There were no indications as to what could've provoked the attack, though Tanglebriar must've appeared prosperous enough, clean and ordered, the tapestries in front of the doors displaying a wealth that could easily be misinterpreted. Perhaps the Bulls had found silver seeds and golden jewellery, precious things that were easy to carry away and melt down, loot that would make them search for similar-sized settlements around the area. For once, I couldn't feel my Siblings anywhere. The scorched ground was devoid of any divine spark. I was trying to bring my stomach under control when I heard Werid let loose a strange, inhuman howl.

Too late we understood that it wasn't only old smoke flavouring the air around us. Something was still burning and the sky above the trees was filled with a strange light.

DRAW US AWAY

While my friends charged ahead, I scrambled onto Cirvi's back, not in the best condition for a gallop across challenging forest terrain. My mare pulled the reins from my hands and followed the other horses. All I could do was to hold on to her black and white mane for dear life and let myself be carried along the sharply winding roads. I had to try and make myself as small as possible to avoid branches hitting me in the face; leaves got stuck in my hair and some of them ripped off the trees.

I caught up with my company on an elevation affording a view over the surrounding valleys.

"Fuck," I heard Werid spit. "That can't … that can't be what it looks like, can it?"

They were staring west, back towards where we'd come from. A pillar of dark smoke rose into the skies, much farther away than I'd thought at first.

"What's back there?" Raz asked my master.

No one wanted to say it, so I did, my voice choked up with terror. "Goldenlake. Goldenlake is burning."

Werid's dark eyes shone with unshed tears. "How can this be? They left before us!"

"Which might've been a ploy to draw us away," Cathil said.

"You shouldn't have killed the priest," Werid said to him. "You gave away the only leverage we had."

"There was no other option," Qes protested. "You know that. It's no use to lash out. What do we do?"

All of them turned around to face me.

"We were supposed to go east," Lilyis said. "But …"

"We need to go back," I decided, not sure why I was suddenly saddled with the decision.

Tears began to spill over my master's dark cheeks. "We need to go back," Werid repeated, their voice thick with emotion.

"Qati is in Goldenlake," Raz said. "We need to help Qati."

"Do we follow the road back west or do we try to reach the lake by cutting across?" Eleas asked.

"We should be able to reach the lake from here," Qes said, fussing with the reins of his gelding. "I'm sure I can lead us."

There was no way we'd be able to make it back to Goldenlake on the same day, though Qes pushed us on relentlessly, and at dusk we came upon the broad belt of birches around the Golden Lake itself. The horses climbed slowly down from the ridge towards the water, Cirvi swaying her rump underneath me to carefully place her hooves, her neck curved back for balance. She was covered in patches of dried and fresh sweat; all the horses were exhausted. The peaceful sound of the water lapping at the pebbled shore was at odds with the threatening glow over the lake, mirroring itself over and over again. We were at least a day's ride away, but from our vantage point the fire seemed much, much closer.

"We'll leave at first light," Qes decided. "I'll take last watch and make sure you are awake."

We rode into the lake to let the horses drink before returning to a sheltered dip amidst the birches, where some of them had fallen and formed a protective fence where our mounts could be tethered. Drawing together, we shared the last of the bread, gone so stale that we had to soften it with water before attempting to chew. Lilyis, who'd ridden at the front of the group for most of the day, sat next to me, clearly tired to the bone. She stared at a piece of dried apple with an empty expression on her dirty face. As

I reached out to her, she looked up almost in astonishment that I should presume as much, but she pushed herself closer.

"This isn't how it should have gone," she said as she leant her head against my shoulder. "They shouldn't have been able to dupe us so easily."

"Goldenlake is full of people able to fight," Eleas reminded her.

"We won't be able to make much of a difference," Cathil said.

"Not you," Lilyis said.

Cathil huffed with offence, the fire across the lake reflecting in his eyes. He shrugged his broad shoulders.

"Good point, though," Werid said. Their face was streaked with dust and tears. "We need to talk about what we can do. We can't just ride into town and let Sloe and Eleas loose on them."

"We should approach them as stealthily as possible," Cathil agreed. "Raz and I could go in first to assess the situation."

"I'm in," the Owl warrior said.

"That sounds like a plan," Werid said firmly. "I will take first watch, get as much rest as you can. It's going to be a short night."

I wrapped my cloak around Lilyis, holding her as close as I possibly could. She'd fallen asleep after we'd lain down under the overhanging branches of the birches, the summer night hazy. There was too much light in the sky and in the waters for me to doze off, even as bruised and drawn out as I felt after the horrific journey back to the lake. It would've been selfish to wake Lilyis to try and get my mind off things, to distract me from the ruins we would find on our return to town. The hours felt endless until Raz woke me to start my watch.

"I'll stay with you," she said. "There's no chance I can go back to sleep. Not when I'm to go on a secret mission with Cathil fucking Cloud. Can you imagine him being stealthy?"

"At least he won't be immediately recognized."

"We shall see. I must say, my life wasn't half as interesting before I met you."

"Are you sure that's a good thing?"

"I'll have so many stories to tell my children," she said with grim satisfaction.

I turned towards the light of the burning town. "I'm glad you don't hate me for it."

"It was my choice to come along. How can it be a bad thing if I can say I was here when the shit hit the ceiling?"

"You have a weird idea of fun."

She gave me a little push. "I dare say if I survive all this, I'll finally feel sated enough to settle down. I could imagine giving Qati another spin if he gets his act together."

"I don't know, Raz. The Siblings are feeling far away from me today and there's no saying what will happen tomorrow. This may be the day we lose one of our holiest places."

"They can't set fire to the lake," Raz disagreed. "As long as there are water and birches, the essence of the Golden Lake will remain and all the Tall and all the Small Gods will join us at the shore." In the half-darkness of the reflected flames I saw her eyes widen. "Should we wake the others?" she asked. "It seems light enough for us to find our way along the lakeside."

"Give them a while, before we boot Qes out of his blanket. It feels …"

"It feels like the night before the battle of the Stoneharp," Raz confirmed. "Though this time we know that we're riding towards a fight."

"What if it's not a fight? What if it's a big coincidence?" I added, desperate to convince myself.

"You believe that after seeing Tanglebriar?"

"I want to consider all eventualities …"

"We can both sense it," she said matter-of-factly. "We can wish for a simpler explanation, but that isn't what we're going to get. I'm going to wake Qes."

We quickly saddled the horses and though there was an awful lot of yawning, no one uttered a single complaint. The sound of hooves on pebbles was awfully loud as we made our way back to the narrow road leading around the waterfront. The shore was squigglier than we'd first believed it to be, and it took a long time to get close enough for Cathil and Raz to split from the group and ride ahead.

"How long can a town like Goldenlake burn?" Eleas asked quietly as we brought water to the resting horses, aware that we needed to be careful not to show up in full view at the waterline. A group of five horses would be easily spotted.

Goldenlake looked strange from such an angle. I'd expected the houses fronting the shore to have disappeared, but they were still standing, and piles of stuff lay lined up aside the water. People had tried to save their possessions. We were too far away to identify them as more than silhouettes, but we saw what they were doing: they stood in long chains, handing along everything that could hold water. Others filled skins and vanished, heaped with them as if they carried braces of birds or fish. No high flames were visible anymore. Perhaps we'd reached them just as they were getting things under control, though they continued to fetch water, unceasingly.

I'd wanted to wait a good long time before returning to Goldenlake, but standing in the shadows of the birches watching felt deeply, terribly wrong.

Werid took me by the shoulder. "You'll have the opportunity to help. Plenty of them are alive."

"And plenty of them could be already dead," Qes said bitterly. "We should've been here."

"There's no point beating yourself up about that. We need to wait for Raz and Cathil. Everything else would be utter foolishness." Werid gave me a shove. "We'll pray."

"We should," Eleas said softly.

Both wizards took me aside to prepare, while Lilyis and Qes started to tend to the horses. Werid cleared a space between the roots of one of the older trees and pulled the amulet they wore for travelling from their clothes. It was a smooth stone, wrapped in silver wire, and of a deep, surprising purple. They placed it on the ground and added a golden circlet.

Eleas knelt and laid the folded shell cape next to Werid's offerings, its iridescence dulled under the summer canopy of dark-green leaves. I disentangled my own tokens and arranged them neatly: Qes' pebble, so unassuming, the silver amulet that had been with me through it all, the key, the bracelet, and the wolfstone, my master's gift.

It was an odd collection of things, both incredibly precious and seemingly worthless side by side, all five tokens representing stages of my path and ties to the most important people in my life, alive and dead, near and far. My love for them induced these objects with their own glow of importance.

My master touched the items lying between us and the birch they'd chosen for our impromptu ritual, murmuring soft words, as if they had to try and soothe the gods before the three of us started to try and get their attention. As they laid their palms against each other, it was Eleas who spoke.

"Sister Storm—protect us."

WHATEVER COMES OUR WAY

It took me a few breaths to understand what my master and our second wizard were trying to achieve. Eleas took up every object that we'd placed on the ground to bless, in the name of one of the eight Siblings. While we knelt among the trees, I could feel the circle around us tightening again. It was behaviour designed to pull the gods' gaze in our direction. When once I'd felt the distracting pressure of them, now it was a welcome feeling, like an embrace. We put the ornaments back on, one by one. Eleas donned the shell cape dedicated to Sister Storm, Werid the purple stone given to Brother Rain and Sister Sun's golden circlet. The rest found their way back to me: Brother Brook in his silver likeness, Sister Stone in the pebble, Brother Flame in the wolfstone, Brother Moon in the Queen's milky blue bracelet, and Sister Soil in the tower key.

As the last of them settled on my chest, their familiar weight grounding me once again, Eleas reached across my numb knees and clasped Werid's hand in hers. I felt what Raz had meant. There was love between them, love I hadn't noticed before.

My master pulled Eleas' hand up and kissed her dirty knuckles, making tears rise to my eyes. "This is my promise to you. To you both. I will have your back, whatever comes our way. Today and forever. This ritual has bound us in place. Stop sniffling, Sloe."

"But my legs hurt so much. I've had cramps since you were on the pebble."

Werid laughed, an unexpected sound given the seriousness of our situation. "Then let's get ready."

Cathil returned alone. "The fire started at the boat station and has made its way southwards through town. There was no outright attack, but everyone suspects the fire was started with the intent of catching all of Goldenlake on the back leg. The warriors are patrolling the outer ring of houses. No one has been apprehended yet."

"Then we need to reinforce them," Qes said. "I might have to borrow a longknife from someone."

"Take the moon blade," I said to him. "I haven't handled it since the crown prince had the idea of making me such a useless gift."

"Calm down," Werid said, stepping up to take the reins of leadership. "Let's get there first and discuss with Qerla Badger what she needs us to do. We have to be careful. It only stands to reason to assume that men from the Cities are close by. Cathil, we need to ride a few zigzags on our way back."

Qes' fiancé gave them a curt nod. "Understood."

Werid turned to face Lilyis. "Are you comfortable with me taking over?" they asked bluntly.

"This isn't a situation we can enter divided amongst ourselves," Lilyis said. "It's a matter of the families in which I get to support the Moons, not the other way around. Go right ahead, Werid."

Raz was with the guards who kept an eye on the main road leading into town. All of them had sooty faces, dark around the nostrils and eyes, as if they'd been up all night fighting the fire before starting their duties.

"There you are." Raz sounded deeply relieved. "I'd almost thought you'd left me behind and got the fuck out of here."

Werid gave a short huff. "Which would probably have been the smarter thing to do, instead of trapping ourselves in a town waiting to come under siege."

"I gave my word to the wizards." Raz scrunched up her nose. "They seemed reluctant to count on you coming back."

"How many of them left?" Werid asked.

"They wanted to, but Qerla Badger started throwing curses around, so they changed their minds. They have bolted themselves into the Roundhouse."

"Why am I not surprised? Get up behind Sloe's saddle, we'll take you into town."

One of the guards helped Raz onto Cirvi's broad back. My mare snorted but allowed her to settle on the saddle cloth. Raz put her arms around my waist. "Don't try anything weird," she warned me. "It's been a while since I've been on a horse this wide. I'm going to walk funny for days."

She held on tightly as we trotted into Goldenlake, passing the water chains that kept going. On almost every street corner more heaps of stuff were in the process of being brought down to the water. It was what Cathil had talked about: all people in Goldenlake were distracted by the fires in one way or another, and the Bulls would only have to ride along the shoreline to loot the place in the end. We were playing into their hands.

Many of the people engaged in saving their town stared at us and let us pass, some grumbling about 'bloody wizards', some exchanging a few hopeful words, which made me feel worse. How could we be responsible for turning away a whole town from the same fate that had done for Tanglebriar? As yet, the fire had spared the central quarters. The Roundhouse stood far enough away from any other buildings, which was undoubtedly why the wizards of the lake had gathered there. A group of warriors blocked the entrance, keeping the ordinary people away. Their eyes narrowed in determination as we approached them on horseback. When we crossed the dark circle where Bjor's pyre had burned a few days earlier, I felt Raz squeezing my middle.

Qor Badger pushed one of the guards aside. "The two wizards can enter," she pronounced, glaring at Qes as if she waited for her cousin to object.

"Fine—but Sloe Moon needs to come with us." Werid dismounted and threw the reins at Qor, which the apprentice let fall to the ground with an expression of disdain. One of the guards bent to pick them up, and I saw Werid thinking about something mean to say to Qor, before deciding to not give her more attention than she deserved.

Raz slid down to allow me space to swing my leg over Cirvi's back. I felt my knees shake as I landed next to her. I knew that my presence would be disputed as soon as we entered the house.

Eleas, in her splendid shell cape, turned around and took me by the wrist. At least I wouldn't have to explain the ritual we'd bound ourselves with to the wizards of Goldenlake. The Roundhouse was filled with fragrant smoke; the apprentices must've burned dried sap and herbs since they'd arrived. The Goldenlake Roundhouse was the largest I'd ever known, but it was stuffed full of people, decked out in their best, and with the hollow look that comes from too much praying with too little reward. A few seats had been moved apart. On one sat the first wizard of Goldenlake, her staff with its cluster of freshwater pearls gripped tightly in her right hand, like the weapon it was.

Werid seemed to grow a handbreadth in size as they stepped forward to meet the disapproving gaze of the older wizard.

"We thought you'd be clever enough to keep away in times like these," Qerla said.

My master smiled at her and inclined their head for the tiniest of fractions. "There is still loyalty among us. We came back to assist you."

"Now that the fire is almost out," Qerla said sourly, "you can afford to be generous with your time, I suppose."

"Cut the crap," Werid snarled and the whole of the Roundhouse gasped. "You're lucky we're here. You can thank Sloe later. What do you know about the fire?"

"That it spread three nights ago, from the boatshed at the station and the northern end of the quarter of the Bears. If the wind hadn't changed direction at dawn on the first day, Goldenlake would be little more than ash."

"But no one was caught?"

"No." Qerla sounded angry. "Though we all know who is behind it."

"It makes sense to assume the men of the Cities employed the same tactics here as with the Badger village they destroyed further east. But why would they wait for the fires to be brought under control?"

Qerla scoffed. "We must assume they will try again. When everyone is starting to allow themselves to hope, the next fires will be started. We have organized a watch and constant patrols along the outer walls of Goldenlake, until the palisades are up."

"Did you speak to the Elks?" Werid asked.

An uncomfortable murmur ran through the rows of wizards in the murky house.

"They claim not to have been informed of either the plans or whereabouts of their guests, but they have lived among us long enough to have scouted out the most vulnerable places of this town. We are paying a high price for the Elks' hospitality and as much as I want to appreciate your return, Werid of the Far Side, you bring us four longknives and little else." Her brows arched in a silent warning.

"Four blades can make a significant contribution if wielded by the right people. Don't forget that I also bring Eleas and myself. More qualified voices to call on the Siblings to bestow their mercy on us all."

Qerla fiddled with a loose pearl on her staff, not meeting Werid's gaze. "There is no shortage of wizards in Goldenlake. There never was."

"Fine. We'll be at hand if you change your mind." My master turned around and pushed gently against Eleas' arms. We stepped out of the dark perfumed interior into bright sunshine, squinting against the light. Our horses were still standing on the square.

"And?" Lilyis asked.

"The welcome was as frosty as expected," Werid said. "We can't anticipate any great gestures of gratitude, I'm afraid." Their words echoed my own resentment. "Let's go and see if the guesthouse remains empty, and we need to find some fresh food to eat. Qes and Cathil, can you see to provisions? Raz, go with them, you might find Qati while you're at it. Take the horses and bring as many victuals back to the house as you can. This might not be a situation easily or quickly resolved, and they won't feed us, not until Qerla finally pulls her finger out and is prepared to acknowledge what help we can offer to the whole of Goldenlake."

❦

FIRE WITH FIRE

The guesthouse was as we'd left it, not swept, not tidied. I stared at the scarf that lay squashed in the corner.

"That was Bjor's, wasn't it?" Lilyis asked.

When I picked it up to push it into my bag, my throat was too tight to get out a useful word. The thought that he'd been alive when we'd last been there was enough to shake me, though the tears I was waiting for didn't rise.

"Can you see to our horses, Sloe?" Werid asked.

I was grateful to be given a task. Lilyis followed me into the stable, leaving the house to Werid and Eleas.

"Why does Goldenlake feel like a trap this time?" she asked as we put the saddles away and checked the hooves of the horses over before digging out the brushes.

"Because it is a trap," I murmured, combing the sweat-spikes out of Cirvi's black and white coat. "Werid would never have brought us back if they didn't expect Eleas and me to explode us free if push comes to shove."

Lilyis tread a heap of hay aside to step in front of Eleas' mount and reach the dirt between the front legs. "What they wanted to do was to force Qerla Badger's hand."

"I made the decision to turn back," I said pointedly. "It's my fault."

"Don't be foolish. If Werid had disagreed, they would've pushed eastwards. They're your master after all, and relish taking control of the company." She looked up at me, half-crouched under the belly of the horse. "How could I have refused for them to take over? Since we've lost Bjor, I've had no real say in anything. This isn't a mission of the Sun anymore," she stated. "Maybe the Sun will take away a few contacts, but it has become about something else."

"I'm sorry about that."

"You don't need to be." She put the brush aside and walked around Cirvi to my side. "I know it is a difficult situation for you, but lately … it has all changed for us, hasn't it?"

I looked up, anxious for what she'd say next. "It's become too serious overall, is that what you mean?"

"I find myself missing you, though you ride but a few paces behind me. We don't talk much, apart from exchanging practical information." She took my left hand and with the right I put down my own brush. She pulled me to her and as we kissed, I felt her frustration, the pent-up hunger that had been pushed aside to make space for grief and fear and anger at our current circumstances.

She slammed me against the dividing wall. It felt like wrestling a flame and it was so incredibly tempting to let myself be consumed, to forget about everything that scared the breath out of me. Her hands were already under my belt, raking over my arse, and though I felt myself reacting in the way she wanted me to, my heart felt numb.

"Lilyis … Lilyis, listen …"

"Don't tell me you don't want me all of a sudden."

"Of course I want you. I love you! But … I'm not sure I'd do this for the right reasons. I don't want you to be a mere distraction because I'm frightened and need something to take my mind off the fires eating their way through town, or our friends being out there, trying to scrape some food together so we can survive being holed up for more than a few days." I cupped her burning face. "I know we won't have many opportunities in the coming days, but … I don't feel up to it."

She pressed her thigh between mine. "I'd say you're up for it all right."

"Please," I pleaded softly. "It wouldn't be fair to either of us. I need to focus on what lies ahead."

Our foreheads met, and I heard her groan.

"I've been waiting to jump you for days."

"I know and I'm sorry."

"No. Sloe, I should've realized how unsettled you feel. I'll take care of myself, as it were." She gave a joyless chuckle. "This almost feels like my marriage—aw, gods. That was an incredibly mean thing to say. I wanted to make a joke. Forgive me."

We kissed again, gently this time.

"As soon as I feel different about it, I will come and find you," I promised.

"Even if we're in the middle of an attack?"

"Especially then. I'll run to you, belt flapping."

We both laughed, and she gave my arm a little pinch. "I'm sorry you feel so conflicted," she said. "Talk to me."

"Are you sure you want me to lay it all on you?"

"I'm still your girlfriend, right? It's sort of my job to listen to you, provide advice if you need it and a shoulder to cry on. Is that the problem? I haven't seen you cry since Bjor died. Apart from when you puked your guts out in Tanglebriar, but I don't think we can count that."

"Actually, since Sjunil died I've gone hollow again, like I did in the battle. Back then it helped me to survive the horror of all that, but now? I should've cried for my aunt. I should've been able to do it for someone I loved as much as her and for a friend as hard-won as Bjor."

"You can't blame yourself," Lilyis said. "It helps you to get on your horse and fight. Too much has happened to you, I understand that. Ever since you've left your home things have been piling up on you."

"Yes, and … what happens if I can't do what Werid wants me to do?"

"Which is?"

"I don't know, but they haven't bound me to Eleas and themself for nothing. Just the fact that they haven't thrown our ritual into Qerla Badger's face makes me wonder what they haven't told me yet. Maybe I'll have to defend the whole town with Brother Flame's assistance."

"I doubt they go for fire, but perhaps …"

"Exactly. Fighting fire with fire might be what they have in mind, to demonstrate how big of a mistake Qerla made to discount Sjunil's hidden talents. Everything is political with wizards, every fucking thing."

Lilyis hugged me to her, and for a few precious heartbeats I was able to push away the thought of impending doom.

"That's a *lot* of smoked fish."

Cathil grinned at Werid. "We were acting on your instructions."

"There are other things too," Qes said, dumping a bag of bearnuts on the table. A few spilled across the top, their dark shells gleaming.

"That's going to be fish porridge for the foreseeable future." My master winced. "Wonderful."

"There's flour and honey, and Raz is out searching for cheese."

"Thank you both," Werid said. "That should see us through a few days." They glanced at Eleas who sat on the edge of one of the sleeping platforms, patching up a tunic, her head bent over her work with a smile playing at the corners of her mouth.

"Is there any news in town?" Werid asked.

Cathil and Qes shrugged simultaneously. "They're expecting the next fires to start, so they're as jumpy as a herd of goats,"

Cathil said. "We put our names down on the watch rota. Seems only fair."

"Yes," Werid said. "Any sign of Qati?"

Qes worried his bottom lip. "No, but maybe Raz will have more luck in finding him. Our first watch starts in a couple of hours."

"Go and rest," Werid commanded, before addressing Lilyis and me. "Sloe, you'll remain here with us. It's important that the tokens are kept in close proximity to each other. Lilyis, do you want to join the watch? I wouldn't recommend it, but I appreciate how difficult it'll be to sit and wait with us."

Lilyis squinted at my master. "What exactly did you do to Sloe's amulets?"

"Never you mind."

"Was it a risky spell to cast?"

Werid's face flushed. "That's wizard business."

"I've let you take control of the company, but I won't let you endanger the one I love more than anything in this world." She said it so matter-of-factly that it took me a heartbeat to understand the statement.

"Sloe's not in more danger than any of us," Werid said, deliberately. "While I applaud the vehemence of your affection, please don't underestimate my own concern for them. I'll protect them with my life, as will Eleas."

"Fine." Lilyis crossed her arms. "Just so that we're all on the same page."

"It's no use to anyone if we start snapping at each other's heels. Go and rest up too." Werid shooed her away, then rolled their eyes at me. "We should plan out a prayer schedule, to be on the safe side."

Eleas cleared her throat, putting down her bone needle. "You do not believe all these wizards in the Roundhouse are doing enough of that? It would make more sense to get on with practical things."

"Such as what?" Werid bit back, and I was astonished to see them react like that, given how things had developed between them and Eleas. "Believe me, you don't want to deal with me when I'm getting stressed out of my head waiting for the attack to start. There's one thing I've been trained for, and that is to pray. The wizards in the Roundhouse have been at it for days and you've witnessed their exhaustion. Someone needs to jump in and keep it going."

The whole house was still. My master, usually so graceful and collected, vibrated with irritation. Eleas came to her feet and took Werid by the shoulders, in a gesture that would've been impossible for the wizard Lilyis and I had first met months ago.

"We will pray," Eleas promised. "But you said it yourself, we must not lose sight of what is truly at stake. This is the holiest place in the east, and we have to defend it with more than our hearts. Have you ever trained with a blade, Werid?"

"No." They sounded resentful. "I never needed to."

"You should divide up the schedule between praying and letting Cathil, Raz, and Lilyis show you a few things to defend yourself."

Werid made a disrespectful noise. "Perhaps."

Dissonant clangs of longknives rose, banging onto shields, of pots slamming against pots.

Raz almost wrenched the guesthouse's door off its hinges as she bellowed at us. "It starts! Get up, get dressed—they're here."

FRIENDS AND FOES ALIKE

"We managed to come back just in time," Lilyis groaned. "Hurrah for us."

Werid shot her a warning glance, pulled the golden circlet from their cloak, and pushed it firmly onto their head. The effect was stunning: Werid of the Far Side was dressed like a ruler worthy of being followed into battle, even in their plainest tunic and their hair in a long greasy braid. We all stared at the wizard.

"Yes," Werid said. "This is what they'll be up against." They faced Raz. "Did you see how many of them are coming?"

"There are a shitload of them, and they're arriving from the western side."

Cathil pulled on his boots. "They needed to attack before the palisades were up," he said.

Werid held out their hands. "Listen to me. You all have to be careful out there. Don't try to be heroic. We need every single one of you alive."

Cathil and Lilyis were the first ones out of the house, followed by Raz.

Qes bound his curls out of his eyes. "Where's your blade, Sloe?"

I stared at my best friend. He was impatient to go, to leave me behind with the wizards, flushed and hopping from one foot to the other.

"It's with the rest of my stuff, I …" I'd flung my gear into the corner that morning, thinking there'd be ample time to sort everything away. I disentangled the sheathed blade from my spare cloak and held it out to him. "Qes, you haven't trained properly for months, and it's an unfamiliar weapon …"

He obviously wanted to follow his fiancé, burning to run after Cathil, but our gazes met. "I will be careful," he promised. "As Werid demanded. You need to keep a cool head as well when you're out there." He took the longknife from me, his dark eyes wide and filled with the same fear I felt rushing towards me, finally breaking into my numbness.

"I'll try my best," I promised. "After all this is over, I want to see you get married."

We stared after our friends through the open door.

Eleas gave a last tug to her shell cape. "Are we ready?" she asked.

Werid wore the circlet, and I clutched the blue stone on the bracelet. "No, but let's do it anyway." My master stepped close and kissed me on the cheek. "Don't do anything unless I tell you to. The surprise will be our most important card to play."

I nodded, feeling ready to cry.

Of course it hits now.

Werid wiped their thumb under my left eye to capture the tear spilling from it. "This is what we were meant to do," they said quietly. As they turned around to Eleas I saw their hands shake with emotion. "And we can't do it without you," they said to the other wizard. "Do you hear me?"

As they rose to the tips of their toes to kiss Eleas' cheek too, the Cormorant caught their mouth with hers. Werid didn't hesitate to kiss back; for a few moments they clung together, their sudden happiness radiating from them so at odds with the shouts and screams reaching us from the town.

When they released each other, Werid said, "This is something to fight for. Something to live for." They checked the position of the circlet on their brow. "Sod it. Let's go."

The noises of arrows thrumming into the roofs of the outer buildings brought back images of the battlefield around the Stoneharp, the stench of hot blood and shit mixed with sweat and piss. The thatch had been drenched in preparation and most of the burning arrows fizzled out quickly, though some struck the walls with a *thump* that made me flinch at every single one. There were horses in front of the ditch dug for the palisade, in one line, and at first glance the riders appeared like members of the families, in green or soil-coloured cloaks. Many of their weapons were familiar longknives, not forged in the style preferred on the Continent. They waited for something, for a signal, keeping themselves away from the small group of archers trying to reignite the fires of Goldenlake, the faces under their felted hoods deep in shadow.

Werid stretched their arms out to keep Eleas and me behind them. Among the warriors and citizens who'd rushed to the edge of town to face our enemies we were the only wizards, and our objective in coming where the blades would start to clash in a few instants was to protect the others, the ones in the Roundhouse, with everything that we had.

"This is a provocation," my master shouted at the defenders of Goldenlake. "Keep your nerves!"

Werid's arrival was met with cheers. They swooped in like a vision of grace, their cloak billowing out behind them. I glanced around but couldn't spot Cathil, Qes, Raz, or Lilyis anywhere near us.

This can't be the only group of riders looming so close. They might be all over the western side of Goldenlake, with their blades drawn …

"What are they waiting for?" Eleas muttered next to me.

"They want us to back off," Werid said. "They must know how many people there are in Goldenlake who'll throw themselves at them, if they try to break through."

"That makes no sense," I barked back.

The thin wail of a horn sounded from our right, further towards the road.

"Oh fuck," Werid said—and the horses stepped forward, a line of gigantic, glistening bodies, more horses I'd ever seen in one spot.

The first defenders attacked their front legs and necks, and suddenly we were enveloped in a clash of blades, screeching animals, and bellowing people. My master grabbed my left hand, Eleas' right hand, and when Eleas and I touched each other, the Siblings came down on us amidst the chaos and the spatters of blood.

The first barrier we threw up was of light: a warning, blazing out from the golden circlet on Werid's brow, making the horses recoil and stumble backwards. The fighters on both sides flung up their arms to guard their faces. The wind came after, flattening the warriors closest to us, friends and foes alike, but the water rose, a thin wall spreading out, dousing the buildings behind us, drowning any flames that had been kindled.

Werid started to pull us forwards, along the ditch, and everyone tried to get away from us in a panic as the storm snatched at them, the light stung them, and the water drenched them to the skin.

Riders started to come at us from the right-hand side, trying to push their way through the bodies. Whatever they'd been trying to do, whether it'd been an attempt at intimidation or ridicule, mocking the deluded people grabbing any kind of weapon available to defend their town smouldering from its last ordeal, whatever order they'd been planned, had long since broken down.

Werid started to run at them; I heard my master laughing, actually laughing, as the power of the eight Siblings bound to us unfolded in a maelstrom of confusion. There were only a few men of the Cities among the attackers. Wherever they'd found their alliances, their supporting warriors were confronted with three wizards throwing their collected powers around. Cheers went up again among the defenders as warriors started to cluster behind us, ready to take on anyone who was stupid enough to come at us, sweeping along the ditch.

I saw Cathil roar encouragement a few feet away, leading the group with him into the fray. Somewhere in there was Qes with the moon blade, taking out all his anger, all the fear I'd seen in his face, on the attackers. Lilyis was too short to be easy to spot, and Werid couldn't be stopped, still running and still laughing, until we reached the back of one of the longhouses at the edge of the next quarters, where five men in sandals had flocked together, their stars displayed on their chests, the long staffs they carried pointing unmistakably at us.

Before that moment I hadn't felt true hate. Having experienced the world the men of the Cities were born into, I knew exactly why wizards made them uneasy, why they'd consider the families as savage and depraved. Their ignorance had angered and saddened me, but I'd never felt such an incredible burning wave, swallowing me in the very instance as the staffs were coming towards my master, targeted without hesitation at the circlet on their brow. Werid of the Far Side was everything the Star was afraid of, if based in Eastbay or Applebeck, and they turned to Werid to punish them in front of the defenders.

The call of the kites should've warned them. Just before the weapons turned into blue flames in their hands, the raptors dropped from the skies above our sacred town, snatching at them with their talons. I pushed myself in front of Werid, in front of Eleas, prepared to take the attack upon myself, as I'd done in the *Sprat*, the Siblings' strengths flowing into each other. The expressions on the priests' faces were worth it: shock, outrage, pain, as they flapped their scorched palms.

"Get the fuck away from them." The words of the Cities sounded hard in my mouth, as hate-filled as was befitting.

"Demon!" The word they spat back at me I'd heard from time to time, without understanding what was bound up in it for them. "Demon!"

I didn't waste any thoughts as I broke the bounds with Werid and Eleas and clasped the weapon closest to my heart, the weapon I'd used to kill before. The key, Sister Soil's token and embodiment of my aunt's powers, felt heavy in my hand.

"Sloe—no!" Werid managed to catch the back of my collar, pulling me back from the five priests, choking me. The leather cord snapped, and the key came loose in my hand, the eyes of the priests glued fast upon it. I was Sloe of the Blue Cloak once more. The heavy piece of iron dropped into air, the cord secured in my hand.

The beard of the key smashed into the first mouth as I whipped it around, spraying blood and teeth.

MINE TO COMMAND

The howl breaking from the priests had something unearthly to it, but with the hate had come calmness. Though my fellow wizards had fallen behind me, I saw them covering themselves with anything at hand. I'd probably broken my master's spell for good and hoped we'd be able to connect ourselves when we had the chance to regroup. I was barely aware that I'd bitten down so hard on my own lip that blood started to run down my chin. I savoured each contact of the key with flesh and bone, thrashing and slashing, until I'd injured three of them, hit one of them unconscious, and caused the fifth to flee. When I bent down and pulled the Star off the neck of the one I'd felled, Werid decided to become involved, startling me upright and out of the bloody fog that had settled over my mind.

"That's enough," they shouted at me. "Save your strength for the others. There are many more to vanquish and we need you." They gave me a sharp shake that made my teeth clash together. "Snap out of it, snap out of it *now*."

I spat blood, clutching the star pendant to me, giving the priest a kick while he was down.

"That was unnecessary," Eleas said but I ignored her.

We were no longer surrounded by a wall of light and others had moved closer, with the aim to pick us off one by one. They wore the felted hoods of the families and had complexions similar to Werid's own, their eyes dark and full of dreadful curiosity. On none of them I could spot family emblems, but their boots hadn't been made in the Cities. They were allies brought in to help, bribed with promises of riches, like the Clouds had once been lured in when getting me out of Goldenlake. I growled at them, though Werid's fingers were still hooked into my collar.

One of the warriors swung his silvery horse around. The animal's foaming spit flew from its bit as his left hand wrenched at the reins. The longknife in his right hand was already dripping with gore as he prepared to ride us down; the horse reared up and his hood fell back, revealing short hair, bleached with limewater at the tips and spiked with grease.

"Hedgehogs." My master released me so suddenly I pitched forward, half falling under the hooves. Whatever feelings I'd thought to experience as I faced the priests were nothing to the icy inevitability in Werid's voice. "They brought Hedgehogs to Goldenlake." My master, who'd confessed to never having been properly trained, launched themselves at the rider, nails first. It was Eleas' turn to lunge after them, trying to hold them back. As they both stumbled into me, light exploded out of the circlet. The silver horse, already at the end of its tether, jumped up with all four legs at the same time, snaking its neck around to escape the rider's hand. We saw it keel over and fall sideways, trapping the Hedgehog beneath it. Werid rushed in, kicked the bloody blade from him, and started on his face, the circlet slipping over their forehead, the light sputtering.

"Get off him!" Eleas pulled them back. "We all could use a lesson in self-restraint. There are more of them to deal with."

Werid picked up the Hedgehog blade, flicking off as much of the blood as possible. "Only Hedgehogs could be persuaded to attack Goldenlake," they panted, their face covered in red spatters, leaving little of the beauteous vision they'd presented. "I should have known. They always were the greediest of the families in the steppes, the quickest to move in on territory that didn't belong to them. We can't let them get their paws on the lake, Eleas, we can't!" Their voice, usually so full and melodious, broke into a desperate rasp.

"I am well aware. Where are the others?"

Werid had swept us past our friends and they were nowhere to be seen.

"So many Hedgehogs …" Werid's gaze flicked feverishly over the fight around us, then their snarl was back, raw and undignified. "Where are your kites, Sloe—get them back! Let them tear the Hedgehogs into strips."

"They're not mine to command!" I protested.

My master snorted, pushed the circlet up. "Let's fuck up the next one," they decided.

We got back into formation. Werid had pushed the Hedgehog blade beneath their belt and the key dangled from my wrist like a dripping charm, with splinters of teeth clinging to its beard. In a pinch I could've caused damage with any of the tokens I carried but the key to my tower was by far the heaviest. It dragged at my arm and my shoulder ached as I clutched at my two companions.

Word had spread across the ditch. By that point the attackers were no longer fleeing but turning towards us, eager to distinguish themselves against the wizards who'd slapped the priests down. It wouldn't be long until they'd try to come at us from all sides. We heard the horn again, less feeble and much closer. It drew us on, eager to seek out the centre of command.

"Come with us!" Werid bellowed at the defenders around us. "Come with us and kick the bastards out of Goldenlake!"

The unorthodox battle cry was taken up, echoed, "… kick the bastards … kick the bastards …"

Werid laughed in delight, sounding worryingly deranged but nonetheless drawing the warriors with us to where we hoped to find more priests and more men from Whiterivers. The next blare of the horn sounded near, from a group of riders who obviously hadn't been involved in any of the fighting yet. The man carrying the shiny instrument wore red and his braided hair was as golden as Bjor's had been. Next to him we saw a familiar face under a blood-red hood: Revael da Relian was sunburnt, his new beard so blond that it was almost white, but it was him, and next to his dappled mare, on a gelding that was all too well known to us, Qati Badger, with a strip of red linen knotted around his right arm.

The light flickered out, though we still held hands. Whatever had kept the spell in place sloughed off us. It was Eleas' turn to crack.

"Why?" She pushed herself forward.

Qati sneered down at her. "Because people never really change that much."

"You do not have to do this! Whatever they promised you, they will never keep their word!"

He seemed unmoved, but his horse squirmed underneath him, proof that his rider was agitated enough under the surface. The remains of the stitches holding his eyelids closed were dark with blood; he looked bruised overall, as if the Bulls had welcomed him into their ranks with a beating.

"Why?" Eleas asked again.

Revael made an impatient gesture and the Bull turned to me. "Where is your precious princeling?" he asked. "Hiding between the wizards like the frightened brat he is?"

"Not hiding," I said, my heart fluttering with an onrush of panic. I had no idea where Lilyis was—somewhere in the middle of it all, in the thickest of it, bashing about in the elation gifted to her by Cousin Blade ...

"This time things are different," Revael da Relian gloated. "This time we are taking out the evil by its roots."

"Goldenlake won't die." My voice quavered. "Whatever happens today, it's the centre of it all, however many priests you want to chuck at us."

He sniffed. "I'm not concerned with priests," he said. "I leave that to my allies, who are much more invested in the whole … issue." He glanced aside to the rider on his left, wearing traditional Whiterivers headgear.

"Then what are the Bulls' objectives?"

"To pull out your heart through your throat, Sloe of the Blue Cloak."

I stared at him, too stunned for words. "You're doing this to get back at *me*?" I croaked out eventually and turned to Qati, who lifted his right shoulder.

"Fuck if I know," he said.

"At you, and Bjor, and the prince, conveniently absent, as so he so often is."

"I'm here."

We spun around.

Lilyis emerged from the chaos behind us, her long tunic soaked, her eyes bright-green jewels against the blood drying on her face. The cord of her braid had broken, and it was slowly unravelling on her sweat-drenched back. She was a mess, while Revael looked as fresh as a dewdrop, perched above us in the saddle, his smile the expression of a predator anticipating its killing bite. There was a slump to Lilyis' shoulders that told me exhaustion was catching up with her.

"This is not your place," she said to the Bulls in front of us.

"It's not yours either, though reliable sources are telling me you have begun to make yourself at home in the west. You can't deny us to do the same in the east. The steppes are sadly lacking in most commodities, which may be why we found such open ears to our proposals. Turns out you don't always have to fuck your way in." He spat at his horses' hooves. "Knowing you, Nian da Nileon, that was probably the part you enjoyed the most. Spreading your legs to forge your own alliance."

Lilyis laughed in his face, angling the point of her longknife. Qati must've traded in all our secrets, and if it became known throughout the Eight Kingdoms, there was no option of return left for the Princess of Crooked Hill. Lilyis jerked up her blade, but standing behind her, I saw her left hand reach behind her back.

She pulled out the knife so quickly that none of the riders facing her realized what was about to happen to the leader of the Bulls. Revael da Relian was punched back by the impact of the dagger hitting him, underneath the right eye.

We saw Qati wrench the head of his gelding around, kicking it into a gallop before anyone had truly understood what had just come to pass. Lilyis had cut the head off the snake. One of its heads, at least.

FALLING INTO PRAYER

The leader of the Whiterivers men, his face covered with grey stubble, stared at the Bull bleeding out in last year's leaves.

"That was an unhonourable way to go about it," he drawled. He had eyes as blue as dirty ice, and his build reminded me of Arif, thick-necked and ridiculously muscled. If he decided to get off his horse and take on Lilyis, she would've barely reached his breastbone. "We've had the pleasure of getting rid of one of yours already, and in that case, we didn't concern ourselves much with his honour either. Savages belong with savages, if from the west or the far west." His teeth flashed at the man with the signalling horn. "Pick up your cousin—be quick about it!"

The man from Whiterivers stepped into the position of command. Lilyis had done him a favour.

"Where are the rest of your priests?" he asked me.

"Protected."

"Behind the swords of hapless heathens."

"This is the land of the families. You are the heathens here."

Lilyis took my elbow, trying to pull me away. "That's an argument he won't understand."

"It's an argument I don't *need* to understand," the man corrected.

The men from Whiterivers started to flock to him, the Bulls pushed aside, as covered in blood and dirt as the rest of us were, each and every one wearing a star pendant on their chest.

I shook out my arm, changing the cords of the key over to the left hand, the bracelet slipping down to touch the edge of my right palm.

The kite slammed onto my arm, its talons gripping me, penetrating my skin.

I heard Werid give a *whoop* of delight as I flung the bird beak-first at the rider before me.

Had he brought his horse over from the Continent it surely would've been used to raptors coming close to it, but the stocky bay he rode had been bred from the herds of the families and freaked out hard. The black wingtips of the kite trailed bright flames behind him; the smell of scorched hair rose sharply to our noses and the sound of a dozen men of the Cities falling into prayer drowned out the roar of their leader, trying to get his mount back under control, to beat out the fire licking up its mane.

The Bull with the horn, crouching over his fallen cousin with the handle of Lilyis' dagger sticking out of his face, was almost trampled as he tried to drag Revael's body away. The kite flew a loop over the treetops and returned to my arm. I was more prepared for the weight of my Sibling settling, though his talons were still as painful as they gripped me.

"A useful trick," Lilyis said next to me, and I heard the smirk in her voice. "Can you do it again?"

"Let's see if he wants to talk some more first. Or call us other names. He probably has a whole fucking list of them."

The last time I'd been so close to Brother Flame had been in my aunt's cottage. There was a smoky odour to him and something feral beneath it, similar to the untamed musk of a fox.

I felt the stares of the warriors circling us. The families didn't train raptors to hunt from their fist and the sight of me with the bird on my arm, its jerky movements and abruptly blinking eyes must've been as disconcerting as the wall of water we three had carried before us. Wizards were in league with the gods, that was how things worked, but carrying the embodiment of one of the Siblings around … Sloe of the Blue Cloak was adding to the legends.

More Bulls had left the fight to come and check up on what was going on, at least three dozen of them in their red tunics. No wonder they'd been able to overrun Tanglebriar; the ship with the red sails had brought more of them to Birkland than we'd been aware of and all of them had followed Revael da Relian into battle.

Angry shouts rose. I glanced back and noticed the defenders had fallen in line behind Lilyis, Werid, Eleas, and me. Cathil was close, as was Qes, breathless with effort. It was a long inhale on both sides, a reconfiguration, in which the Whiterivers men were pushed behind the Bulls, most of them shaking with rage after seeing their leader felled by a dagger.

Werid and Eleas still clasped hands, though the spell had worn off; I looked at the Cormorant, and she held up her empty hand before sweeping it down in a sharp motion. The cheeks of our adversaries flapped with the impact of Sister Storm's fury, helmets were blown off, beards whipped about like banners. We'd lost the circlet's light, but I struck them with a blast of rain drops, close enough to freezing to cut skin. Steam rose into the air around us, where hot flesh and ice clashed with the force lent by Sister Stone. The defenders yelled as I threw the kite up and flames spread out behind it, drawing a wall of fire between us and the men from the Cities and their Hedgehogs, who finally fell back. Brother Flame circumnavigated the town, the ditch around us dancing with his gifts—Goldenlake was enveloped in a palisade of fire—unquenchable but controllable fire. I groaned in pain as the kite came to me for the third time.

"I'm going to make you a proper falconer's glove," Lilyis promised as blood ran down my wrist. "If you plan on doing this all the time."

"By all the Tall and all the Small Gods …" Qor said behind us.

The group of apprentices rushing over the battlefield froze when they saw the state of us.

Qes' cousin was one of the first, her bushy hair standing up in all directions.

Brother Flame took off with a piercing cry. I wrenched the left sleeve from my tunic and started to wrap it around the right arm to take care of my slashed skin.

"We've pushed them back for the moment," Werid said. "You can tell your masters we've given them a problem to solve, but that we need to think about how we want to play the situation."

Qor slumped. "Please, would you come with us to explain, Master Werid? This … this is above any of our responsibilities."

"Your master shouldn't be surprised it has come to that, but yes, please take us back to the Roundhouse. I think we're all going to enjoy it."

The tree sap was on its last puffs of smoke; it had already started to lose its sweet smell and specific bitter note. The wizards jumped to their feet as we entered and a whole forest of staffs were lowered at our chests. Qerla Badger was the only one who remained seated, exhaustion drawing deep lines into her face. Her right hand shook so hard I could hear the pearls rattle.

"We need a good explanation," she said.

Werid straightened the circlet on their brow, their face filthy with ash, mud, and blood, their hair full of broken bits of leaves and twigs, and still Werid of the Far Side appeared like the only one in control, with a backdrop of frightened apprentices and Eleas and me, both panting with exertion, my arm dripping blood.

"There isn't one," my master said bluntly. "Unless you take into consideration that something like this situation was inevitable. Goldenlake would have fallen today. The Hedgehogs have come from the steppes, joining their blade skill to the might of the men of the Cities, holding up an alliance set on crushing the wizards of the east. There will be no other solution than to call on all talents we have available to us. If any of you possess strengths you have kept secret to this day, master or apprentice, we need you to join the defence of our sacred place."

A shaking hand was put up in the last row of the wizards. A youngish man in the colours of the Bears cleared his throat. "Does controlling fog count?"

"Most definitely." Werid held out their own hand to him. "Come and stand beside us."

"And freezing the water in a washbowl?" one of the apprentices piped up.

"Yes," Eleas said, turning around and giving the slight girl a pat on the shoulder. "We need your strength to assert our right to the lake."

Protesting murmurs arose from the master wizards, starting to drown out the excited chatter of apprentices.

Qerla Badger bellowed, "Shut the fuck up—all of you!" She threw herself back into her seat and glared at Werid. "This is most irregular."

My master grinned at her, with the hint of the fox I'd seen so often in my aunt's face. "Well, what can you do?"

"I suppose there is no easy way of keeping this quiet?"

"Do you really want to hush up such accomplishments? When we are in the midst of the battle for Goldenlake?"

"*If*," Qerla spat at my master. "And it's a fucking big 'if'."

"The men of the Cities and the Hedgehogs would be standing on this very spot if it wasn't for the forbidden spell I used to make resistance possible."

I gawped at them. "I didn't know it was forbidden," I admitted, starting to feel queasy.

Werid winced. "Your aunt thought I should know it, just in case. And, as usual, she was right. I wish she hadn't always been right. She was so bloody irritating sometimes … I remembered the words and bound us and here we are. Still alive. I will perform it again, gladly."

Qerla snorted. "I can't stop you."

As soon as we retreated from the Roundhouse, our two new recruits in tow, angry shouts followed us into the central square of Goldenlake.

"What are they on about now?" Qes asked. He'd tried to wipe the worst of the grime off his face and made it greyer.

"They'll calm down," Werid said dismissively.

We heard Qerla's voice again, trying to overpower her fellow wizards.

My master winked at him. "Soon. It was to be assumed they'd have a hard time adjusting to such an unexpected set of circumstances." They smiled at the young Bear wizard and the even younger apprentice. "Don't be afraid," they said. "That will be my second try at it."

BITTEN TO BLOOD

I felt the bond forming between the five of us, like a golden thread winding its way through our bodies, connecting fingertips to fingertips. The wizard, who went by the name of Hano, gave a silver amulet in the shape of Brother Rain as a token and the apprentice, a Magpie called Mayiel, offered a flint with multiple natural holes, similar to the pebble I wore. Werid dedicated the stone to Brother Brook. Mayiel was thin and jittery, with fingernails bitten to blood and brittle hair cut to her chin. It was a small miracle she'd brought up the courage to confess her talent so publicly, and I noticed Eleas made a big thing of ensuring she felt as comfortable as possible as we knelt in a line at the shore of the lake, where flames hovered above the waterline, burning searingly hot and without discernible fuel. At some point the fire would be spent; at some point the palisade of flames would fall and our adversaries flood into town. It was merely a respite, the chance for us to rework the spell and draw enough breath to fight the next round.

The ground hurt my knees. I couldn't help but utter a soft curse as I bent forward again and again to take back my own tokens. Hano seemed apprehensive as Werid placed the amulet on his chest, but a few heartbeats later, when he hadn't burst into a squall of rain, he smiled, the corners of his big brown eyes creasing.

Werid had barely concluded the ritual as we heard the pebbles shift behind us. Qerla Badger had come, watching as we accepted our tokens.

"What do you want to do?" she asked Werid outright.

Werid glanced at me. "We should ask Brother Flame to pretend a collapse of the flames—a narrow breach that is defendable for our warriors. I don't want to go in with all our talents blazing. The last time the spell fell apart and we need to preserve it as best as possible." They squinted at the first wizard. "Have they calmed down?"

"They're still shouting," Qerla said, transferring her staff to her left hand to scratch under the silver-grey hair at her temple. "If this doesn't work, they'll kick me out of town. I'm depending on you. Are you really that confident, Werid of the Far Side?"

"Not at all." My master took a shuddering breath. "But these are the talents we've been given." They gestured towards us. "I'm little more than a leech, making use of them. What would happen if Goldenlake fell to the Hedgehogs? No one could tell. They have always looked more towards the mountains of the far east and the council in Cloudhome. And if Goldenlake fell to the men of the Cities? Tell her, Sloe."

I rubbed my aching knees. "They'd build a temple of their own over our holy town, like they did in Eastbay. Something with a dome, so big that it can be seen across the width of the lake. They'd fix a big copper star to its top, proclaiming their victory over the Tall and the Small Gods. They'd transform our gods into evil spirits, demons, and call their conquest a triumph of civilization. They have a pattern to follow."

"Do you want to risk it?" Werid asked the older wizard.

Qerla stared at me. "Is this the truth, Sloe Moon of Tall Trees? Would we abandon our gods to mistreatment and misrepresentation?"

"I've spoken with some of the Siblings while I visited the Continent. They all suffered different fates, and there might be some pockets of secret believers hidden away, but most of it lies buried under new legends, rituals that used to mean different things, places that once were of similar importance as Goldenlake and nowadays lend their significance to newer gods. On the Continent everything intermingles, but it feels too early to submit our faith just yet …"

Qerla scratched her head again. "I certainly don't want that to happen under my watch. Thank you, Sloe. There are some things Sjunil taught you well." She frowned. "Where do you want to open up the fire, Werid?"

"Near the boat station, where most of the buildings have already burned away. It needs to look like an accident though, so it can't be too convenient for us."

"Yes," Qerla said. "The headland will be narrow enough to control the ones who make it through."

"Exactly, and we need to release our warriors slowly, so they don't realize immediately it was a prepared situation."

Qerla straightened her shoulders, her blue and brown eyes shining with new resolve. "Then that is how it will be. I leave you in command, Werid of the Far Side."

It took some time to find Raz. It felt wrong to pull away from the other four, and I was coated in cold sweat when I finally spotted her crumpled against one of the half-burned houses, pulling a bandage tight around her wrist.

"Are you all right?" I asked, and she shrugged.

"I've fought with worse." She gestured to the crusty sleeve around my own arm. "That looks nasty."

"I'll live. Werid sent me out to find you."

"I was worried you'd say that. What do they want to yell at me for? Qati took me in like the rest of us. I had no fucking clue." Her face was full of self-loathing. "I sure know how to pick them."

"This isn't about Qati. We need to sort him out later, and then you're more than welcome to rant at me for hours about your awful taste in men. This is about commanding the warriors of Goldenlake."

"What?" she asked, perplexed.

"You've spent a lot of time with Rawil Owl, you must've learned a thing or two."

She drew in a sharp breath. "What makes them think I could grasp command?"

"Qerla has stepped aside and asked Werid to take her place."

Raz slowly shook her head. "Funny, how things work out like that."

"By their own admission, Werid hasn't a lot of experience with blades."

"Is this a real request?" She still sounded suspicious.

"It is."

"Fuck. All right, but I'll need Lilyis' help."

"Don't make it too obvious where the orders actually come from." There was a glow around Lilyis.

"They've seen you fight on our side all day," Raz reminded her. "They won't reject you. Not the ones who saw your skill for themselves."

"Be careful," my master said softly. "Don't get too carried away by the possibilities presenting themselves. What can go wrong will go wrong. I'll leave the matter in your capable hands. Sloe, gather the others—we should walk up to the boat station together and look at what's left to play with."

Hano and Mayiel were flushed and excited as we made our way across town. Members of various families stood at street corners to hand out food to the defenders, and everywhere people had collapsed against house walls, sleeping as much as they could in anticipation of the next flare-up. The apprentices had organized medical stations to see to the wounded; from time to time their masters joined in to help with salves, bandages, and stitches.

The circle of fire around Goldenlake made everyone appear sweaty and exhausted, and its heat crisped the thatched roofs and let the rafters crackle. What unfathomable strength Brother Flame needed to keep protecting his people … I couldn't bear to consider the effort, and how could the Hedgehogs stand against us, seeing the demonstration of favour? Perhaps my master's reasons to despise them had solid foundations, and were based on more than rivalry between two families living too close together.

"I need a staff," Werid decided as we came upon the first swathe of flattened houses, still smoking, with ashes soft beneath the soles of our boots.

We were close to the fire; flames swooped around the headland, jumping across the outlying jetties of the boat station. The ground formed an arrowhead pointing east into the waters, crowned by a cluster of boulders. Someone had laid down an offering of summer flowers, already charred around the edges and ready to burst into flames, to mingle their ashes with the others.

The destruction was astonishing. It'd been a long time since I'd visited the station, but I remembered it as a bustling part of town, with many storage sheds and racks for drying fish, baskets to wash mussels and process the goods brought over the lake from Coldharbour.

Everything was gone, apart from heaps of jumbled charcoal and smouldering fabrics, the wool resisting the fires. There was nothing much to hide behind, and as Werid started to search through what was left for anything that could be fashioned into a symbol of their new power, the utter strangeness of the scene struck me. The town of Goldenlake had withstood centuries, and we were gathered among a desolation of rubble and ash.

While Mayiel cried softly into Eleas' shoulder, Hano stared out at what had once been such an integral part of the sacred place, the most human part of it, where trade had been more important than wizard business. My master crouched amidst the spoilage and pulled at this and that, flinging away unsuitable options. The light of the fire washed over their graceful frame and ash-caked hair. Werid of the Far Side had transformed into a scavenger; the vanities that had ruled their life had been discarded.

Eleas cleared her throat. A grey coating of ash clung to her dark skin and her mouth was weirdly pale. "This is what could happen to all of it," she said roughly. "This is what we fight against."

Mayiel sniffled and Hano touched her shoulder briefly, but in the gesture was so much care and gentleness that my throat constricted.

"Hah!" Werid's shout of triumph rang out over the wasteland. As they straightened up to display their find, we gasped.

They'd found the unburnt remnants of a tall drying rack, one of its branches singed but serviceable, with a tangle of wire fused around its end. A hole had been cut to slot into the other parts of the rack. It seemed right, something that escaped destruction and had been moulded by circumstance into beauty. Werid's dirty face shone as they ripped the purple stone off their neck and jammed it into the opening, pushing the wire around it to keep it in.

"This will do."

ALL THAT COULD HAVE BEEN

The flames fell in the hours of the early morning, just before dawn, and our enemies rushed out onto the headland. Our defenders had stationed themselves in different places at the eastern edge of town to give the impression of arriving group by group on the scene, and the breach was small enough to only let in a couple of Hedgehogs at a time. For a while we saw our fighters pick them off comfortably, until a sudden blast of ice subdued the flames, widening the gap.

Werid spat out a curse. The next man stepping through the breach sported much longer hair spikes than the warriors, and his robes were embroidered with stylized flakes of snow. He had a faint limp, using his staff as much as a crutch as a weapon. A faint bluish light hovered around him, and I heard Mayiel gasp, as if her talent recognized the strength within the wizard. He brought seven others with him; based on their plainer clothes they were lower in rank, but bound to him as we were to Werid, holding him up. The Bulls had come to Birkland to find more sorcerers and had unearthed at least a single formidable one.

As the flames fell away around them, Werid pulled us forwards, the defenders following with a roar. The Hedgehog wizard whirled his staff up, punching my master full in the chest with a stormy gust. It was Eleas who screamed in pain, her Sibling turning on her. I heard myself panting in shock. Sister Storm had never been close to me, but what would happen if Brother Brook withdrew his allegiance? Or Brother Flame? The circle could well close in on us and finish what the men of the Cities started.

Werid countered with a blast of blue fire. The wizard ducked but one of his bound apprentices went down with a screech. He drew his strength from them as he hurled out an icy fist of wind, no fire, no light. While Werid had harnessed our talents to use them, as varied as they were, he was the one with the connection to Sister Storm. Werid rammed the circlet onto their head and sun streamed forth to bring down the veil of ice crystals.

Eleas was breathing hard, her face streaked with tears. Werid's attack brought another of the Hedgehog apprentices to their knees. My master was trying to incapacitate them one by one, having understood his spell as soon as I had. Werid's new staff flicked around, focussing our gifts into a mixture of stone and soil, a deadly composition of brute forces to smack the next Hedgehog squarely between the eyebrows. She fell back without making a sound, as straight as a tree. There were four of them left at his back, propping him up, but I read unguarded fear in their faces. He had likely compelled them and though three had fallen, his spell didn't shatter, and he didn't attempt to pull in any of the other fighters around him to replace the fallen apprentices. There was a chance he had a different way of setting it up, and it was only Werid's second try. When Werid launched another beam of light on them, I clutched at the hands of my companions, and we surged on.

Mayiel was pale and covered in sweat, and Hano's breath came in great painful gasps. He'd bitten his lips bloody, trying to withstand the sensations my master subjected us to, the purple stone flashing, bundling the light of Sister Sun.

"Don't kill him!" I heard myself scream at Werid, fear of what could be lost taking over.

They spun around to me, the small distraction enough for our adversary to step in and shower us with ice crystals sharp enough to lacerate our skin. Werid howled in frustration, wrenching their arm back in time to save their face from being cut to shreds.

"Fuck—Sloe!"

"We need to learn from him—don't kill him!"

Blood sprayed off their wrist as they raised their staff again. "There might not be another way!"

"You'll find one!"

"He's a Hedgehog, for fuck's sake!"

"He's one of us!"

A wave of half-frozen water punched down on us, breaking the binding that held us to my master. Werid blanched, realizing by how much they'd overplayed their hand, when the Hedgehog wizard came after them. Eleas and I pushed ourselves in front of Werid, our shoulders colliding with a painful *whump*. I almost threw Eleas off her feet, but she raised her hands to ward off the onslaught. I heard her fingers break as the ice crunched down on us, Sister Storm once more withdrawing her favour.

I shoved Eleas back as she cradled her hands against her chest. Mayiel and Hano were at my back, the two most inexperienced ones, the ones who'd possessed the courage to volunteer in a house filled with resentful wizards … I bared my teeth, clawing at the key. Even if it was pure superstition, I felt stronger wielding it. Winding its cords around my wrist to secure it, I squared my shoulders.

I was too far away from the Hedgehog wizard for the key to reach and hurt him. I had no staff and knew better than to pick up my master's. He snarled at me. It was the right leg he favoured as the butt of his own staff squelched into the sodden ground, where pieces of ice melted around us. Sister Stone stood with me as I hurled all I had at his left leg. He tried to retreat behind his apprentices but one of them stumbled and I struck him, the noise sickening as he faltered. I set the hair of the closest apprentice aflame, while Hano blinded the others, wrapping the mist rising from the ground around them like a sheet. I drew on Mayiel to form our own ice scythe, slicing across the group, before Sister Soil exploded the ground before them.

The Hedgehog wizard had only grunted as Sister Stone hit him, but Sister Storm hurt him more. Like Eleas, he seemed troubled, for the first time since the wizard-off had started. All his strength relied on the faithfulness of one single Sibling, and as my aunt would've been quick to tell me, Sister Storm never had been the most loyal of them. I heard her laugh as she hurt him, and his left leg started to buckle.

"Are you sure you want to keep him alive?" Brother Brook asked me. He stood before me, radiating the crisp coolness of a deep river, his hands clasped behind his back, his green eyes mocking me. "It won't take long for my brother to exhaust himself fully and the fire will fall. Look around you—they're still coming through, and some of them haven't joined the fight yet. It would make more sense to get rid of him once and for all. He hasn't any qualms about pounding you into the ground."

I stared at the wizard in front of us, gathering the strength of Sister Storm around him like folds of a glittering cloak. His face was distorted in rage, the spikes of his bleached hair sparking with wrath—the wave crested above me and the others, building itself up higher and higher.

"You need to decide now," Brother Brook said. "This is the moment you need to know your heart."

"Save them," I said, as my arms stretched out to shield Hano and Mayiel behind me. "If this goes wrong—save them."

The key flew from my hand, breaking its cords, striking the Hedgehog across the bridge of the nose. I'd meant to knock him out, but as his face exploded into blood and snot, he came up and at me, his weakened legs straightening up in one last desperate push. I raised my arms, the fingers curled inwards to keep them from shattering, the outside of my wrists colliding with ice and bone.

A shout tore from my throat as I expected to be overwhelmed, trying to pull in Sister Soil's last wisps of purplish mist. There was a bright flash, a cloak fluttering across my eyes, clean and woven in stripes of grey and black. A fan of liquid mud sprayed up as the first wizard of Goldenlake barrelled into the man who'd tried to kill me with everything he had.

Freshwater pearls came loose from Qerla's staff and pinged against my forehead as she mowed down the last of his apprentices. I saw her mouth, set in a decisive frown, her eyes squinting against the glare of the ice in the air. A blade sprang out of the side of her staff, opening the Hedgehog wizard's head up from jaw to ear, and he fell into the mist.

Qerla sneered down at him, her silver braids flecked with his blood.

"Are you completely *insane*?" Werid shrilled.

The old woman grinned at her, whirling her staff around in a way that was clearly meant to show off, the smeared blade cruelly hooked. "Goldenlake has been my town for all my life," she said coolly. "There is no way you can keep me from fighting for it."

The Hedgehogs quickly realized the wizard they'd sent to deal with the biggest threat to their enterprise had failed. Instead of falling back they came at us with everything they had left; riders galloped through the ever-widening breach to surround us.

"Get back!" Qerla barked at us. "Can you repair the spell, Werid?"

"No, of course I fucking can't!"

"Then get out of the way, if you don't want to be trampled."

My master picked up their own staff and wiped the mud off the purple stone. "Come and make me."

"This is not the time." Eleas held her arms across her chest to protect her smashed hands from further damage. "The spell has broken but we can still fight—with tooth and nail if necessary."

A shadow sailed across my face and the call of the kite drew our gaze up to the skies. Brother Flame glided through billows of smoke, ruffled, but still flying, a glow emanating from every feather.

"The gods are with Goldenlake," Qerla Badger rasped, before the first wizard turned to face me. "No wizard will ever admit lightly that they were wrong," she said. "This is for Sjunil Moon and all that could have been." She spun around and charged back into battle.

A NEW CONSTELLATION

We found Qerla Badger later, after the fire circle had broken down to expose us once again. She'd fallen into the ditch, her body wedged against the edge of the unfinished palisade, with an axe sticking up between her shoulder blades.

Cathil retrieved her staff, buried under the last Hedgehog she'd killed and trudged back to us, his right leg hastily bandaged. The defenders had corralled the surviving men of the Cities in front of the Roundhouse. Only four Bulls were left alive, as well as three priests of Whiterivers: men who'd been known in town and who'd surely be blamed for the uproar caused by Bjor's death.

Raz and Werid stood shoulder to shoulder, surveying what was left of Goldenlake, the piles of rescued goods and possessions littering the shore of the holy waters. From as far away as the centre of town, many collapsed houses were visible. Three quarters had been completely destroyed in the fighting lasting from dawn to dusk. It'd taken a while for the attackers to understand their attempt to overrun us had failed; the frantic movement had slowly petered out as everyone had become aware that the instigators, easy targets among the Hedgehogs, had been brought down one by one, the scant survivors bloodied and so exhausted in their defeat they were barely able to keep their eyes open.

In my mind, the last few hours had become one large blur. After the Hedgehogs lost their wizard to Qerla's blade, we'd broken apart, everyone fighting their way back as best as they could, retreating towards the Roundhouse filled with uncounted wounded and the last of the wizards of Goldenlake, stubbornly praying.

Qes was with the prisoners, sporting a deep gash on his forehead that would have to be stitched up sooner or later. The right side of his face was swollen and discoloured. We hadn't fallen into each other's arms when we found each other again. There was nothing to celebrate. Too many members of the families lay dead: Hedgehogs, Bears, Badgers, Ravens … all of them in a tangle with the men who'd thought to make their mark on our lands, to light a beacon that could be seen all the way across the sea and fuel an uprising that had nothing to do with us. Still, it was difficult for me to continue hating them, shivering and bleeding as they were. Even the star amulets around the priests' necks couldn't rouse me anymore.

Together, Raz and Lilyis had managed to keep a grip on the situation, preventing the defence from succumbing to utter chaos. As they stood with Werid, the new wizard in command, the people of Goldenlake beheld the trio with unexpected reverence. An Owl, a Wolf, and a Princess of Crooked Hill would reap the praise and rewards for the victory. The far west, the steppes, and the Cities had entered into an unlikely alliance on both sides and combined their expertise to save the day for all of us, for the pilgrims and the fisher people, everyone living a life between ceremonies and arguments over theories. Lilyis had acknowledged me with a quick smile of relief before vanishing back into the huddle of commanders, while I'd crumpled onto a bench at the wall of the Roundhouse and was trying to catch up with myself. Allowing myself to feel everything would've been too overwhelming, so I welcomed Sister Stone's hand upon my heart.

Apprentices walked around with waterskins to offer a drink to the surviving defenders; the first children started to appear between the houses, no longer willing to be cooped up inside, though there were bodies sprawled out on the streets of their town. Goldenlake would have to be rebuilt, and it would be a different place afterwards. Qerla Badger had been right: it had been her town, and it was scrambling back to its feet, finding itself scorched and beaten into a pulp, but breathing.

As I buried my face in my palms, my eyes felt as if someone had filled them with burning sand. Someone poked me in the shoulder with a sharp elbow.

"You should be happier."

Eleas Cormorant, her fingers bandaged and splinted, and with a faint green sheen around the scrapes on her face and neck, stood next to me. "You saved Goldenlake."

I laughed in disbelief. "Horseshit."

"You had a large part in saving Goldenlake, does that sound better? They might look to the three back there, but everyone who has seen you launch the circle of flames knows what truly happened." She slowly settled next to me, awkwardly with her bound hands. "I stood next to you throughout it all. I can tell them."

"Don't you dare."

"I heard Qerla admit she made a mistake with you. Who knows what might come of that?"

"Shut up, Eleas—please. Be glad we're still alive, though I don't think that's enough."

Her black eyes narrowed. "Not enough? What do you need to be finally convinced that you did not make a mistake in letting us return to help?"

"Look at your hands, Eleas."

"My hands are my problem and they will heal. I was stupid enough to risk my limbs, this is not on you. Whatever the Siblings whisper in your ear, whatever *he* says to you ... I cannot shake you out of it, but I am still tempted to try. Breathe, Sloe. The smoke is lifting." She gestured around us. "We will find a new constellation."

"What constellation?" I asked bitterly.

"In a year, this town will be very different. People like Hano and Mayiel will not have to worry about their shameful secrets being exposed. They will know that it is simply another way to serve the gods—a more calamitous way, but nothing the council can make you feel less about. Nothing you could be punished for."

"Will you stay here to make sure the vision comes true?"

She held up her bandaged hands. "It will take a while for me to be truly useful, but you know Werid needs someone to look after them, to prevent them from getting giddy with the power that was given to them. The wizards of the west have laughed at them all their life, have called them a dung beetle and barred the way to the Harp for them. If they are in charge of the council of the east, I can only imagine how tempted they will be to make them all regret ever having snubbed them."

"That sounds like something Werid would be prone to do," I admitted. "They won't be an easy person to be around."

Eleas gritted out a laugh. "No, they will not."

"But you'll try, right?"

Eleas' shell cape gave off a silvery sound as the polished pieces shifted against each other. "I will try. I never expected to be granted a chance at love, so it would take all Eight Siblings, Brother Fear *and* Sister Courage to pry me off. This is something I need to thank you for. If you and Lilyis had not come to Westlight, I would still be stuck in the village, marrying off other people and weaving silent prayers. Each year I would have become more resentful." She winced as she tried to fold her hands against her chest. "There will come a time when I miss the sea too much not to ride down to the coast, but for now I can make do with a sacred lake. And we have a wedding of our own to prepare for as long as both grooms recover from their cuts and bruises." She turned towards Qes and the broken men of the Cities, towards Cathil, who stood with Lilyis and Raz, his leg wrapped in the dirty bandage.

"You're right. It is far from the end." I pushed myself off the wall and onto my aching feet. One of the soles of my boots had started to peel away during the fight and it was arduous business merely to walk towards the few men we kept under such close observation.

Qes' eyes widened in alarm as I came closer.

The eldest of the Whiterivers priests flinched away from me, clutching at the star on his chest. As dented and soiled as the amulet was, he wasn't prepared to do without the love of his gods, while I felt hollowed out, so much had my Siblings drawn out of me in the last hours. As our dead were being washed and prepared to cross over to the land they would from now on call their own, I stared down at the frightened man. He'd seen me wield flame and ice, had witnessed my bound friends kill his comrades—he was scared. For him I was all that a wizard could be, not something gone wrong, someone who'd strayed so far off the path that there was no redemption.

"Your gods didn't stand with you today," I said to him, to all seven survivors. "Or maybe they did, as you are breathing and will have food, drink, and shelter, courtesy of the families who rule this town and the lands around them." My voice sounded rusty; my accent much stronger since I no longer used the words of the Cities every single day.

The seven glared at me, as if me speaking tainted them. I felt an impatient wrench in my gut. They longed to spit at my feet; I could see them already sucking in their cheeks.

One of the Bulls decided to speak up. "This is the start," he said. "There are many more cousins of mine waiting to embark on a quest to avenge us."

"And will probably fail. The Hedgehogs have fled, and they won't easily agree to another alliance with the Cities, if Southclere or Whiterivers. Other families will hear of your defeat and shy away from risking something so ill-considered. What did you promise them? Land? A higher cut of the profits while you sell on Birkland goods for three times as much as they are aware of?"

The Bull looked away. "It doesn't concern you."

"I'm curious. Which kind of greed compelled them? Or what kind of punishment did you threaten them with if their help was refused?" I asked, trying hard to control a sneer.

"It doesn't concern you," he repeated.

"But it concerns me." Lilyis swept off her felted hood. Under all that blood and dirt she was still recognizable as of the Cities, her hair too red and curled to belong to a true member of the families. "You are held captive by the Company of the Sun, specifically by someone you should be aware of." Her bright eyes narrowed as she crouched down before them, as she'd done with the priest who'd died by Cathil's knife in Thorndell. "I wield the authority of my forebears and the strength of their name."

"You are Nian," one of the Whiterivers priests blubbered. "Nian da Nileon—I saw you marry my cousin Fiolis, many years ago."

Lilyis smiled at him. "That's right. I am Nian, Prince of Crooked Hill—*and* I am Lilyis Sun, commander of the warriors of Goldenlake."

A VERY SIMILAR STORY

The leader of the Hedgehog delegation coming back to Goldenlake under the protection of their status as emissaries looked decidedly worse for wear. Her right ear had been crudely stitched back to her head and was greasy with salve, her lips split and swollen. She was almost as thin as Mayiel Magpie and her company was made up of women warriors, who sported the same spiked hair style as the men. They wore sage-green cloaks and many of them had pierced ears, with golden ornaments hanging from them. It might've been a deliberate attempt to calm Werid's prejudices against their family by sending beautiful women but I wasn't the only one fearing an éclat.

Eleas pushed through the spectators to reach the Roundhouse where the remnants of the council had reconvened before the delegation arrived, to prepare their new leader for what was coming their way.

"They're wizards," I whispered to Lilyis as they passed us.

She took my elbow. "You should be in the Roundhouse and listen to what they have to say."

"But …"

"You've earned it." She gave me a quick kiss to send me on my way. "Go. Go now, before I push you through the fucking door."

In the days after the battle of Goldenlake, the town was as busy as before; the sounds of chopping axes and clay being mixed with straw in large wooden vats were everywhere. Heaps of sturdy hazel rods lined the streets and groups of citizens went out to cut bracken in the surrounding woods. Compared to the bustle around it, the Roundhouse was quiet, though two dozen wizards shoved in with me to gawp at the Hedgehogs, who'd come with an agenda we were all impatient to uncover.

I saw Hano standing at the back and joined him.

He gave me a relieved nod.

The chair that had been Qerla Badger's for longer than most of us remembered, was covered in Werid's seal skin cloak and my master seated upon it, their feet placed primly next to each other. Werid of the Far Side wore the golden circlet on their brow, and next to them stood Mayiel, in charge of the scorched staff topped with the purple stone dedicated to Brother Rain. Werid's face was drawn, their large brown eyes strangely luminous, as if Brother Moon still stood with them.

"Why did you come?" they asked bluntly.

The Hedgehogs knelt before the first wizard of Goldenlake and with a single motion reached up to their own heads, unclasped their jewellery, and held it out in a gesture of sacrifice.

"We come to apologize," their leader said. As frail as she appeared, her voice was powerful, filling every last nook of the Roundhouse. "To offer payment to assuage the Tall and the Small Gods, and win back their favour, to atone for what was done to the town of sacred waters. We come to offer ourselves."

They placed their gold on the floor of the house, where it lay spilled like a treasure hoard.

I saw the muscles around Werid's mouth twitch. "Atonement is not that easily bought," they said coldly. "We are not men of the Cities to be blinded by trinkets."

"Trinkets that will pay to restore the town to its former glory, and more," she replied softly. "We offer our ties with the far east, with the families who live among the riches of the mountains, their silver, gold, and gems of colours that have never been seen in the west."

"If you are as rich as you claim, why follow men from the Cities? What could they have given you in return?"

"The promise of renewal. Of gods that are easier to please than our own."

Shocked silence spread in the Roundhouse. My master was lost for words.

"Oh no," Hano muttered next to me.

"How?" Werid asked. "You are wizards like us. How could you …"

Their leader came to her feet. "We are the ones who disagreed with the plans. Who were punished for resisting."

Werid snapped to attention. "Please, all of you rise. Tell me—how did it come to pass?"

"You will have heard what happened with the Clouds," the Hedgehog said. "Ours is a very similar story. Many of us have been seduced by the tales reaching us from the Cities," she said, her head still bent. Anger radiated from her, barely suppressed. "About wonders beyond the seas and many favours bestowed upon their populations by *kings*." She spat out the last word with a vehemence that let me shudder. "Now that the Tall Gods have demonstrated their strength in such a memorable way and have thrown down our warriors, everyone rushes to beg for forgiveness, even if it means cowering in front of a Wolf."

Whatever had once happened between the Hedgehogs and the Wolves, both Werid and the leader seemed loath to put their misgivings behind them.

My master's face was unmoved. "Be assured that I sit before you not as a Wolf, but as the wizard who received the right of command from the late first wizard of Goldenlake herself, and that my council does bear you no ill-will. Beyond what they experienced at your hand a few days ago, that is. We know how easily one can be lured in by promises of new, exciting things. Be they treasures of far-away lands or the expectation of finding our circumstances changed in general. The gods of the Star might not be my own idea of fun, but taste—thankfully—varies."

A small shudder ran through the body of the leading Hedgehog, and I understood she'd chuckled at my master's joke.

"One day there will likely come a time when the Star claims the lands of the families or when we find a way to worship in much more peaceful ways, but it seems as if order has been restored." Her rich voice sent a shiver down my back. "As the most prominent wizards remaining to the Hedgehogs, we welcome it."

"I'm glad to hear that, but please don't be offended if I do as you have so kindly offered and ask my apprentice to retrieve the gold from our floor, to provide our working population with the materials to hasten Goldenlake's resurrection as the heart of the Tall and Small Gods."

"It was not meant to be an empty gesture, so please go ahead." On her signal, the wizards took up their gold and held it out for Mayiel to collect in a basket. An appreciative hum went through the Roundhouse.

The leader cleared her throat. "It is also not our only gift. We have in our possession something that might be of more value to you. Or, rather—someone."

Qati Badger had a broken nose, the bruises stretching out under his seeing eye and the one that had been sewn shut. Apart from that he seemed unharmed, though they'd bound him so tightly he was unable to find a comfortable position to sit in. He stared up at Werid, who'd come to him on the back of a golden mare with a swishing silver mane, their long cloak falling over the horse's rear in folds too heavy to be of use at the height of summer. No bead of sweat showed on my master's brow as they sneered down at him.

"You were kinder to him than expected. He'll make our eighth prisoner. I dare say I won't be the only one who will enjoy seeing him bound up like a parcel of cloth."

The Hedgehog wizards had walked with us to the clearing in the forest, onto a slight elevation from which we could see the sun blinking on the waters of the lake, fringed by the dark summer leaves of the birches closest to the shoreline. Werid was the only one on horseback. Qes and Cathil stood next to the head of the golden mare.

The Hedgehog camp showed signs of their hasty departure. Only the wizards and a few others had stayed behind to face the council. They worked hard to keep the look of desperation off their faces.

"You are all welcome in Goldenlake," Werid proclaimed. "We can make use of every hand. Cathil?"

Cathil closed his eyes for a moment, as if he'd been dreading the command he'd received; he stepped forwards and pulled Qati up. Qati's eye roamed over the rows—he was searching for Raz, I realized, but Lilyis had asked her to stay behind in town with her. Eventually, Qati's eye fixed on me as Cathil lashed his wrists to Werid's saddle, then loosened the rope around his ankles so that he'd be able to walk behind the golden mare. He'd be taken back to Goldenlake in shame, a Badger who'd betrayed all Badgers.

As I glanced back at him, I found it difficult to swallow. Once my own father had been in a similar situation. The hate that was in Qati's narrow face had once felt familiar to him, and to me. Werid made a noise against the roof of their mouth to urge their mount on, the rope pulling the eighth captive forward. The tight fetters must have caused his legs to go numb and he stumbled; Cathil walked behind him to prevent him from falling.

Whatever reasons Qati had had for his actions, they must've been plausible enough to risk that kind of humiliation. The way he continued to scan the people around him made me think he wanted Raz to witness his defeat. In handing him over, the Hedgehogs had bought Werid's good will, but he'd been something like my friend; we'd travelled together and it was hard to simply give up wanting to find the best in him, even with all he'd done to deserve being treated like the men of the Cities. But for a few twists of fate, a similar spectacle could've been staged on my behalf. I'd come close, when Bjor had paraded me across Seagard. Back then I'd felt my Siblings around me, like a shadowy guard at my back, but Qati faced the wizards alone. There'd be many people clamouring for his death, for another cage, another pyre, another sacrifice to the waters.

TAKE ON THE NAME

Raz seemed determined to keep her mind off Qati and the seven men of the Cities. "We have far too much to do to get side-tracked," she said and pushed past me to join Qes and Cathil at the newly erected guards' quarters.

"Leave her be," Lilyis said, fumbling with a bandage around her right wrist that was supposed to protect a long cut on its underside, where one of the Bulls had slipped through her defence. "She's taking this quite hard and isn't ready to talk about him yet."

"There might not be many opportunities left," I said.

"Because of what they're planning to do to him? I'm sure Eleas will convince Werid not to make any rash decisions. Qati is a Badger, after all."

"They will pick a deliberately horrible punishment to warn off any others."

"He betrayed you, too." She sounded disapproving.

"It isn't about me."

She raised a brow at me. "Are you sure?"

"What are you saying? That I'm selfish? I'm trying so hard not to be."

"No. Just that you see everything in your own way and your first prejudice is always against yourself, despite a thousand people congratulating you on your victories. I'm getting slightly fed up with that attitude." She snorted as I stared at her in dismay. "You haven't understood that it's over."

"For now," I said cautiously.

"And the last thing we need is to get sucked into another family conflict."

"Yeah," I scoffed. "Good luck with that. Even if it should've been the hardest lesson for us to learn, it will happen again and many times over. As long as there are family members that feel hard done by or overlooked, there'll always be uprisings and broken alliances, divorces that throw the whole of the forests out of balance … it will never end. Never ever."

"Because it's not supposed to." She pulled me down by the collar. "The only thing I need you to focus on is that we've made it out of the battle alive, when so many others didn't. That we have a wedding to plan and that you've watched your own master ascend to a position of power. These are good things, Sloe." She kissed me gently. "Even if Werid will need someone to keep an eye on them. They strike me as someone who might be a bit too enthusiastic."

Lilyis gasped as I threw my arms around her. Someone cheered as they saw us snogging in front of the guards' quarters and Lilyis started to laugh.

"We need to decide how to make the most of the Bulls' failure. Perhaps they wouldn't protest too much if I relieved them of any goods they've amassed so far? I can afford to offer them a good price. Or I could requisition their ship, paint it yellow and return home to Seagard with a fleet." She looked flushed and excited. "Before then we need to find some time for us."

"Right." I glanced over my shoulder. "There aren't many buildings left that would suit us, but the Roundhouse is currently empty …"

She grinned. "I'm not going to fuck you on Werid's throne," she said. "We'd never hear the end of *that*."

We'd walked out of town, among the birches. It was a warm day, but the shade provided by the canopy sent waves of goosebumps over my arms and neck. Lilyis pulled me along, not able to restrain herself, and as she pushed me against one of the trunks, its silky silver-speckled bark, I was finally ready to loosen my grip. Suddenly there was no time to get undressed, we shoved out of the way what needed to be out of the way. My head was pressed into the dry leaves of last year as the whole forest crackled and sparked around me.

It didn't take long, but as I started to apologize Lilyis closed my mouth with a kiss. "There will be time," she whispered. "So much time. The *Golden Drake* is all the way back in the west, and you might want to check up on your sister and the baby on our way back to the Stoneharp. You're not getting rid of me so fast." She pinched the skin on my arm.

"Ow!"

"I won't let you start finding fault with that argument just yet, Sloe. I can pinch you all day." She rolled on top of me, her hair filled with broken leaves and pieces of dry moss. "Even if Werid can't really marry us, we can have our own vows—for us. If you'd want to do that." She buried her face on my chest and pinched me again. "Don't let me wait so long to agree!"

"I certainly want to, I was just …" I bit down on my lip to anchor myself before confessing to my feelings.

"Just what?"

"Overcome."

"Overcome?" Lilyis echoed. "Really? Don't you dare play games with me."

"I've seen you handle interrogations. I'd never be able to resist you."

"Damn right. You can't fuck with a Princess of Crooked Hill."

"Well—turns out you can." I felt a weird urge to giggle that I suppressed by clearing my throat. The sweat started to dry on our skin and Lilyis nuzzled into me.

"I wish we didn't have to go back. We could live here among the trees, snare hares, dig out roots, exist off the favour of the gods. There must be people who manage that."

"Have a hut in the woods, like Sjunil? Keep a few apprentices around to do the actual work and read all day? When we're not devouring each other? You'd go stir-crazy after a few days. Remember when we stayed with my aunt and Werid? You hated it."

"I did," she admitted. "Because I knew Sjunil needed me to get out of the way. I think she saw through me immediately. The truth is, I'd be very afraid to disappoint you after all. And I'm lying on a root—something keeps digging into my back."

"Fine—let's go back. I think Qes put me on the watch rota for the afternoon anyway and I don't want to piss him off. He might not let me stand next to him at the wedding."

"Of course he will. If you brush your hair and wear something clean." She picked a piece of twig out of my hair. "You might need a bit of help with that."

The smell of hot vinegar lingered over the central houses of Goldenlake. A row of cookfires had sprung up under the roof of one of the bigger buildings and a table covered in chopped vegetables for pickling and salting waited for the pots to come up to the boil. Members of several families had gathered to prepare the glut of summer for winter storage. Many boats were out on the lake and would bring over goods from Coldharbour, paid for with the gold of the Hedgehogs, as well as aged timber, tanned hides, and tools to replace what had been burned.

The people of Goldenlake seemed all too eager to leave the battle behind them, to sweep up the ashes and prepare for Longest Night and its festivities, though we were many months away. Some of them greeted Lilyis as we passed the guards on the road and made our way across town. As the third-in-command she'd caught their attention, and the fact that she'd defended them against her own people had stuck. Lilyis blushed and waved back. We walked hand-in-hand in the sunshine, with the light bouncing off the lake to our left and setting a glint in Lilyis' green eyes.

For once I didn't think about the Siblings at my back or the cuts we both had suffered, not about Lilyis' eventual departure or that my aunt hadn't been here to take control, that Lilyis would travel home to her father to tell him about our adventures without me, that it was more than likely that I'd never see Nivael da Nileon again, or Hilvis da Ozanil, or the crown prince, even if I'd scraped off the blood from his key to wear it around my neck once more.

As we drew closer to the Roundhouse the vinegar bit the inside of our noses, and I released Lilyis' hand to wipe at my face. I barely noticed the door of the house swinging open and a group of wizards stepping out. Some of them were Hedgehogs, but most of them part of the Goldenlake council, all dressed plainer than usual.

"Is something going on?" I asked. "They're all staring at us."

Lilyis took both of my hands. "Forgive me. Werid asked me to distract you while they prepared the house."

"For what?" My stomach clenched.

Eleas came out into the square and bowed to her. No—she didn't bow to Lilyis, she bowed to me.

"You're making me nervous," I said, starting to sweat again.

My master was the last to come out of the Roundhouse. "You look as if Lilyis has dragged you through the whole of the forest," Werid complained and picked another piece of broken twig off me.

"That's how I always look."

"Indeed." They wore their grey floor-length tunic, their glorious hair in a simple braid closed with a pearl-studded wire, and there was the circlet, gleaming demurely against their dark skin.

"You're scaring the shit of me."

"I know, and I'm sorry, but we all thought it might better come as a surprise." They signalled to Mayiel, who propped the door open. A plume of sweet-smelling smoke escaped from within. The Roundhouse had been cleansed in preparation for something important.

"Surprise me with what?"

Lilyis laid my hands into my masters. "We thought you might like to get this over with before the wedding celebrations."

"Get *what* over with?" I squealed, afraid that I would piss myself in front of all these wizards, as I'd pissed myself in the battle of the Stoneharp.

"The council has met and decided upon the matter, so there's no way we're not going through with it," Werid said. "They have come today to serve as witnesses, and we might need them to hold you down. We have agreed to count the battle of Goldenlake towards your apprenticeship, and as your own Protocols. I've asked for the ink and the instruments to be prepared. Today you will become a wizard, Sloe Moon of Tall Trees. Today you will officially take on the name of Sloe of the Blue Cloak."

ONLY JUST THE BEGINNING

"Does it hurt?" Qes peered at my forehead with kohl-rimmed eyes.

"It just had to get infected. Eleas said that's perfectly normal and that I've been lucky the fever only knocked me out for two days. I couldn't have forgiven myself for missing this."

Qes threw himself into my arms and we held each other.

"I'm glad we can do it quietly," he murmured. "Imagine if they'd made me get married in Thorndell! Mother wouldn't have let me get away with something simple. Maybe it has its advantages to fall out with your family in such a spectacular way."

"You'll be joined by the first wizard of Goldenlake—if that doesn't qualify as a special occasion …"

"Have you talked to Cathil?"

I shook my head. "No."

"But he's still in town? He hasn't jumped on his horse and fled?"

"Why would he do that to you?"

"Because that's usually how it works out for me."

I kissed his flaming cheek. "Not today. Not ever again. Don't cry—you'll smudge the kohl."

My best friend sniffled desperately. "Could you ever have imagined this is how it ends?" His gaze was once again drawn up to my brows. "I'm sorry, but I can't get used to that. How did it feel when they put the mark on you?"

"I fainted pretty quickly, so I'm not sure. I say fainted—the Siblings pulled me under, so who knows."

"Did you ask them for a double mark?"

"No. It's one of Werid's ideas."

The mark that had been inked into my skin resembled two teardrop shapes over each other, one pointing up and one pointing down, overlapping in the middle of the design. The skin around it felt hot to the touch, though Eleas had checked the tattoo every day and asked Mayiel to mix pastes and salves while she watched, her broken fingers grotesque in their bandages. The muscular woman who'd marked me had been a master of her craft, had marked many apprentices ascending to their wizardship in Goldenlake. I'd seen her work on Hano afterwards. She'd been quiet and gentle and hadn't questioned what had been asked of her. In a few days, Eleas' tattoo would be amended and when Mayiel passed her Protocols, she'd be the fourth bearing the double-drop.

The changes came fast to town and with Lilyis eager to bring the seven captives west, I sometimes needed to force myself to stop and breathe deeply, not to allow myself to fall down the panic spiral. All my life being marked as a wizard had seemed the one thing to relieve my apprehensions, but since I'd been inked, I needed to find something else to direct my future at.

Both Cathil and Qes had wanted to marry before we started travelling again and though the square was full of dark circles left over from the funeral pyres, Goldenlake was more than ready for a joyful feast. Deer roasted in the communal kitchens and the first lot of pickles had matured; bowls and plates of fruit and fresh cheeses stood on the tables, as well as towers of flatbreads. Though by comparison Qes was correct to call it a simple wedding, there were more people waiting for him than in the whole of Tall Trees. As we stepped out of the Roundhouse to make our way to the shore, we were being followed by a gaggle of children wearing wreaths of summer leaves, who skipped along the streets, and members of many families, scrubbed almost as clean as me and in their finest. Like me they wore their amulets and ornaments openly. It was a windy morning, the breeze tearing at hairpins and curls, drying the beads of nervous sweat on Qes' forehead. He looked stressed and happy in equal measure as he turned back around to me.

"When we set off from Tall Trees, this wasn't what I imagined," he said quietly. "Or planned in any way."

"I understand."

"When we were here last, I hadn't realized how much your friendship would come to mean to me—with everything that it couldn't be after all."

"You'll make me cry," I warned him, feeling the inside of my nose itch with the oncoming tears. "I'll probably cry anyway at some point, but it would be nice to start the ceremony off without snot running down my face."

Again, he stared up at the mark. I'd also have to get used to that; many people would be unable to see the person behind it. "Qes—eyes down here."

"Oh, sorry … it's … you look so different."

"More important?" I asked with a smirk.

"Probably. A bit more grown up, but that might be because you actually bothered to do something about your hair today."

"Lilyis braided it up for me."

"It looks nice."

We stood behind the guests who'd come together to see a Badger marry a Cloud. Even at the Stoneharp I'd never seen a mix of so many colours, of members of so many families.

I spotted the delegation of Hedgehogs near the altar that had been carefully rebuilt after the battle and draped in garlands of soft blue flowers gathered from the grassy edges around the lake. Many children had come, tired of waiting for the ceremony to start, splashing about in the shallow waters.

Werid of the Far Side stood at the ready, the hems of their grey tunic and the ends of their loose hair swirling about them in the gentle swell of the waves. The sun circlet shone on their head as they greeted us with a discreet inclination of the chin. Next to them stood Eleas, her bandaged hands hidden behind her back, the shell cape picking up the colours of the lake around her. Lilyis and Raz were waiting too, both appearing unfamiliar in loose tunics, with their hair braided into crowns. Two bright spots bloomed on Lilyis' cheeks and her eyes were already brimming.

Qes clutched my hand and squeezed as Cathil approached from the other side of the altar, in the silver-grey cloak of the Clouds, his hair pulled up into a knot pierced with a curved bone needle. He hadn't seemed more like himself in a long time, though bearing tiny scabs from the nicks he'd come by during the battle covering his face and neck. He was the man who'd once caused my life to descend into chaos and who'd do his utmost to ensure my best friend's happiness.

"You fuckers really play your own game," I hissed at no one in particular, or rather, every Sibling who was prepared to hear some of the truth. Brother Brook's silvery laugh rose from the lake.

We walked through the shallows to the front of the altar.

Werid gave their scorched staff to Mayiel to free up both hands, and as I placed Qes' hand in Cathil's, we were finally ready to start.

"I can't believe they had that much honey beer squirreled away in Coldharbour. Ah—fuck." Raz cursed as she splashed beyond the edge of the last bowl and used her sleeve to wipe up the overspill.

Our table was close to where the wizards had been placed, but any attempt at a formal seating arrangement had long since been given up. All wedding guests were deep into their bowls, most of the food had been devoured, and the braziers placed around the benches fired up to illuminate the faces of the revellers and guide everyone who wished to walk across the square towards the remaining quarters of Goldenlake. Guards who'd been relieved came back to join in, so there'd been uncounted rounds of toasts on the future happiness of Qes Badger and Cathil Cloud that had made me start to cry several times. I was stuck between Lilyis and Raz, desperate to wiggle out for a pee but not sure whether it was a good idea to move at all. I was stuffed to the gills and just drunk enough not to start blathering.

"This is stronger than the usual stuff," Lilyis said, eyes shining. "Or I'm not used to good quality beer anymore—Sloe, are you still awake?"

"Barely. Stop jabbing me with your elbow, I can feel that down to my bladder."

"You stop whining. Ask the Siblings to sober you up enough to start on your next bowl."

"Actually, I think I've had enough."

"Aw," Raz wailed. "We wanted to see if we could make it until sunrise!"

"No one is stopping you."

"Why are all wizards such spoilsports?" Raz asked, but she grinned from ear to ear.

"Because they need a wee." I started to push myself up from the table. My knees were wobbly, but I was able to get up. As I extricated my legs from the gap between table and bench, I had to hop on one leg as the heel of my boot caught. "Fuck—sorry."

"You're coming back, right?" Raz called after me, as I made my escape. "You can't leave your girlfriend all alone at a wedding!"

A roar of laughter went up, but on my feet and walking I began to realize that I'd left it far, far too late and hurried into the shadows between the houses surrounding the square. I found a stable. The grey horse in the first stand didn't mind too much as I relieved myself with a groan, the crown of my head pressed against the clay wall. The smell rising from the floor made me gag and the horse snorted, starting to snuffle at my tunic, long since rumpled and covered in stains. I patted the soft coat of its flank before trying to exit the building. There was nothing more to wait for. In a few days I'd climb onto Cirvi's back and it would only take a few more until I was once more in Tall Trees …

"I don't want to go back," I whined.

"I know." Sister Stone stepped out of the space between the thatched roofs, the young face of my aunt pale in the falling light. "You don't need to, you know. You have been made a wizard of Goldenlake. There are very few people you need to answer to. My brothers and sisters of course, but you will have to make your own rules."

I felt a great weight settle on my heart. "Why does that scare me so much?"

Her shoulders rose. "Perhaps because new things have so rarely meant a change for the better for you, and sometimes any sort of freedom is difficult to understand and to take full advantage of. You know that we will be with you, wherever you choose to go, whomever you choose to be with. This is only just the beginning. Lace yourself up and go back to your friends."

I straightened my own shoulders, tied a firm knot to secure my trousers, and turned around—to face my future.

EPILOGUE: STILL ME

The kite took off from my wrist with a shriek. The strength with which it pushed up caused me to make a soft *oooof* sound. Most people around the Stoneharp camp were used to the sight of me carrying the raptor around, resulting in a few more nicknames I pretended not to be bothered about, though they gave me a weird little glow inside.

We'd travelled back west slowly, with the Sun's cart full of prisoners dictating the pace we'd been able to move at, until the bleak towers of the Harp had greeted us from across the grasslands. The skies above us were grey, though it was mild for the time of year and the vendors at the market were wearing the summer cloaks and hoods studded with water drops. It had stopped raining a mere hour before and the smell of dying grass and wet kelp was in the air.

"You're sure?" The commander of the west had draped their wrists over the pommel of the saddle, leaning slightly forward in their usual slumped way that hid fierceness and determination. "The ship is still here—just about."

I rubbed my numb right arm. "We've talked about it at length, and we'll both have come to the same conclusion. Multiple times."

Rawil Owl pulled a grimace. "I think you're making a mistake. She might have promised you a hundred times to come back, but things happen. Not only storms and sudden illness, but why would she want to return to a life that doesn't suit what she is?"

"She'll make it suit her." At that point, Eight Tall Gods couldn't make Lilyis Sun bow down. The thought made me smile.

We both squinted at the prow of the *Golden Drake* rising up before us. That morning I'd slept in Lilyis' arms, but there she stood on the deck, wearing one of her Cormorant necklaces, with a thick shawl wound across it and a braid studded with pins and rings above the yellow tunic of the Sun. Of the crew rustling around her, she was the only one with ornaments of the families on display; even from the beach I could see her mouth set with determination. She was the person in control.

A few hours before, we'd exchanged promises and letters, a whole pile of them cinched together with a leather strap, directed at her father, Hilvis, and the ladies in Blackfields, to my father and brother separately. I'd also written to Lauron Wolf at the *Rotting Pear*. The letter to the crown prince was the only one not folded into a neat square. I'd shed a tear or two as I'd carefully wrapped up the key to the Hidden Tower with a piece of soft barkcloth and secured the message with a narrow tablet-woven ribbon.

I missed the weight of it around my neck, though Werid had dedicated another token to Sister Soil to replace it, a broken blade picked from the Goldenlake battlefield, blunted and formed into an arm ring that I wore above the blue stone bracelet, a rough ornament that had felt familiar from the first moment I'd put it on. Lilyis would carry the key back to Crooked Hill.

The seven prisoners had been the last to be brought to the ladder and made to climb into the *Golden Drake* where their shackles were refastened, the Whiterivers priests still in their sandals; the Bulls had been given new clothes to replace the ragged red tunics and trousers. The eighth prisoner … I turned around.

Raz was back among her cousins, laughing and telling stories about her adventures in the east, but though she smiled a lot among people, I could often catch a line furrowing her brow. Qati had been subjected to the fate he'd courted for so long, though Raz had managed to dissuade the council from drowning him in a cage. On a muggy late summer morning she'd had three guards bring him to the altar where Qes and Cathil had been married a few days before. We all had witnessed Werid pronouncing the verdict on the man who had started the first fires of the battle of Goldenlake.

The longknife had been sharp, the Badger warrior who'd been chosen to wield it strong, and Qati quiet as he'd bent the neck to receive the blow. His blood had swirled around our boots, had washed in and out to the shore and stained the pebbles while Raz had stood next to Lilyis and watched the Tall Gods claim him.

I flinched as a horn sounded on the *Golden Drake* and only a few breaths later the oars were run out to move the ship away with the tide.

Lilyis stepped to the rail, frowning, lifting her right hand, while the left stayed clamped around her side. I answered with the same gesture.

Rawil studied me from the side. "I'm not happy about this," they grumbled as the waters churned around the oars and the *Drake* began to cut through the waves, its sails starting to unfurl to catch the winds coming around the coastline. The horn sounded again and then Lilyis withdrew from the rail, from my sight.

"Believe me, I tried to fight for her. I have cried buckets, but she wouldn't be persuaded. I get it. At least, I think I do. On the Continent, she has a lot waiting for her. I tried to convince her to go further east, make good on our plan to travel the steppes, maybe all the way to the eastern mountains and to the coast beyond."

"What did she say to that?"

"That she wanted to see them the next time." And she would, I was sure of it.

The commander sniffed. "Do you want to wait?"

"No—let's go." I pulled my mare around.

Cirvi started to make her way through the market on the beach, while Rawil and their entourage of Owl warriors followed. As we reached the gatehouse I couldn't resist and put my right hand on Cirvi's piebald back. From up there the yellow ship seemed close enough to the beach for me to gallop down and swim over, but I saw Raz' face, her determination to not break down and hastily faced forward again. Lilyis had promised to come back, and princesses were supposed to honour their word.

The guards greeted us by lifting their pikes and stomping the ends on the flagstones before letting us pass into the first yard that was glistening with the recent rain and impeccably clean. We dismounted, gave the reins to one of Rawil's Owls, and started to walk across the Harp as we'd done so many times.

The Apprentices' Yard that had once been so lively only sported two tents. The washing lines were empty, the little group of chickens sheltering under the empty benches.

"Have you thought about taking on an apprentice?" Rawil asked me.

I swallowed. "It's much too early for that. It will take me years not to feel like an imposter."

"Not many wizards have earned their mark in battle, but it doesn't mean you are any less."

"Tell that to my sister. One of the reasons I haven't gone back home yet is because I can't face the drama. She can't be the only apprentice working her arse off for a decade and not having received official recognition, though she's taken on the full workload long ago."

"But you'll go back soon?" Rawil scratched their scarred temple under one of the firm buns that denoted the Owl family hair style.

"Yes. I'll need to meet the new baby."

"Don't put it off too long, Sloe."

"That's what Qes said when he and Cathil split from our group. I feel a bit bad about using him as my envoy, but he basically volunteered."

"*Basically*?" Rawil made another one of their disapproving noises.

"He needed to officially end the cousin exchange, and while he's there he can give my whole family the good news."

"Hmhm." Rawil stopped walking. "How can you go through that much and be afraid to stand up to your mother? Sloe of the Blue Cloak, Sloe of the Fire Kite—it won't take long for all the families of these lands to know your name."

"But I'm still me. Somehow, after all these miles and all the blood and the loss of so many friends … that's still what I'm working with." It felt odd to realize that I could say those words and not be disappointed. I had learned to trust that despite being me, I was loved.

As we stepped into Yuna's Yard, one of the Harp's administrators stood by the kitchen door. "We expected you sooner."

"Blame the tide," Rawil rasped.

The kitchen smelled of fresh tea and sweet toasted bread. Yuna Elk sat at the scarred table over a piece of grass paper covered in oily fingerprints. Next to her sat the Sun Lilyis had left in charge of the rented tower. Knowing the man held the post Bjor had been prepared to take on had made me resentful towards him at first, but he was polite and reasonable. He'd served as a steward under her father.

"There you are." Yuna pushed the paper aside. "I can make another pot of tea."

"Let me do it," Rawil said.

Yuna laughed. "The commander of the western grasslands will not make their own tea. Sloe—you do it."

I laid down my shoulder bag and while Rawil settled into their seat next to her I found the jar with the herbs, located a spoon, and was grateful to be allowed to distract myself from the fact that while I waited once again for the water to boil, the *Golden Drake* was getting further and further away from me.

I heard Yuna and Rawil talk behind me.

"When are they leaving?" Rawil asked.

"Next spring. The council has officially been disbanded. There are a lot of bets going on where it will pop up again, but as long as there are families in the grasslands, the administration centre will be kept busy with the storage yards. We signed a new contract with the Clouds a week ago."

"I heard about that. Soon there'll be a lot more Clouds and a lot more Squirrels in the camp—how's that tea coming along, Sloe?"

"Water hasn't boiled yet."

Yuna stood up and came across the kitchen to stand beside me. "How are you feeling?"

"Horrible. Sad and already lonely."

"She said she will be back. You know she will do everything she can to keep that promise. She has many people to catch up with, not just yourself. She will also come back for Qes and Raz, for Cathil, Werid, Eleas, and your sister."

"I know." Finally the water started to clamour against the sides of the small iron pot, and I poured it over the herb mixture.

Yuna eyed me critically. "How are your healing skills developing? Are you taking lessons?"

"I will when I'm back in Goldenlake. What do you think will happen with the council of the west?"

We both breathed in the fragrant vapour rising off the pot. "There are many special places in our lands. Someone will make a choice, brush off an old legend, and the wizards will flock to it. It will probably not be a port this time, but somewhere secluded and safe, where they can restrict access and keep all people out they do not deem worthy enough to be taught. They will have a lot to say about the new first wizard of Goldenlake." Her gaze flickered up to the double-mark on my forehead. "It will take them time to accept a fresh idea, as always, but in the meantime, any wizard who has shared a piece of your experience will know where to turn. I would say that is worth it, wouldn't you?"

I glanced towards Rawil Owl, who sat at the table with an expectant smile. Seeing them content in their new position made me hope to find my own feet.

Yuna gave the herbs a stir and brought the pot to the table, calling to me over her shoulder, "Don't forget the spice cake."

THE END

SUN & FLAME
VOLUME I
EVERYTHING
the SUN
TOUCHES
C. M. Kuhtz

As the only daughter born into one of the most prominent merchant families in the south of the kingdom, Qonna has always known that one day she would have to marry–but she has never fallen in love and she isn't really sure that she can.

Cisir falls in love with everyone he meets and has left his noble family in the north to start a new chapter in his life, after everything has gone terribly, embarrassingly wrong.

When Qonna and Cisir meet in the flourishing trading port of Seagard, neither of them knows that they have been given a very specific magical gift that will force them to work together and that their destinies will become irrevocably intertwined with the fate of the bustling and politically volatile city they both try to survive in.

As a queer twist on the marriage of convenience trope, *Everything the Sun Touches* is a tale of chosen family and deep, complex friendships, perfect for fans of *Gwen and Art Are Not in Love* and *Little Thieves*.

RELEASING ON 15 MARCH 2026
IN HARDBACK, PAPERBACK, AND EBOOK

WOLLSCHWEBER
PUBLISHING

More information on
www.wollschweberpublishing.com
www.cmkuhtz.com

AUTHOR NOTE & ACKNOWLEDGEMENTS

As I am sitting down in June 2025 to write the Author Note for this volume, the world has become a different place. When I finished the first draft of *Goldenlake* at the end of October 2022, I honestly had envisioned a brighter future. But while the state of the world does its best to rob me of any surplus energy beyond survival, it has also shown me the importance of the Wollschweber Publishing venture.

Sloe Moon has cost me uncounted hours, endless tears of both grief and joy, and many, many hand cramps as I filled twelve A5 notebooks in the process, but I wouldn't have it any other way. There were incredibly tense times, especially when I needed to abandon the original cover concept for the series halfway and pivot, but working with artists has always been one of the most enjoyable aspects of publishing for me and I love the three watercolour covers by @karlskunstkrempel with all my heart; missing out on them seems inconceivable now.

Since 2022 I have established a hefty pipeline of new projects—all are set in Sloe's world, though at different times and in different locations, slowly painting in the blank spaces of the storyverse. This means at any given time I'm working on books in different stages of the process, usually handwriting one first draft, prepping documents for beta-reading and copyediting, typesetting, and proofreading. Each and every day I learn more about marketing and what mistakes I've made in the past and the instinct that let me throw so much time, passion, and resources at the series and all subsequent books has begun to dig in its heels.

The recent global wrench to the political far right and especially the resulting inhumane treatment of trans people in the UK where I live, have brought to the fore that reading is, and always has been, deeply political. Anyone who claims otherwise is firmly blindfolded by privilege.

The world of Sloe and the families has been my sanctuary for decades at this point, and despite being very far from perfect, it has been a lifeline that I hope and long to share with others as they are made to doubt their humanity. I hope with all my heart that by the time *Goldenlake* releases in November 2025, things have begun to look up and I would be able to write a sunnier note to wrap up this labour of love.

I live my life as a tall, fat, visibly queer person who is stared at for merely existing wherever they go and despite there being days when doing so feels like my skin is slowly being peeled off, I have come to think of this visibility as resistance.

I wrote Sloe's story as a matter of representation, because I had never seen someone like me portrayed in my favourite sort of books when I was growing up. Fantasy literature is notorious for serving wish fulfilment and for a long time I used it to escape into a reality where I could get rid of my body and my sneaking suspicion that things were so much more complicated than I was led to believe. For me, Sloe's magic is their insistence on being worthy of love, worthy of being seen, worthy of being a hero just because they are human—and their story is far from over.

Many people accompanied me along the way and need to be thanked:

Isa, who has lived in the Eastern Cities with me for almost three decades and is probably the only person on this planet who can read my handwriting without breaking a sweat. You're the Sloe to my Qes.

Marlen, who is never afraid to go deep. For knowing me too well to let me have the easy way out and for showing me where the best cake lives and where the fairy waterfalls are.

Dorit, graphic designer and flatmate extraordinaire. For the many late nights in our wonky Hildesheim kitchen, talking about our lives to come—and our Isle of Skye adventures!

Diana, Nicole, and Bouke, who continue to go on the adventure with me. For being friends, fellow writers, and first readers, and for believing that all that bloody effort is worth it.

Elena and the Marshalls, who took me in as part of their bubble and have become my found family in the UK.

Lorna, who teaches me about art and shares my enthusiasm for extraordinary places.

Claudia and the Cabbage Club, who help me make sense of the bewildering country we have all come to live in.

Jenna, fellow writer, who gave me so much encouragement when I needed it most and managed to rein in my panic when things didn't move quickly enough.

Gobion, Hannah, and Ariadne Rowlands, fellow writers and avid readers, who have been of more support than they will ever know. I am so grateful that it's never too late in life to make amazing friends! I'm so excited to work with you on projects that nudge me out of my comfort zone.

Rachel, Tanner, Ronan, Laurie, and Aliya for their invaluable beta-reading and sensitivity-reading insights and giving me so much to think about.

Britt, for an amazing and endlessly rewarding copy editing experience.

Casey, for capturing the spirit of the series in her beautiful cover illustrations for volumes one to three.

Karla, for fearlessly jumping onto the cover image design from volume four onwards!

My parents, for coming around to support the choices I make. For teaching me that life is too short to live in a cage. For being role models for adventurous cooking and travelling, for making me interested in how stuff works and all the books, art, and love—and French cheese!

My brother Henry, who shares the story-telling bug. For all the road trips into the wilderness, storm or no storm, snow or no snow.

Hamish, the one true Prince of Crooked Hill, who is missed in every single moment.

And everyone who picked up the book and found something in my flawed, passionate, yet anxious hero to relate to.